EIGHT NIGHTS OF FLIRTING

HANNAH REYNOLDS

RAZORBILL

To friends-my-friends,
for getting me through this last year

RAZORBILL

An imprint of Penguin Random House LLC, New York

First published in the United States of America by Razorbill,
an imprint of Penguin Random House LLC, 2022

Visit us online at penguinrandomhouse.com.

LIBRARY OF CONGRESS CATALOGING-IN-PUBLICATION DATA
Names: Reynolds, Hannah, 1988– author.
Title: Eight nights of flirting / Hannah Reynolds.
Other titles: 8 nights of flirting
Description: New York: Razorbill, [2022] | Summary: Sixteen-year-old Shira is on a mission to
find the perfect boyfriend over Hanukkah, but after getting snowed in on Nantucket
with her nemesis-slash-former-crush, her plans begin to go off the rails.
Identifiers: LCCN 2022019076 | ISBN 9780593349755 (hardcover) | ISBN 9780593349779
(trade paperback) | ISBN 9780593349762 (ebook)
Subjects: CYAC: Friendship—Fiction. | Dating (Social customs)—Fiction. | Hanukkah—Fiction. |
Nantucket Island (Mass.)—Fiction. | LCGFT: Novels.
Classification: LCC PZ7.1.R4865 Ei 2022 | DDC [Fic]—dc23
LC record available at https://lccn.loc.gov/2022019076

ISBN 9780593349755

Printed in the United States of America

1 3 5 7 9 10 8 6 4 2

BVG

Design by Lori Thorn
Text set in Maxime Pro

ALSO BY HANNAH REYNOLDS
The Summer of Lost Letters

CHAPTER ONE

When I saw Tyler Nelson at Nantucket's tiny airport, I ignored him, because Tyler Nelson was the absolute worst. I watched him from the corner of my eye, feigning indifference as I brushed away the snow clinging to my coat from crossing the tarmac. He took the prime position at the start of the baggage carousel, so I moved to the far side and stood with my back to him. Outside, white flakes swirled madly. The wind—which had spurred nerve-racking turbulence—howled like a lone wolf given wild, maniacal form by motes of snow.

My phone buzzed, and I pulled it out. "Hi, Mom."

"Shira?" In just two syllables, Mom's tone conveyed worry and bad news. "Where are you? Did you land?"

"I'm at the airport. Are you at the house?"

"We're still in Boston. Our flight was canceled."

"What?" I'd expected her to be at Golden Doors by now,

along with the rest of the family, lighting up my grandparents' house with laughter. Their plane had been due to arrive an hour before mine. "Did you get another?"

"They're all canceled—the winds are too strong. We're going to take the Hy-Line tomorrow, if the ferries are running. Will you be okay alone tonight?"

I'd been looking forward to seeing my family, to burrowing into their warmth. The idea of being alone for an extra day made my stomach feel hollow. But it wasn't worth telling Mom and stressing her out. "I'll survive."

"Make sure you pick up something to eat, okay?"

I glanced outside again. I'd be lucky to get home in this storm, let alone get takeout or delivery. But surely Golden Doors had food in the pantry. "Will do. How was Noah's ceremony?"

"Good, lots of speeches. Noah looked very grown-up. How did you do on your midterm?"

"Aced it," I said, because if your daughter had expensive tutors, she damn well better ace her exams. "Are Grandma and Grandpa okay?"

"Oh, well," Mom sighed, "Grandpa's complaining about how we should have predicted the weather, and Grandma thinks he's being foolish. She's worried about the decorations, though. She thought she'd be back today and have them up before the littles arrive tomorrow, but now everyone will show up at once . . ."

Mom lacked even the smallest drop of subtlety. "You want me to decorate."

"Not if you don't have time . . . But you *will* be there . . ."

So would you, I wanted to say, *if you'd stayed home and flown out of JFK instead of going to Noah's thing in Boston.* But I'd told them it was fine, so it was fine. "Sure."

"Okay, great, darling. We should be there around three tomorrow. You're sure you'll be okay?"

"I'll be fine," I said. "See you tomorrow!"

When we hung up, my fake smile fell away, and I stared blankly at the swirling snow. Alone for the first night of the holidays. I could do this.

Only I was so lonely.

Nope. Nope, I was fine. Besides, I didn't have time to be lonely. I could work on my plans for this break. Because I had big plans. Plans involving Isaac Lehrer.

If my life were a movie trailer, the voice-over would say, *This holiday season, Shira Barbanel is determined to win over Isaac Lehrer no matter what.* A series of slapstick shots would follow of us running into each other in Central Park, flicking latke batter at each other in my kitchen, and ice-skating at Rockefeller Center (where he'd witness me landing a triple axel).

The narrator might add something along the lines of *Shira Barbanel is a lost cause at love*, the appropriate-for-all-audiences version of *Shira Barbanel is a hot-AF mess who can't get a boyfriend*, a situation I planned to change over winter break.

I'd met Isaac—my great-uncle's nineteen-year-old intern—sporadically over the last year, at family and company events.

He was six-three, lanky, and as dreamy as Morpheus. His grandfather and my great-uncle had gone to college together, so when Isaac's parents decided to spend six months traveling through Europe and Asia, my great-uncle offered to bring Isaac to Golden Doors for the holidays. And now (*this holiday season*), I would turn our occasional small talk into a genuine connection.

And maybe I didn't have a *great* record of getting boys to like me, but that could change. Besides, not everything could go as badly as it had with Tyler.

Who, in a cruel twist of fate, was now the only other person left at baggage claim. Also, while I was blatantly ignoring him, I found it insulting that he so easily ignored me. To add insult to injury, our belated bags came out nestled together. I looked pointedly away while Tyler pulled his duffel bag free, and instead of walking over, waited for my slow-voyaging suitcase to reach me.

When it did, I heaved the bag off the conveyor belt and lugged it across the nearly empty room. Nantucket's small airport was almost more like a train station—the whole of ACK could fit inside Grand Central. Still, a broken wheel on my suitcase left me panting and awkward as I reached the doors, where I accidentally made eye contact with Tyler.

He smirked.

While the plane ride had turned my normally impeccable curls both frizzy *and* greasy, and I could feel a zit poking out of my chin, Tyler looked like he'd stepped out of central casting. His soft golden hair gave him the aura of a Disney prince, and even the amusement in his blue eyes didn't detract from his angelic looks. "Hey, Shira."

"Tyler." I dragged my suitcase another few feet.

"Need any help?"

"No."

"Suit yourself." He turned away, buttoning up his woolen coat and tossing one end of a scarf over his shoulder. It was sixteen degrees outside. He should have been wearing a puffer jacket and Bean Boots, like me. But god forbid he look like anything other than an ad for expensive cologne.

Whatever. I didn't care if he froze to death or ruined his fancy leather shoes. Tyler Nelson came in at No. 1 on the list of Shira Barbanel's Disastrous Attempts at Romance, and I wanted nothing to do with him.

The list, in no particular order:

1. Jake Alvarez. Asked him to homecoming last year only to have him blink, stumble backward, and stutteringly tell me he already had a date.

2. Dominic Hoffman from Camp Belman. Mocked him relentlessly in an attempt at flirting. Made him cry and leave for home early.

3. Siddharth Patel from driver's ed. Lusted after him silently throughout the entire course. Finally

exchanged numbers on the last day. No response to my one, brave text (**Hey**).

4. Tyler Nelson. Spent four summers madly in love with him, only to finally make a move and be utterly, devastatingly rebuffed.

Isaac—handsome, smart, sophisticated Isaac—would not be another example of me failing at boys. He was way more grown-up than any of my other crushes, sure to be better at conversation and easier to hang out with. And this time, I'd master the art of flirting. Or I'd at least follow the steps laid out by Google, for as much as they were worth. (*Step three: start talking.* Possibly, Google needed as much help at flirting as I did.)

In any case, I knew better than to expend energy on Tyler Nelson. I tore my attention away from him to check Uber and groaned at the surge pricing. And—

No car available.

Impossible. I tried Lyft with the same result.

With a sense of looming dread, I looked out the windows again. The snow obscured the world. Hard to believe leaves had still clung to trees a month ago, yellow-green and orange-brown. The chill in the air had only been enough to make boots acceptable. But today, a nor'easter had swept the Eastern Seaboard with the reckless speed of Elsa icing Arendelle, painting the world white—even Nantucket, where the sea usually whipped the island wet and bleak.

Outside, a car pulled into the taxi lane, careful on the snow-dusted asphalt. By the terminal doors, Tyler gathered his duffel bag, tightened a hand around his suitcase handle, and walked into the blizzard.

Pride warred with desperation, and the latter won. I dashed after him, heaving my suitcase off its broken wheel. It banged against my legs, the pain and embarrassment warming me against the hideous cold. Snowflakes smacked into my skin, dissolving in icy pinpricks. "Tyler!"

He stood by the back of the taxi, placing his bag in the trunk. "Shira."

"Can I share your car?"

"Let me guess." A close-lipped smile curved his perfectly shaped mouth. "You can't get one. Tough break."

"Tyler, come on. You live next door to me."

The driver pushed his head out the window. "That you, Shira Barbanel?"

"Phil!" I beamed at the driver, who I'd known for years. "How are you?"

"Doing well, doing well. Where's the rest of your family?"

"Snowed in in Boston. Their flight was canceled."

"Really?" Tyler said. "Same with my family. What were they doing in Boston?"

"Noah had a thing. I had to stay home for a final."

"Toss your stuff in the back," Phil said. "I'll give you kids a ride."

Throwing a triumphant look at Tyler, I maneuvered my bag into the trunk, then slid into the back after he beat me to the front.

Phil pulled away from the curb. "You two have a good flight?"

"Some turbulence, but not bad," Tyler said. I made a noise of agreement. I couldn't believe I hadn't noticed him on the plane. Maybe I'd boarded after him, and he'd been in the back. Maybe he'd boarded at the last minute, when I'd already been absorbed in my book. Maybe, I thought with a shot of hope, I was no longer so tuned in to Tyler's presence that I noticed every move he made.

We drove down Old South Road. Though the storm might have been a transportation nightmare, I adored how the snow powdered the pavement white, like we'd been transported to a time when horse-drawn carriages traveled on dirt paths, where people hurried down the streets in velvet capes and fur muffs, and sleigh bells mixed with the sound of laughter. The island already had a quaint, old-timey atmosphere, and winter just heightened it. This was my favorite season on Nantucket: I loved the stark, cold beauty, the snowy beaches and brilliant stars.

The drive only took fifteen minutes, winding past the cedar-shingled island houses outfitted for the season, decked in sparkling lights, yards populated by light-up reindeer. Windows displayed Christmas trees and candelabras whose branches I always counted. There were wreaths twined with pine cones and holly, and red and gold everywhere.

But Tyler's house, when we reached it, was dark. The lawn was a sheet of white, the bushes snowy heaps, and the house—usually an elegant beauty—a blank monolith under the darkening sky.

"Thanks," Tyler said to Phil. When he climbed out, icy air swept in, and goose bumps rose on my neck. Tyler tossed a look my way. "See you around, Shir."

"Shir*a*," I muttered. Being called Shir always made me think of sheep or transparent tops. But he'd already shut the door and gone to unload his bag.

"We'll wait to make sure he gets in all right," Phil said as Tyler trundled to the front door, then stepped inside. Relief broke over me as Phil put the car in reverse. With Tyler out of the way, I could focus on Isaac—on the future, not the past.

"How's Aimee doing?" Phil's nineteen-year-old daughter was a lifeguard during the summers and had just started college in Boston. "Is she home for Christmas?"

"She got back two days ago. Brought a suitcase of dirty laundry." Phil laughed, hearty and familiar. "She's loving college. Next semester she'll have to declare her major, and she's teetering between computer science and physics. Her mom and I tell her—" Phil paused, and I saw his frown in the rearview mirror. "Huh."

I twisted. Tyler was running toward us, waving his arms for attention.

Phil rolled down the window. "You okay?"

Tyler reached the car, his breath coming out in white puffs.

Snowflakes glittered in his golden hair. "The electricity's out. The heat, too; the panel didn't work."

Oh no. Surely he wouldn't *deign* to suggest . . .

He met my gaze and smiled, more ironic than charming. "So, Shira. Can I bunk with you tonight?"

"You want to stay with me. At Golden Doors." *Why don't you stay at a hotel?* I wanted to ask, but I didn't want to bicker in front of an adult. And while Tyler could afford it, why would he shell out money for a last-minute room when he could stay at my grandparents' place for free? Besides, then Phil would have to take Tyler to a hotel, spending even more time driving in these conditions.

Still . . .

But no. I couldn't turn him down. Our families ran in the same social circles; we'd be attending their Christmas Eve party later this week, and they'd be attending our Hanukkah celebration a few days after. "Fine."

"Great." With a flash of his white, even teeth, he retrieved his bag and returned to the car, his long legs once more cramped in the front seat. "We'll have a good time."

I didn't dignify his lie with an answer.

Tyler's moms' summer home abutted my family's ancestral property, the sprawling estate of Golden Doors, so the ride took a scant minute. The house loomed as we pulled up the circular drive, not gold, but gray: gray shingles covered the original nineteenth-century building as well as the modern expansions.

Endless windows reflected the gray-white sky. Someone had plowed and shoveled the porch steps, but even so, a blanket of snow had gently returned.

"Thanks so much," I said to Phil, and Tyler echoed me. Then we were pushing through the drifts, our legs struggling against the snow. On the porch, where a lighter layer carpeted the wooden boards, we brushed ourselves off as best we could.

I let us in to the dark foyer and flicked the light switch, my chest tight—what if the power had died here, too? But the chandelier lit up and the HVAC panel summoned the telltale whir of heat. I stepped back on the porch, directing two thumbs up at Phil. He gave a friendly honk and sped away.

Leaving me and Tyler Nelson alone.

We stared at each other. I had never met anyone else with such perfectly sculpted features, with eyes so blue and hair so gold. This boy could get away with murder or fraud or heartbreak, and people would chuckle and pat him on the cheek and say, "What a rascal!"

"Well, Shira," he drawled, and even his voice was beautiful, damn him. "This should be fun."

CHAPTER TWO

Here's what went down when Tyler and I first met.

Five and a half years ago, when I was a foolish eleven-year-old, I discovered crushes. I'd never had one before, though I'd watched my classmates giggling about kissing, all fascinated by the bewildering and unstoppable advent of puberty. I understood in the abstract but didn't relate.

Then Tyler Nelson showed up on Nantucket.

My god, the first time I saw him. A miracle, on par with a sea parting, the sun and moon standing still, oil lasting eight nights. The world slowed so each indelible second could be printed on my soul. Olivia Phan—my best summer friend—and I sat eating ice cream outside The Juice Bar. The hydrangeas were in full bloom; the air smelled sweet and floral.

A laugh from someone in line caught my attention.

Usually I only noticed embarrassingly loud laughs, like my Uncle Jason's in the movie theater. This laugh, though, came closer to music than anything else. I could no more resist searching for the owner than I could have resisted rainbow sprinkles.

He stood with a trio of others, who faded into the background like so much noise. The laughing boy shone, not illuminated by light but the *source* of light, a miniature sun, brilliant and lustrous. "He's beautiful," I breathed.

Beside me, Olivia wrinkled her nose. Also eleven, she was both more interested in and more cynical about romance. "He's kind of bland-looking, isn't he? Like a Disney star."

"You didn't have to ask who I meant, though."

"He's obviously the most conventionally attractive."

"Yes," I agreed. "He's stunning." I willed the boy to make eye contact with me, though I had no idea what I'd do if he did. But he and his friends took their cones and walked away.

"He *has* to be here all summer." A desperation I'd never known before formed a tight band around my chest. "If he's a day tourist, I'll *die*."

Olivia crunched down on the end of her cone. "Probably you won't, though."

It turned out Tyler would be there for the rest of the season: his moms had bought the Johnsons' old house, west of Golden Doors. Which meant I saw him that summer and the next, my crush surging back each year like a trick candle. I was drunk on exquisite longing, watching him flirt with summer girls and tourist girls and local girls. He belonged to the same friend group as Olivia's sister and my cousin Noah, so we spent the summers tagging along after them, following the older kids to the beach or squeezing our way close at ice-cream parlors. I had no shame, chasing Tyler with all the nuance of a six-year-old who thought her parents couldn't tell when she lied. I adored him, so how could he not adore me back?

After three and a half summers of being wild about him, I thought, *now*. I was fourteen and more than ready for my first kiss; I spent almost every night fantasizing about Tyler. Mid-July, I gathered my nerve, along with the prettiest seashells and smoothest stones and sea glass. I woke early one Saturday to form them into foot-high letters on the beach. *Tyler, date me?*

(I'd originally planned to write *Tyler Nelson, will you go on a date with me?* but quickly realized it would be way too much effort.)

Olivia guarded the words while I found Tyler where he was playing volleyball with a bunch of the other older kids. Everyone looked shockingly adult, their skin slick with sweat and sunblock, the guys with broad shoulders, the girls confident in their bikinis and retro one-pieces. No braces or constellations of acne to be seen. As the game ended, I picked my way over, nervous and terrified and feeling impossibly brave. He stepped away from his friends to grab his water bottle, and I closed the gap between us.

He noticed me hovering. A flash of something—*Irritation?* I wondered in retrospect. *Impatience?*—crossed his face, but then

14

he smiled. He'd always been unfailingly kind to the younger kids. "Hi, Shira."

I tried to say something, but no words emerged.

"Looking for your cousins?"

I shook my head.

He waited a second. "Uh . . . anything I can help with?"

I nodded.

He half smiled, more genuinely this time. "You might have to tell me what it is."

I took several rapid breaths, trying to ease the tightness in my chest. I felt like I might either float off the ground, buoyed by the moment's surreality, or be crushed into pieces by its immense weight. Finally, I blurted: "Can I show you something?"

"Sure."

I started quickly walking back toward the words.

"Shira!" A pained expression crossed his perfect face when I looked back at him, and he pushed back his hair, which was, if possible, even *more* golden after a month of constant sun. "We have to go somewhere?"

"Not far! It's super close."

He glanced back at his friends—who, thank god, didn't include Noah today. Even so, a few watched us, grinning widely. "Have fun, Nelson!" one of them called, and Tyler—hand low, where he probably thought I couldn't see—flipped him off.

Then he turned back to me. "As long as it's quick."

I nodded several times, heart pounding. This was happening. I had taken my fate into my hands; I had made the decision to bare it all. I felt powerful and horrible.

I scurried onward, several feet in front of Tyler, down the beach and past Olivia. She gave me a salute and walked off to give us privacy. I thought I heard Tyler sigh. But it could have been the wind.

We reached the words made of stones and seashells.

I turned around. This was it. I'd been waiting for this moment for years. I'd dreamed up ten thousand different ways it could go, this moment that launched the rest of my life. Tyler and I would become a couple. The moment settled into me, and I knew it would be a perfect, golden memory: the smell of the sea, the caw of seagulls and crashing of waves, the sun on my skin. My mouth split into a huge grin.

But instead of looking at me with a matching blooming smile, he stared at the words with something akin to horror. Then he managed a queasy smile. "Aw, Shir, no."

My stomach swooped. I tried to say something, but nothing came out. How could he say no? I felt *so strongly* for him. It was impossible that such a strong feeling could only go one way.

He scratched his neck, tried for another smile, and started walking away.

What?

This couldn't be it. I could save this—save me, him, us. My hands curled, and I shouted words at him, magic words, a spell to start our future. "I love you!"

He froze. Then he looked at me and laughed.

I'd heard his laugh a hundred times. It was so dear to me, the first thing I'd ever noticed about him. This time it cut through my core like he'd carved me up with jagged glass. "You don't love me."

"I do. I love you—I love you more than Juliet loved Romeo."

"Jesus Christ, I hope not. Look, you don't even *know* me."

"I do too!" I said, shrill and terrified.

"You're a little kid." He was too far away for me to make out the blue of his eyes, but I didn't need to be closer to hear his irritation. "What do you want, for us to hold hands and kiss on the cheek? Come on, Shir. Be real."

"I—no. I want to do—whatever you want to do!"

He laughed again. "I doubt it. Which you'll figure out soon, so I'm gonna put a cap on this."

And this time, he really did walk away.

He just . . . walked away.

I sank into a crouch on the sand, shocked. What had happened? We were supposed to be together. We were supposed to be perfect. I was fourteen and he was sixteen, and we were supposed to be in love.

Humiliated, I avoided Tyler for the rest of the summer. I tried not to notice all the other girls he flirted with and kissed. A hot, tight feeling squeezed me whenever I saw him. He, on the other hand, seemed unfazed. And like he wanted every girl but me.

By the next summer, I'd patched over my hurt with pride and

used it to keep my chin up. We only interacted once, near the end, at a chaotic party thrown by Olivia's older sister. I ducked into a guest room to try to find a moment of peace. Instead—

"Oh my god."

I tried to make sense of the various limbs. When I did, fiery heat clawed my cheeks. A guy's back, shirtless, muscles stark. A girl pressed close to him, arms wrapped around his neck. The girl I recognized—my cousin's almost ex-girlfriend.

The boy turned his head, and it was Tyler, because of course it was Tyler. Tyler, who I'd been madly, innocently in love with. Tyler, who would hook up with anyone, except for me. He looked tousled and sexy and perfect, his skin glowing, his hair mussed. "Of course it's you."

I made a noise of disdain, backed out of the room, yanked the door shut.

And my crush on Tyler Nelson was utterly doused. I had too much pride to waste away over someone who didn't like me, who'd laughed in my face when I told him I loved him, who hooked up with my cousin's *girlfriend*, of all people. He might look good on the surface, but scratch it, and he was pyrite, fool's gold.

And hadn't I been such a fool.

When I returned the next summer—last summer—I was finally free of my obsessive crush. Tyler Nelson was no prince charming, just a boy who wasn't worth my time. So I wasn't going to let him have any of it ever again.

CHAPTER THREE

And now Tyler Nelson and I would be spending the night in my house, alone.

We faced each other, me in the doorway, him a step down on the porch. Snow swirled in glittering eddies around his feet. Wisps of hair flew out from under his hat, and the cold pinkened his cheeks. Had his eyes always been so bright? So uncomfortable to meet? "Come in."

"Thanks." He heaved his bag over the step, bringing a shower of snow into the foyer. He took in the cream-colored walls, the polished wooden floor, the curved staircase leading up to the second floor. A painting of the sea by my grandfather hung across from the door. A vase filled with dried lavender rested on the table below it.

I ignored him and sat on the entry bench to unlace my boots. When was the last time I'd been alone with someone besides family or Olivia? I didn't have close friends; I'd spent most of my childhood either playing piano or ice-skating, and I had the fuzzy impression everyone else had formed their tight-knit friendships while I'd been at practice. Sure, people invited me to parties and wanted me at their lunch table, but mostly because my family was well known. Or because they read my demeanor as aloof and cool—at least according to one girl I'd overheard in the school bathroom—when really I was just awkward and silent.

And here I was with Tyler, who had a million friends, who was the life of the party. He was warm and friendly and popular, and I was cold and prickly and closed off. I had no idea how to behave alone with him.

Boots off, I jumped up, keeping my coat on since the heating hadn't yet beat back the chill. Tyler did the same, though he tossed his beanie atop his suitcase. His hair flew about, staticky and fine. "Do you have a towel I can dry my shoes with?"

I glanced at his shoes, which, in their defense, looked very expensive. "Maybe you shouldn't have worn four-hundred-dollar shoes in a blizzard."

"Six hundred."

I rolled my eyes, throwing a tea towel from the coat closet at him. "Here."

Carefully—almost lovingly—he polished the damp from his shoes, then looked up at me with a smile I had to brace myself against. Too much charm, this boy. "So what's the plan?"

"No plan." I brushed away the crusts of snow clinging to my jeans. Wet dark spots stained the fabric. "We can make tea to warm up, I guess."

"Cool."

He followed me deeper into the house, silence pressing in on us. The mansion sprawled, having expanded through the centuries. It felt weird to be in Golden Doors without cousins rushing around, without parents and aunts and uncles and Grandpa and Grandma at the steady center of it all. I was used to being alone in New York, but I'd never been alone here. Tyler's presence relieved me the smallest bit. Well, not Tyler's, specifically. But I was glad not to be alone.

Still, even empty, Golden Doors had an air of magic. I loved this house and felt at home here more than I ever had in Manhattan. It felt like Golden Doors *belonged* to me. Silly, maybe. But it'd always been a house for Barbanel women: the gardens designed and maintained by women, the blueprints drawn up by a woman. And I was the eldest granddaughter in the current generation of Barbanels. Golden Doors and I fit each other, a key and a lock.

I led him to the great room, where my family spent most of our time, a space that was equally living room and dining room and kitchen. Large windows and French doors took up one wall, beyond which the lawn spread toward gardens before falling in dramatic cliffs toward the sea. Usually, we could see a line of blue from here, but today the storm blurred out everything. Though only four in the afternoon, the sun had disappeared, plunging the world into a bluish haze. The snow continued to fall, the mounds outside shaped by tempestuous wind.

I switched on the light, outshining the outside world. Now instead of snow and darkness, we saw my grandmother's impeccable decorating: clusters of soft seating, small coffee tables, a large table for informal dining, a marble island counter separating the kitchen from the rest. I padded across the room, my thick winter socks slipping once on the smooth floor, and entered the pantry at the far end. Tyler kept at my back, his footsteps silent, his presence palpable.

"You can have whatever." I opened the cabinet where the tea lived: herbal Celestial for Grandma, Lipton boxes for Grandpa, Mom's Bigelow, and tins of loose-leaf tea. I pulled out orange spice and cinnamon, my comfort pick. Tyler studied the choices like I'd asked him to do open-heart surgery, running his fingers along the fine-grained wooden cabinets, then sniffing several options. After that, he picked up an embossed box and turned it in his hands. Finally he filled a metal ball with a scoop of Earl Grey.

If only I'd been trapped alone for a night with *Isaac*. I could imagine exactly how it'd go: He'd be polite and charming and kind. We would cook dinner together (never mind that I rarely cooked). We'd light the menorah, our hands over each other's, our voices mingling. We'd sit on the couch and talk all night. He'd put his arm around me and, then, somehow, we would be kissing . . .

I peeked at Tyler, flushing. I couldn't be daydreaming about making out with someone else next to him. Stomping back into the great room, I set the kettle on to boil and brought two mugs over to the kitchen island. We dropped into barstools across from each other. "This doesn't mean we're friends or anything."

He placed his tea infuser in his cup. "God forbid. No."

"I just don't want you to freeze to death."

"We have that in common." He grinned at me. "I, too, don't want to freeze to death."

How could he be so easygoing while active discomfort pulled at every corner of my body? But then, he'd always been relaxed and confident, where I felt stiff with most people outside my family. How could I survive the night trapped alone with him? "Do you want to watch a movie or something?"

"Nah. Movies are boring."

Tyler had a way of making almost everything he said sound reasonable, and I almost wanted to nod in agreement. I shook it off. "The entire point of movies is to *not* be boring."

He shrugged off his woolen coat and draped it over the back of his chair. The heat had finally kicked in. "Okay, not boring, but a last resort. There's more interesting things to do."

"Like what?"

"You know. Trade our hopes and dreams and plans and secrets."

I scoffed. "And why would I tell you any of those?"

"Because talking is *fun*, Shira."

Was it, though? "Not with strangers."

"We're not strangers."

"Well, we don't exactly know each other, either. Not really."

He studied me with the smallest upturned smile, utterly unlike the wide, open smile I was used to seeing on his face. "You used to think you knew me enough to say you loved me."

I couldn't believe he'd so casually bring up the most excruciating moment of my life. Even after two and a half years, the reference felt like he'd dumped a saltshaker's contents onto my innards.

"I was fourteen. I was in love with a different person each week."

He snorted. "You were in love with me for years."

He was right, and neither of us had ever acknowledged it to the other before. I could feel my cheeks, hot and heavy, but I refused to flinch. "You wish."

He leaned forward. "Admit it. You thought I was the sun and moon."

"For thirty seconds." The kettle began to whistle, and I busied myself with pouring hot water into our mugs. "Don't get too full of yourself." I shed my coat as I dropped back into my seat, suddenly too warm. "And I didn't like you because I *knew* you. It was because you're so—" I waved a hand.

He wrapped his hands around his mug, the steam rising to his face. "So what?"

"So *pretty*," I said. "Your genetics do the heavy lifting. It wasn't because you have a thrilling personality or whatever."

"Shira Barbanel." His eyes widened, and he looked unwillingly impressed. "What a burn."

I shrugged, feeling a little bad but unwilling to back down. "You're the one who went hard, making fun of a crush from when I was a kid."

He had the grace to look embarrassed. "Sorry. I didn't mean to make you feel bad. I guess I got whiplash, going from years of adoration to years of disdain."

I rolled my eyes. "Must be hard, no longer being the center of the world."

"Then you admit I *was* the center of your world."

"Because I was a shallow child, no other reason."

His eyes narrowed fleetingly, but then he flashed me the grin I'd spent years adoring. "If I actually tried, you'd melt at my feet."

"You wish." I took a large swallow of tea, which burned down my throat and spread tendrils of warmth through my chest. I couldn't imagine having so much confidence, and it made me want to take him down a notch.

He stared at me for a long, measured moment. Then his gaze flicked down. "You have tiny hands."

"What?" I said, thrown off completely.

"Your hands. They're tiny."

"They are not," I said, weirdly defensive of the size of my hands. "I played piano."

He smiled, softer. "Really? I didn't know."

"Why would you?" I muttered, and when he kept looking at me, as though intrigued, I cleared my throat. "Um. Yeah. My dad taught me."

"What do you play?"

Why were we talking about this? I breathed in the orange-and-spice steam from my tea. "I don't know. Never mind. I don't play anymore."

"What were your favorites when you did?"

My favorites. God. Had I had favorites before piano became too much work, one more activity in a long line of things grinding me into dust? Vivaldi and Debussy and Schumann, those had been who I *played*, but *favorites*—

"You know, I really liked *Cats*."

He let out a startled laugh. "Seriously?"

"Yeah, I loved it. 'Memory' did me in."

"Wow. Who would have thought?"

"I was six, okay?"

"Young." He raised his hand, fingers spread apart. "But pianists are just known for long fingers, not large hands."

I raised my hand so he could see it. "It's a perfectly normal-sized hand!"

He placed his against mine, palm to palm. A jolt of energy went through me at his touch. His hand was, in fact, much larger than mine, and warm. He curved the tops of his fingers around mine. "See?"

"Hmm." Heat flushed my whole body. "Anyway, it doesn't matter—"

He intertwined his fingers with mine.

I lost all capacity for speech. He smiled. His thumb stroked my palm.

And I yanked my hand out of his. "You're an asshole."

"Come on, Shir, you basically dared me. You said I had no personality."

"It's Shira. And that wasn't *personality*, it was . . . being smooth." I sipped my tea, picturing Isaac to calm myself down. Isaac would never play games like this; every time we'd talked, he'd nodded seriously. Of course, our conversations never lasted long and were usually about school or the weather, but he wasn't the kind of guy who would mock me. "Being charming doesn't count as a character trait."

"Why not?"

"I don't know. Because it's not real. It's a surface thing."

"What's real, then?"

"I don't know." I was, in fact, not entirely sure *I* had a personality, as opposed to just conforming to all the expectations of the people around me. "Your aspirations, I guess? Your passions."

"Okay." He leaned forward, resting his forearms on the countertop. I was hard-pressed not to notice the golden dusting of hair on his skin. "What are yours?"

Oh no. My least favorite question, and I'd walked right into it. "Maybe I'll save the sea turtles," I said lightly. "They're having a time of it."

"The sea turtles," he repeated.

"Yep." I liked turtles; they were like cute old men with flippers. I'd learned if I mentioned sea turtles, people often laughed and moved on. Which was, in fact, my end goal. Because I didn't like to talk about my future or what I wanted out of life.

I used to think I knew my dreams and aspirations. I knew I wanted to be *great*. Only it turned out I wasn't.

Not at piano, not at skating, despite the years and practice I'd sunk into both. Now these things, which I'd once thought might be my life's passions, hurt too much to get close to. I used to sting with jealousy when I watched professionals, hungering for their talent, their medals, but I could bear the envy because it egged me on, it made me want to be better. I could study and learn from them, and eventually, I would emerge from my own chrysalis, transformed.

Only I never had, and now skating and piano just made me sad.

My phone buzzed. Mom, probably checking to make sure I'd made it to Golden Doors. I hopped off my seat and walked into the hall so we could have a semiprivate conversation. "Hi."

"Hi. Did you get to the house okay?"

"Yeah. I'm fine. Um—I split a taxi with Tyler Nelson. His house didn't have power, so he came over here."

"Oh." Mom sounded startled, but not unpleasantly so. "Do you two have food?"

"I think so. We haven't looked yet." I winced at the admittance. "I'm sure there's pizza in the freezer or something."

"Okay, good. Everything's working?"

"Yeah, it's totally fine, Mom. What are you guys up to?"

"We're back at Aunt Liz's—we got takeout, since no one expected to be here. We're about to light the menorah. Do you want to FaceTime?"

A deep ache opened in my stomach. Part of me wanted to see her, see the whole family. On the first night of Hanukkah, we always sang "Sevivon" and "The Dreidel Song" and "Light One Candle." It hurt, the idea they might sing without me. But if I watched everyone from a distance, I'd feel even worse when I hung up. "No, thanks—I need to start decorating anyway."

"Are you sure? Here, I'll—"

"Mom, it's fine. I'll see you tomorrow."

"Why did you snap?" she said immediately. "What's wrong?"

I sighed. "Nothing's wrong. I don't want to leave Tyler alone."

"Okay. Well. We'll be there tomorrow."

"Okay. Love you."

"Love you, too," she said, and hung up.

CHAPTER FOUR

Back in the great room, I plopped back down at the island counter across from Tyler. "Here's the deal," I said. "It's the first night of Hanukkah, and tomorrow my family's arriving."

"Happy Hanukkah."

"Thanks." I strove for a tone of practical briskness. "So. We have to do a couple things."

"Light the menorah?"

I pulled back. "No. Decorate the house."

Though I would like to light the menorah. How hard could it be to find? At home, our menorah lived on a bookshelf in the living room year-round. Menorah on the bookcase, Elijah's cup in the cupboard, Shabbat candleholders on the sideboard.

But I'd never lit a menorah without my family surrounding me.

Would it be weird with Tyler here? What would he do—*watch* me sing the prayers? Awkward. Also, I was not exactly vocally gifted.

Then again, I already felt guilty after snapping at my mom, and not lighting a menorah would only increase the guilt. A pickle: guilt or awkwardness.

Obviously parental guilt smashed everything else flat.

"Maybe we'll light the menorah, too," I relented. "But first we have to carry boxes down from the attic. Think of it as your rent."

I unearthed a box of candles and a matchbook in the pantry and found the brass menorah in the formal dining room. Next, I led Tyler upstairs. He looked curiously at everything as we moved upward through the house, trailing his hands across painting frames and couches and even stroking the curtains.

"You keep touching things."

"I'm a tactile person," he said offhandedly. "When I was little and my moms took me shopping, I used to touch all the fabric in the stores."

"No one ever told you to keep your hands to yourself?"

"Maybe." He laughed. "But I don't think I listened."

And I could tell how, with his charming laugh and beautiful smile, people would let Tyler Nelson get away with whatever he wanted.

We reached the third floor, a smaller level with lower ceilings. The littles and middles—all the cousins twelve or under—slept in one giant room up here tucked beneath the eaves. Near the center of the house, I paused and pointed at a trapdoor in the ceiling. A thin string hung down. "I present: the attic."

Tyler squinted upward. "How do we get in?"

I squinted, too. "Usually there's a ladder." Bending my knees, I jumped and caught the string, pulling the door open and the attached ladder down.

"Ladies first," Tyler said. I hesitated, imagining him staring at my butt as I climbed up, and then I decided—whatever. I had a damn good butt.

The attic was a low, crowded space with slanted ceilings. Up here, the wind sounded even louder, knocking against walls that had little insulation. The cold, too, seeped inward. In the dark, I could clearly see out the windows on either side of the low, triangular space. Snow fell steadily in the blue light of the sunken sun.

Tyler followed my gaze. "It's beautiful."

I only nodded, not ready to share a moment admiring nature with this boy, and pulled on yet another string. A single light bulb lit up, casting stark shadows across the long room. "Let's see if we can find the decorations."

We circled the attic, peering at endless boxes: white mailboxes and brown cardboard boxes, clear plastic boxes and the occasional wooden trunk. Abandoned furniture was interspersed with the storage: a rocking chair and horse, a few old lamps, a mirror.

"How long has your family lived here?"

"Since the 1800s," I said, and when he glanced at me, I smiled. "Guess we've had a long time to accumulate stuff."

He suddenly crashed to the floor, a startled look on his face. "Ow!"

I skirted around a large stack of boxes between us. "Are you okay? What happened?" Had my smile been *so* surprising he'd fallen flat on his face? Wow, I really needed to work on being friendlier.

He pushed himself to a sitting position, rubbing at his ankle. "I'm fine. I just tripped on . . ." His voice faded, gaze hooked on the floor where he'd been standing. A board of wood had been tugged away from the others.

Oh no. We broke the floor. "That's what you tripped on? Eesh."

"You think it's on purpose?"

"I—what? Do I think the floorboard tripped you on purpose?"

He laughed. "If it's *loose* on purpose. If it's been pried up before."

My interest was instantly piqued. "Like a hidey-hole?"

"Only one way to find out."

He scooted over, and I sat with my knees tucked beneath me so we could both peer in. Then I paused. "What if there's mice?"

"You're bigger than them."

"But not half as scary." I took a deep breath. "Okay. Let's look."

We peered into the darkness. And there, nestled within the small, dusty space, lay a box.

No bigger than a shoebox, with the elegance of a jewelry chest.

It had a curved top of dark, polished wood and intricate carvings on the sides. I lifted it out of the depression and set it on the floor. "Look at this," I breathed, tugging at the top. It failed to open. "Hidden treasures!"

"It looks old." He studied it. "I wonder how long it's been there."

"Is there a key?" I shone my phone's flashlight into the corners of the hole but only came up with dust.

"I'm sure we can figure out how to open it. Let's take it downstairs."

"Okay," I said, excitement rising, though I reminded myself not to get distracted. "But first we have to find the decorations."

Tyler raised his phone so the flashlight shone on a pile of boxes in front of us, illuminating a label reading *Hanukkah* in my grandmother's handwriting. He circled the phone's light so it took in a dozen similar boxes. "Uh, do you think it's all of these?"

It took twenty minutes to carry the large plastic boxes downstairs. We brought down the wooden chest last, setting it on the marble countertop next to our tea. Tyler tried to pry off the top with his hands. "Maybe we can pick the lock."

"Sounds aggressive. Someone probably hid it for a reason."

"Yeah, like a hundred years ago. I don't think we're breaking anyone's trust."

I wanted to open it, I realized. I hadn't been excited about something in a long time, not the way I had once been excited and enchanted by skating and piano. Sometimes I was so *bored*, and the afternoons stretched interminably, filled with homework and papers and studying. At least my job as a café barista, though mind-numbing, allowed me to lose myself in the pattern of button pressing and milk frothing.

It would be nice to be captivated by something again. I googled *how to pick a lock* and both Tyler and I craned our heads toward the first result on my phone. "Apparently we need a tension wrench," he read.

"There's tools in one of the closets . . ."

A few minutes later, we'd secured a wrench, and with the help of bobby pins and a decent amount of cursing, the lock clicked. The box seemed to sigh as the lid released its death grip.

Tyler and I stared at each other. Then, ever so carefully, I opened the box.

I didn't know what I'd expected: Something magical and instantly fulfilling? A treasure map, a pile of jewels? Instead, a jumble of items lay tangled together: an arrow, a piece of wood, an oval metal case, and a tiny glass bottle filled with seashells.

"Someone's keepsakes," I murmured. Some son or daughter of the house, probably a distant ancestor of mine, had hidden these away. I picked up the arrow; it was made of wood and had a long, thin tail. I frowned at it and handed it to Tyler to examine before lifting out the piece of wood. It was about eight inches long and four wide, sharp and precise at one edge, ragged and broken on the others. Bits of two letters filled it, barely recognizable as part of an *O* and an *S*. "What do you think this is?"

"No idea." He put the long arrow with its tiny head down and took the wood. "Looks like it used to belong to a way bigger piece of wood, given the size of the letters."

Next, I reached for the oval case, about two-by-three inches and thin. It clicked open to reveal a miniature painting of a handsome young man. Tyler leaned close. "Think he was a Barbanel?"

"I don't know," I said. "Maybe. But I think it's more likely you'd keep a portrait of a—of someone you liked, not of yourself."

He looked thoughtful. "You think it's one of your great-great-grandma's old boyfriends who didn't make the cut?"

"Could be." We both peered at the young man, who wore a white shirt with a wide collar and a tie with both tails hanging down his shirt. A dramatic mustache covered his upper lip. "Maybe she didn't want to forget him, so she squirreled everything away. A breakup box."

"A breakup box?" He grinned at me. "Sounds like something you give a friend. Filled with chocolate and alcohol and Amy Winehouse albums."

I bit back a smile. "Sort of like those baby boxes Nordic countries give people. State-sponsored supplies for dramatic events."

His brows rose, and he smiled at me. It was a different smile than the large, polished one I usually saw him flash around—smaller, quirkier. "Exactly. A public service. I think people would pay real tax dollars to receive breakup boxes."

I smiled, charmed despite myself, and looked back at the portrait. "When do you think this is from?"

He studied it, too. "Dunno. When were miniatures common? Probably before photography was invented, right?"

I pulled up the Wikipedia page. "Okay, photography got big after the Industrial Revolution—after the 1850s. It got really trendy in the 1880s. I'll have to ask my grandparents who lived in Golden Doors before then."

"You think they'll know?"

I carefully placed the items back in the chest. "The house has been in the family since it was built, so yeah."

"Right, I briefly forgot you were Nantucket royalty."

"Please." My family had been on the island since the early 1800s, true, but while the Quakers here had been much more open than the Puritans on the mainland, my Jewish family still hadn't been entirely taken into the fold.

I pulled out the glass jar and unscrewed it. How old were these seashells? I felt nervous to touch them and carefully pulled a few out. An eclectic mix filled the jar: small white shells and large, colorful fans—rather like the gray scallops I often saw here but with the gold and orange of a sunset.

"Those don't look like they're from here," Tyler said. "But I guess in the 1800s, people from Nantucket were going everywhere because of whaling. Maybe it was a gift. Maybe the Barbanel girl's lover was a sailor."

Blushing at the word *lover*, I looked away, glancing at our empty mugs. "Want more tea?"

He unspooled himself from his seat. "Maybe something stronger?" At my expression, his mouth twitched. "If you don't mind."

"Of course not," I said quickly. Drinking didn't bother me; just drinking alone with Tyler Nelson wasn't a scenario I'd exactly envisioned. I led him to the bar cart, stocked high with liquors.

He crouched down to examine it. "Anything we shouldn't touch?"

"They don't keep their good stuff here. And so many people come through, I don't think anyone will notice."

"Sweet. I'll have the brandy."

"Are you an eighty-year-old man?"

He laughed. "So judgmental. Not only old dudes have brandy."

"Hmm." I handed him a glass, then poured myself a straight shot of Godiva liqueur.

Tyler blinked at me. "Seriously? *You* were mocking *me*?"

"It's liquid chocolate! Much better than brandy."

"Well." He raised his glass. "Here's to you, taking in a stranger."

"And it's not even Passover."

"What?"

"Never mind." I sipped my drink, which really was like liquid chocolate—though with a much stronger bite. I didn't love alcohol, but I liked the fuzzy feeling from tipsiness, the way it blunted my edges and made socializing easier. "Come on. We should get decorating."

We popped the covers off the boxes. Decorations pressed up and out: tinsel and ornaments, pine cuttings and dried eucalyptus. White plates filled one entire box; blue tablecloths and white runners stuffed another. There were candles and twinkle lights and bags of dreidels and glittering Stars of David.

These decorations contained sixteen years of my Hanukkah memories. For Passover and the High Holidays, we rotated city homes, but for winter break, the Barbanels came to Golden Doors. Even if Hanukkah had come and gone, my grandparents made the house feel festive.

"What's the plan?" Tyler regarded the pile of goods with some dismay.

"Er." I had no idea how to translate this mess into Grandma's Pinterest-worthy interior design. I took a bracing sip of the Godiva. "Maybe we start with the wreaths?"

Tyler took his own sip, looking a little wary. "Seems easy enough."

We both regarded the pile uncertainly. And took more sips.

"Okay." I banged my drink down on the table. "Wreaths are easy. Let's go."

"You're the boss." He tapped at his phone. "I'll DJ. There's a Hanukkah playlist."

Wow, was he going to get an earful when he realized our songs were more about smiting enemies than decking halls. "Cool. Biggest wreaths on the front door and foyer, and the French doors here, I think? And then the smaller ones throughout the house."

There were two full boxes of wreaths: blue-and-silver wreaths, wreaths made with ribbons, or metal balls, or evergreens, or all of the above. We hung them everywhere we could find a nail or a hook. "This house is *massive*," Tyler said as we trotted upstairs and down, winding our way through the music room and the library and the rooms without names.

"It's great for hide-and-seek."

When we returned to the great room, we heard "for the terrible sacrifice justice and freedom demand" coming from the phone's speakers, and Tyler shot me a look. "Festive."

Actually, the song *did* feel festive to me, though I could never manage the key change. "I mean, ninety percent of Jewish holidays are about trying to survive and the rest are about trees, so we take what we can get."

"Trees?"

"Sometimes, they're about surviving *and* trees." I dug my laptop out of my bag, pulling up photos from past years so we could try to replicate Grandma's decorations. "Let's put runners on tables throughout the house, and we can arrange plates with ornaments and greenery. Like this, see? Around a candle or something."

Tyler's shoulder brushed against mine as he leaned close to see the screen. I pulled away. This wasn't as horrible as I'd expected, but I imagined again being snowed in with Isaac instead, Isaac helping me decorate, Isaac's shoulder touching mine. "Let's go."

With Tyler's phone blasting "Sevivon," we wove tinsel around banisters and tacked silver-sprayed leaves over paintings and mirrors. We filled vases with ornaments and sprigs of eucalyptus spray-painted white and placed dried bouquets of blue baby's breath in slim glass containers. We sprinkled dreidels and gelt on the hallway tables.

Next up came the great room. I studied old photos of Grandma's house. "Let's move the stuff off the fireplace mantels—we can put them on the bookshelves—and then we can try to replicate this picture. See?"

He knelt down by the drink cart again. "More brandy first, though. For creativity."

"For creativity, shouldn't we be drinking absinthe?"

He grinned up at me, doling out two more fingers of amber liquid. "Do you have absinthe?"

"I don't know," I admitted. "I just like *Moulin Rouge!*" I poured myself more Godiva, feeling pleasantly buzzy. "Game on."

We lined each mantel with a blue table runner, then placed the prettiest dreidels on top, along with candles and ornaments.

We scattered more decorations around the room and strung up sparkling Stars of David along the French doors. Nothing looked as classy as Grandma managed, but it certainly looked festive. *Hanukkah, oh Hanukkah, come light the menorah. Let's have a party; we'll all dance the hora . . .*

With everything satisfactory, I verified the existence of frozen pizza and preheated the oven. Then I glanced at the menorah. Technically, I should have lit it at sundown, but better later than never. "Are you, um, cool, if I light the candles?"

"Course." He watched as I slid two candles from the box and placed them in the menorah. "I thought it was the first night?" he said hesitantly. "Why two candles?"

I felt overly on display. "There's one candle for each night, and this candle, the shammash"—I nodded at the slightly raised candleholder—"is used to light the rest."

"How come?"

Oh no. Questions. I dredged my brain on the off chance answers had been caught in the nooks and crevices over the years. Surely I'd learned this in Hebrew school? *Because you do* didn't seem like a sufficient answer. "It's like—the other candles are too important to touch a match to them. So you light one candle, the servant candle, and it lights everything else."

"Does it matter what colors you use?" He nodded at the white shammash and blue candle.

"No, or only for fun." Arranging the candles was a big deal in my family. I was into patterns, Grandma liked alternating, and Noah was exacting, though one year he did all orange candles on the eighth night, and I still hadn't forgiven him. But to be fair, we always had more orange candles left over than any other, and we had to get rid of them somehow.

Tonight, I'd picked white for the shammash and blue for the first night. Classic. "Okay, um. I'm going to . . . sing. You don't have to pay attention or anything."

He frowned at me. "Why wouldn't I pay attention?"

Now I felt weirder and more flustered. "No reason. I don't know."

"Cool." He hesitated, hands in his pockets. "Should I do anything?"

"Um. Nope." I struck the match and fire bloomed out of nothing, accompanied by the faint scent of char. "Barukh ata Adonai," I sang, intimately aware of my thin, reedy voice alone in the silence. Usually, my voice blended with the voices of two dozen family members, collectively sounding strong and true and right, instead of my singular weak and hesitant voice. Still, I carried on, warbling on some notes, breaking on others. "Eloheinu melekh ha'olam, asher kid'shanu b'mitzvotav v'tzivanu l'hadlik ner shel Hanukkah."

I touched the match to the shammash, then the shammash to the first candle. My family always raced to light all the candles and replace the shammash before we finished the prayer. By the seventh and eighth nights, this meant stretching out the last words of the song like a college kid with quarters. But on the first night, the lighting could be leisurely, no rush, plenty of time.

With a practiced flick, I extinguished the match and set it on a small plate, breathing in the nostalgic scent and watching the lights flicker. In the Hanukkah story, the oil lasted for eight nights instead of only one. The Hanukkah miracle. The Festival of Lights.

A massive *crack* boomed through the house, and everything went dark.

CHAPTER FIVE

With the great room plunged into darkness, the two candles flickered boldly. Now instead of seeing our faces reflected in the large French doors, we could see snow still falling, piling high in navy-blue drifts while the moon and stars shone bright.

"Man." Tyler sounded slightly impressed, like he was pleased nature had pulled one over on us. "I bet a power line went down."

"Do you think the heat's still on?"

"Yeah, why wouldn't it be?"

"I don't know! Your heat wasn't." I padded over to the doors, mesmerized by the snow—and nervously aware of Tyler in a way I'd almost shaken off in the past few hours. What a difference darkness could make. "What if our families can't get here tomorrow, either?"

"Then I guess we'll have to forage in the pantries of the Nantucket elite for food. Speaking of." He glanced at the oven, the planes of his face cast into stark contrast by the candlelight, as intense as a Caravaggio painting.

"Oh no." The oven's power had been cut; so much for pizza. "Let's see what else we can eat."

Our phones' flashlights cut through the dark, keeping us from crashing into chairs and walls as we made our way into the pantry. I could feel Tyler behind me. We ran our beams of light over the shadowy cupboards, inspecting cans of diced tomatoes and chickpeas and black beans, containers of couscous and spaghetti and orzo and rice. An alphabetized spice rack lined one wall, and rows of unopened condiments filled a drawer.

I regarded the bounty. "PB&J sandwiches on stoned wheat thins?" I spied a maple leaf–shaped glass bottle on the shelf. "Oh! And we can make candies."

"What?"

"You know. Maple syrup on fresh snow. Didn't you do that when you were little?"

I could see the dark shape of his head as he shook it.

"Come on, then." I grabbed the maple syrup, while he carried the other supplies into the dining room. "Put the stuff down and follow me."

Tyler hesitated, looking at the menorah. "Should we blow the candles out?"

"No!" I whipped my body back toward him. "You can't blow out the candles."

"Why not?"

"Because . . . because you can't. You let them burn down all the way."

"Isn't it a fire hazard if we leave?"

Certainly it would be unfortunate to burn down my grand-parents' two-hundred-year-old mansion. However. "They've never tipped over before."

"Your funeral," he said skeptically. The darkness seemed to intensify the sound of his voice, giving it greater weight and depth. At least the lack of light also hid the shiver down the back of my neck, the goose bumps on my arms at being cocooned in the dark.

I led him to the foyer, where we stuffed our arms back into our coats and shoved our feet into boots without bothering to lace them. On the porch, the snow sparkled like fallen starlight, swooping in hollows and hills and lying thick on the front lawn. The air was cold and fresh, like drinking ice water. Even though the storm had kept my family away, I couldn't help but love what it had created: the gentle silence, the calm that stole into you when snow blanketed the world.

I poured two lines of syrup, and gave the amber liquid time to seep through the ice crystals and harden. Then I peeled my mitten off and scooped up the soft candy, popping it into my mouth. Sweet and sticky. I laughed. I hadn't done this since I was ten.

When I looked at Tyler, he watched me, bemused. I nodded at his line. "Try it."

He did, closing his eyes, his mouth moving as the ice and sugar melted on his tongue. Flushed, I looked away and focused on the far-off moon drifting through hazy clouds, a luminescent, misshapen pearl.

"Tastes like maple syrup," he said.

"But funner, right?"

He laughed. "Yeah."

For a silent moment we stayed there. The wind whisked up fine sheets of snow, twirling them through the air. The night felt the way the poets tried to describe but could never quite capture. You could only sink yourself into it until your fingers were numb and you couldn't stop shivering. And then you drank in one more gulp of the cold night, and went back inside.

In the great room, the menorah still glowed, both candles shrinking while their flames danced long and bright. We topped off our glasses, my chocolate liqueur bringing a warm ball of fire to my stomach, and lit the other candles scattered around the great room, until light flickered everywhere.

Tyler glanced at one of the fireplaces. "Do they work?"

"Yeah. My grandparents use them all winter."

"Let's light a fire, then."

"I hope you were a Boy Scout." I sipped my drink, feeling more dazzly and generous toward Tyler than I had in years. "Because fire lighting is not part of my skill set."

"I was."

I gaped at him. "You were not."

"Why so skeptical?" He examined the logs and bin of kindling next to one fireplace. "Not all of us were raised in concrete jungles. Got any old newspapers?"

"You were raised in LA. And you go to NYU." I found him an old stack of *The Boston Globe* in the recycling.

"Keeping track of me, Shir?"

"Shir*a*. And it's not 'keeping track' to possess ears. They accumulate knowledge whether I want them to or not."

He crumpled up several sheets of newsprint and placed them strategically around a tent of twigs over the logs. "The lady doth protest too much."

I rolled my eyes. "Anyway. Being a Boy Scout seems so *wholesome*."

"You don't think I'm wholesome?" He struck a match; blue flame appeared on the end, and he held it toward a sheet of newsprint.

Half a dozen images of him played through my mind, ending with the time I'd walked in on him half naked two summers ago. "It's not your brand."

"Brands are created, not born." The fire took hold. "Aha!"

I let out a laugh of sheer pleasure at the success, then bit it back. Had I had too much to drink? I felt loose and happy as I watched the fire grow, as we sat on the floor and assembled our peanut-butter-and-jelly dinners on a low coffee table between us.

Tyler picked up one of the dreidels we'd placed on the table earlier. "How do you play?"

"It's easy." I took the dreidel, a classic of my childhood: wooden, with each letter slightly engraved and painted in a different color. "Each player puts in a penny at the beginning of a turn, then spins. The side you land on determines what you do." I gave the post a quick twist and smiled, pleased with the length of time it took to topple.

When it did, gimel lay on top. My smile widened. "This is gimel, the best. It means you get all the coins in the pot." I turned the dreidel to the side. "This is hey. You get half the pot." Another two turns. "Nun, so you get none; and shin, when you have to put a coin in. The worst."

"Do you speak Hebrew?"

"Not really. Not like my grandparents or Isaac." Shoot. No reason for me to mention Isaac. I hurried on. "But I can read it phonetically, and I know one or two phrases."

"Like what?"

"Oh, I don't know. The first line of a lot of the prayers is the same—blessed are you, lord god, ruler of the universe, et cetera, et cetera."

"Quite the sobriquet."

"Have you heard what they used to call the Pharaohs? People *lived* for these names back in the day."

He grinned. "Okay, let's play."

"We'd need gelt or pennies."

He cocked his head, firelight flickering over his face. "I'm sure there's drinking games without either."

For some reason I flushed. "Probably. But none I know."

A smile danced at the corners of his mouth. "I bet there's some kind of strip dreidel, too."

I took a quick sip of Godiva. The alcohol burned in my belly, low and warm. "Would be a pretty quick game if you landed on gimel."

He laughed. "Well, what would it mean? What's the pot—the other person's clothes or your own?" He gave the dreidel a whirl. It spun haltingly, then toppled over.

Of course he'd get gimel. He raised his brows at me, and I gave him my stoniest expression. No stripping for me.

He looked down with a small, private smile. "What's the story?"

"The Hanukkah story?" He nodded. I regarded the burning candles, low now in the menorah, wax spilling over the sides. "There was a lamp. With only enough oil for one night—but it burned for eight instead. A miracle."

"Then why don't you burn oil instead of candles?"

I looked at him sharply, then let out a brief laugh. "I don't know."

He smiled, his expression soft in the candlelight. I was struck by the moment's intimacy, like we were the only two people in the world, like we'd been this close a hundred times before and would be a hundred times again. Delusions from the alcohol, probably.

"Do you believe in miracles?" he asked. He faced the candles, their light dancing across his cheekbones and brow.

My instinct was to say no, to almost scoff at the idea, but he looked . . . almost fragile. "I don't know," I said instead. "Do you?"

"Maybe not in *miracles*. Not divine things delivered on a silver platter. But . . . miraculous events? Maybe."

"Like what?"

He glanced at me, then smiled again. It was a bright, wide smile, the one I was most used to seeing on his face. He'd pulled it out so quickly, like a switch had been flicked. Could a smile deployed so suddenly be real, or was it more a curtain whisking shut to hide what was really going on?

I'd never noticed before how many smiles he had.

"You know," he said easily. "A perfect GPA. Being able to sleep, party, *and* study."

The way he'd pulled out his smile, the way his voice had been vulnerable and now sounded smooth, made me sure he lied, sure he wanted something more than good grades and eight hours a night. "You're sure those are the only miracles you want?"

Something hardened under the planes of his face, but then it was gone. He leaned forward, a gleam in his eyes. "You know, you're actually sort of cute."

"Excuse me, *what*?" I sat back, cheeks burning.

"I never noticed before. I'm used to thinking of you as . . . young. Pesky."

"Gee, thanks," I said, mortally offended. "You really know how to boost a girl's self-esteem."

"We've got this whole house to ourselves." He spun the dreidel idly. It landed on gimel, *again*. "Imagine if we were on the same page about how to have fun."

I shook my head. "You'd hook up with anyone you were snowed in with for a night, wouldn't you?"

He shrugged. "It'd pass the time."

This boy. What would it be like, to be so comfortable with hooking up? "So would Bananagrams."

He laughed. "True. You wanna play Bananagrams?"

Actually? "Yeah. Let's."

We played Bananagrams until long after the menorah's candles had burned down, leaving puddles of wax in the holders. The fire burned low, embers glowing. "How are you so good at this?" he asked after I won for the third time in a row.

"Years of playing Scrabble with my grandma." I yawned and checked my phone, surprised to see the hour closing in on eleven. "Bedtime?"

We blew out the candles around the room and turned on our phone flashlights as we crept once more through the dark house. Our phones illuminated paintings and mirrors, then the stairs, then the doorknob of the guest room I'd picked for him. Not too far from my own, actually. The house was dark and a little scary; I wanted a human body near mine. "Here we are."

I pushed the door open. We pointed our phones inward, their two beams of light haphazardly piercing the darkness. Two twin beds, a dresser. I headed to the closet, where I found a clean towel ready for guests. I grabbed it and turned back.

But Tyler had moved forward, and in the darkness, I didn't see him quickly enough. We collided. I dropped the towel and my phone and almost fell. Tyler caught me, his hands on my waist, his own phone dropping to the bed, the flashlight going out.

"Whoa." He steadied us. "You okay?"

It was dark except for the blue rectangle of night outside the window. I could hear his breathing. I could hear my own heartbeat and hoped he couldn't. One of his hands burned hot against my hip.

I didn't *like* Tyler Nelson. He didn't like me; he liked entertainment. Yet I didn't move. I listened to his breathing, felt the feathering of his breath across my face.

Then he inhaled jaggedly and stepped back. "Sorry."

Thank god for the dark, blotting away the redness of my face. "Right. Yeah. Um, here's your towel."

"Thanks."

"Right. Okay. Are you all set?"

"Yeah. Thanks."

"Yeah." I cleared my throat. "Good night."

After rapidly brushing my teeth and washing my face, I retreated to my room, opening the window and sucking in the night air: delicious and sweet and refreshing, more liquid than oxygen, intoxicating enough to get drunk on. I smoothed my hands out on the windowsill. Usually, Nantucket calmed me, the eye in the middle of the storm. But nothing could calm me in the face of Tyler Nelson.

I dropped into bed, head cushioned by the soft pillows, less firm than the ones at home, and tried not to think about him. I pulled the familiar blue quilt up to my chin and closed my eyes.

As I drifted off to sleep, I wondered what kind of miracle perfect, golden Tyler Nelson could possibly want.

CHAPTER SIX

I woke from unsettling, titillating dreams I couldn't remember.

From bed, I could see an expanse of distant blue sky outside, unlike the low white ceiling of yesterday. The storm had blown over. Snow glittered beneath the early sun, piled in heaps across the lawn and frosting the tall pines. In the distance, the sapphire sea sparkled brightly.

Sapphire sea like sapphire eyes. Oh god. Tyler Nelson was here.

I changed from my actual pajamas to cute flannel bottoms and a black Henley and holstered my hair in a ponytail before heading downstairs. The decorations we'd put up made me smile. No wonder Grandma did this every year; a hint of festiveness could lift your whole mood. The wreaths made of silver and blue ornaments, the dreidels scattered on tables, the HAPPY CHANUKAH! sign strung across one doorway, handcrafted by the triplets out of construction paper and glitter a few years ago—it made December feel right.

As I entered the great room, I heard the crackle of the fire. Surprised, I turned to the fireplace and found Tyler in his own flannels. He held a Dutch oven and stared at it with intense concentration.

"Um. Good morning?"

He looked up and hope flared on his face. "Good, you're up. Is this a Dutch oven?"

"Um. Yes. Why?"

He gave me a woeful look. "If I don't have coffee before noon every day, I'll die. I can put this in the fire, right?"

"I . . . think so?"

Good enough for Tyler. He placed the Dutch oven in the fireplace, and used a poker to nudge it into the embers. "Do you want any?"

"Um." I watched, bemused. "No. Thanks. You're boiling water?"

"It was either this or hold a pot over the fire itself. Which I tried, but my arm got too hot."

"Wow. Commitment. We could make oatmeal, too."

He brightened. There was something soft about him right now, sleep-tousled and slow. "Good idea."

With the water sufficiently hot, we assembled coffee and oatmeal, dusting the latter with cinnamon and honey. "We're regular pioneers," Tyler said happily. "God, I love coffee. It's great your oil lasted for eight nights and all, but if I had to pick a miraculously unending power source, it would be coffee."

"You're an addict." I smiled slightly. Tyler Nelson—weirder than I had thought. "Have you heard from your moms?"

"Yeah, they'll be here on the three o'clock."

"Same with my family."

He ate a spoonful of oatmeal, then spoke, very lightly. "I could go home now."

"You could." I aimed for the same airy tone. It was harder, in the bright light of morning, without the support of alcohol, to sound casual and open. "Or you can stay. It's not like I have anything urgent to take care of." It felt almost indulgent, to not have to run off to math tutoring or a café shift or homework.

"What an indolent life you live."

"Please," I said, slightly insulted. "I have a job."

"Seriously? What?"

"I'm a barista."

He shook his head. "You're joking."

"I'm not." Unlike most things I used to fill my time with, there was no pressure in making coffee. I didn't have to beat myself up if I got an order wrong. Fine, yes, I had in the beginning, but I'd figured it out. It turned out you could perfect coffee making faster than a double axel. Now I never disappointed anyone.

"I would've guessed you'd be interning at Barbanel or something."

I made a face. "There's nothing I want less than to work in accounting."

He sipped his coffee. "Doesn't your family also have a media company?"

"Danziger Media, yeah. My grandma's family." I let out a sigh. "Isaac makes it seem like a lot of work, though."

Tyler's brows rose. "Who's Isaac?"

Oh no. Oops. "No one."

He put his mug down. "Are you *blushing*?"

"No," I said quickly.

"Why are you blushing?"

"I'm not. I wouldn't. I was just thinking."

"Liar." He leaned forward and smiled a taunting, beautiful smile. "Isaac?"

I looked down at my bowl, trying to find an extra oat I hadn't yet scraped up. "He works for my uncle."

"You've been holding out on me," he drawled. "You like him."

I shrugged and held myself stiffly, posture perfectly correct.

"Wow. Okay. What's his deal? Why are you into him?"

I didn't need to think; I'd gone over this list so often. "He's smart and ambitious and driven." Every time I saw Isaac, even at a corporate event my family was sponsoring, I was blown away by how impressive he seemed. He knew exactly who he was, exactly what he was doing. I—someone who had no idea who I currently was—found that intoxicating.

"And hot?"

"It doesn't hurt." Hot in a completely different way than Tyler; less Hollywood, more Byronic. Like someone you could take seriously, who would talk about important things, not someone who would flit around from girl to girl like an indecisive hummingbird.

"Smart and ambitious and driven," he mulled. "Are those the most important traits someone can have? What about funny? A good listener? Kind?"

"Sure," I agreed. He was probably all of those, too. "And he seems serious. Like someone who commits."

Tyler made a face. "*That's* the most important trait?"

I straightened. "It's pretty much the only important one if you actually want to be in a relationship."

"And that's the most important thing to you?" He tilted his head. "Why do you want it so much?"

"What do you mean, *why*?" I lifted my chin. "I don't know. I'd like someone to make out with."

His eyes locked on mine. "You don't need a relationship to make out with someone."

My cheeks were as fired up as I was. "It's what I want."

"Right." He looked away, breathing a little harder than before. "Okay, then."

"I take it you don't want a relationship." As though I hadn't already figured that out by watching him over the years.

He shrugged. "I don't see what's the big deal about committing to someone while we're young. We're not going to meet our soul mates right now, so why not have a good time?"

"Some might call being in a relationship a good time."

"Fine. We're at an impasse." His gaze roamed away from me, settling on the French doors. "Want to go outside?"

I looked at him, startled. "It's freezing out."

"It's twenty-seven degrees. Warmer than yesterday."

"Technically, twenty-seven is still freezing."

"We'll wear thick socks." His eyes shone with an almost childlike delight. "Come on, it'll be fun."

I looked at him. Really looked at him. He radiated excitement about frolicking in the snow, with me of all people. He wasn't trying to charm me. He just wanted to play in the snow.

So we bundled up. Hat low, gloves on, boots tight. "Okay. Here goes." I slid the French doors open and we stepped outside.

The air hit the exposed bits of my face, cold and bracing, but not biting. After temperatures in the low teens yesterday, twenty-seven really did feel practically balmy. Or, at least, my chin didn't feel like it was being burned with frozen fire.

We waded out. A thin crust of crystal had formed on the snow's surface, and each step sent our feet plunging through. I moved carefully, testing the safety of my boots and snow pants, watching how deep my legs went into each drift. Tyler, however, tromped gleefully toward the edge of the lawn, where a hedge separated the yard from the gardens. "What's through here?"

"I'll give you the tour."

Crossing under an arch in the hedge and entering the garden always had reminded me of passing through the wardrobe into Narnia, and never more so than today, with the winter wonderland spread out before us. On either side of a narrow path, fir trees and junipers rose high, crowding out the sky. Ice coated the needles of the evergreens, encasing each in a thin, glass-like layer. Snow weighed down the branches. Nearby, a wind chime sounded, its bell-like melody cutting through the air.

"You'd never know we were so close to the sea," Tyler said.

"You can see it if you continue down the path to the cliffs." I placed my hand on the trunk of an evergreen. "Or I used to climb this when I was little, and there's a spectacular view. Bet I still could."

"Not with the snow everywhere."

"Could too." I hadn't climbed the tree in years, and the branches appeared more spindly than they used to. Still. Placing one foot on a thick branch close to the trunk, I hoisted myself up.

"Shira, I wasn't daring you—"

"Chicken?" I tossed down, taking a step upward. It came back to me, the slow, steady climb, testing my weight against each branch before stepping onto it, keeping one hand anchored around a secure limb at every moment. How to climb with your legs, not pull with your arms.

"What if you break your neck?" Tyler hollered.

I grinned down at him. "Then you'll be arrested for my murder!"

He sucked in a laugh, then placed his foot on the first branch. We climbed two stories, then paused in a gap between the branches. We could see the gardens, the gazebo, the dunes, the sea. I sat on one of the sturdier branches, hooking my arm around another, and sighed contently.

"Shira Barbanel." Tyler shook his head, white puffs of breath coming from his mouth, his head a foot lower than mine as he stood on another branch. "Who knew?"

"Knew what?"

"That you're a daredevil."

No one had ever called me that before. I wasn't used to thinking of myself as someone who took risks. But I wanted to be, didn't I? I wanted to win over Isaac, even if it meant putting myself out there. Like Tyler did.

A slow, insidious idea began to work its way into my thoughts as we climbed back down and headed inside, then pulled off our coats and boots and hats. The electricity, to my relief, had returned, so I started heating up hot water for cocoa.

Tyler was so easygoing, so confident and relaxed. He knew how to make people feel warm and comfortable and special—all the reasons I'd fallen for him in the first place. I wasn't in danger of falling for him again. He liked casual hooking up, while I craved an actual relationship. But he knew how to get people to like him. He knew how to flirt.

I had no idea how to flirt, but maybe I could learn if I approached it the same way I'd approached skating and piano and any school subject I did poorly in: with study, discipline, and training. By hiring an expert as my teacher.

We sat at the kitchen island, now clear of the wooden chest, which I'd brought to my room to keep it safe from the littles' imminent arrival. We mixed hot cocoa into our mugs. "I was thinking."

"A monumental feat, I'm sure."

I clutched my mug, inhaling the rich scent of chocolate, and tried to speak delicately. "I'm not very good with boys."

"What do you mean?"

Okay. The blunt version, then. "I suck at flirting. I don't know how to make guys like me."

"Just be you."

"I've tried." My voice came out sharper than I'd intended. "It hasn't worked."

His smile had an edge. "I suppose your other option is to be someone else, then."

"Huh?"

"Nothing. Never mind. Shira, you want to be with someone who genuinely likes you."

"Right. Yeah. But how do I get them to like me? I could use

help. And when you need help, you get a tutor." I took a steadying sip of hot chocolate. "So. Tyler. I have a proposition."

"A *proposition*?"

"You're easy to get along with. Everyone thinks so. And you're good at hooking up."

"I feel like I'm about to be insulted."

"I don't mean it in a bad way. But you've had a lot of practice. More practice than me, obviously."

"Where's this going?"

I pinned my gaze behind him, at the blue and silver tinsel we'd arranged around blue and silver ornaments. "Look—I've never even been kissed."

He looked taken aback but reined it in quickly. "Okay."

"I don't even know how to get there. *You* know how. You understand the whole flirting game. So teach me."

Sheer astonishment took over his face. "Are you serious?"

"Please." I turned imploring. "I *know* Isaac and I would be a good fit, if I could only figure out how to talk to him instead of chatting about the weather every time I see him."

"God." He shoved his hair. "Right. Isaac."

"He's going to be here this week. And I don't know how to switch from being his boss's grandniece to a romantic prospect, let alone how to get to the about-to-kiss point."

He kept frowning. "So what are you asking for? Kissing lessons?"

"Don't get ahead of yourself," I said, alarmed. "No. I don't think so? I want you to teach me how to flirt. How to talk to boys. How to make them like me romantically."

"Wow." He stared at me a moment, stunned. "Why would I agree?"

"I don't know. Maybe you could get something out of it, too. What do you want?"

He studied me, and I thought he was considering this bizarre, inane idea of mine. But then he shook his head. "Noah would murder me."

"You need a better reason to say no than my *cousin*."

"You might not believe this about me, but I try to live my life as stress-free as possible, and dealing with Noah is stress-inducing."

I blew out a breath. "*Please*, Tyler. This would be perfect. It won't piss anyone off because there's no emotions involved—I'd never fall for you again, and you're not interested in me, so no one can get hurt. Tell me. What would it take?"

He paused, his gaze falling to his mug, then rising again. "Your great-uncle is Arnold Danziger, isn't he?"

Oh. I could feel myself emotionally retreating, wary. "Yes."

"CEO of Danziger Media."

". . . Yes."

"I could use an internship with him."

I was almost disappointed. I don't know what I'd expected—when your family was appallingly wealthy, everyone wanted a piece, even people also from well-off families. Still, I'd hoped Tyler would ask for something less tangible, more along the lines of him teaching me to flirt—a little silly, a little entertaining, but not a real-world monetary asset. "I can't promise you an internship."

"An interview, then."

"I didn't know you were interested in media."

He hesitated, then shook his head. "You know what—never mind."

"Never mind which part?"

"All of it."

All of it seemed a bit extreme. "What about meeting my great-uncle?"

Tyler shook his head. "One meeting doesn't leave an impression. In marketing they say you need seven impressions before advertising sticks."

"I can't get you *seven* meetings! They're only here a week."

"Five, then."

"Two."

"Four."

"Three."

"Done." He nodded slowly. "Three meetings, and I'll teach you to flirt."

My shoulders slumped in relief. "Thank god. When can we start? Tomorrow? I could come over around one."

"Okay. Should we shake on it?" He raised his brows. "Or kiss to seal the deal?"

I narrowed my eyes, aware he was goading me. Determined to get the upper hand, I leaned across the island and bussed him quickly, my lips glancing against his fleetingly before I pulled back.

His eyes went wide and surprised. Then he broke out in a wide grin. "You desperately wanted me to be your first kiss, didn't you?"

"You're so full of it." I gave him an arch look. "And honestly, I wasn't so impressed."

His grin widened. "Shira Barbanel." He shook his head at me, and then a laugh burst out of him.

And try as I might, I couldn't stop myself from joining in.

CHAPTER
SEVEN

An hour after Tyler left, my family arrived in a rush.

They poured into Golden Doors, pushing and yelling, a shifting mass of cousins and luggage and babies and chaos, and I could feel my heart expanding, my whole soul brightening. The triplets rushed in, followed by aunts and uncles, toddling Steffie trailing in their wake. She hadn't quite mastered walking and shuffled briefly before falling to the ground, rump in the air.

I picked her up so she wouldn't get trampled. She wore an elephant suit, soft and plush, and her brown eyes blinked up at me. I stroked her tiny head, her hair still soft and fine but already that familiar Barbanel brown. "Hello, Steffie. You can't keep up with the big kids; you're too little."

Thankfully, her normal impulse to burst into tears at any

given moment was overridden by surprise at seeing me. She stuck her thumb in her mouth and sucked.

"Hey, Shira." Noah walked in, followed by Abby, his girl-friend. He looked half-pleased and half-disinterested by the sight of me—his standard reaction, which was annoying given how all I really wanted was to hang out with him. But affection dwarfed my irritation. He'd left for college in August, and save visits at the High Holidays and Thanksgiving, I hadn't seen him in months—a lonely switch, since I used to see him almost every day.

I shifted the baby to my hip and one-arm hugged him. "How was the ceremony?"

"It was fine."

Abby nudged him. "It was a very big deal," she corrected. "There hasn't been a freshman who won in a decade."

"It was mostly because of my advisor," he said. "I just helped out."

Noah had spent his first semester of freshman year interning with a professor at the Arnold Arboretum in Boston, and had received a special award for his contributions. This was just like Noah, to not only know exactly what he wanted to do, but to also win awards for it. "I wish I'd been there." I glanced at Abby. "Did you go?"

"Barely made it," she said. Abby was a senior in high school, a year older than me. "My dad drove me into the city after my last final."

Weird how Massachusetts people called *Boston* "the city," but okay. "Cool."

The wave of relatives pushed them on, up the stairs with their bags in hand. Abby would share my room, but I wondered how much I'd see her. I didn't know her well, but she seemed fine so far. Nosy, but she made Noah happy.

They were followed by Aunt Liz, who removed her offspring from my arms with an "Oh, good, you found her," and then by Grandma and Grandpa. Grandpa tolerated a hug from me; he was ninety—impossibly old—but still moving. Grandma wasn't much younger but still seemed spry and spoke crisply. "How are you, dear? Survived the night in this drafty old house?"

"She was *fine*, Helen," Grandpa said. "She's not a child."

Grandma rolled her eyes (which she swore she'd picked up from me) and swept on, while Grandpa turned in the opposite direction. I watched them, unease curling in my stomach.

When Noah and I were little and my grandparents lived in Manhattan, we used to see them all the time. But a few years ago, they moved to Nantucket full-time, so I saw their interactions less. Their marriage had never been filled with PDA, which I'd always assumed was because they were old and prudish. But lately . . .

My parents appeared. Mom pulled me into a tight hug before setting me back and studying me, as though expecting to find a broken limb or other injury. "Are you okay?"

"It was only one night." Sometimes I wished my parents had had more kids, so they could spread the worry around.

Dad gave me a brief hug before returning to his conversation with my uncle Harry, Noah's father. Dad always had Very Important things to discuss with his siblings and parents, which apparently was what happened when you were an executive in a Very Important firm. Mom swept my hair out of my face. "How did your midterms go?"

"They went."

Her eyes narrowed. "Shira—"

"Mom."

She sighed. "You said you were fine with Dad and me going to Boston."

I shrugged.

"Are you upset we missed the first night of Hanukkah?"

I unbent, since she looked so concerned. "You couldn't help it."

She hugged me. "Honey, I'm sorry. You know we would've rather been here with you."

"I know. Anyway, the tests were fine. I just missed you."

"Well, by the end of the holidays you'll be sick of us," she teased.

Unlikely. I never got sick of my family.

"Shira!"

I turned at the familiar voice, and threw my arms around my cousin David. He lifted me off the ground, squeezing tight. At sixteen, he was the closest cousin in age to me, the middle of three boys. He was the only Barbanel to alter our ubiquitous glossy brown curls and currently had them dyed dark violet. "How was the wild night alone in Golden Doors? Meet any ghosts?" He waggled his brows. "I hear Tyler Nelson stayed the night."

"It was entirely innocent." We headed upstairs so he could dump his things in the room he'd be sharing with his younger brother, Oliver.

"To your utmost regret, I'm sure."

"Are you kidding? I don't want anything to do with him."

"What's wrong with you, then?"

I flopped down on one of the twin beds covered in a green-plaid duvet and groaned.

"Ah." Realization dawned on David's face. "I forgot Isaac's coming."

"Don't say a word," I warned him. The idea of my family knowing about any of my crushes killed me.

He pantomimed zipping his lips shut. "He gets his own room, you know. Ethan's with Noah." Ethan was David's older brother, and I wasn't too surprised by the setup. Grandma would consider Isaac a proper guest, which meant he'd get plenty of space.

And if Isaac had his own room . . . With all the family here, it could be hard to find a private space. But maybe . . .

I'd never been alone in a boy's room before. I'd never even seen Isaac in casual clothes, just the nice slacks and button-downs he always wore when I ran into him at events. Now I pictured him wearing a simple T-shirt and sitting on his bed and saying, *Hey, Shira, come in.*

David interrupted my daydreams, making a face at the other bed. "Maybe I should bunk with you and Miri."

"We've got Abby with us." Abby, interestingly, did not count as a proper guest, but I wasn't sure if that was because Grandma had accepted her into the fold or because the adults wanted to make it hard for Abby and Noah to hook up. "And Oliver's not bad." David's fourteen-year-old brother would rather wander the grounds, dreamy-eyed and lost in his own head, than cause any trouble.

"He's going through a Billie Eilish phase, god help me."

"Excuse me, we *love* Billie Eilish."

David pointed to himself. "This part of 'we' loves Billie Eilish in small doses. Also, he keeps jerking off to her."

"Ew." I held up a hand. "I don't want to know."

As David unpacked, other cousins routinely barged in. Noah wanted me to show Abby the room we'd be sharing; eight-year-old Kate needed help untangling a necklace; fourteen-year-old Miriam and twelve-year-old Gabe wanted me to settle an argument; Oliver drifted in to lie on his bed. Warmth spread to every nook and cranny of my body. *This* was what Golden Doors was, a gathering of all the people in the world I loved. This was what made the holidays special.

"Kids!" Uncle Jason shouted from the bottom of the stairs. "Come help with dinner!"

Downstairs, I joined the latke-making crew. Noah and Abby grated potatoes and squeezed water from the shreds—my least favorite task, given how the starchy liquid ran in rivulets over your hands and dried out your skin. Aunt Liz tossed McIntosh chunks into a pot with hefty doses of cinnamon, sugar, and lemon juice, their heady and sweet scents perfuming the air. At another burner, her husband tossed a slice of onion into a thick layer of oil, waiting for tiny bubbles to froth over the translucent sliver before sliding in latke patties.

I was about to start chopping more onions when Grandma swept by. "Shira, come along."

I trailed in her wake, feeling a surge of pleasure at being chosen. "Where are we going?"

"I brought fresh flowers from Boston. You can help me arrange them. I want everything to be perfect when my brothers arrive."

It was a big deal, Grandma's brothers and their wives coming for Hanukkah. The Danzigers lived in New York and usually hosted their own celebrations—which we occasionally attended—but Grandma's brothers had never come to Nantucket before. Why would they, when they had their own kids and grandkids in New York?

The adults had freaked out when they'd heard the plan. They thought Grandma's brothers, who owned stock in Barbanel, wanted to convince Grandma to give them her shares. And the adults thought Grandma might, if she was mad enough at Grandpa. Personally, *I* was freaked over the idea that Grandma might be mad enough at Grandpa she'd help wrest control of his company away from him.

We entered Grandma's sunroom, a large, rectangular space off the east side of the house. Plants hung from the ceiling and grew in pots around the room. In one corner, she had a table of carefully tended orchids, which all seemed to thrive at her touch and her careful regimen of sunlamps and water. I loved this room, so uniquely Grandma, elegant and clean and minimalistic. The light in the room changed with the seasons: in the summer, Nantucket light felt rich and golden, like you were soaking up Kerrygold butter, but winter light felt crisper and sharper, capable of shattering at any moment.

I perched on a green settee and watched Grandma sort through her flowers. White roses and white lilies. Belladonna delphiniums, the dusky purple-blue of the darkening sky. Blue hydrangeas, the flower a staple of Nantucket. A basket of white carnations, half of which the little and middle cousins would dye tomorrow by sticking them in water with blue food coloring.

She handed me the roses, and I started slicing stems diagonally, knife biting through and into a wooden board. Grandma had told me that when she first came to Golden Doors, her favorite part was the sprawling gardens behind the house: all flowers and a rose garden, which bloomed each summer in a cascade of color.

"Are you excited for your brothers to get here?" I asked.

She glanced up. Her eyes were hazel, unlike the deep brown

of the rest of the family. "'Excited' is not, perhaps, the word I'd use."

In movies, grandmothers were soft and sweet or zany and loving. They baked cookies and wore cozy sweaters. *My* grandmother was like iron, tough enough to break any fairy-tale notions. Grandma, if she'd been a holiday candle, wouldn't be cinnamon-and-nutmeg scented but something cool, like snow and pine, amber and lavender. She twisted her hair in a chignon, wore necklaces and earrings every day, and drank an inch of Grand Marnier after dinner without fail. *Excited*, perhaps, would never be the right word for her. "What word, then?"

"I'm . . . interested. In how people will behave."

"People? Like Dad and Uncle Harry and the others? Or like your brothers?"

She shrugged. "Everyone, I suppose."

"Like Grandpa? Is this all because of him?"

"Not everything's about a man, dear."

"I know." Who was the twenty-first-century woman here? I changed the topic. "I found an old box when I went up to the attic to get the decorations. Filled with old stuff. I brought it to my room, but I thought you might want to see it."

"What's in it?"

"Things from the 1800s, I think. A painting and seashells and some other things. I think maybe it used to belong to a Barbanel woman. It was hidden beneath a floorboard."

Her brows rose. "A floorboard? Well. This house is full of secrets."

"Not unlike this family," I said, and her lips quirked up. "Do you know any old stories about Barbanel women from back then? Like if any of them had forbidden lovers?"

"Who didn't?" she asked dryly.

I gaped at her. "Did you?"

"No. If *I'd* been in love with someone, I would have married them." She gave a bouquet of white lilies a final touch in its slate-blue vase, her movements jerkier than usual, her expression tight. "There's plenty of books in your grandfather's study about the family. Let's see what we can find."

I followed her in silence. She'd clearly been alluding to how Grandpa used to be in love with Abby's grandmother, which had all come out last summer. I wanted to say *I'm sure Grandpa married you because he loved you*, but I wasn't sure he had, was I? It made me sick to my stomach to think of the two of them being unhappy.

Grandpa's study was in the original wing of the house, a low-ceilinged room with dark wood and heavy furniture. Grandma knocked once, firmly, then opened the door.

My grandfather looked up from behind his desk, his weathered face surprised. "Helen."

"Shira wants to look at some of the old family history," Grandma said coolly. "I thought you could help her."

"Of course," Grandpa said, but before he could say anything

more, Grandma had glided out the door, regal as a queen.

I smiled tentatively. "Hi, Grandpa."

Grandpa was old, even for a grandfather—he hadn't had his kids until he was in his thirties, and the next generation had done the same. Every time I saw him, I was surprised anew by how ancient he appeared.

Also, Grandpa and I didn't, like, hang out. I liked to sit next to him on the couch and read silently, and I helped him walk around the house when he needed an arm, but I didn't have much to *say* to him, other than *Yup, school, still happening. New York, still there.* "Um, so like Grandma said, I was hoping we had a family tree from the 1800s. I found this old box in the attic . . ."

He looked pleased, and I immediately felt bad. Maybe I should have tried harder earlier to find common ground. "What sort of box?"

I pulled a chair over next to him as I told the story again, and his creased face brightened. He stood—a slow, laborious moment in which I wasn't sure if I should assist or not. His back was bent as he made his way to the bookshelves, scanning through them and pulling out one volume after another until he found the one he wanted. "Here we go," he said, reseating himself with a long groan. He placed a binder before us and flipped through to a family tree.

"It sounds like you're looking for our family on Nantucket but before photography, then," Grandpa said. "Joseph Barbanel came to Nantucket at the turn of the nineteenth century. His father had a successful accounting office in New Bedford, which Joseph's older brother inherited. Joseph came to Nantucket, since the towns had a strong connection to the whaling trade." He flipped a page, showing me a sketch of a small house. "At first the Barbanels lived in town, but in the 1830s, Joseph's son, Marcus, had Golden Doors built."

I flipped back to the family tree, peering at the names. Joseph and Esther Barbanel were connected by a line at the very top, and two children descended from them: Marcus and his sister, Naomi. Marcus had three daughters; the family line descended from the eldest, Shoshana.

I pointed at Shoshana's name. "What's going on here? How come she kept her last name, and we have her name, not her husband's?"

Grandpa smiled, his finger wavering slightly as he tapped the page. "Shoshana married Nathaniel, her father's apprentice. He took the name Barbanel to continue the family line, and he helped her lead the business."

I studied the dates. Shoshana had been only eighteen when she married, and she had had five children. The eldest, Rebecca, would have been twenty in 1860. So we had three generations around before photography really took off: Marcus and his sister, Shoshana and *her* sisters, and potentially Rebecca and her profusion of siblings and cousins. Didn't exactly narrow down possibilities for the owner of the box. "Can I take pictures of these?"

"Of course, sweetheart."

I'd barely finished when Aunt Rachel, Noah's mom, poked her head inside. "Edward, dinner's ready—oh, hello, Shira."

"Hi, Aunt Rachel." I pushed to my feet and hovered until Grandpa was also standing, then looped my arm through his, offering silent support as we made our way to the dining room.

Most meals were taken in the great room, but when we wanted the whole family to be able to sit inside, we ate in the older, central portion of the house. The formal dining room had enough stately chairs around the mahogany table to seat a dozen adults. Opened doors led into a parlor, where we had seating for the cousins.

My table consisted of the older cousins: me, Noah (and Abby), David and his brothers, and Miriam. The middles and littles sat at the other table, and two-year-old Steffie sat in a high chair with the adults. Grandma and Grandpa had six children, which struck most people as excessive, but I loved having over a dozen cousins and almost as many aunts and uncles.

As Grandma picked up the matchbook at the main table, I picked up the one on ours. Iris, the triplets' ringleader, picked up the matches at the younger kids' table. Then I hesitated, gaze flicking to Abby. I'd fight the boys tooth and nail to light the menorah first, and Miriam would always give me precedence, but Mom and Grandma would 100 percent expect me to give this to Abby, a guest. I held the matchbook out. "Want to?"

Her eyes widened, and she shook her head quickly. "Another night."

This shouldn't have made me think more favorably of her, but it did.

"All right, everyone," Grandma said. She looked around the room to confirm our attention, then struck her match, light flaring at the tip. Iris and I followed. "Baruch atah Adonai . . ."

We sang the blessing, each table a half step off, laughing and chattering as the shammash was reinstalled. Then, from ancient, stapled packets of paper, we sang everyone's favorite songs before diving into dinner. I breathed in deeply, inhaling the smell of hot wax and fire and latkes and applesauce and cinnamon. If I could bottle a smell, I would bottle this one.

After dinner, everyone traipsed back into the great room. The adults drank wine and the kids ate milk chocolate gelt. The triplets started distributing the gift bags and packages that everyone had placed by the fireplaces. We ripped in, no orderly manner for us: the littles and middles went wild, the adults more measured, the older cousins in between. People called out in excitement and thanks, shouting over each other and waving gifts.

I'd made everyone DIY sugar scrubs and gotten Mom and Dad matching slippers and coffee mugs. I got a book from Noah and Abby, and from Grandma and Grandpa a pair of earrings. The various aunts and uncles gave gift cards, lotions, and candles. Grandma received two one-thousand-piece puzzles, which we'd all work on throughout the week.

I unwrapped a white cardboard box from Mom and Dad and opened it to find an elegant white sweater. I turned to Mom, beaming. "This is so nice! Thank you!"

"Happy Hanukkah." Mom kissed the top of my head.

Happy Hanukkah.

Once all the gifts were opened and the chaos had quieted into mild disarray, Iris, the oldest of the triplets, waved her arms. David and I shot each other wary looks. Triplet trouble: you couldn't avoid it. "I'd like everyone's attention! Can I get all the cousins upstairs?"

"One of these years, I'm going to get her a bullhorn," David muttered to me.

"Don't you dare."

Pushing to our feet, we trailed through the labyrinthine halls and staircases to the cousins' hang-out room. Situated on the second story, it had a sweeping view of the lawn and gardens and sea. Couches and beanbag chairs and board games and an entertainment system filled it, and the adults generally left us in peace here.

I squeezed onto one couch alongside Miriam and David, while Ethan—second oldest, just shy of eighteen—claimed one of the coveted recliners. "What's up, triple threats?" he asked.

Iris nodded as though Ethan's question had been in earnest. She clapped twice for everyone's attention, Lily and Rose perched on either side of her like a row of identical caryatids. "We've decided to put on a play."

A play. Of course. We were lucky it wasn't a musical; the triplets' bat mitzvahs had been Broadway-themed.

"It's a Hanukkah play," Iris continued. "I will be the director and narrator and General Holofernes. Rose will be Judah Maccabee. Lily will be Judith."

"Sounds fun." Noah made to stand. "Abby and I will bow out, though."

Iris threw a pillow at him with deadly accuracy. "Sit down. You're not getting out of this. You're Mattathias. Don't worry, he dies at the end of the first act."

Noah sat down.

"What is *happening*?" David hissed in my ear as the triplets handed out scripts with character names scribbled at the top. "Why do we give them so much power?"

"It's your fault," Miriam said from my other side. "You guys are the oldest. You should have pulled the plug years ago."

I gaped at her in betrayal. "*Noah* is the oldest! And Ethan!"

Lily arrived, handing me a script. "You're my handmaiden."

Judith, I was familiar with; her handmaiden, less so. I had the vague feeling she showed up in paintings and looked beleaguered. "What do I do?"

"You help me—I'm Judith—defeat the bad guys. I seduce the enemy and chop off his head."

"Do I get to chop off someone's head?" David asked.

"No. You get to be very bad at military defense. That's why

Judith needs to step up, because the men suck at getting anything done."

David took his script, looking resigned.

Iris waved her arms once more for attention. "Tonight, we'll do a read through. There're two story lines—Judith, who beheads General Holofernes, and the Maccabean Revolt. They're both about fighting imperial conquest, set hundreds of years apart. We start with a joint monologue between the kings, while behind them everyone acts out the bad stuff, like a statue of Zeus being put up and pigs slaughtered in the Temple." She nodded at six-year-old Jack, five-year-old Connor, and four-year-old Eva, who were currently squabbling over a pair of stuffed bears. "They'll be the pigs."

I blinked and tried to exchange a skeptical glance with Noah, but he was busy exchanging a skeptical glance with Abby.

"To be clear," Noah said, "you're going to dress the littles up as pigs and pretend to slaughter them?"

Iris nodded. "Yes."

Noah's mouth twitched. "Just checking."

"They *will* look pretty cute in pig outfits," Abby murmured.

"David, you'll be the statue of Zeus in this scene, so you need to work on a toga situation."

David and I began shaking with silent, unstoppable laughter. The triplets gave us icy stares.

"As the narrator, I start," Iris said. Stately as an orator in ancient Greece, she began to speak. "After twelve years of rule, Alexander the Great died, and his officers crowned themselves rulers in his place, and from them came many great and terrible evils . . ."

✸ ✸ ✸

At ten thirty, I called rehearsal. The littles had already gone to sleep, and the middles were drooping. "We'll practice more tomorrow," I assured the triplets, and hustled everyone off to bed.

I headed to my room alongside Miriam and Noah's girlfriend. When Abby left to brush her teeth, Miriam and I regarded the air mattress skeptically. "What do you think the plan is?" Miriam asked. "Think she'll stay here or sneak into Noah's room?"

"I don't know. Noah's sharing with Ethan." The rooms the Danzigers would stay in were currently empty.

Which reminded me. "Are we going to do this play in front of the *Danzigers*?" In front of Isaac? I felt sick. Isaac was adult, so polished—would he think a kids' play was fun and charming? Wait. Yes. Of course he would—it *was* fun and charming. Surely Isaac would agree.

"I guess. Uncle Arnold's bringing his assistant, right? The hot one?"

A jolt of competition shot through me, but I tried to sound casual. "Isaac?"

"Yeah. Him." Miriam giggled. "He's gorgeous."

"I guess." I reminded myself Miriam was fourteen, and Isaac was nineteen. Right. Calm down, self. *I'd* be lucky to get Isaac's attention—he wasn't going to hit on a fourteen-year-old.

The door opened, and we both flinched as Abby entered, looking slightly nervous. "Hey, guys."

"Hey."

"Hope you guys don't mind me crashing with you." She sat on her neatly made air mattress.

"Course not," I said. "Though we won't tattle or whatever if you go off with Noah."

Miriam clapped her hand over her mouth to stifle laughter.

Abby flushed, but she met my gaze, her own steady and evaluating. "Oh?"

Surprisingly, I wanted to end up in her good standing. "No. I mean, our parents might pop in to check on us since it's the first night, so wait until after then. But we're not going to be weird about it."

"Okay." She nodded slowly. "Thanks."

My mom and Miriam's did pop their heads in, making sure we were settled and wishing us good night. Soon after, Abby slipped away, leaving Miriam snuffling lightly on the other side of the bed. I closed my eyes, feeling warm and cozy and sated by the presence of so much family, like I'd been wrapped in a blanket.

For the first time in ages, I fell asleep without any trouble at all.

CHAPTER EIGHT

I woke to a text from Olivia, my best friend on the island. **I'm here!!** she wrote. **Are you free today? Meet for hot chocolate??**

Yes! I answered. **Have a thing at 1—how's 10?**

Olivia: Perf yes can't wait

I snagged a towel and headed for the bathroom. The smell of last night's fried potatoes clung to my body and my hair, saturating my curls like I'd wiped the latke pan with them. Latkes: great for smelling, not for smelling like.

I returned to my room in a cloud of rose and herbal scents, my body soothed by lotion, my curls lovingly tended with mousse and hair spray. Careful not to wake Miriam, who lay sprawled across half the bed, or Abby, who lay comatose on her air mattress as though she'd never left, I pulled on leggings and a sweatshirt and slipped out again.

Downstairs, Mom sat on one of the couches by the fireplace, nursing her coffee and reading on her phone. "Morning, sweetie. You did a wonderful job with the decorating."

I smiled, pleased, looking at the centerpiece on the coffee table before us, a glittery blue plate with a white pillar candle surrounded by ornaments. "Thanks." I sniffed the air, inhaling hints of butter and vanilla. "Are there pancakes?"

"Rumor has it," Mom said, smiling.

I drifted past lentils soaking in bowls of water for tonight's dinner, past a half-empty pot of coffee, to where Uncle Gerald flipped pancakes with the concentration of an ice-skater determined to stick their landing. Bubbles formed and popped on top of the batter, which sizzled when he slapped them down in the pan. I sidled up to him. "Those smell delicious."

"Flattery will get you everywhere." He nodded at a plate on the other side of the stove top. "You're in luck, there's a fresh batch."

"You're the best." I forked four golden-brown ovals onto a plate. They were thick, fluffy, and still steaming. I drizzled maple syrup on the side and carried my plate back to the low coffee table by Mom, sitting on the floor so I'd have proper leverage.

She eyed the pancakes hopefully. "Is one for me?"

One, in fact, was. "You're lucky I love you."

"Yum." She snagged a pancake and ate it plain. She said syrup or jam "drowned out the flavor," which, okay, incorrect. "Why are you up so early?"

"It's only eight thirty. I'm up earlier for school."

She raised her brows. "Not on weekends."

"Olivia and I are meeting up." I cut up my pancakes, salivating as I popped a piece into my mouth. I loved pancakes, especially Uncle Gerald's recipe, which used sourdough discard and tasted amazing.

I'd practically finished by the time David entered the room and flopped down next to me, rubbing his eyes. I turned away from Mom and Aunt Liz, who'd joined us, and studied David's wild purple hair. "You need a haircut," I told him. "It looks alive."

"It *is* alive. It is the source of my strength."

"That's Samson, not David." I pulled at one long strand. "Even if you want to keep growing it out, you need to trim it so it stays healthy."

"Whatever. Are there more pancakes?"

I nodded at the stove.

He came back and joined me on the floor before the coffee table. "How're you and Tom?" I asked.

"Tom?" David said, and the instantaneous disdain on his face made me wince. "Tom who?"

"Oh no."

"Tom *dumped* me three weeks ago." David slashed viciously at his pancakes.

"What happened?"

"Tom said he simply didn't 'feel strongly' enough for me, and so it wouldn't 'make sense' to keep dating, because he didn't think he could 'get to the same place' I'm at."

"Did you commit his entire breakup speech to memory, by any chance?"

"Maybe. Now he wants to be 'friends.' Legitimately. We went to the movies last weekend and got dinner after."

"Wow, no, do not be friends with him."

"We're being 'mature.'" He stabbed three stacked squares of pancake.

"Oh no."

"Oh yes. He asked if I still wanted to exchange presents because he'd already bought me mine, and he thought I would 'really like it.'"

"Please tell me you shot that down."

He smiled savagely. "I said sure! Because we're being civil. But I hadn't actually bought him anything yet, so I *went out and bought him a present* so we could exchange presents *as friends*."

"I hate all of this. Stop."

"I can't. I'm still in love with him. How do you stop being in love?"

"I think you stop seeing the person."

"I'm not that strong. Not if he still wants to see me."

"Ugh, I'm sorry. That sucks so much. He's an idiot."

"An idiot with a GPA of three point nine and a full ride to

Yale." David put his fork down so forcefully it spun off the table, clattering to the floor. "Fuck."

"Still an idiot," I said loyally, picking up the fork. "And IQ is different than EQ. He's a fool to let you go. You're amazing."

David pinched his nose. "That's true. I'm a fucking catch."

David's brothers wandered in, both in their pajamas: Ethan, tall and sleepy, Oliver, dreamy-eyed as always. "Morning, beauties," Ethan said, ruffling both David's and my hair.

I pulled away. "You'll mess up my curls."

He clasped his hand to his chest and staggered backward. "The horror!"

I couldn't quite suppress a smile as I shook my head. "You're ridiculous."

"Ridiculously . . . amazing? Handsome? Smart?" He paused briefly, then decided he had more good things to say about himself. "Adventurous? Sexy? Inspiring? A real leader among men?"

David, Oliver, and I stared at him.

"Ridiculously confident." I pushed my plate away and stood up. "Anyway, I'm off to see Olivia. Try not to have too much fun without me."

❋ ❋ ❋

Nantucket often looked like something out of a Hallmark movie. In the summer, tourists and locals alike marveled over the sandy beaches and quaint shops, the cobblestone streets and ice cream parlors. The island excelled at summer, all snapping American flags and sailboats and balmy breezes.

The off-season, on the other hand, could be desolate. The tourists rolled out and the fog rolled in, wind dashed waves against the shores, and slashing rain compounded the cold and gray. My grandparents swore they loved all seasons on Nantucket, but as David once remarked, parents also said they loved all their children equally.

On a day like today, though, Nantucket winter was at its best.

My breath formed merry puffs as I walked through town, dropped off by Aunt Liz on her way to Stop & Shop. Cotton-like clouds dotted the blue sky, and Christmas trees lined the streets. Merriment filled the air as people bustled about, bundled in scarves and bright coats. Parents tugged along their kids, groups of friends laughed and yelled. A child walked by me, hand in hand with her father, matching antlers sprouting from their hats.

One would think most people wouldn't want to visit a far-flung island during the darkest days of the year—and one would be, for the most part, right—but people occasionally came to Nantucket. Not just for the Stroll in early December, when carolers dressed up in Dickensian costumes and Santa arrived with the coast guard to hang the giant wreath on the lighthouse at Brant Point, but for the holiday, too. I understood why. Nantucket felt like a fairy tale, and as I walked through town, I peered at each window display, admiring the tiny figures of Santa and Mrs. Claus, the fake snow and elaborate dangling snowflakes, the tiny trains and nutcrackers and wintry jewelry.

Every so often, I'd see a menorah or dreidel, and they lifted my heart like a hug, calmed me like the sun after days of rain. I liked Christmas; I loved the happiness it brought to so many people. But it could feel overwhelming: the ceaseless music, the way people acted like I must be as excited about Hanukkah, a minor holiday, as they were about Christmas, but never noticed Passover or the High Holidays.

Turning off Main Street, I entered one of my favorite cafés. Inside, golden lights twinkled and two small trees stood in corners. The scent of chocolate perfumed the air, rich and decadent, with hints of vanilla and cinnamon and cherry. Olivia sat at an elegant round table with gold siding. The whole café was elegant, all gold and celadon green like a Parisian macaron shop. Olivia had slung her favorite blue peacoat over the back of her chair and was now finger-combing her sleek bob. We'd known each other since we were six, and despite not seeing each other for months at a time, our friendship always fell back into place as easily as a door snicking shut.

Still, for a moment I froze, nerves sweeping through me. I was so happy to see her, and yet after each long separation, I always worried she'd no longer be as excited by me, no matter how often we texted.

But I was being silly, so I made myself step forward. "Olivia! Hi!"

She jumped up, her scarf whipping behind her, dangly earrings spinning as she did. "You're here!" She threw her arms around me. "I'm so happy."

"Me too." My arms tightened around her, and I could feel my body relax. God, I was glad to see her. There weren't too many people I hugged: my family and Olivia were about it.

With eyes bigger than our stomachs, we ordered buttery croissants, half a dozen macarons, a gingerbread latte for me, and a peppermint mocha for her. We carted our treats back to the table she'd snagged. "Tell me everything," Olivia said. "I missed you! How were your tests? Is Isaac coming for sure?"

I cut the macarons in half and offered them to her for choosing, like Noah and I had done when we were little. "He'll be here tomorrow. I'm freaking out."

"When was the last time you saw him? The benefit thing in September?"

"And once in October at a museum gala. But I barely spoke to him then, just said hi." I ate a pistachio macaron half. "It's like, every time I'm in a circle with him, I want so much for him to notice me and be impressed by me, but I lose the ability to talk. So I smile and nod along with everyone else. *I'm* so impressed by him, but I can't tell if he even notices me."

"You'll make him notice you now."

"I hope so. I'm . . . preparing." I wanted to tell Olivia about the flirting-lesson plan, but not quite yet. Not until I'd had some gingerbread simple syrup to ramp me up. "How are you? Jackson's coming for New Year's, right?" This year, Olivia's parents had opted to spend New Year's on Nantucket instead of in their South End brownstone and planned to throw a Nutcracker-themed party.

"Ugh. Yes."

"Why the face? What's going on?"

"Oh, it's nothing. We're fine. But like I told you, Jackson's freaking out about college." Her animation rose, color filling her cheeks. "And I still can't do anything about it. My parents are Brown or bust, so it's not like I can follow him to another city. But he keeps saying there's no way he'll get into Brown, so I should apply to some of the New York schools he's looking at."

I tore off an edge of croissant covered with almond slivers. "Obviously I'd love for you to come to New York. But do you want to? I thought you also really loved Brown, not just your parents."

"I do! And I love Providence." She took a swig of her peppermint mocha. "It's not like I don't *want* to go to the same school as him. I just don't think it's important. I think we could do long distance, and I'm pissed he doesn't." She turned her mug in her hands. "Maybe that's the real thing bothering me. He's apparently decided if we're not at the same school, we're doomed. What—if I'm not *right there*, our feelings would fade? He'd hook up with other girls? What the hell?"

"He wouldn't. You know he's obsessed with you." I offered a tentative smile. "At least the party will be awesome?"

The parties thrown by Olivia's family were on a different level. Her dad was an event planner, and her older sister, Kaitlyn, threw an epic themed party every summer. Only looking at Olivia's expression made me think this party might be less than awesome. "What's wrong?"

She exhaled deeply. "My parents want me and Kaitlyn to dance at the party."

I blinked. "I'm sorry, what?"

"Mom's going to play 'The Nutcracker March'—you know, do, do-do-do do, do, do, doo, doooo—and we're going to dance."

I burst into laughter.

"Stop," she moaned, sinking her face into her hands. "It's horrible. I hate performing in front of people I know."

"You're really good," I assured her. "Everyone will be impressed."

"It's embarrassing. This isn't a recital. I hate being trotted out." She sighed. "Also, Kaitlyn always manages to look hot dancing, and I look like a five-year-old."

"I'm sure you look hot, too." I nibbled on my rose macaron half and closed my eyes. I loved roses. To look at, to use as lotion, to eat. Weird, but true. "'March of the Nutcracker,' huh?" I remembered playing the famous song when I was younger, when the middles were the littles and they'd marched around like toy soldiers. "How long's the dance?"

"Only three minutes. But *still*." She sighed, then took a sip of her mocha. "So what's it like with Noah being gone?"

Noah being gone . . . We'd grown up two blocks apart in the Upper East Side, and our families had Shabbat together every Friday. He'd been the first boy grandchild, me the first girl, and while our other cousins had siblings, we had each other. "I don't love it. I remember when he started high school and I was still in middle school and we didn't walk to school together for two years, which I *hated*. But I still saw him a few times a week. And now he's . . . gone. Too busy for us. And why wouldn't he be? He has a new girlfriend."

"I thought you liked Abby?"

"I do. She's nice and makes him happy. I guess I'm . . . jealous he's spending time with her instead of us. I know it's not fair or rational. But it's how I feel."

I felt lonely. I'd lost my support, my pseudo-brother, and I didn't have a best friend to lean on. I actually, secretly, thought of Olivia as my best friend, not just on the island, but anywhere. I wouldn't *tell* her; god forbid she had her own best friend back home. But she was the one I could text at one in the morning, the one I sent selfies to when I needed cheering. The one I asked and told about relationship drama.

Seeing her made me almost as happy as seeing my mess of cousins.

When we finished our coffees, we drove over to Brant Point

and walked toward the lighthouse. The cold wind bit our faces, and we ducked our chins into our scarves. A thin layer of crunchy snow covered the hard sand, and the water was a strange white-blue. The froth had frozen against the beach. Seagulls cawed, soaring through the air.

In the summer, tourists would have crowded around the light-house, children *ouch*ing as seashells bit their feet, fishermen with their lines in the water. Now, though, we were the only people here. How different Nantucket was in the off-season, and I loved it. I loved the space, the cold, the uncrowded vistas.

I raised my face toward the thin sunlight. Now or never. "I did something stupid."

Olivia pulled her jacket tighter. The wind whipped a strand of hair across her eyes, and she pushed it away. "My favorite way for stories to start."

My favorite thing about Olivia was her lack of judginess. At home, I'd never admit to being messy. Whenever I'd even *slightly* mentioned messing up, people seemed too amused, too pleased, which made me shrink into myself and swear to never own up to being less than perfect. Olivia, on the other hand, reveled in my messiness and shared her own disasters. "I told you how I'm, uh, getting ready to see Isaac."

"Yes . . ."

"So obviously I have no idea how to talk to boys, and I don't want to mess up with Isaac. I feel like if we could get over the awkward getting-together stage, we'd be so perfect. He's just so . . . competent, you know? He's so driven, he works so hard, he gets this cute furrow on his face when he's trying to get something handled, he already knows about my family . . . Anyway. I don't want to mess up my chance with him." I swallowed. "So to help me win Isaac over, I asked Tyler Nelson to teach me how to flirt."

"You did *not*." She practically crowed with delight. "Oh my god, Shira."

"I know. I'm a mess. But Isaac is just so perfect. I have to do *something* if I want a chance with him." I told her everything as we picked our way over to the giant rocks at the base of the short lighthouse and stared up at the Christmas wreath with its giant red bow.

By the time I finished, it was closing in on one—time for me to get to Tyler's and for Olivia to meet her family for lunch. "One thing," she said as we headed back toward her car. "What if you fall for him again?"

"For *Tyler*?" I laughed. "I'm not an idiot. Fool me once, and all that. Besides, I wouldn't want Tyler if I could have Isaac."

"Love your energy," she said, both skeptical and amused. "Guess I'll have to wait and meet the guy."

"He's great," I said. "You're going to be blown away by him."

Now I just had to ensure Isaac would be blown away by me.

CHAPTER NINE

Nervous energy ricocheted through my body after Olivia dropped me off at Tyler's house. Was this ridiculous? People didn't ask for flirting lessons outside of rom-coms, did they?

No. This made sense. When I'd needed to improve my math SAT, my parents got me a tutor; for piano and skating, I'd taken lessons. Practice made perfect; practice was practical. Besides, what was my other option with Isaac arriving tomorrow? Treat him the way I'd treated all the boys I'd liked in the past? Because I'd clearly done so well then.

Unlike last time I'd been here, Tyler's house now looked alive, candles in the windows, wreath on the door with pine cones and a red-plaid bow. Icicles hung from the roof, and the blazing blue sky made the house look friendly and picturesque. I rang the bell, listening as chimes echoed inside the house. My stomach clenched.

A moment later, one of Tyler's moms, Elena, opened the door. She looked surprised. "Hello, Shira."

"Hi." Ugh, I should have texted instead of ringing the bell. "I'm meeting Tyler?"

"Come on in. He's in the morning room." She led me inside. The aroma of freshly baked goods enveloped me: butter and sugar and cinnamon and nutmeg and ginger. "So nice of you to let him stay at Golden Doors the other night."

"Of course," I chirped. Sometimes I wondered if adults lived in a different universe than the rest of us, where they thought all teens got along. "What are you baking?"

"Gingerbread," she said cheerfully. "It's cooling now. A hassle, but Robin would kill me if I ever stopped the tradition. Would you like anything to drink? Water, tea?"

"Oh, um, a glass of water would be great."

Armed with a LaCroix, I followed Elena past the living room, where a seven-foot-tall Christmas tree stood decorated in warm golds and reds, presents piled at the base. She stepped into another room, and I paused behind her, nerves stretched thin enough to snap. Tyler and I might have struck a bargain yesterday, but it hadn't erased years of strain.

"Tyler, Shira's here," Elena said, then abandoned me.

I entered a room filled with light and low couches and plants.

Tyler couldn't have arranged himself to better advantage if he'd tried—and who knew, maybe he had. Sun streamed over him, picking up glints of gold in his wheat-blond hair, gilding his mysteriously tanned skin. (Shouldn't his tan have died after a semester at NYU?) He wore a robe over his T-shirt and flannel pants; his feet were sheathed in slippers edged in cozy wool. A steaming cup of coffee sat on the end table beside him. He looked both decadent and laid-back, and I felt like throwing up.

"You're wearing a robe," I said instead, and instantly regretted it. Why couldn't I have said something clever? Or even *hi*.

He looked up, his eyes blazingly blue, which I'd somehow forgotten in the twenty-four hours since I last saw him. "You sound surprised."

"Well—it's one o'clock. I would have thought you'd be dressed. Since you knew I was coming over."

"Aw, Shira." He stretched out his legs, crossing his ankles on an ottoman. "I would have dressed up for you if I knew you cared."

"I don't."

He held his thumb and forefinger an inch apart. "Maybe the teeniest bit?"

Tyler reminded me of a cat playing with a mouse, not for food but for entertainment. "Why do you keep teasing me?"

He grinned, those perfectly orthodontically straightened teeth blinding. "I just want to win your affections."

This boy. He could get under my skin like no one, and it made me want to do the same. "I think you tease and you flirt because you think it makes people like you. And I think you hate the idea of anyone not liking you."

His mouth parted slightly and he leaned back. "Shots fired."

"Am I wrong? You didn't like me not liking you."

"We're here to psychoanalyze you, not me." He took a long sip of his coffee. "All right, let's cut to the chase, then. What are we working with?"

"Um. Excuse me?"

He gestured at me broadly. "If we're going to do this, I want to know how much work we have cut out for us. You wouldn't teach someone calculus without figuring out how good they are at math, right?"

"Not at all the same." I sat down in an armchair kitty-corner from his couch. "But fine. What do you want to know?"

He sipped his coffee as he appraised me. "You said you hadn't kissed anyone. So . . . no past relationships? No hookups?" He waited as I shook my head for both. "How comfortable are you flirting?"

I tried to smile, but it felt tight and brittle on my lips. "I'm not. I can't flirt."

"Huh." He leaned back.

I was uncomfortably aware of the way his shirt rose slightly and the ripple of skin over his stomach. "What does 'huh' mean?"

"Nothing. I'm taking everything into consideration. Making

a game plan." He tilted his head. "Why do you think you can't flirt?"

I tried not to sound curt. "Obviously I've failed every time I've tried. And like I said, I've never had a boyfriend."

"That's the outcome. It doesn't help us figure out what's happening with your flirting. How do you usually flirt?"

Embarrassment tightened all my muscles, like I was trying to compress myself into nothingness. "I'm not sure I do. It seems so . . . obvious."

He tilted his head. "What seems obvious?"

"I don't know." Heat crawled through me, and I tugged off my sweater. "I don't want to seem—I don't want—"

I didn't want people to know if I had a crush on them. Which hadn't seemed so weird until right now, as I articulated the feeling. "I don't want anyone to realize I like them."

Tyler looked genuinely confused. "Why not? If you want to date someone, don't they *have* to learn you like them for anything to happen?"

True. I realized, in a blinding, obvious epiphany, that I wanted the person I liked to pursue me without me, personally, having to bear any vulnerability. Shamefaced, I said, "I guess I just want them to realize they like me and ask me out."

"You don't want to make the first move," he said easily. "Classic fear of rejection. You have to get over that hump."

Easier said than done. "How?"

"Hmm." He tapped his fingers against his thigh. "You need to flip a switch in your brain. Get yourself to see most people are *flattered* when others express an interest in them. No one's going to laugh at you for putting yourself out there."

I let out an actual laugh, sharp and high and bright. My voice came out as pointed as the icicles glittering outside the windows. "Are you serious?"

Horrified realization flashed across his face. "Oh."

"Yeah. Pretty sure getting laughed at is a possibility."

He rubbed his hand across his face. "I gave you PTSD."

"No." I didn't want to give him so much weight in my life. "No. I'm just . . . cautious."

"Let me think." He pulled on his fine hair, making it float about his head. "Okay, you don't have to go straight to asking anyone out or anything. Maybe . . . you should reframe how you think about flirting. Don't think of it as having an end goal, where you have to tell someone you like them, where someone could reject you and you could get hurt. Think of it as having a good time. Hanging out, chatting. Low stakes. Fun."

"Right." I could see his point, only . . . "The problem is, I'm not fun."

He frowned. "Why would you say that?"

"I don't know. I come off as too sharp. Too stiff. Cold."

"So you have walls up." He shrugged. "Everyone has walls."

As high and solid as mine? I wrapped my arms around my knees and pulled them to my chest. "Why is dating so easy for some people and so hard for others?"

"What do you mean?"

What did I mean? I meant I didn't understand why this seemed so much harder for me than it seemed for everyone else. I meant I felt broken sometimes, watching how easy other people found dating, which I found painfully distressing. "One of the girls at school, Kaylee, is always sliding in and out of relationships. She hasn't been single since we were thirteen. I don't even know how to start. I feel like I'm standing on the outside looking in, with no clue what to do. How is this something people *know*? How does the whole human race manage to pair off?"

He finished off the dregs of his coffee, looking thoughtful. "I guess anything new feels bizarre and unnatural at first. It's probably easier to flirt and date if you always have and harder to start the longer you haven't. Like Newton's first law of motion. You need a force to act upon your body at rest."

I stared at him. "That's the nerdiest thing I've ever heard you say."

He looked wry. "You will be shocked to hear I'm not just the good-for-nothing playboy you seem to think I am."

I smothered a smile. "True. A good-for-nothing playboy would never use those words."

He ignored that. "These lessons are going to be the force you need to knock you into the dating arena."

"Great. How?"

"Maybe you're so uncomfortable because you don't have any practice at this, at flirting and dating. You're not confident. If you were, you'd feel a lot better about all of this."

I didn't disagree; I'd read *Be confident* in a hundred different dating-advice articles. But it felt like a chicken-and-egg problem: How did I *get* practice if I was too terrified to start? "So how do I magically get confident?"

Tyler stretched one arm along the top of the couch. "Confidence comes from being comfortable with something. Like, I was always comfortable about sex and relationships because my moms were open about it; talking about dating never felt like a big deal to me."

I would rather go through another lockdown than talk about sex with my parents. "Okay."

He placed his hand on the arm of the couch, palm up. "Take my hand."

"What?" My heart lurched.

"Take it."

I regarded his hand the same way I would a live wire splayed across the road. "That seems like a lot."

"Or seems like something pretty reasonable if you want to be comfortable touching people, a standard part of flirting."

"Maybe I'll invent a new kind of flirting where you stand six feet away and shout at each other."

He smiled but said nothing. His bright gaze held mine.

This seemed like a no-good, very-bad idea. Ever so slowly, I leaned across the gap of our seats and placed my hand in his. His palm was warm and his fingers cool and I'd never held hands with a boy before, except when Tyler and I had measured our hands against each other's two nights ago. My heart beat as quickly as a hummingbird's wings.

His fingers closed around mine. "Not so bad, right?"

"I don't get the point. I'm not just going to pick up someone's hand." My words came out monotone. No, worse: rude. My self-defense mechanism.

"The point is for you to relax. I can tell you how to flirt, but if you don't have the experience, the muscle memory, all the intellectual knowledge in the world won't help your game. If you've never held hands before, the first time you do is going to feel a lot harder than every other time."

So the next time I held someone's hand, my heart wouldn't feel like it was about to explode? "Okay."

"It's like—to prepare for interviews, you're supposed to picture yourself doing well, saying hello to the interviewer, being confident. Picture yourself in situations and imagine them going well. And mimic the actual conditions, if you can. I read an article about a kid who wanted to get into Juilliard, so he'd go running before practicing to pump himself full of adrenaline while he played, like he would be at the actual audition."

I blinked. Popular, devil-may-care Tyler, getting excited about articles on interviewing? "Interesting."

A knock on the door sounded, and Elena poked her head in. I jerked my hand out of Tyler's so violently, I flailed and almost fell sideways in my armchair.

Elena, kindly, pretended not to notice. "How would you kids like to decorate gingerbread houses in a bit?"

"Mama." Tyler rolled his eyes.

"It'll be fun!" To me, she said, "We do it every year. It's a tradition."

"Mama, no."

I, on the other hand, already needed a break from hand-holding. What would he want me to do next, sustained eye contact? Good lord. "I've never decorated gingerbread houses before. Sounds fun."

Tyler groaned.

"Good!" his mom said. "Wonderful! The gingerbread will be done cooling in about an hour. I'll get you guys then."

When she left, I turned to Tyler. "Decorating gingerbread houses with your moms is pretty freaking wholesome."

"They're just making sure we're not having sex, you know."

I blanched. "What?"

He shrugged.

"Why would they think they needed to?"

"It's their standard policy when I'm alone with a girl."

"Even *downstairs*?" A flash, again, of Tyler twined around a girl. Embarrassed heat twisted in my stomach at the memory of his lazy grin and all that naked flesh. A reminder how the Tyler before me, focused solely on me, was not the Tyler I usually saw out and about. "They've never walked in on you, have they?"

"Not quite."

I gaped at him. "'Not quite' sounds way too close for comfort."

"It was fairly scarring, yes."

"Though—you said they're cool with sex?"

He made a face. "In theory. They're less cool now when it's actually happening."

"Why do they even *know* you're having sex?"

He laughed. "They insisted I be open with them. But also, they said I'm not as good at hiding things as I think I am."

"Sheesh."

"Right?" He shook his head. "Parents. Real ego killers."

"Like you have a problem with your ego."

He shot me a sharp smile. "Like you do, either."

I flinched. "What's that supposed to mean?"

"Oh, come on," he said. "You're *Shira Barbanel*."

I flushed. "Excuse me?"

"Rich, pretty Shira Barbanel," he said lightly. "The world's at your fingertips."

"It's not 'at my fingertips.'"

"Really? What do you want that you don't have?"

What did I want? Isaac. Being with him would make things so much easier. I'd never have to go to a party alone, never skip a dance for fear of feeling awkward, never be lonely on the weekends. And more than Isaac, I wanted to be comfortable in my own skin, to know who *I* wanted to be instead of letting everyone's expectations mold me into their own platonic ideal of me: daughter, pianist, skater, student, Barbanel. "I just want . . . I want to be more comfortable. In flirting but also, I don't know, in everything."

He studied me with a strangely piercing expression, and I swallowed hard.

"Okay, then." He placed his hand back on the couch arm between us. "Let's figure out what we need to do to get you comfortable." When I gingerly placed my hand back in his, he squeezed it. "First: eye contact."

I *knew* it. All of a sudden, I couldn't meet his eyes. I forced myself to for one second, then quickly refocused out the window, on the snow lying in glistening mounds, on the sharp blue sky, the afternoon sun. "Uh-huh."

"Come on. Back at me. Actually—sit on the couch."

"What?"

He rolled his eyes. "Shira. You're the one who asked for my help."

Swallowing deeply—not oxygen and nitrogen but fear and pride—I resettled on the couch next to him, our hands resting between us. Reluctantly, I met his gaze. I'd thought of his eyes as a cool blue, but really they were warmer, like friendly water instead of far-off sky. His lashes were a shade darker than his hair, like honey, and longer than I would have expected.

"Not so hard, see? Angle toward the person you like. Don't look away or aim your body in another direction. Lean in." He did so, his free arm stretching along the back of the couch behind me, coming perilously close to my body.

I, on the other hand, sat perpendicular to him, my knees pointed straight out, only my face turned toward him. Slowly, with excruciating awkwardness, I angled the rest of myself toward him.

He watched with obvious amusement. "You're not dead yet, right?"

"Yet."

"It's almost refreshing, how freaked out you are. People usually *want* to be close to me. This is like a whole new world."

"Thanks a lot." I tried to yank my hand out of his. He held on to it, and I scowled and stopped fighting. "I feel like I'm going to throw up."

"Wow, thanks."

"Sorry. Not because of you."

"Breathe, okay?"

"Okay."

We sat there, hand in hand, angled toward each other, and breathed. I breathed in Tyler's cologne and the scent of his conditioner, and I looked at his face. And slowly, slowly, my body acclimated to being so very close to his. I could still feel my heart thudding away at my rib cage, but I wasn't so hot I wanted to rip my skin off.

"Out of curiosity," Tyler eventually said, after a minute or an hour, "when you were super into me, what did you want to happen? Because this obviously makes you uncomfortable."

Valid question. My daydreams had never contained the same awkwardness as in real life—the exact opposite, actually, I'd imagined being swept away by passion. I flushed, remembering the extraordinarily vivid daydreams I'd had about Tyler for years. "I liked you then. It wouldn't have made me uncomfortable if I knew you liked me back." Right? Or was I only comfortable in dreams, not reality?

Would I be uncomfortable holding Isaac's hand? God, I hoped not. All I wanted was to curl up next to Isaac, blissfully happy, cuddling on the couch and smiling at each other. Surely I'd be comfortable if he initiated it, at least. Could *I* initiate? A terrifying thought.

"Okay. So you'd be more into this if I was also into it? Because for the record, I think you're hot, and I'm very happy to sit here holding your hand."

"Tyler!"

He looked startled by my shout. "What!"

"Don't *flirt* with me! We don't like each other!"

He started laughing while I stared at him, appalled. "Sorry—sorry," he said, trying to catch his breath. "I forgot. You're right. The only flirting allowed is businesslike flirting. No sincere compliments or anything else."

An unexpected giggle made its way out of me, and I didn't think of myself as a giggler. "When you put it that way . . ."

He put his hand over his heart and looked up at me like a Pre-Raphaelite knight swearing allegiance to his lady. "On my honor, I'll never flirt with you again."

"Stop it." I gave his shoulder a little push. "Okay, fine. You can, I suppose, say flirty things if you *need* to, for training purposes."

"Thank you. I'm really honored that you'll let me do this thing you asked me to do." He grinned, and another laugh escaped me. "All right, next up—conversation. I'd go with asking a lot of questions and scattering in some compliments."

Right. Knowing how to have a conversation with boys without freezing up entirely seemed important. "One sec." I pulled my hand out of his and opened the Notes app on my phone. *Eye contact, body angled, compliments, questions.*

"You're taking notes?"

I flushed. "I want to get this right."

"You're a dedicated student."

"Practice makes perfect." You didn't get anywhere in life without putting in your ten thousand hours. Or maybe some people did, the naturals in life. Tyler probably never had to *practice* getting people to like him. But I did. I could be good at piano, at skating, maybe—god help me—at flirting, but only if I studied the hell out of it.

"Right. Which means you actually have to practice. Put your phone down and give me your hand again. And look at me."

Phone down. Hand in his. Eyes locked. Could he feel my pulse? Could he tell he made my mouth dry? Of course he could; he knew he was brilliant at this.

He studied me so intently I forgot to be embarrassed. "You have beautiful eyes."

I swallowed, and it did little to help my parched throat. I could feel my heartbeat in my neck, the rush of blood in my ears. This was a game. A lesson. Give people compliments. Nothing more. "Okay."

He smiled slightly. "You're supposed to say thank you."

"This isn't real, though."

"No, it's practice. And you need to practice not going on the defensive."

I wanted to strike back at him and only barely realized that would be cutting off my nose to spite my face. I managed a tiny nod.

"And you *do* have beautiful eyes. What color are they?"

"Um." I pushed some of my hair behind my ear and tried to sound measured. "I'm not going on the defensive, but you don't have to go this hard. Especially since no one's going to say anything about my eyes, because obviously they're brown."

"No." He leaned closer. With our hands clasped between us, it felt like we existed in a small intimate circle, possibly also because my vision had narrowed into a tunnel and I couldn't see beyond him. "They're a little orange at the center."

A flare of surprise and pleasure jolted through me. No one had ever commented on the tiny orange flecks, an inheritance from Grandma. Then again, no one had ever looked into my eyes so deeply. "Oh."

"I've never seen anything like them."

This was too much. I pulled my hand out of his, hard. I felt flustered and hot and uncomfortable, the exact opposite of what this exercise was supposed to establish. "That's overkill."

He sat back. "That's flirting."

"I'm not going to sit down next to Isaac and start talking about his eyes. There must be some sort of lead-in we're missing."

His eyes narrowed. "Do you want my help or not?"

"I do!"

He captured my hand again. "Then listen to what I tell you." He stroked a finger up the inside of my wrist, halfway to my elbow.

God, my breath was going haywire. "I *am* listening. But, um, if you want me to pay attention now, that's a little distracting."

He gave a small, satisfied smile. "I know. It's effective."

"I don't think I'm going to be stroking Isaac's arm," I said over my embarrassingly short breaths.

"Maybe not at first. But you have to get comfortable enough to not bolt out of your chair whenever someone touches or compliments you."

"Exposure therapy?"

He laughed. "Pretty much. Now. Say something nice to me, and try to sound like you mean it."

Right. "Okay. Um. Your eyes are incredibly blue." I waited, nervous, for a response, and when he gave me none, I kept babbling. "Like a . . . like a lake in the summertime."

His mouth twisted up. "Not bad. It sounds like the words are being pried out of you, though. Not like you want to kiss me."

"I *don't* want to kiss you!"

He gave an exaggerated roll of his eyes. "You want to kiss Isaac, don't you?"

Yes. The amount of times I had imagined somehow, somewhere, kissing Isaac, having all his serious, intense concentration focused on me . . . It was worth it, all this discomfort, if I could make Isaac notice me. But Isaac wasn't like Tyler; he wasn't flippant and focused on hooking up and partying. "I don't think Isaac's the kind of guy where complimenting his eyes will work."

Tyler stopped running his finger up and down my forearm. "What's that supposed to mean?"

"I don't know. He's not shallow?" I let my head fall back in dismay. "Isn't there a way to make him fall madly in love with me without having to, I don't know, talk?" Had I honestly thought

I'd be able to reinvent myself as a seductress in a few short days? I yanked my hand out of Tyler's and repositioned myself on the couch so I was farther away, my back against the couch arm, my legs between us. "This is never going to work."

Tyler looked, of all things, a touch put out. "What's so special about this guy? Why is he worth all this effort?"

"I told you. He's smart. He's ambitious. He's . . . he's basically perfect."

"Everyone seems perfect when you don't know them. You can imagine they have whatever qualities you want because they haven't had a chance to prove otherwise."

My brows shot up. "I like him, okay?"

"He seems like a lot of work."

"Um, *anyone* would be a lot of work for me. Isaac is worth it."

"Right." He looked away, breathing a little harder than before. "Okay, then."

I looked away, too, at the sun glinting on the snow outside, at the slide of water down the icicles, the droplets falling off the points. "Why are you doing this?" I asked. "I mean, I know I agreed to introduce you to my great-uncle. But I didn't really expect you to . . . follow through."

He flashed me a smile, the one I'd started to notice as being his charming, overexposed one. "It's an interesting challenge, playing Professor Higgins."

"Who?"

"*My Fair Lady*? Eliza Doolittle? Audrey Hepburn?" At each shake of my head, he sighed. "It's an old movie where a professor trains a flower girl to act like a lady."

"Wow, rude much."

He grinned. "And I guess—" He stopped.

"What?"

"Nothing."

"You were going to say something."

He shook his head. I waited him out.

"Okay." He tugged at his hair. "I feel . . . a little sorry. For hurting your feelings back then."

I reared back. Pity.

He *pitied* me.

My stomach folded in on itself while my voice frosted over. "Got it."

"I shouldn't have laughed when you told me you liked me. I was just surprised."

"Surprised?" My voice hardened, though I wasn't sure if it was because of his years-old action or his current pity. "Because, what, fourteen-year-old me did such a good job at hiding my emotions?"

"I had no idea you'd make a *move*. I thought you'd lust silently from afar."

I gave him a brittle smile, wishing I could be as laissez-faire as him. "Thank god I didn't. Think how big your ego would be if it had gone on even longer."

He raised his brows. "What, you think your disdain didn't feed my ego, too?"

I gaped at him. "What?"

"Come on." He grinned. "It meant you still cared, how mad you stayed at me."

"Are you kidding? Are you saying you've thought I was *still* obsessed with you for the past three years?"

"Am I wrong?"

"Wow," I said, aiming to puncture his swollen ego. "It must sting to realize the lengths I'm willing to go to to get Isaac Lehrer's attention."

His eyes widened, and he flinched.

"And I didn't still like you," I said. "I realized we're nothing alike. I want a relationship, and you want hookups."

His expression hardened. "I've always been honest about what I'm looking for. I've always laid my cards on the table."

"Great. Good for you." I shrugged. "But I also know what I'm looking for. I want a relationship. A person to hang out with all the time. A best friend I get to kiss. I wouldn't have to worry about making plans or being lonely." I winced as the last word slipped out. Admitting I was lonely felt stupid and silly and like something I should get over. And, I realized, shoulders slumping, Tyler probably couldn't relate, since he had a million friends.

"Huh," he said. "I guess . . . I don't look for that kind of connection in romantic relationships. That level of friendship."

"Why not? Because you get enough of it elsewhere?" I could almost see, actually, how if I had more friends I might not care quite as much about having a boyfriend.

He shifted uncomfortably. "I guess."

The silence stretched too long; Tyler stared at his empty mug, then out the window, and I stared at him, until he looked back at me and our gazes clashed. He cleared his throat. "Uh, so did you ever find out more about the box?"

Thank god. I'd had about as much of talking about emotions as I could handle for one day. "Yeah. I got the names of the Barbanels around before photography became popular. But there's a ton of them."

"I actually had an idea," Tyler said, straightening. "You know the piece of wood? I thought it might be part of a quarterboard."

My brows shot up. Quarterboards were common decorations on the Cape and islands: long, narrow planks of wood bearing the name of pretty much anything these days, from houses to restaurants to shops, tacked up as nautical decoration. Back in the day, they'd been nailed to ships. "You think it's from an actual ship? Not decoration?"

"If the box is from the 1800s. People used quarterboards a lot then, right?"

"Yeah, actually." I'd taken pictures of all the objects in the chest, and now I pulled up the photo of the plank. "If we think it's real . . . it's broken. Didn't quarterboards wash ashore after wrecks? And people could use them to figure out what ship went down?"

"Right," Tyler said. "So . . . why would your ancestor keep a quarterboard from a shipwreck?"

We stared at each other, the answer between us. "She could have known someone on the ship," I said slowly. "Someone who . . . didn't make it."

"Probably a sailor, if they were out of Nantucket in the 1800s," Tyler said. "A whaler, probably."

I shuddered. True, Nantucket had been the epicenter of the whaling industry, but I hoped the man had been some other kind of sailor, or even a passenger on a vessel. "God, I hope not."

"What's wrong with whalers?"

"Besides the whole *hunting whales* thing?"

"Oh. Right." He leaned against the sofa's back. "If we could find out what ship the quarterboard belonged to, the time frame and people would get narrowed down. There must be a list of shipwrecks from the 1800s, right? We can see if any of them included 'OS'—those were the letters on it, right?"

It took very little googling to find an online resource of sailing vessels from Nantucket, aptly titled *Catalogue of Nantucket Whalers: Their Voyages from 1815 to 1870*. Included, too, was a publication concerning wrecks around Nantucket, over five hundred in total.

"It's a lot of wrecks." Tyler sounded dubious. "Even if we search for 'OS' . . . it's over fifty hits."

We scanned the document anyway. The doomed ships carried rum and gin and soap; live oak and coal; bales of cotton and bushels of salt; spices and flour and raisins. There were schooners and steamships and brigs and more schooners, from Plymouth and Puerto Rico and New Orleans and New York.

"What *is* a schooner?" I asked. "And why are they so bad at not getting wrecked?"

Tyler laughed. "It's a type of sailing vessel. With at least two masts, lined up along the keel."

"The . . . keel?" I made a confused face.

"Don't you spend your summers on Nantucket?"

"I'm a landlubber. Come on, be excited, you get to explain something to me."

"Something you should already know," he said, but a smile slipped out. "The keel runs through the center of the ship—the hull's built around it. Well, now some ships are prefabricated, but laying down the keel used to be the first step of a ship's construction."

"So what I'm hearing is you're a boat boy."

He gave one of my curls a gentle tug. "If a ship is fore-and-aft rigged, it means it has its masts—its sails—up and down the keel's line, instead of being square-rigged."

I was so distracted by the hair tug, it took a moment before

I gathered words. "What's a square-rigged ship?"

"Like a brig, or a cutter can be. Actually, schooners can be square-rigged, too, if you have a topsail schooner—"

I decided we'd gone too far and too deep. "Okay, so what do schooners do? They're not whaling ships, then?"

"They can be. I think small whaling ships could be schooners. But they were often merchant ships, or passenger vessels, or pirate ships . . ."

"So maybe he was a sailor but not a whaler," I said, relieved. "Maybe he worked on a merchant's ship. I wonder . . . Abby talked to a bunch of historians last summer. Maybe we could do the same. To us this quarterboard is just two letters, but if we found experts, they might recognize it."

"You're into this."

This was both embarrassing and correct. "I like learning about my family. You don't have to help."

"Nah, it's fun. Maybe someone at the Whaling Museum could help us."

"Tyler Nelson." A smile played at the edges of my mouth. "Are you trying to come up with an excuse to go to the Festival of Trees?"

He grinned. "Look, I don't have a million small children to go with and pretend it's for them. I have to take what I can get."

"Ah, yes, a Christmas tree exhibit, the highlight of the Hanukkah season."

He looked startled. "So you've never been?"

"Of course I've been! I appreciate a good Christmas tree."

A knock sounded on the doorframe, and we both swiveled toward Elena, who smiled at us. "The gingerbread is ready."

Tyler sighed, transitioning to an embarrassed son. "Mama . . ."

"It'll be fun," she coaxed. "You always love decorating the houses."

I could have sworn roses bloomed in his cheeks.

We followed Elena into the dining room. Drafting paper covered the table along with baking sheets filled with gingerbread and tubes of frosting. There were bowls of gumdrops, snowdrops, red and green sprinkles, miniature candy canes, M&M'S, and peppermints. Christmas carols played from glittery speakers. "Chestnuts roasting on an open fire . . ."

Elena disappeared back into the kitchen, and Tyler caught my arm before I sat. His hand froze me more than his lowered voice. "You don't have to do this."

I arched a brow. "Are you kidding? I've never decorated a gingerbread house before."

"My moms—they want"—he rubbed the back of his head—"they're into this kind of stuff."

I couldn't swallow my grin. "It's cute."

"It's not what you came here for."

"No," I said serenely. "It's not."

And yet I didn't mind the idea of making gingerbread houses.

Maybe I enjoyed seeing Tyler discombobulated. His parents made him human, fallible, in a way I wasn't used to. And I liked it.

Elena and Robin bustled through the door from the kitchen, each of them holding two steaming mugs. "Do you like hot chocolate?" Robin asked.

"It's Robin's family recipe," Elena said. "Cinnamon, nutmeg, cayenne pepper—and both cocoa powder *and* melted chocolate."

"Sounds delicious," I said, because even if my stomach probably shouldn't have two cups of milk in one day, what the hell.

Robin set one mug in front of me, red with white lettering. "It's so nice to have you here," she said. "Usually it's just the three of us for the holidays."

I'd been vaguely aware Tyler was an only child, but were there no grandparents? No cousins?

"You need two of each of these—the long walls, short, and these are the roof tiles." Robin indicated different trays of gingerbread. "We used to have competitions when I was a kid. The whole extended family, day after Thanksgiving."

"This is her way of warning you how competitive she is." Elena handed out the pieces.

Kids my age could make me nervous, but I'd always gotten along with adults. "Do you have a big family?"

The women exchanged glances. "Big enough," Robin said lightly. "Not as big as the Barbanels, though!"

"I blame the triplets," I said. "As soon as people see three identical faces, they think, 'That's it, too many people.'"

Tyler's parents laughed politely and asked a few more questions about my family before turning to the serious business of gingerbread-house construction. "Here's what you do," Robin said. "This icing's the mortar. If you want to cheat—"

"It's not cheating!" Elena turned to me. "We have milk cartons you can use for structural integrity, so your house doesn't collapse."

Tyler leaned close. "It's cheating."

Elena threw her hands in the air.

I swallowed a smile. "What's the icing made out of?" I watched as Elena carefully applied it to the edge of a gingerbread piece. "It's strong enough to hold the house together?"

"Confectioner's sugar, egg whites, and cream of tartar," Robin said. "And crossed fingers."

"Here." Tyler picked up a bag filled with icing. "Hold those two walls perpendicular, yeah, like so—I'll put the icing on and then you hold them until they set."

Building and decorating the houses was more comfortable than I would have believed. Elena and Robin chatted with me in the way parents always did, about school and my family and interests, and Tyler behaved—Tyler behaved like a boy with his parents: younger and more open than I had seen him before, a little annoyed, a little affectionate.

"Tell us about this jewelry chest Tyler said you found," Elena said, crushing candy canes in a Ziploc bag with the back of a spoon. "He said it was under a floorboard?"

I wasn't sure why, but I found it sweet Tyler had told his parents about the box. "Yeah. We think it might have belonged to one of the first generations at Golden Doors, in the mid-1800s."

We were telling them about our afternoon research when my phone lit up with a call. I scrambled for it. Only family called instead of texting. *Noah*, the screen said. "Hi?"

"Where are you?" He sounded aggrieved.

Aggrieved meant he'd been roped into something and thought I, too, should have to deal with it. "Out?"

"We're taking the middles and littles sledding."

"Ha," I said. "Have fun."

"*We* are," he enunciated.

"The others can't help?"

"Ethan and David have vanished," he said. "And we need you to drive the second car."

"Abby can drive it."

"*Shira.*"

I rolled my eyes. Clearly he meant he needed me to help babysit and didn't want to be separated from his girlfriend for two seconds. "I'll meet you at the hill," I said, a compromise I knew he'd be desperate enough to take. "And you owe me."

CHAPTER
TEN

omehow, Tyler wound up coming sledding.

"It'll be good for you," he said as I pulled on my coat in his foyer. "And I'll get to see you in your natural environment."

"I'm not going to flirt with you," I said. "Not in front of my family."

"Relax." Tyler rolled his eyes. "I'd never, ever expect you to flirt with me. But Isaac's staying with your family, right? This'll be good practice, interacting with a guy with your family around."

Tyler was very different from "a guy," but I saw his point, so we drove together to Dead Horse Hill. We parked off the street and headed to the top of the sledding area, a small enclave surrounded by trees, not far from the hospital. I felt more nervous with every step and froze completely as we passed Grandma's car. "I don't know if this is a good idea."

"Why not?"

"All my cousins will be there. Noah has a grudge against you."

"You have a grudge against me, and you're with me right now."

Despite being several inches shorter, I did my best to look down my nose at Tyler. "We have a *deal*," I said. "And you hit on Noah's girlfriend last time you saw her."

"Come on, Shir." He took a step closer and rubbed his mittened hands up and down the sleeves of my puffer jacket, the white puffs of our breath mingling. "This is a great idea."

He was *too* close, so close I could feel the heat of his body and had a front-row seat to the Obnoxiously Perfect Beauty of Tyler Nelson whether I wanted it or not. I gave his chest a firm push with my own mittened gloves, feeling like we were two Pillsbury Doughboys in a fight. "Just remember, I warned you."

I hurried to the top of the hill, Tyler not far behind, trying to outpace him as I located Noah and Abby. They watched the littles absentmindedly, their heads bent together.

"Hey, guys," I called, and they turned. I lowered my voice as I approached, so only they could hear me. "Don't be weird."

Noah looked confused, and then his gaze fastened behind me. His brows snapped together. "What are you doing here?"

I hated when Noah used that tone. He sounded like Grandpa. Like Grandpa right before I fled the room. "I invited him."

Noah's lips pressed together. "Why?"

"Hey, Noah," Tyler said easily, reaching my side. "Abby." His gaze lingered on her with too much fondness, and Noah didn't miss it.

"Hey, Tyler." Abby sounded amused more than anything. "How are you?"

"Great." He elbowed me lightly. "Hanging out with my favorite Barbanel."

"Didn't you get enough time together the other night?" Noah asked shortly.

Tyler slung his arm around my shoulders. "Never enough."

I shrugged it off immediately and focused on Noah. "Behave."

He shook his head and stomped away through the snow. Abby threw me an unreadable look and followed him.

I scowled at Tyler. "Are you going to go around touching me for the rest of the day?"

"Does it really count as touching with fifty layers of goose down between us?" he mused, then took in my expression. "I'll stop."

"No," I said slowly. "You're right. I want to be comfortable with casual touch. You can . . . put your arm around me, or whatever. If you need to."

A slow smile spread on Tyler's face. "Your generosity is astounding."

"Hmph."

He surveyed the mess of Barbanels running and screaming around the hill. "Are these all yours?"

"A baker's dozen."

"A fairly uncreative baker," David said, wandering up to us. His purple jacket matched his hair. "Everyone's always getting us confused, and only three of the batch are genuinely identical." He gave Tyler a nod. "Hey, man."

"Hey." Tyler gave a bro-nod back. "How've you been?"

"I thought you weren't coming," I said to David.

"Me too. But Oliver ratted me out." He surveyed Tyler. "Surprised to see you here."

Tyler spread his hands. "Shira begged me to come."

I gaped at him, then at a laughing David. "What's wrong with you two!"

"A question I ask my therapist every week," David quipped. "I thought you were hanging out with Olivia today."

"I was." I spoke as repressively as possible. "Then I ran into Tyler."

"We made gingerbread houses." Tyler sounded far too happy to be having this conversation.

David smirked. "Is that what the kids are calling it these days."

I reached down and formed a snowball, not even bothering to throw it but mashing it into David's face. He howled and lunged at me.

"You had that coming," I yelled, skipping backward.

Unfortunately, I promptly tripped. David took advantage, wrestling me to my knees and stuffing snow down the back of my neck. With a scream, I hoisted an armful of snow at him, missed, and hit two of the triplets, who regarded me with blank, awful faces before declaring war.

In minutes, we were a mess of cousins, snow flying through the air everywhere along with laughter and shrieks. The air in my lungs was so crisp it almost hurt, and the missiles lobbed by my cousins' strong throwing arms were occasionally painful, but it felt good to run and yell and act like a little kid as long as I didn't bowl over any actual children. I paused briefly when Miriam knocked into Tyler, but he only laughed, helped her up, and conferred with her about who to attack next. I'd almost forgotten that about him; he was good at making people comfortable, putting them at ease.

This was why I loved Nantucket. I got to have this riot of cousins around me, this clan to which I belonged and which belonged to me. I didn't have to monitor anything, didn't have to try, could simply breathe—or gasp for air, as the case may be. With my last snowball thrown, I collapsed backward into the snow, holding my hands up to plead mercy to anyone still in the fight.

Tyler dropped down next to me, also short of breath. His cheeks were rosy with pink undertones, unlike the bronzed gleam on all the Barbanels. "Wow. I haven't had a snowball fight in years."

"I'm too old for this kind of thing," I said. "The middles are violent."

Tyler laughed, watching the triplets—still full of energy—board their sleds and whisk off down the hill. "It's fun."

"Yeah." I grinned. "Can't deny that."

God, he was beautiful. The thought crashed up, unbidden and unwanted, but not exactly deniable. He looked like a perfect Christmas angel, here on this snowy hilltop capped by ice and laughter. No wonder I'd developed such a crazy crush. I'd spent years watching him like this, all good-natured in group settings, doling out charm and attention and kindness.

I remembered how often I used to gaze at him and think, *I am smitten.*

Now it was Isaac I daydreamed about, but it was different somehow. Isaac didn't feel as . . . raw as Tyler had. Isaac felt steadier. When I'd obsessed over Tyler, I'd been overcome by emotions, but when I thought about Isaac, I pictured a future. I pictured us together at lunches, walking down the street, in the park. It felt more real, less like a fever dream.

I turned to watch as Noah sat on a sled, Abby between his legs. They sped away down the hill. I watched them flatten out before the trees with their long shadows. Although it wasn't even five o'clock, the sun was sinking, the light growing weaker. "Can I ask you a question?"

"Go for it."

"Why are you guys here, at Christmas, instead of with one of your moms' families? A few of the summer families come for the holidays, but most want to be with their extended families."

Tyler pulled one leg up to his chest and wrapped an arm around it, his gaze locked on the kids lying on their stomachs and plunging down the hill. "My grandparents on Mama's side are in Mexico, and we see them at Easter. And Mom's parents . . . we see them, but not more than we have to."

"Oh." Seeing my family had never seemed like a choice. "Why not?"

"They don't get Mom. Whenever we see them, everyone ends up shouting. A few years ago, Mom and Mama decided they would take a break from weeklong trips and holidays and we'd do shorter ones."

I hadn't known you could simply decide not to spend holidays with family. The wonders of being an adult. "It sounds hard."

"Yeah." He toyed with a button on his coat. "They make Mom feel bad, like she did everything wrong. Even though she's this major producer, they think since she didn't go to college she lucked out instead of working hard. It's like she's always trying to prove herself to them. That's why my parents bought the house here, actually. Mom wanted to prove—I don't know—she can fit into the old money thing if she wants."

"I would have thought—after grandkids . . ." I gestured vaguely at him. "Your grandparents didn't chill out?"

He let out a white cloud of air. "I'm how it started. Mom left home when she was eighteen and pregnant and moved to LA. So it's not like I was a mark of her being settled and adult or anything."

"Wow." I was a little surprised I'd never heard about this. "Do you—are you in touch with your bio dad? Sorry if I'm prying—"

"It's fine. We have a fine relationship. He's still in Raleigh and works in cleantech."

"Oh. Cool. I didn't know." I immediately felt foolish, because of course I hadn't.

"I don't talk about it." He gave me his bright, polished smile, the one I was beginning to realize wasn't real but maybe part of the wall Tyler himself had up. *Everyone has walls*, he'd said earlier. Even him. A mirrored wall that kept people from realizing there was a wall at all.

"I tell everyone things are fine all the time, too," I said impulsively. "I'm usually lying. It's okay if it's not fine."

Now he gave me his smaller, more crooked smile, the one that felt more real. "Okay. Yeah. It's more complicated than fine. But it's not bad."

"Not bad seems like the best we can hope for half the time."

"True." He laughed, then turned his sparkle on me, his good mood restored. "Come on. Our turn."

"Our turn for what?"

But he'd already jumped to his feet, striding toward the triplets as they returned with a sled in tow. A moment later, negotiation complete, he returned.

I stared at the sled. "I don't know . . ."

"What do you mean?" he asked innocently. "It'll be fun."

Sledding was fun, true. But sledding with Tyler? I could feel my body heating up. An excellent way to fight the winter cold: keep yourself perpetually flustered. "How do we do this?"

"Easy." Tyler settled on the sled, his legs wide. "Sit down in front of me."

My throat convulsed. "You've got to be kidding."

He grinned. "Scared?"

And damn if his taunting didn't work. I sat on the sled before him, stretching my legs straight ahead so they wouldn't brush his.

"You're gonna fall out of the sled if you don't hold on to anything." His voice was amused, his breath brushing the back of my head.

I reached over his legs for the edge of the wooden sled. Tyler, damn him, scooted closer, his long legs bracketing my own. He put his arm around my waist and suddenly my back was flush against his front, his chest warm and hard. I sucked my breath in.

"Wow," I said lightly, because I didn't know how to handle this besides through sarcasm. "I would have *loved* this three years ago."

"Admit it, Shir," he said, mouth alarmingly close to my ear. "You love it now, too."

"Get over yourself."

He laughed. "Never. Ready?"

"Sure."

He pushed off, and the sled tipped over the edge of the hill and onto the incline, gradually increasing in speed until we whipped recklessly downward, wind flaying my cheeks and tearing a shriek out of me. Tyler laughed. His arms tightened around me, and I clutched him. We were going so fast, it was impossible to be in control. The sled careened from side to side, snow slashing up at us, the world a blur of white and blue and green. Tyler's warmth seeped into me, his body the only steady thing . . .

And then the hill leveled off, the sled slowing and turning, and we fell off it, laughing, lying in the snow.

"Shira . . ."

I grinned at him, trying to swipe hair out of my eyes, getting snow on my face instead. "Yeah?"

For a moment, his face was very still, unreadable, which was odd because I was used to Tyler being so expressive. But then he let out a huff of laughter and smiled wryly. "It's too bad we want such different things."

I stared at him, trying to figure out what he meant. *Such different things . . .*

He looked away, squinting at the sun. It glowed orange and low in the trees, casting skeletal shadows. "It'll be dark soon."

"Right." I swallowed hard. "We should head out."

We trooped up to the top of the hill, Tyler's long-legged stride weirdly graceful, unlike my clomping steps. "Did you learn anything observing me with my family?" I asked.

He glanced over. "Are you going to get mad if I tell you?"

"Only time will tell."

His mouth turned up in a small smile. "Fair." He studied me, that look of his I'd noticed before, so unlike his charismatic smile. Had Tyler been watching everyone for years and just done a good job hiding it? "With your family, you're sweet and open and warm, but usually when I see you at parties or wherever, you kind of come off like an ice queen."

"Excuse me?" What a term.

"I don't mean it as an insult. But no one sees you and thinks, 'Oh, she's awkward and uncomfortable joining in—'"

"Thanks," I said dryly.

"They think you're bored and aloof and not in the mood to flirt."

I frowned. "So you're saying my anxiety manifests as bitchiness instead of, I don't know, making me look like an endearing, twee rom-com heroine."

His lips twitched. "Pretty much. Look. If I've learned one thing over the years, it's that no one's as obsessed with me as I am." He grinned. "Well, maybe you were."

"Thank you," I said, "for shoving a finger in that old wound."

He continued. "What I'm trying to say is, no one pays as

much attention to you, or judges you, as harshly as you judge yourself. I think you get stiff around other people because you're overthinking how to act. Imagine you're hanging out with your family, and act like you do with them." He nudged me with his shoulder. "Be sweet."

"*Sweet?* How horrifying." I was gratified by his laugh. "Okay, so with Isaac, I'll be sweet. The sweetest. Like meringue."

We reached the top of the hill, where Noah had began corral-ling the cousins into gathering up sleds and far-flung hats. "I'll give you a lift," Tyler said.

I glanced at my mob of cousins, weighing the comfort of being squished in the back seat with an elbow in my ribs and another in my eyes, versus the interrogation I'd get if I not only arrived with Tyler but also left with him. Then Gabe ran by, and I got a giant, sweaty whiff of his armpits. "Yeah, okay."

In the car, Tyler blasted the heat and the radio, the synthesiz-ers and electric guitars of the Trans-Siberian Orchestra belting out "Carol of the Bells." We pulled out ahead of the others, pass-ing houses lighting up the night with fairy lights and glowing Christmas trees.

"Why *did* you like me when you were a kid?"

I turned sharply toward him, but he stared straight ahead, both hands gripping the car wheel. "What?"

"Why'd you have such a crush on me?"

There was a strange relief to being able to talk about this

massive part of my life out loud with the object of it. Still, I didn't know what to say. "I thought I'd covered that already. You're pretty, if you didn't notice."

"Right." His voice was flat.

I frowned, surprised. "You wanted a different answer?"

"No one loves the idea that people only like them for their looks."

"Tyler, you're the most popular guy I know. You don't need to be worried about people only liking you because you're pretty."

"Mm," he said. "Though you just said that's the only reason you liked me."

Wow. This really bothered him. "I mean—no, it wasn't the only reason."

"Then why else?"

I stared out the windshield at the snow-heaped pines flashing by. "You're easy to like." I tried to keep my voice neutral, objective. "You're friendly, and you make people laugh and give people your full attention. It's addictive. Who wouldn't like that?"

"So you do think I have a personality. And you like it."

"It's acceptable," I said, making a face at him. "God, Tyler, why are you badgering me for compliments?"

A small smile hovered on his lips. "Maybe because I know how rarely you give them."

We'd reached Golden Doors. He pulled up the circular drive and turned off the engine. Outside was all darkness and sky and snow. Above, the stars scattered across the velvet black. There were more stars above Nantucket than you'd ever see in Manhattan, more stars than you'd realize existed.

"You really like this guy?" Tyler asked as we idled in front of the porch. "The one coming tomorrow?"

I conjured Isaac's face, brow smooth, eyes dark. He was exactly what I wanted. "I do."

"Okay, then. What time does he arrive tomorrow?"

"Four, I think?"

"Let's meet up before for practice." He spoke more assertively than I would have expected from someone acting out of necessity. "Text me in the morning."

"Really?"

"Never let it be said I don't hold up my end of a bargain." He shot me a smile. "See you tomorrow, Shira."

"See you," I said, and I hopped out of the car, humming softly as I walked to the door. *Hark how the bells, sweet silver bells, all seem to say, throw cares away . . .*

Maybe I would actually have my own miracle this Hanukkah. Maybe I would get exactly what I wanted.

CHAPTER ELEVEN

The next day was game day.

Isaac would arrive today. Isaac would be here, at Golden Doors, staying down the hall from me.

After showering, I worked my curl-enhancing mousse through my hair with precision and massaged my favorite rose-scented body·lotion into my dry skin. Wrapped in a towel, I returned to my room, hesitating briefly in the hall to listen to the sound of adults scrambling, getting last-minute preparations ready for the Danzigers' arrival.

Miri lay curled up in bed, reading a book featuring a girl in a fancy dress wielding a sword. She looked up. "Morning."

"Sounds like chaos downstairs." I perched at the vanity, where my pots of creams and powders sat in satisfying clusters, and glanced briefly at the air mattress. Abby had already left before I went to shower—or had never come to our room.

"Want a CLIF Bar?" Miri offered. "I keep a bunch in my drawer in case I'm starving and don't want to face the music."

"Good point. They're probably drafting everyone into cleaning." I smoothed primer over my face, then pulled out my foundation. I wanted to look good today but natural; Isaac shouldn't be able to tell I wore makeup.

In the mirror, I saw Miriam cock her head. She'd always been the most watchful of the cousins. "Tyler came sledding yesterday."

"He did," I said carefully, dabbing on some highlighter.

"Is . . . anything going on with you guys?"

I pinned her with my most Grandma-like stare. "No. We're friends."

"Oh." She frowned. "I thought you hated him?"

"I don't *hate* him." Miriam was only two years younger than me; she'd definitely noticed the rise and fall of my affections for Tyler. "I'd . . . He embarrassed me when I was little. But it was a long time ago."

"He seemed into you. He was smiling at you and touching you a lot."

Because of our agreement, not because he liked me. "That's just how Tyler behaves with girls. It doesn't mean anything."

"If you say so," Miriam said skeptically.

"I do." Turning my head from side to side, I studied the final result. I looked cool, mature. Definitely like someone who could date a nineteen-year-old.

Next, I regarded my closet with some dismay, suddenly worried I had nothing to wear. My dresses felt too fancy. *I* knew I wore dresses as a matter of course, but would Isaac think I was trying too hard if I wore one? I settled on an oatmeal-colored sweater and my favorite jeans. Time enough for dresses with all the parties coming up.

Downstairs, I piled a plate high with toast and eggs and sat alongside the triplets. They spoke over each other to tell me about all the travesties of being twelve, which, to be fair, were many. I listened and gave what advice I could, all the while aware of the knot in my stomach tightening, my toast losing taste. What if I froze up in front of Isaac? Last night I'd been so sure I could do this, but what if I couldn't?

Tyler had offered to meet up today, before the Danzigers arrived. I pulled up our message thread. **Around for more practice?** I texted. And then, because I was still curious about the contents of the box and because I wanted to kill every last hour before Isaac arrived: **Could also stop by the Whaling Museum after, if you're interested.**

Tyler replied right away.

Tyler:
Hell yes I'm interested

how often do I get to investigate
drowned sailors

we probably need to figure out how
he died or he'll haunt the shores of
Nantucket forever

I smiled, then tried to concentrate as the triplets told me about the injustice of other kids winning a history fair project.

"This is *ridiculous*."

Our heads swiveled toward the fireplace, where Grandpa scowled at Dad and Uncle Harry. All three of them looked like steam might burst out of their ears any second.

The triplets' faces swiveled to mine. "Do you think everything's okay?" Iris asked.

I gave them my brightest, most genuine smile. Who said they were the only actors in the family? "Of course. You know how people get at the holidays."

But now I noticed the tension radiating from the adults like distorted air around a fire. Everyone seemed tauter, sharper than usual. Like the adults, too, were preparing to put on a play, and their story line was *Everything is perfect in the Barbanel family.*

Uncle Harry's voice boomed from across the room. "I am *not* going to move my car!"

The triplets scattered.

I wasn't far behind them.

✳ ✳ ✳

Outside, the world was still, as though a raging storm hadn't swept through a few days ago, sending the sea into a temper, churning the waters and sky. Today was almost warm, the sky a few shades lighter than a robin's egg, and no breeze rustled the air. I strolled across the lawn, inhaling deeply. Everything smelled like pine and the sea.

I texted Tyler as I walked up his drive, and he opened the door as soon as I reached it. In his pajama pants and cotton shirt, he looked like a sleepy Prince Charming. I couldn't help but smile. "Hi. Get your skates."

He yawned and rubbed his hair. Some of the fine strands rose straight up as he lowered his hand. "Has anyone ever told you you're bossy?"

"Yes."

He let me inside. "Give me a sec to grab my stuff."

I waited in the entryway, taking in the decorations: a few holiday candles surrounded by holly; a worn rug, ancient but impeccably made; and a painting I hadn't noticed before of a blonde in her underwear, insouciantly pushing a vacuum cleaner, red-lipped like Marilyn Monroe.

"The dealer called it 'perfect for intimate spaces,'" someone said behind me, and I turned to see Robin, bundled up in a cozy sweater depicting a polar bear drinking a hot beverage. Robin, too, held a mug, a hazelnut scent wafting from it. "Code for 'you might not want to hang it where everyone can see it.'"

"But you did."

"She's too good to hide." Robin sipped her coffee. "What are you two up to today?"

"We're going skating."

"Are you?" Her brows rose. "Fun."

Tyler bounded back into the room, now wearing jeans and a cabled sweater, skates in one hand, phone in the other. He drew to a stop. "Hi."

"Morning." Robin gave him a once-over. "Do you have your gloves?"

Tyler must have been stronger than me, because he forbore to roll his eyes. "Yes, Mom."

Soon we were in his car, pulling out of the drive. "Where are we headed?" he asked.

"Maxcy Pond. You know the turnoff?"

"Of course." He looked insulted.

I suppressed a smile, glancing out the window at the long stretches of snow-covered lawns and hedges. In barely any time at all, we pulled over into a little parking space alongside Cliff Road. A narrow path cut through the thicket to Maxcy Pond. The Nantucket Anglers Club had owned it for years before selling it to the Land Bank, which cared for much of the island's nature. Now it was a popular ice-skating spot.

By the trunk of the car, I swapped my boots for my skates. Tyler sat down next to me. "Ice-skating, huh."

"You said the best kind of practice mimicked actual conditions. I figured I could get my adrenaline pumping to mimic how nervous I'll actually be talking to Isaac," I said. "Skating seems perfect."

"Fair warning"—slower than me, he removed his boots and tugged on his skates—"I can't skate."

I stared at him, appalled. "But—you own skates!"

"What kind of bougie New Yorker would I be if I didn't?"

"I guess you're not a real bougie New Yorker," I said. "You're from LA."

He laughed up at me as he tied the laces. "I'm trying my best."

"It's easy," I promised, though I remembered when skating hadn't been, when I'd wobbled each time one of my feet left the ice, when I'd toppled over at the slightest provocation.

"Promise to catch me if I fall?"

I grinned back at him. We were in my territory now, and it made me feel light and pleased. "Not a chance."

We tottered down the short path through the brambly sur-roundings, which opened to frozen water. I took off my guards and launched onto the ice, pushing off against the uneven surface of the pond. Dried yellow marshes and trees ringed the shore. How long had it been since I'd last skated on a pond? When I'd been serious about skating over two years ago, it'd almost always been at the rink, and most of my practice had been off the ice:

core training, balance, strength training. I hadn't been out on a pond, breathing in bracing, icy air, in ages. In a lifetime.

I took a few gliding steps, my legs at first unwieldy, no longer familiar with the proper way to carry my weight. But though it had been years, a faint memory lived in my body, the ghost of a girl who used to be excellent. Each time my skates moved against the ice, she came back. I *knew* this: not just the movements but the cold on my cheeks and in my lungs, the bright sky above, the bumpy ice. Before I'd been a serious skater, I'd skated on ponds like these, on *this* pond. And it'd made me happy.

I skated back to Tyler. He'd managed to get onto the ice, holding his arms out for balance in a surprisingly endearing way. I circled around him, laughing. He laughed back. "Not fair!" he shouted.

"No?" I skated a few paces backward, reveling in the tension in my calves, the kick and give, the way my muscles responded exactly the way I wanted them to. Why had I waited so long to do this again? How had I given this up?

I picked up speed. It had been ages since I tried this, but my body remembered. While I didn't have the same control I once had, skating didn't feel as foreign as I'd been afraid it might. I executed a few waltz jumps, remembering how to hold my body, adding speed and crossovers. I'd forgotten the sheer joy of this, the magic of having control over my body, of reaching unexpected heights.

Could I still do an axel? An axel jump meant taking off forward and landing backward, one and a half rotations in the air, which made it the hardest edge jump. I'd been good at them once. I breathed in the crisp air, so much more invigorating than the air in the rink, then moved into a series of backward crossovers. Oh, I could do this. This had been my bread and butter. Bending my knees, I lifted into the air, rotating with that familiar feeling like flying, the world a blur as I shifted my balance.

And I felt an instant of brief, painful fear. Landing could be the hardest part, and my legs weren't as strong as they'd once been. What if my muscles no longer had the strength to hold me up? What if I collapsed in a tangled pile of limbs?

But then my right foot connected solidly with the ice, my leg wobbling slightly but holding, and I was skating backward and laughing.

God, it felt good.

I returned to Tyler, smiling so broadly my cheeks hurt. He brought his hands together in several loud claps. "I get it now."

I shook my hair out of my face, spitting out a strand of curls. I'd forgotten to tie my hair back, so I performed a quick and effective French braid. The wiry nature of my hair meant I didn't need an elastic to hold it. "Get what?"

"Why you wanted to skate. You're good."

"Thanks." I grabbed his hand. "Come on!"

"I don't know—"

"Bend your knees and keep your toes pointed out. Shift your weight back and forth. Don't look down. Let's go!"

I looped him about the pond until we were out of breath and rosy-cheeked. Tyler, to his credit, made a valiant effort despite his lack of coordination. We were doing decently until one slightly too enthusiastic push-off. Windmilling his arms, he tottered, yelped—and fell sideways onto me.

We hit the ice, hard. Tyler bore the brunt of it, twisting so he landed with a *thump* and I merely fell over him. He let out an involuntary cry. "Ow!"

I couldn't stop laughing, even as I pushed up to a seat while Tyler remained sprawled on his back. "Are you okay?"

"I think I ripped my pants," he said mournfully. "They're my best raw denim."

"Poor boy." I patted his arm. "But you had fun, right?"

"Yeah." He grinned up at me, and my heartbeat sped up. I wanted—

I wanted Isaac. We were here to get my heartbeat up so I could practice flirting so I'd be prepared for *Isaac*.

I cleared my throat. "We should practice. Now that we're all . . . filled with adrenaline."

His grin faltered, but then came back. He waved a hand. "Fine. Flirt with me."

Eye contact. Smile. Compliments and questions. I flashed a

grin, trying to mimic the same casual, comfortable one Tyler gave out so easily. "Hey, Isaac."

Tyler winced.

My smile fell immediately. "What? How did I already mess up?"

"No—nothing—sorry." He held his hands up. "It's weird, having you beam at me and say another guy's name."

"Oh. Sorry. I thought it would be helpful if I . . . pretended this was the actual situation."

"Right. Sure. Let's try again."

I took a breath and forced a smile. "Hi, Isaac."

"Hi." Instead of smiling, Tyler looked almost austere.

"Welcome to Golden Doors." Questions. Casual touch. "Um— is this your first time on Nantucket?"

"Yeah."

I leaned forward, trying to radiate warmth, joy. "Why don't I show you where to put your bags. This way." I touched his arm. I didn't think I could touch *Isaac's* arm, but I could at least practice the motion on Tyler.

Tyler stared down at my hand. "I'll put them away later, thanks."

I scowled. "You have to play along. The triplets say the first rule of improv is to always say yes."

"Maybe this guy won't be friendly."

I hadn't even considered that. Surely Isaac would be

friendly—he always had been before. But I'd never flirted with him before. I fell backward onto the ice. "Then what do I do?"

"Just be who you are. That should be enough."

"Well, it hasn't been so far," I snapped.

"Then maybe he's not the right person for you," Tyler shot back.

I pressed my lips together, feeling jumbled up and almost like crying. Isaac was the right person—wasn't he? I thought he might be like me, reserved on the outside but only until you got to know him. But if he didn't like me—if the people I liked never liked me in return—it seemed like the problem lay with *me*, not them. In which case, I couldn't just be me. I had to change.

"Sorry," Tyler said abruptly. "I didn't mean . . . I'm sure he'll like you."

"Whatever."

"But . . . you don't *need* to make this guy like you, you know. The world won't end if you give this a pass."

"Right, I know." I looked down at the ice, the foggy white of the frozen surface, the thin lines and strange bumps. "But I can't always give things a pass. I can't avoid whatever scares me. Maybe it's . . ." How to explain this? I took a deep breath. "Okay. When I do something, when I want to learn something, I practice endlessly. So I know this situation seems weird, but it's how I do things." I looked up to find Tyler's intense, relentless gaze on me, so searing I shifted nervously. "What?"

"I wish this could just be fun for you."

"Afterward will be fun, the actual relationship. I just have to get there." I sighed. "How did you get so good at this? At flirting, at people, at getting everyone to like you?"

His mouth twisted briefly. "I decided to be."

"What?" I tilted my head, confused.

He looked up at me briefly, his eyes darker blue than the sky. "I was bullied pretty badly in middle school."

The words were so unexpected, it took a moment to parse them. "Really?"

"Yup." His mouth flattened. "I was quiet and dressed badly and had bad skin and my hair was very fine and it lay flat and greasy."

I tried to picture any of those things but found them impossible to see in the easygoing, perfect, popular boy before me. "Hard to believe."

"Believe it."

I'd never really been bullied; people might not care to get to know me, but they definitely wanted to hang out, especially in public. I found school lonely and stifling, but not . . . bad. Or bad in a different way. "I'm sorry. That sucks."

"Yes." He gave me a tight-lipped smile. "It really sucked. Then I went to high school with a different group of people. And I didn't want to be bullied anymore, so I decided to be popular."

"How?" *Decided to be popular.* I barely understood the concept. The way people saw me felt so out of my control. I was quiet, so people thought I was aloof. I was a Barbanel, so they thought I was a snob. The idea of trying to control how people saw me was alien.

"I noticed if I dressed like the popular kids, people were nicer to me. If I had the same hobbies as the popular kids, people were nicer to me. If I was a little more basic, people were nicer to me."

I stared at him. "Are you serious?"

"Yup."

"That's *terrible*."

"That's people." He stretched his long legs out in front of him.

I wasn't sure whether to find this depressing or brilliant. "But so—you changed who you were?"

"I didn't change *who* I was. I changed how I presented myself— got better hair supplies, stopped reading comics at lunch, stopped bragging about baking. It worked."

"Wow." I paused. "But—if you're never really real—it sounds lonely."

A muscle in his jaw twitched, like he was tense, angry, a way I'd never seen him before. "It's not."

"But if you're hiding parts of yourself . . ." I didn't feel like people at school necessarily knew me, but I also never felt like I pretended to be anything other than who I was. If I *did* have more friends, I felt sure they'd know everything about me. "What about your best friends? They must know all about . . . comics and baking and everything."

For a moment his face was open and surprised and—I don't know, sad?—before it blanked and he flashed the polished smile I was coming to hate, the one he gave to everyone. The one I didn't want him to give to me. "Sure."

Which made me think that, maybe, Tyler Nelson—the most popular boy on Nantucket, never without a friend or a girl or a party—might not actually have very many close friends.

I looked out at the yellow marshes, not wanting to prod deeper at the soft spot he'd revealed, not wanting to bruise him. "You still like comic books and baking?"

He shrugged. Then nodded.

"Like what?" I asked. "I've read *The Prince and the Dressmaker* and *Heartstopper.*"

"Those are good. My moms like those."

I gave him a light shove. "Here I was feeling so cool, and I'm reading the same stuff as middle-aged women."

He grinned. "I won't tell them you called them middle-aged."

I laughed. "So what do you like?"

"Oh, uh, I like *Green Lantern.* And *Far Sector*—which, uh, I guess you would *also* say is *Green Lantern*, but, um, actually . . ."

I watched, fascinated, as his cheeks pinkened. Tyler Nelson was *embarrassed.* He was *shy* to tell me about the comics he liked. And yet he did tell me. As he spoke, the pink of his cheeks mellowed and his tone became excited instead of flustered.

"Would you ever write comics?" I asked. "Or draw them? Since you like them so much."

"Nah, I don't think so. But I like how stories dig into how

and why people behave the way they do. I'm actually studying psychology for the same reason, I guess. I like to understand what makes people tick."

"Cool." I tilted my head. "Do you think it's because you spent so much time thinking about that when you were younger?"

"Maybe." His voice was thoughtful. "I think . . . the more time I spent trying to understand why people behave the way they do, the more interesting I found it. And I think if you're interested and passionate about something, you should pursue it."

I watched the clouds drift, felt the cold seep through my coat and into my arms. "What if you're not passionate about anything, though?"

He rolled onto his side and looked at me. "Everyone's passionate about something."

I shook my head. "I'm not."

"You're passionate about skating."

I let out a white puff of laughter. "Thanks. But I'm not really."

"What? Yeah, you are."

"No, I'm not. I'm *good*—but you need to be great, or it doesn't count." I wrapped my arms around my legs and rested my chin on my knees. "And I'm not great."

"How do you know?"

I pretended to be nonchalant. "I used to compete and stuff. But I wasn't good enough to be real."

"Good enough to compete still sounds impressive."

"Thanks. It was just regional level, though." I gazed at the sky, which looked like ice with snow spread across it in sweeping lines, all one level. "Then it got to a point where it was only about competing, which made me hate it. And then I wasn't good enough to keep going, so I had to stop, and then I hated myself."

He sat upright, pinning me with his blue gaze. "I'm sorry."

I forced a laugh. "Sorry, that makes it sound very dramatic. It was fine. It's just . . ." I traced my mittened hand against the ice. "Sometimes I watch skaters on TV and I *ache*. I feel like I could have been them. If only I were better. If only I was good enough."

"How long did you ice-skate for?"

I fixed my gaze on one of the clouds, a cotton puff drifting across the sky. "Eight to fourteen. I started being serious around twelve—basically when I realized I wasn't going to get better at piano."

"When did you start piano?"

"Oh, I must have been around four."

"And now what?" he asked warily.

"What do you mean?"

"You can't tell me someone who spent a decade playing piano and skating suddenly gave up trying to be best at something."

"Now I'm a barista," I said. "It's much more relaxing."

"Okay . . ." he said slowly. "Do you like it?"

"I like not being under a microscope all the time." I shrugged. "Do I really need to throw myself into yet another activity?

Can't I have some time to myself? To make coffee?"

"If it makes you happy."

"Skating and piano used to make me happy," I said. "What if . . . you found your purpose, the thing you love and want your life to be about, and it turned out you were wrong? You weren't good enough to go any further, weren't talented enough, weren't *enough*? Then who are you?"

Our eyes met. I felt, for whatever reason, like he understood me, understood this strange, purposeless weight I carried around. "Then I guess you get to decide," Tyler said slowly. "You get to pick who you want to be next."

I didn't know what I wanted to be next. I didn't know what I wanted to do with my life or even what made me happy. Except for Nantucket, except for my family. Except for Olivia, and, bizarrely enough, Tyler Nelson.

And what did he want?

"What about you?" I gazed up at the cloud-brushed sky. "What's this miracle you're looking for?"

"Why do you think I'm looking for a miracle?"

"Everyone wants a miracle." Who didn't crave a touch of magic, a sudden, wondrous change to their everyday lives? It felt more possible miracles existed at this point in the year than at any other, as though the goodwill at the holidays generated a kind of magic. The days were long and dark, but people came together with light and joy, and that was a miracle in itself.

I wanted a hundred miracles: to be less stiff and less awkward, to be better at skating or not care about it at all. To know what I wanted to do with my life. To live at Golden Doors with all my family year-round. "Besides, you asked me if I believed in miracles."

"Just a—psychological curiosity. Because you said Hanukkah is all about miracles."

"All right," I said archly. "Don't tell me the miracle you want. Tell me what you want more than anything else in the world."

He scoffed, and I thought he'd push back. It was a deeply personal question, after all. Instead, he frowned at the ice, tracing a line in the cold dust. "I wish I could get my mom her family back."

"What do you mean?"

"Mom had a giant family growing up. She loved it. Especially at the holidays. Now—she gets kinda morose. That's why we came to Nantucket this year, actually—to try to change things up. Make her happier."

"But you said they chose not to spend time with your grandparents at the holidays, right? So they could if they wanted to."

"Sure, technically. But they always get into huge fights about how Mom screwed everything up. Especially my life. I think they read it as this huge insult that she dared to leave the nest and have a job they don't approve of and marry a food critic, which they also think isn't a real job, and live in LA, land of vice and terror, and send me to public school instead of Phillips, which, like, god forbid."

"Are they . . . Emily and Richard Gilmore?"

He snorted. "Yeah, maybe."

"Oy."

He smiled wryly. "But you know what they do approve of? What they watch every night? Channel 9 News. Danziger Media. And you know what they read? *Today News*. Danziger Media. If I can get an internship, a job—a real *career* with a company they respect—maybe they'll lay off my parents. They'll think I've course corrected and won't fight about my moms' parenting. Maybe they'll relax all around, and we'll be able to have Christmas with them."

"Tyler . . ." My heart hurt for him. "That's why you want an internship with my great-uncle, isn't it? You think it'll bring your family back together?"

"I think there's a decent chance, yeah."

"You tell your moms this?"

"God, no." He shuddered. "They'd tell me I was overburdening myself. *That* would burden *them*, which is the exact opposite of the point."

"But they'd be right. It's not your job to make your parents and your grandparents happy."

"Maybe not my job. But if I can, shouldn't I?" He squinted at the sky. "And isn't it, maybe, a small miracle if a way to get an internship at Danziger Media drops in my lap? A way to meet Arnold Danziger, my grandparents' hero?"

"I think a miracle would be if it made you happy, too."

He shrugged. "Well. Miracles probably don't exist."

Maybe not. But maybe they existed if we made them, if we helped them into being. Maybe lightning wouldn't strike from nowhere and tell me what I should do with my life. But maybe I could go after what I wanted. I could give miracles a nudge.

I thought once more of the strange little mystery of the wooden chest. Hadn't the Barbanel girl gone after what she wanted with her secret lover? What had ended it—death, departure, loyalty to her family? Had she been happy she'd had her romance? I thought she must have been. Tennyson had probably been right: "'Tis better to have loved and lost than never to have loved at all."

"Come on," I said, jumping to my feet. "Let's go check out some Christmas trees."

CHAPTER
TWELVE

The Whaling Museum was located on Broad Street in a collection of buildings including an old candle factory. Back in the day, Nantucket had had a gazillion candle factories due to the whole whale oil thing. White columns flanked the redbrick entrance, and long banners announced exhibits.

Inside, we bought our tickets from one of the Nantucket Historical Association employees, a woman in her forties with a short bob and a blue vest. "I have a kind of weird question," I told her. "We were wondering if you had a curator or someone we could talk to? We found a box of old things in the attic and wondered if someone could take a look . . ."

Without blinking, she said, "You'll have to make an appointment at the Research Library."

"Oh." I exchanged a glance with Tyler. "There's no one here who can look?"

"Nope," she said.

Okay. Welp. "Are they open?"

"They will be after the new year."

Of course. "Okay. Thank you."

As we headed into the museum, we heard her say to her colleague, "Everyone thinks they have treasures in their attic."

I glanced at Tyler glumly as we passed a giant map of Nantucket engraved in the wall. "So much for that."

"You know what?" Tyler said. "We're smart people. We can research shipwrecks ourselves."

"I like your optimism. I'm not sure I buy it, but I like it."

Every December, the museum transformed into a winter wonderland, decked with wreaths and filled with trees. We wandered through the rooms, admiring them while also looking at the actual displays. As a kid, my favorite part of the museum had been the interactive exhibits about women who'd lived on the island, holograms of reenactors telling their stories. Noah had liked the giant skeleton of a sperm whale in Gosnell Hall, while Grandpa, an amateur painter, had loved the seascapes. Tyler, I quickly discovered, was obsessed with the miniature boat models, with their tiny, impeccably made sails. "I want to make one of these," he said as we passed the first.

I studied it, all the masts and rigs and sails. "Seems

complicated. And like they'd take up a lot of space."

He grinned. "If I lofted my bed, I bet it could fit."

Tucked between ship replicas and standing tall in gallery rooms were Christmas trees, designed by local nonprofits, artists, and businesses. Some were classically decorated, others goofy, and some weren't trees at all but tree shapes made out of buoys. We wandered about, picking and changing favorites, ducking into the old candle factory and craning our heads back to take in the tree toppers.

I must have been in the museum a hundred times, on rainy days especially, as the adults tried to find ways to distract all the cousins. There'd always been exhibits about nineteenth-century Nantucket, the heyday of whaling and its downfall, but I'd never paid intense attention. Now, in between admiring trees, Tyler and I pored over each plaque. I focused on the nineteenth-century women, as though tucked away might be a mention of one specific Barbanel lady. I read about Petticoat Row: modern-day Centre Street, which had once been a hotbed of women-owned businesses. One temporary exhibit discussed women who'd gone to sea themselves. Some disguised themselves as men, like Rebecca Anne Johnson, who used her father's name when she joined a whaling ship, but many wives of whaling captains also accompanied their husbands.

A poem had been transcribed, titled "The Nantucket Girl's Song." A few of the lines jumped out at me:

Then I'll haste to wed a sailor,
and send him off to sea,
For a life of independence
is the pleasant life for me.
But every now and then I shall
like to see his face,
For it always seems to me to beam with manly grace . . .
But when he says Goodbye my love, I'm off across the sea
First I cry for his departure, then laugh because I'm free.

"Harsh," Tyler said.

I gave him a fierce smile. "I love it."

Tyler trailed his finger over the second couplet. *For the life of independence is the pleasant life for me.* "And is that what you want? I thought you wanted Isaac."

"I *do* want Isaac. To date, not to center my life around. Welcome to the twenty-first century, bro."

"Guess I deserved that."

In the candle factory, we read about sperm whales, saw old oil lamps and glass bottles filled with yellow spermaceti, admired portraits and paintings and newspaper clippings. In one case, I saw a small wooden arrow, remarkably similar to the one we'd found in the chest. "Tyler! Look!"

I read the plaque as he joined me. "'Boatsteerers—or harpooners—used oak pins known as chockpins to secure

168

harpoon lines to a whale boat. They held one of the highest-ranked positions on a whaling ship and were likely to become officers or captains themselves. According to legend, they wore their pins to let the young ladies of Nantucket know they were whale hunters and, therefore, highly eligible bachelors.'" I made a face. "I wouldn't want to marry a dude who killed whales."

"You're only saying that because of modern sensibilities," Tyler said. "You would have in the 1800s. You would have thought it was hot."

"I would not!"

Tyler raised a brow. "Guess you'll never know, will you?"

I frowned. "So if the guy had one of these pins—it meant he was a whaler, didn't it? A harpooner."

"Seems likely."

"What did the harpooner do?" I looked around the room, as though the information I wanted would jump out at me. "Why were they so fancy?"

"Oh." Tyler brightened. "How familiar are you with how whaling worked?"

"Apparently less familiar than you."

"Follow me." He led us back into the hall with the sperm whale's skeleton attached to the ceiling, diving down at the boat on the floor. I'd seen them a million times before, but most of my thoughts were along the lines of *big whale, small boat, scary,* before I'd move on.

"This is a whaleboat," Tyler said. "They launched from ships after a whale was spotted. They'd row up quietly, and the harpooner would stand at the front of the boat and stab the whale."

My stomach turned over. "That's horrible."

"The harpoon got embedded in the whale's blubber on one end, and attached to a line secured to the whaleboat on the other." He took a few steps over to another exhibit with an inset paragraph titled *Nantucket Sleigh Ride*. "The whale would be pissed, and dive and swim, towing the boat behind at about twenty miles an hour."

I studied the sculptures of whales and boats resting below the display, their tiny detailing exquisite, the whales caught in motion, small figures on the boat ready to attack.

"They'd whip along the ocean until the whale needed to rest, and the whalers would use the line to pull themselves close, and the boatheader would take their lance and stab the whale until it died."

I stared at him, appalled. "I hate this." Why did people go so far in pursuit of oil? Light, power? A true miracle would be the Hanukkah miracle on steroids—a tiny bit of oil that lasted forever, instead of having to wreck our planet for more.

"You know what?" I said to Tyler. "I think Hanukkah's the holiday of renewable energy. It's all about energy efficiency, how it's so amazing the oil lasts eight nights. I'm gonna tell the triplets to put that in the play."

"The play?"

"Oh. The triplets are doing a Hanukkah play, and it is a *thing.* All the cousins have been drafted. I play the handmaid. I carry a decapitated head."

He blinked. "That sounds . . . really nice."

"It is," I said agreeably. "I assume you're talking about the play, not the head, though. Otherwise I might have to call the police."

He laughed. "Yeah. The head just sounds heavy."

I considered. "How heavy do you think a decapitated head is?"

"You google it," he said, crossing his arms. "I don't want that in my search history."

I laughed. "Fair. Okay, so, anyway. If our guy was a harpooner, it meant he was on a whaler, right? It could narrow down his ship."

Tyler nodded. "We should look again later at the list of wrecks and see the whalers with OS in their name."

We kept wandering. I'd forgotten how big the museum was, how many rooms, how many exhibits. I'd forgotten how spaces smelled different, the main building, the candle factory, the second floor over from the factory, with its exhibits of artifacts from far-off places. There were bells and fans, baskets and head-rests, from India and China and Japan—all from places Nantucket whalers had reached.

And a necklace made from seashells that looked familiar.

"Tyler!" I called excitedly. "Jewelry made out of seashells from the Pacific."

"Cool." Tyler peered at them. "Wait—do you have a picture of your shells?"

I pulled up pictures of the seashell jar. "I don't know anything about seashells."

"Me neither," Tyler said. "But yours look like these ones in the case. And—wait, are those puka shells? Like from the nineties?"

"I guess?" I studied the small white shells in my photo, which certainly did look like the old necklaces. A few of the other shells were smooth and dime-size, with a curl through them. I'd also photographed the beautiful scallop-shaped shells, vibrantly colored in pink and orange and yellow. "You look up puka; I'll look up the others."

"Puka shells are naturally occurring in Hawaii," Tyler said after a minute. "When do we think Nantucket ships made it to Hawaii?"

"I think one of the boards in the candle factory mentioned a date," I said, already looking it up.

We fell into a rapid rabbit hole. An American whaling ship first visited Hawaii in 1819; afterward, Hawaii quickly became a common stop for resupplying on the way to Japanese waters. "In 1834, one hundred whaleships stopped in Hawaii," I paraphrased one article. "Twenty years later, over seven hundred stopped there in a single year, mostly from Nantucket and New Bedford. A lot of Native Hawaiians ended up as crew on Nantucket ships and came here."

"Look at this." Tyler turned his phone to show me a picture of a seashell that looked like mine. "This is called a sunset shell, native to Hawaii. Very fancy. You have two of those. I bet the sailor found them and decided to bring them back to his girl."

"So we're looking for a whaleship that made it to Hawaii," I said. "With an 'OS' in its name and that wrecked near Nantucket."

"I'm down to look it up," Tyler said. "But maybe over more coffee?"

We headed a few blocks to a Portuguese bakery with white-washed walls and blue paintings of the sea, almost enough to make you feel like you'd been whisked away to the Azores. Nantucket whalers had been in contact with those mid-Atlantic islands since the 1700s, but I hadn't thought much about contact with Pacific Islands.

Tyler ordered a cappuccino and I got a hot chocolate. We both got egg tarts and settled in. I scooted my chair closer to his, so I could peer over his shoulder as he pressed the search button on the old book we'd found of Nantucket wrecks, typing in *OS* and paging through the results, looking for a whaleship. First *OS*: schooner. Second: brig. Third: schooner. Fourth: schooner. Fifth: schooner.

Sixth: whaler.

I squeezed Tyler's shoulder. "Look! There!"

"Slow down," he cautioned. "Let's go through the rest. There might be more."

There were, but the two other whaler wrecks occurred before

1820, before whaling ships had made it to Hawaii. Only one whaler remained with an *OS* in its name: the *Rosemary.*

"Let's see her deal," I said, and with a few more taps, we'd pulled up an article.

In April of 1845, the *Rosemary* had been coming in late at night in heavy fog and mistook Sankaty Head Light on Nantucket for Gay's Head on the Vineyard—both lighthouses worked similarly. The ship steered as though approaching the Vineyard and went ashore near Long Pond, bilging and breaking apart. Five crewmen died, including the first mate; the rest were brought to shore.

A quick search brought up another article. The *Rosemary* had been returning from South America, with crews out of New Bedford and Nantucket. She'd been sailing for twenty years. She'd navigated so many difficult waters and had been so close to home on her final voyage.

"Jesus," Tyler said. "I bet your girl was in love with one of the sailors who died. And she was so brokenhearted, she couldn't get rid of his stuff."

"Maybe," I said. "Though statistically, it's more likely he survived."

"Sure, but would she really be keeping his shipwrecked quarterboard if he lived and they broke up?"

"Fair point." It made me sad, thinking of one of my ancestors losing a loved one in a deadly shipwreck. I'd rather she hid away the belongings of a guy she wanted to move on from, not someone she'd been forced to give up. "If this ship went down in 1845 . . ."

I pulled up the photo of the family tree on my phone and we scanned it. "Joseph and Esther were the first Barbanels who came to Nantucket," I told Tyler. "They had Marcus and Naomi, who would have been in their forties and married in the 1840s. But Marcus's daughters . . ." My gaze fell on Shoshana—my distant ancestress who had continued the family line in lieu of a male heir—and her younger sisters. I did some quick math on my napkin. "In 1845, Shoshana would have been nineteen, Josephine seventeen, and Louisa sixteen."

"Sounds right to me."

"So we're looking for a sailor in his teens or twenties, I bet."

"Why so limited?" Tyler said, grinning. "Don't be ageist."

I made a face. "Okay, I *hope* he was close to their age, but who's to say. Still, he looks young in the picture, right?"

"I guess," Tyler agreed skeptically. "It's a painting; can you really tell?"

I swiped back to the photo of the painting. "Yes. He's young and hot."

Tyler rolled his eyes.

On a new napkin, I scribbled dates.

1819: ships make it to Hawaii (seashells)
1850s/60s: photography shows up (no need for painting!)

1813–1845: Rosemary whaling
1845: Rosemary sinks

"So we can expect our sailor and his lady love were together before his last voyage, right?" Tyler said. "And these trips took two or three years—so how old would the Barbanel girls have been in 1843?"

Nodding, I scribbled down their ages.

1843:
Shoshana—17
Josephine—15
Louisa—14

Tyler peered at my napkin. "I bet it's the oldest girl."

"Can't be." I shook my head. "Shoshana married her dad's apprentice the year before the *Rosemary* returned. If she'd been waiting for a sailor, she wouldn't have married someone else."

Tyler raised his brows. "She might have."

I winced. True, but I hated that option. Why would she have done it? Unless she'd been forced to by her family. "It could have been one of the younger girls."

"A fourteen-year-old or fifteen-year-old?" Then he smirked. "You know what, sure. I'd never say a fourteen-year-old couldn't stay obsessed with the same guy for years and years."

I kicked him. Not softly, either. "Get over yourself."

"We should look up if either of them never married."

"I hope they did! Unless they didn't want to. But no one should stay in mourning *forever* because of a teenage boyfriend."

"Hey, maybe she ran a shop on Petticoat Lane, happy with her independent life."

"I'm fully pro–independent life, but I'm also pro–getting your happily ever after, too, if you want it." I scrolled through the family trees on my phone, but didn't find any more details about Josephine or Louisa. "I'll check with my grandparents to see if they have more records. And maybe there's a list of the crew, and we can see how old the sailors were, see if we can narrow down who he was." I froze. "I mean, obviously, I will. You don't have to be involved."

"I don't mind," he said easily. "I bet it was the first mate. Probably started off as a harpooner, then got promoted for this voyage and gave his oak pin to his girlfriend. He would have had to have been on at least one trip before this one, too, to have reached Hawaii and gotten the shells."

"Good point." My phone buzzed, and I started, a little surprised to remember it did anything besides research family trees and shipwrecks and seashells. Olivia, checking to see if I wanted to meet up before Isaac arrived. I hesitated. I did, but I was oddly loath to leave Tyler. "My friend wants to meet up."

"Kaitlyn's little sister?"

Right, he'd know who I meant. Olivia and I had always been two peas in a pod. "Yeah."

"Tell her to come here."

I glanced at him, startled. "You don't have to hang out with us."

He gave me a slightly sharp smile. "Maybe I want to."

"Okay . . ."

"Unless you want me to go." His smile changed, became a shell projecting friendliness. And my thought from earlier in the day cropped up once more: maybe Tyler didn't have so many people he really liked to hang out with.

"Stay," I said. "And we'll order more food."

✳ ✳ ✳

Olivia greeted Tyler pleasantly enough, though she widened her eyes at me when we hugged. "What have you guys been up to?" she asked as she sat.

"We went to the Whaling Museum." I hesitated. "And skating."

She cut her eyes at me. Olivia knew my whole history with skating. "Really."

"Yeah. It was . . . fun."

"That's great," she said sincerely, then turned to Tyler. "Are you much of a skater?"

He put his hand to his hip and grimaced. "Definitely not."

As they talked, my gaze kept darting between the two of them, nervous about how they'd interact. Tyler, at first, treated Olivia to his large smile and easy laugh, to his undivided attention and good questions. I hadn't realized, before this week, how he really did have a polished, impenetrable wall up. He told entertaining, nonpersonal stories, deflected anything genuine about himself, and asked plenty of questions. And it worked; I could see Olivia opening up to him, chatting about her boyfriend, Jackson, and the New Year's party and college. But Tyler himself didn't open up or drop his polished smile.

Not until I jumped in, taking over the conversation with Olivia. "I read a pretty decent zombie apocalypse book recently," she said. "Usually I don't like zombies because I like smart villains, and zombies are so dumb. But this was about a start-up trapped at a retreat on the Cape, and how the different departments behaved, like content and marketing and engineering, and who survived, and how they defended the resort from zombies."

"Love it," I said. "I'd like to read one of those set in high school, about all the different cliques."

"Jocks could probably mount a good defense," Olivia said. "But the nerds have the tactical advantage. They should probably team up."

"And one person from each group who hated each other would have to work together and fall in love."

"One hundred percent." She took a bite of her malassada, a fried-dough pastry covered in cinnamon and packed with lemon zest. "I think the theater kids are dead right away, though. Too loud. And they keep pausing to monologue."

"What about the stoners? Are they so slow the zombies get them or so utterly still the zombies don't even notice them?"

"I assume the zombies can detect heat, so they're probably done for. Unless the weed confuses the zombies?"

"Quite possible."

Tyler's gaze flickered back and forth between us, and I could see him slowly relaxing, as though he was realizing he didn't have to entertain anyone. And then his other smile appeared, the smaller one, and he leaned forward. "What about the artsy kids? They could probably camouflage themselves, like Peeta."

After that, the rest of the afternoon felt wonderfully easy.

I was the one who actually had to call it, realizing with a start the Danzigers would be arriving soon. We stepped outside into a light flurry of snow and almost ran into two laughing girls—one of whom was Abby.

"Oh, *hi.*" Her eyes widened as they flicked toward Tyler, and I felt like I was doing something illicit.

Tyler's expression, of course, remained unaffected. "Hey, Abby. And—Jane, right? What are you guys up to?"

Jane linked elbows with Abby. "Gossiping about boys," she said. "And how much trouble they are."

We chatted for a few minutes, even though I wanted to spontaneously combust, and Abby and Jane looked like they might break into giggles any second. "See you at home," I said to Abby as soon as politely reasonable, and hurried the rest of us along.

"I'll give you a lift home," Tyler said as we walked down the street, as though driving together was the most natural thing in the world.

"Cool," Olivia said before I had a chance to answer. "Good to see you, Tyler. See you soon," she said to me, with a waggle of her brows when Tyler couldn't see. She peeled away.

Tyler glanced at me as we walked back toward the car, past the Christmas trees lining the streets, the shops with holiday displays, the lampposts twined with ivy. "You guys have been close forever."

"She's basically my best friend," I said, then flushed. "I mean, we don't call each other that, and it might sound weird since we only see each other during the summer. She might not think we are, actually."

"You don't talk about it?"

What, ask Olivia if she thought we were besties and risk the mortification of being gently let down? "No, thank you. Anyway, she probably has a real best friend back home."

"Don't you?"

"No. I don't really have close friends other than Olivia. And my cousins, I guess."

"Really?" He sounded surprised. "Why not?"

I shrugged. "People like to have me around, but they don't really want to be my friend, you know?"

He frowned. "No. What do you mean?"

What *did* I mean? "Like . . . for semiformal," I said slowly, trying to articulate it, "no one invited me to get ready with them. I had to—to ask what they were doing, and everyone had already made plans with their micro groups. They said I could join, but I didn't want to crash. It felt weird, not initially being included."

"What did you do?"

"I got ready on my own. No big deal." We'd reached the car, and I busied myself climbing inside, hiding my face with my hair as I buckled my seat belt. It'd been a very big deal.

Tyler started guiding the car through the streets and toward the gentle incline of Cliff Road. "Maybe they didn't know you wanted to hang out with them."

I snorted.

"Seriously. You should tell them. It's the same deal as flirting— you have to let other people know you like them."

"Look at you, psychoanalyzing me one semester out of college." I shook my head, silent for a minute, then I sighed. "Maybe you're right. But I feel pathetic, asking people to do things. What if they think I'm a loser?"

"Then you don't want to hang out with them in the first place, and you'll find better people." His voice softened. "Hey, look. They should be flattered you want to hang out with them. It's flattering when someone expresses interest in you."

"Maybe." I glanced over at him, hesitant to pry but deeply

curious. "What about you? Do you have a lot of good friends in college?"

His mouth twisted, and he made the turnoff toward Golden Doors sharply. "Quantity over quality. I haven't had a best friend since I was ten."

"Oh." I gnawed on my lip. "Because . . . people were mean to you? And then you never let anyone get super close?"

"Now who's psychoanalyzing who?" He pulled up in front of Golden Doors. "I've never thought about dating the way you put it earlier," he said slowly. "About your partner being your best friend. I mean, obviously everyone says that all the time. But I didn't consider what it would be like."

"I don't think your partner *needs* to be your best friend," I said. "Or not your only good friend, because that's probably codependent. But I think it would be really nice."

"Hmm." He nodded toward the house. "You feeling ready for this?"

I took a deep breath. I didn't want to climb out of the warm, safe bubble of his car. "Not really. But I'm going to do it anyway."

"You're going to do great. I'll see you tomorrow?"

"Tomorrow?"

He looked amused. "My moms' Christmas Eve party?"

Oh, right. I opened the door, letting in a rush of cold air. "See you then."

CHAPTER
THIRTEEN

In the hour before the Danzigers arrived, Golden Doors maintained a heightened level of stress as Barbanels darted about, putting last touches on charcuterie boards and wiping down counters. In the great room, an aunt and uncle were talking in strident tones about health care with Grandpa, who looked bored and somewhat disdainful. Four of the younger cousins lay on the floor, working on a thousand-piece puzzle and determinedly ignoring Uncle Gerald as he vacuumed up crushed Cheerios around them.

I escaped to Grandma's sunroom, where she was arranging the last few bouquets. "Hi, Grandma."

She looked up. "Good. I can use another pair of hands."

I held lilies and roses as she measured stems and compared colors; I stripped off thorns and leaves from lower stems.

"I hear you've been spending time with the Nelson boy."

Sometimes I thought gossip ran through my family's veins instead of blood. "Not 'spending time' in any real way."

"Why not? You liked him so much when you were younger."

"When we were *kids*."

"He's always been such a sweet boy. So friendly. When I was your age, I was swooning over Roger Klein." Her gaze softened. "He was a real charmer."

I shot her a startled glance. I'd known Grandpa dated before Grandma, but I'd had no idea she'd done the same. "Who was he?"

"He went to Columbia for law, and we used to go into the same deli at the same time every Tuesday." She smiled a small, private smile.

"What happened?"

She made a soft moue. "We liked each other, but he was never the kind of boy I was going to marry."

Harsh. I thought, briefly, of the Barbanel girl and her sailor—another unlikely match for matrimony. "Why not?"

Her mouth twisted slightly. "Perhaps we were both too easily influenced by who our parents thought we should marry."

"How did it end?"

"Your grandfather and I became serious." Her scissors snapped together. "I thought."

"Do you . . ." I clamped my mouth shut.

"Finish your sentences, Shira."

Sometimes I thought Grandma reminded me to finish my sentences because she was nosy, not to teach me manners. "I know Grandpa dated Abby's grandmother when they were young. And I know he was, um, pretty shaken last summer to find out . . . she'd passed away. Do you know what happened to your old boyfriend?"

"He died fifteen years ago," she said in her cool, practical voice. "I learned from Facebook."

Oof. "I'm sorry."

"Well, *most* of us don't stay hung up on childhood romances," she said flatly, definitely alluding to Grandpa and Abby's grandmother. "Hold the flowers higher, please."

I did. I watched her work, listening to the quiet *snick* of the scissors, breathing in the scent of plants and blooms. "You're really mad at Grandpa, aren't you."

"Pardon?"

"Because he dated you and Abby's grandma at the same time. And never told you about it."

"It was a very long time ago."

"You can still be mad."

"I'm not mad, darling," she said firmly. "Just . . . disappointed."

Disappointed. I thought about how furious and humiliated I'd been when Tyler rejected me, and we'd never even been a couple. "Hell hath no fury" and all. Could you ever trust someone again if you felt betrayed, even if it had been a very long time ago? Did time truly mend all wounds, or were some too deep?

"Hand me half a dozen delphinium stems," she said, and I did, and we moved on.

✳ ✳ ✳

An hour later, the doorbell echoed through the house. I checked my lipstick in a hallway mirror before slipping to the front of the house, where Grandma, Grandpa, and a few of the aunts and uncles welcomed the Danzigers. Both Great-Uncle Arnold and Great-Uncle Harold stood in the foyer alongside their wives: a quartet of octogenarians, younger than my grandparents but no less stubborn. No children or grandchildren accompanied them, only Isaac.

"Arnold." Grandma nodded at her brothers. "Harold."

As they greeted each other, Isaac lingered behind everyone, holding a duffel bag and looking a little lost. A week ago, I would have avoided his gaze and kept my face blank, all the while hoping he'd magically decide to come talk to me. Now I made myself smile when his eyes met mine and lifted my hand in a little wave.

He looked relieved and crossed the entrance to me.

All the individual muscles in my stomach clenched tight like they were squeezing anxiety into my esophagus, where it rose fast and closed my throat. I tried to pretend none of this paralyzing fear was happening. "Isaac. Hi."

God, he was good-looking: chiseled jaw; windswept hair; dark, serious eyes with long black lashes.

"Shira, hey." He looked slightly surprised, like maybe he hadn't expected to remember my name. "Didn't realize you'd be here."

Okay, not the *best* way to start, with the reminder he hadn't been counting down the days until he was in my presence, but it took some of the pressure off, didn't it? I recited my list of tips: smile, eye contact, compliments, questions, casual touch. Tyler gave people his full attention; he was warm and genuine and centered on you. I gave Isaac my fullest smile. "Good trip over?"

He returned the smile, small but still there. "Yeah. Nice of your uncle to bring me. And of your whole family to let me stay."

"Are you kidding?" I said lightly. "We're thrilled to have someone not in our family to mix it up. And there's already a couple dozen people, so what's one more?"

Immediately, I winced. Had I made it sound like we didn't want him here? Because I definitely wanted him here.

Luckily, he didn't seem to be overthinking my words to the same degree I was. "You do have a huge family."

"Sometimes too huge," I joked, then couldn't think of a single other thing to say. Nothing. Nada. What were words? I hoped Isaac couldn't sense my rising panic. My hands were slippery with sweat and I had to consciously keep from wiping them on my jeans.

Okay. What was I supposed to do? Give a compliment or ask a question.

Compliment: *You're so beautiful, and I think we'd make a fantastic couple.*

Nope. Nope. Okay. Question. If I asked a question, I didn't have to talk. I cleared my throat, fearing it might be so dry I'd croak. "Um. Your parents won't miss you for Hanukkah?"

"Nah, they're off traveling."

Right. God, I knew they were traveling. "Where are they now?"

"Paris."

"Wow, how cool! I love Paris!"

"Have you been?"

No. No, I had not, which made it weird I'd made a statement about loving it. "No, I've only left the country once, when we went to Italy when I was fourteen." Did I sound boring and inexperienced? He'd probably been all over the world. "But I love croissants," I said brightly, then wanted to die. *I love croissants?*

Luckily, he smiled like I'd said something cute. Or childish. Potentially both. "Same."

I smiled back, relieved he hadn't given me a look of scorn. I felt like I'd run a marathon.

Oh no. I'd run out of things to say *again.* Why hadn't Tyler made me make a list of conversational gambits?

I never ran out of things to say with *Tyler.*

"Um, you haven't been to Golden Doors before, right? I'll show you around." I turned to find my grandmother, who'd know where Isaac's stuff should go, then remembered one last piece of advice.

Casual touch.

Oh god, no. The thought of touching Isaac made me want to vomit. Well, no—I would *love* if we *magically* touched. But I couldn't bring myself to initiate a touch of his arm.

Or.

Could I?

I beamed at Isaac as bright as I could, hoping it would blind him to my nervousness. Then, fleetingly, I touched his arm at the elbow. "I'll be right back."

I walked toward Grandma and Uncle Arnold, internally screaming. *Ahhhhhh!* My whole body started sweating, liquid springing from pores I hadn't known existed. I had done it. Good lord. I had *touched Isaac.* I was a superhero.

"Hello, Shira," Uncle Arnold said, urbane as always, as I approached.

"Hi, Uncle Arnold." Standing on my tiptoes, I kissed his dry, papery cheek. "Happy Hanukkah." I turned to Grandma. "I thought I'd show Isaac his room. Where do you want him?"

She gave me a sharp glance, which quickly transitioned to the politest of smiles. "Thank you, dear. Next to Noah and Ethan."

I nodded and turned to Isaac. "This way."

He followed me up the grand staircase, his bulging messenger bag over one shoulder, a duffel bag in the other hand. If people liked Tyler because he made them comfortable, I should try to make Isaac comfortable. Only Isaac wasn't the ill-at-ease person here; he seemed fine trooping after me in silence.

"How's work?" Surely a benign question, given how I mostly encountered him in his work settings.

"It's good."

I waited a beat. Never mind. "You're at Columbia, right? What are you studying?"

"Business."

"Cool." A man of few words. At least we weren't talking about the weather. "What do you want to do while you're on Nantucket?"

"I don't know. I don't really know anything about the island."

"There's a ton to do!" I beamed at him as we walked down the hall, then my smile fell away. "Well, since it's winter, a lot of things are closed for the season. But the island is gorgeous. And there's still some restaurants open and walks you can go on." I swallowed. Okay. It was *okay* to put myself out there; no one would be insulted by this offer. "I'd be happy to show you around."

He smiled back. "Thank you."

Wow. I might *show Isaac around*. I wanted to shriek and throw myself on my bed and pant until I'd recovered the breath currently fleeing my body. Instead, I paused at the door to his room. "This is you. The bathroom's at the end of the hall."

"Thanks."

"Great." I smiled, a touch maniacally, and walked away.

I detoured to my room, where I did throw myself onto my bed and screamed into my pillow. Oh my god. I'd *done* it. I'd spoken to Isaac, and I hadn't been sharp or rude or anything other than nice and polite, and I'd offered to play tour guide, and he'd *smiled* at me. I could do this.

I wanted to tell Tyler. I wanted him to be impressed by how well I'd done. Grabbing my phone, I texted him: **Managed to behave like a human being.**

I waited, buzzing with excitement, but it took him a solid three minutes to respond. **Cool.**

I frowned, unsatisfied. But what had I wanted? Follow-up questions, an exclamation point? Tyler didn't *actually* care about the details of my flirting—he was giving advice per our bargain. And he'd just spent half a day with me; I shouldn't expect more from him.

I had to get ahold of myself. Taking a breath, I moved to the vanity and began retouching my makeup. This, I had control over, and the actions soothed me. I strengthened my eyeliner and redid my lipstick, plastered over a zit and brushed on some bronzer. "You can do this," I told my reflection. "You're doing great."

I headed downstairs and was immediately drafted into dinner duty. The adults had perfected a masterful scam: they never needed to cook at Golden Doors as long as they could corral their offspring into the great room. They relaxed on the couches and armchairs, trying out Aunt Liz's latest Hanukkah cocktail, a chocolate drink with a piece of gelt on the rim.

Across the counter from me, Oliver and Miriam chopped

onions, peppers, cucumbers, and tomatoes for a horiatiki salad, while I attempted to master a cheesy-mustardy cauliflower side dish, modified from a Yotam Ottolenghi cookbook.

"Can I help?"

Isaac appeared next to me, and my heart performed a series of Olympic-worthy acrobatics. "Sure. We can always use more hands."

It was actually more work to tell Isaac what to do than to do it myself, but I didn't mind. "If you measure the curry, cumin seeds, and mustard powder into a bowl, we can add it to the sauce along with this cheese." I nodded at the cheddar block I'd picked up to grate.

"Cool." He pulled the curry toward himself and picked up the measuring spoons. "How much?"

"Actually—um—" A stroke of sheer brilliance occurred to me, blindingly bright. "What's your number? I'll text you the recipe."

And just like that, Isaac Lehrer was in my phone.

David came over as we brought the sauce to a simmer. He leaned against the island with extra flair, displaying his self-proclaimed good side in Isaac's direction. "Hey, Isaac."

"Hey," Isaac said. "Uh—Dave, right?"

"Right," David said, though no one called him Dave on pain of death. "I see you've already been put to work."

"It's no problem." Isaac paused his stirring as I added the steamed cauliflower to the pot, where it took on the golden yellow of mustard and curry. "I like cooking."

"Really?" I said. "Me too!"

"Oh yes, Shira is *quite* the cook." David popped a crumb of cheddar in his mouth, smirking as I narrowed my eyes at him. I only cooked on Nantucket, as David knew; otherwise, my parents and I ate Sweetgreen or sushi for dinner at least four times a week.

Eventually everything had been cooked and plated, the tables set, the water and wine poured. We sat, surrounded by Greek salad with slabs of feta cheese, fresh-baked sourdough, roasted sweet potatoes with figs, and the cauliflower dish Isaac and I had labored over. I glanced at Noah, expecting him to make a grab at the candle lighting tonight or at least to fight with the other boys and Miriam about it.

Instead, all the older cousins looked at me, then Noah's eyes flicked toward Isaac, who'd joined our table.

Was I supposed to ask—Isaac?—if he wanted to light them? Why couldn't one of *them* ask? Why did I have to be the de facto host? I mean, I was bossy and in charge, yes, but I'd rather one of them asked, so it didn't look like I was pandering.

Or maybe it would look like I was being nice? Was this why I was so bad at flirting, because I always tried to not seem like I liked my crush, which meant I was never friendly, only coolly polite?

"Isaac." I smiled, though it felt forced. "Do you want to light the candles?"

He glanced around the table, finding polite go-ahead expressions on everyone's faces—even Abby's, who, by dint of no longer being the newest newcomer, felt more like one of us. "Okay." He lifted a match and, when my grandmother gave the signal, dragged the head against the striking surface.

Four candles tonight. These ones were all alike, red wax at the bottom, blending into orange and finishing with yellow. The flame at the top, though, put everything else to shame. I watched them as we ate, the shammash tilting, the candle on the far right shrinking, the leftmost candle flickering.

I looked up and saw Isaac watching me. Flame licked at my stomach. He was *looking* at me. You only looked at people you liked, right? I should smile. I should say something.

But Ethan beat me to the punch, asking about Columbia, and Isaac turned away. I sat back, disappointed in myself for missing the opportunity.

It's flattering when someone expresses interest in you, Tyler had said. Was he right? Would it be easier to talk to Isaac, to make friends, if I stopped being afraid of being judged? I could reach out to the girls at home, try to strengthen our friendships. Only I didn't know how. Liking all their photos? That seemed easiest, but also like it might scream desperate.

I could text them. Text Meg, who I liked talking with the most at lunch. Text Lou, the girl in art class whose commentary made me smirk.

I opened up my texts with Meg, but my heartbeat spiked at the mere idea of texting. Pocketing my phone, I took a deep breath.

Never mind. I had Olivia and my family. And I *was* friends with the kids at school. It was fine if we didn't want to get BFF tattoos.

After dinner, Grandma had the triplets pass around blue-and-white gift bags. One for Abby, too, and even Isaac. At a nod from Grandma, we all unpacked them: hunks of beeswax and coils of wick. I brought the wax to my nose and inhaled. I loved making candles, loved the sense of accomplishment, the smell, the wax on my skin.

Normally, I would turn toward David, but I made myself turn toward Isaac instead. "Have you ever made candles before?"

He shook his head. "Do you do this every year?"

"Maybe every other? It's fun."

"Nice."

Once more, my conversational skills dried up. How was anyone supposed to respond to *Nice*? I fumbled for something else to say. "Do you have any crafty hobbies?"

I winced. *Crafty hobbies?* What? Why did everything I say sound so awkward?

Isaac, fortunately, was either too oblivious or too polite to notice. "Not really crafting. I used to play the violin in high school."

"Oh, cool! Do you still?"

"Nah. I don't really have time anymore."

"I get it. I used to play the piano." And I still had the time, just not the motivation.

We followed the crowd back into the great room and set up

our candle-making stations. Isaac was into a lot of indie folk music I'd never heard of, but he certainly had plenty to say about them. I asked questions, and after noting a wince at my mention of Taylor Swift, avoided talking about my own favorites. Which, sure, I didn't want my dream boy to scoff at my taste, but to each their own.

We dropped our hunks of beeswax in old Chock full o'Nuts cans, then set those in pots filled with water to melt into a gleaming mass. I loved this part, loved Miriam's intensity as she tried to make her candles absolutely perfect, loved Ethan's laissez-faire attitude, loved the way the triplets made candles as individual as their personalities. I even loved how Abby made Noah laugh, especially after he'd spent the last year being so serious.

"Ow!"

I spun. Isaac had dropped his candle and clutched at his hand, surprised pain on his face.

"Quick!" I pulled him to the faucet and ran cold water over his hand. "Stay right here. I'll be back with Neosporin."

I dashed off to the closest bathroom, feeling weirdly on top of the world. I was Florence Nightingale saving my man. I mean, Isaac wasn't "my man"—gross—and also I wasn't sure Florence ever married, but whatever.

When I returned, Isaac was still standing by the kitchen sink, and he made an apologetic face. "I'm such an idiot. I wasn't paying enough attention."

"Could have happened to anyone." I handed the Neosporin over.

"Thanks."

I smiled, trying to convey *Anytime* and *I would give my lifeblood for you* and *You are my one true love* all at once, in a non-creepy manner. "No problem."

Unfortunately, once more I couldn't think of anything to say, and Noah said something to him, and so much for Florence and her Crimean War soldier actually getting anywhere.

At the end of the night, the candles had been made, we'd eaten enough of the chocolate Great-Aunt Shelbie had brought to be sick, and I found myself next to Abby. Isaac was wrapped up in an intense conversation about AI with some of the other cousins, and the littles and middles had gone to bed.

"So," I said to Abby, a touch hesitantly. "I remember, last summer you were looking into your grandmother's past . . ."

She nodded. "Yeah."

"I found this box. Well, Tyler and I did." I told her the whole story, ending with the visit to the Whaling Museum. "What would you do next? To figure out which of the girls it was?"

"Hmm." She leaned back on her hands, looking pleased to be asked. "It would be easiest if they'd kept journals or if their letters survived . . . but even if they didn't, other people around them might have written down gossip. Nantucket contemporaries, or maybe even newspapers."

"Good idea. Thanks." I hesitated. "You want to be a historian, right?"

"I think so. I want to major in history, at least. Maybe I could be a curator or an archivist or someone who does research—I don't know yet, but I liked looking into everything. I liked connecting the dots." She shot me a wry, self-aware smile. "Some might call me nosy."

"You are nosy."

"Fair." She paused, then added, "Most of my friends don't know what they're going to major in, though."

I swallowed. It felt like everyone I'd ever talked to had their careers mapped out for the next twenty years. "Really?"

"Yeah. My best friend is studying engineering, but the rest are undecided. My mom says that's what college is for. Figuring things out." She shrugged. "Better than making the wrong choice prematurely, right?"

"Right," I agreed slowly. It hadn't really occurred to me I could take my time to figure out what I wanted to do—I felt like I was already behind, not knowing my major and my school and my life plan. But maybe I could slow down. "Much better than making the wrong choice."

CHAPTER FOURTEEN

The next morning, David plunked down next to me on the sofa where I was eating toasted sourdough slathered with butter. "I think Isaac's into me."

"Are you trying to poach my Hanukkah fling?"

He shrugged and picked up a piece of gelt, peeling off one metallic side of the wrapper, then the other. "Just calling it like I see it."

"Wishful thinking, more likely."

David popped the chocolate coin into his mouth, then chased it with a mouthful of coffee. "A boy can dream. Surprised you're picking him over Tyler, though."

I rolled my eyes. "Why don't you go after Tyler, if you think so highly of him."

"I don't know," he mused. "He's not really my type. He's too . . . blond."

"How can someone be too blond?"

"It's like . . . his hair is just *so* golden. It's practically singing the national anthem. You can see the flag glistening in his waves of grain."

I snorted a laugh. "Okay."

"And he's too hot. I couldn't date someone so hot *everyone* was obsessed with him, it'd stress me out. Isaac, though—Isaac is attainably hot."

"What does that even mean?" I asked.

"You know. He feels like a real person. As opposed to, say, a Ken doll."

"Good morning," the non–Ken doll object of our conversation said. I started violently.

"Morning." David sipped his coffee and took in Isaac's black jeans and black sweater. "You realize you're not in New York, right? You don't have to wear all black."

"David!" Maybe I sucked at flirting, but at least I didn't insult people's outfits. "You look very nice," I told Isaac, then wanted to bury myself beneath a hundred blankets. *You look very nice?* I both sounded like Grandma and a suck-up, which David's smirk confirmed. "Ignore David, he's just jealous he's not from the city."

David rolled his eyes. "Only New Yorkers think people from other places are 'jealous' of them."

"Where are you from?" Isaac asked politely.

"San Francisco."

Isaac lit up. "I grew up near LA."

This devolved into a classic *Name every town in California and share your opinion on it* conversation, with an addendum of theoretically-friendly-but-slightly-edged discussion of the differences between NorCal and SoCal and the classic *Let's bond over In-N-Out and the East Coast's attempt at Mexican food* exchange.

"Shira!" Iris ran up to me, interrupting the boys. Thank god. "We need you upstairs. Gabe *refuses* to practice his part, and if he doesn't rehearse the scenes with Ethan where they speak in tandem, it's going to be a mess. And Oliver keeps wandering off, and Noah says he and Abby aren't going to even *be* here for half the day—"

"Iris. It's nine forty-five."

"So?"

Right. "The triplets are putting on a play," I told Isaac.

Iris scowled at David. "Why aren't you upstairs?"

He pointed at me. "Shira's not upstairs."

"What's the play about?" Isaac asked.

"It's about the Maccabees and Judith," Iris told him. "And imperialism and assimilation and female empowerment. Oh, and we're writing in some stuff about renewable energy, for Shira."

"I'll leave you to it." Isaac took a step back. "I've got some papers I should read."

Rehearsal took us through to two o'clock. When I wasn't

running lines or maintaining the peace, I looked up Nantucket in the 1840s, curious about what life would have been like for my ancestor and her sailor boy.

Sperm whales had been discovered off the island in the early 1700s, and their oil provided an astonishingly clean light. Nantucketers specialized in hunting them. The whaling capital of the world, they called Nantucket, and the early 1800s had been the height of the island's cosmopolitan glory. Money, people, and fame poured in.

But by the 1840s, more than half of the whaling vessels in the world were based out of nearby New Bedford instead. The Atlantic whales had all been killed, so ships had to travel farther afield, and larger ships were necessary for the voyages that now lasted years instead of months. Larger vessels called for deeper harbors than Nantucket's shallow waters, so the industry moved to New Bedford.

In 1845, when the *Rosemary* sank, Nantucket had been at the end of its glory days, a civilization heady with success and unknowingly on the brink of crashing. There had been mansions and balls and celebrities, and three daughters of Golden Doors, one who had been in love with a harpooner—an ambitious man with a career set to skyrocket, before he had died.

If he had died. If he hadn't, instead, gone to the oil fields of Pennsylvania. Because the death knoll to Nantucket's whaling days came in 1859, with the discovery of oil in Philadelphia. Many former sailors headed there or out west in search of gold. Maybe it was part of the human condition, to chase oil, money, light. To chase whatever could push back the night.

I snuck out of rehearsal and headed to Grandpa's office, knocking gently before entering. "Hi, Grandpa."

He looked up. "Well, hello there, darling."

"Can I ask a few more questions about the early family?"

"Of course you can."

I pulled up a chair next to him, opening my computer. "We think the chest came from the 1840s, when Shoshana and her sisters were my age. I thought I'd see if you knew anything else about them? Or about who Shoshana's sisters married?"

"Let's see." He leveraged himself out of his chair, peering at his bookshelves. He ran his finger along the albums. "Aha! This should be it."

He passed me a binder, which included family trees of the families both Louisa and Josephine had married into. I snapped a few photos. "Thanks, Grandpa. This is perfect."

I returned to the cousins' room, settling on the couch again next to Miriam and pulling half her blanket over me. I googled each of the sisters' partners. Shoshana's husband, her father's apprentice, came from New Bedford; Josephine married a New York merchant; and Louisa ended up in Ohio.

I wanted to share the news with Tyler, then hesitated. I was supposed to be getting to know Isaac.

But what was I supposed to do, catch Isaac up on my whole family history? Besides, I knew Tyler would find this interesting. No reason to think Isaac would.

> **Me:**
>
> **<Family tree.jpg>**
>
> **All the girls got married**
>
> **No lovelorn ladies forever**

Tyler:
Guess not everyone is as loyal as Mrs. Muir

It took me a minute to catch the reference—Mrs. Muir, the widow who moved into a house with a hot ghost. Good thing my dad loved old black-and-white movies.

> **Me:**
>
> **Not everyone can stay loyal**
> **to a dead sea captain**

Tyler:
You know what they say—50 percent of
ghost/human relations end in exorcism

> **Me:**
>
> **What happens to the other 50%**

Tyler:

I assume they're deeply frustrated individuals

I smiled, then set my phone aside to follow Abby's suggestion of checking out old primary sources. Plenty of websites included scans of old letters and diaries from nineteenth-century Nantucket, and some had even digitized the text. Even so, most of what I read was a bust. The Starbucks and the Coffins and the Folgers entertained each other, but the Barbanels were not mentioned at all.

My phone buzzed again.

Tyler:

So how's the great flirtation going?

Wooing him with poetry about

absent sailor-husbands?

Me:

Yes I memorized the whole poem and recited it

It was epically romantic

Tyler:

I'd pay good money to see you do that

Me:

You think I wouldn't

But

You haven't seen the stuff we're
saying in the triplets' play

Tyler:
I thought you were a silent handmaid?

Me:
Please I'm not SILENT
I'm Judith's hype woman

Let's! Behead! Generals!

Tyler:
Wow and you pretend not
to be bloodthirsty

Me:
Only bloodthirsty for evil generals

Never for nice friendly whales

Did you know sperm whales are
matriarchal and the ladies live with
their calves in a nice family group

Tyler:
They oust the boys?? Jesus they're
like the Nantucket sailor girls

Me:

**They don't OUST the boys the boys want to
do their own thing, like the whaler boys**

And they let the boys back to sleep with them

Tyler:
Mm yes like the Nantucket sailor's girl

Me:

Don't knock a good thing

Tyler:
So scandalous, Shira Barbanel

I bit back a wide smile. Because Tyler made me feel scandalous, and playful, and capable of being ridiculous and sexy and fun.

Energy I needed to bring to my interactions with Isaac.

I headed into the hall, toward the room where Isaac was staying. My feet slowed as I approached the door, and I made myself take a huge breath. Okay. Isaac probably wouldn't scream in horror at my presence. I knocked.

Isaac opened it.

For a moment I forgot to breathe, but then mustered up a smile. "Hey, Isaac. What are you up to?"

"Hey. Catching up on some reading." He nodded at a thick textbook on the bed. "What's up?"

"Oh, nothing. You know." I took a deep breath, then forced it out. Okay. As Tyler had told me, no one was going to be insulted that someone wanted to hang out with them. Even if Isaac didn't want to, it would be flattering, not an insult, not something I needed to hide. "I was planning on going for a walk—if you wanted to join? See the beach? If you wanted to see more of Nantucket or whatever."

His face brightened. "Sure."

Sure. I had asked Isaac to do something and I had *succeeded.* Victory!

I hadn't precisely thought about what would happen after I succeeded, though. In my daydreams, I went from a silent infatuation with Isaac Lehrer to a steady, lasting relationship. These intermediary steps felt deeply wonky. "We can cut through the back."

We suited up and stepped outside. Though early afternoon, the sun had disappeared behind the trees, washing the sky with pale streaks of colors. Pinkish lilac colored the horizon, faint and rare, peeking between the barren tree limbs.

"My grandmother spends a lot of time on the gardens," I said as we walked through them. "Do you . . . Are you good with plants?"

"No."

Cool. "Uh, me neither, really. Noah is, though. But I'm too much of a city person." Which was dumb. Noah was as much a city person as I.

"Same. You live in Manhattan, right?"

"Yeah, Upper East Side."

New York, at least, was easy to talk about. Everyone had ten favorite restaurants and cafés, hated the congestion, and loved the diversity. We talked about our neighborhoods as we reached the top of the bluff and descended the securely attached staircase to the shore below, then talked about shows we'd seen as we walked along the sand and how New York compared to other cities.

On Nantucket, you could walk forever, rounding one bend, then one more, envisioning yourself walking all eighty miles of coastline. Once, Noah and I'd decided to do it, setting out in the morning, our little-kid backpacks—mine the Little Mermaid, Noah's Superman—filled with snacks. We were convinced we'd made it halfway around the island before we finally gave up and called Noah's mom, but it turned out we'd gone less than two miles. She didn't even drive to come get us. She walked out, and she made us walk back.

Now I was intimately aware that however far I walked with Isaac, we'd have to walk the same length back, and I would have to think of how to fill the silence. So when one of the lulls in our conversation stretched slightly too long, I said, "We should turn back. We'll want enough time to eat before the party."

"Sure," he said amiably, and we pivoted.

The warm colors had disappeared from the sky, pinks melded into a brief purple, which quickly turned blue, then bluer still, blue everywhere. Even the clouds were blue, visible only by the grayish tones that gave shape to their snow-like texture. I shoved my hands deep in my coat's pockets. I'd been so focused on getting Tyler to teach me to flirt—had I skipped other crucial steps? How did you connect with someone? I felt positive Isaac and I had a ton in common, so why were we only talking about surface things? "So, um—what do you do besides work? And school?"

"I guess that's mostly what I do," he said. "I'm into snowboarding, when I can get away for the weekend. Do you snowboard? Or ski?"

"I ski a bit," I hedged. I'd *been* skiing. But growing up, my winter sport had always been skating—and then it had been my summer sport, too. Sometimes people assumed I was into various sports because I'd skated so much, but in reality, practice and conditioning didn't leave me with much time for others. And god forbid I wrenched or broke anything in another activity. Theoretically, I could have taken something up after skating, but I hadn't wanted to. "Where do you go?"

"I grew up going to Tahoe, but I've been doing some of the Northeast with friends this year. I've got a trip out to Colorado in February."

I nodded along as he told me about the upcoming trip. "What about in the summer?" I asked when he lost steam. "What do you do then?"

"I'm big into hiking."

I perked up. "Me too!" Though by hiking I really meant wandering the windswept mid-island moors, gazing across at Altar Rock and up to Sankaty Head.

"Yeah? Where do you go?"

"Oh. Um, here, mostly."

"Right, yeah. You come here every summer?"

"Yeah. And every winter break. What about you, where do you like to hike?"

It was easier to listen to Isaac talk than to talk myself, maybe because I was still nervous he'd dislike whatever I said. Not that I was terribly into all his descriptions of carrying tents on his back and going on multiday hikes, but maybe I could be. Hiking was trendy, and I definitely loved nature. I just loved showering, too.

"And I like to rock climb," Isaac said. "You ever done that?"

"Once?" I offered. We took a few more steps on the wet, hard-packed snow. "I don't really have the arm strength, though . . ."

"It's all about your legs, not your arms." His gaze dipped, and even though I knew he couldn't even see my legs beneath my long coat and jeans and leggings, I still blushed. "It's fun. There's a bunch of good places in the city for it."

Was that . . . a date? I held my breath, willing him to say *We should go.* I supposed I could have said it, but that felt too terrifying. Still. Good to know what he liked. Maybe when we were back, I could suggest we go rock climbing.

Even though, honestly, I'd rather go for a walk. For some reason, I'd thought Isaac would be way more into sitting around and brunching, which was clearly not the case. Though it was good he had so many hobbies. Maybe they were fun hobbies. Maybe I could like them.

Beneath our words, the ocean roared, containing two tones: both a dull, gathering strum and a higher scrape against the dun-colored sand. The wind whisked my hair around and in front of my face, turning curls into kinks and knots. I gathered it up as best I could, like a bushel of unruly hay, stabbing it through with a pin against my nape.

Do you miss your parents? I thought about asking. *Do you like working for my great-uncle?* Maybe if I wanted our conversation to go any deeper, I'd need to be the one to lead it, but that felt almost insurmountable at the moment. Baby steps. I'd asked him to come on this walk, and that was enough for now.

"There's our staircase," I said instead, and we turned to climb back up the bluff.

CHAPTER FIFTEEN

ive candles lit, prayers sung, and a quick dinner, then everyone separated to their rooms to get ready for the Nelsons' holiday party. The sea wind had tangled my hair irreparably, so I brushed it into compliance and forced it into a French twist.

As I smoothed down the last few strands with a touch of lotion and sprayed them into place, I could feel my stomach twisting. Sometimes I felt so stressed, though I couldn't pinpoint why. I tried to pull apart a twisty, tangled knot of possible causes. Was it because I might have to flirt with Isaac tonight for real, initiate something romantic? Or did the idea of Isaac and Tyler being in the same room terrify me? Or was I worried about . . . something else? Why couldn't I tell what I was worried about?

Deep breaths.

I picked my ensemble carefully: a wintry lilac dress with a very low back, silver heels, and pearl-drop earrings. I used a frosty palette for makeup; silvers and the palest pink lip. From the bed, Miriam watched wide-eyed. "I wish I could pull off makeup like you can."

"Of course you can. We have the same exact coloring. Come here. Open." I carefully primed her lips, then smudged on the pale pink. "See? Gorgeous."

Rather than walk a scant five minutes, the whole family stuffed ourselves into a caravan of cars to avoid the cold and snow. Warmth and light spilled out of the Nelsons', their windows glowing cheerily. As we climbed the steps, Pentatonix's "God Rest Ye Merry Gentlemen" slipped out the front door, voices twining and twisting around each other.

"Hello!" Tyler's moms beckoned my massive family inside. "So good to see you! So glad you could make it!" People darted about, pressing cheeks and shaking hands. Cinnamon and vanilla and mulling spices floated through the rooms. I would have assumed it came from candles or fragrance diffusers if I hadn't learned this week how much Tyler's family baked.

Coats discarded, we dispersed into the rest of the house, a mob of Barbanels and Danzigers. I wandered into the main living room behind the triplets, my gaze searching every corner. Guests milled about, their outfits all greens and reds and golds, beneath wreaths of pine cones and evergreens. I knew most of them: local families and a few seasonal islanders. Olivia's family couldn't make it, since they had relatives arriving tonight, but otherwise the crowd looked similar to the one I expected for my family's Hanukkah party in a few days.

"Who are you looking for?" Ethan arrived at my side. Somehow, my cousin had already armed himself with three delicately balanced appetizers.

I helped myself to the cream-cheese brownie he had the weakest hold on. "No one."

Ethan ate a miniature spinach-and-mushroom quiche in one bite, talking around it. "These things are so *boring*. I dunno why we have to come."

"Gotta show that Barbanel face." I grinned at him. "Missing the swashbuckling of the high seas?"

"You're making fun, but I am *very* swashbuckly, I'll have you know."

Ethan was arguably the most adventurous of the cousins, prone to mountain biking and water skiing and spending large swaths of time trying to break limbs. Interning for a historian for the past three summers had not calmed him down in the slightest; it seemed to make him think he could be Indiana Jones. He'd gone so far as to declare his major in archaeology at the University of Chicago, where he'd gotten in on early decision.

"I bet Tyler will sneak us some shots if we ask." His eyes lit up, and I followed his gaze to a pretty girl smiling at Ethan from across the room. "I bet she can get me shots."

"You do?"

He waggled his brows at me. "Shots of *dopamine*."

"Please don't make jokes ever again." Shaking my head with amusement, I watched him make his way across the room. Unlike at a party of my peers, I was perfectly comfortable being alone in a party of mostly adults—especially since I knew I could find half a dozen cousins at a moment's notice.

From behind me, I heard a familiar, melodic voice. "Hey."

I wasn't even surprised; I'd expected him to make his way to me. I turned, a faint smile still on my lips, to find Tyler appraising me with his own arch expression. He wore a white sweater over burgundy pants, wintry in a festive way, blond hair staticky, the wispy tendrils floating like a halo. He handed me one of two champagne flutes, clinking his glass against mine.

I took a small sip, the bubbles bursting on my tongue. Crisp and fresh and sweet. "Thank you."

His gaze ran up my lilac dress, taking in my hair, drawn up to elongate my neck, the pearl drops in my earlobes. "You look nice."

"Thanks. You too. Is this cashmere?" I reached out to stroke his forearm, the soft fabric cloudlike under my fingers.

"Early present. To ensure good behavior."

"Is it working?"

"Depends on your definition of 'good.'" He led me over a few steps to a high table with round, two-layer miniature chocolate cakes covered in a chocolate ganache with a cranberry on top and a decorative green sprig. "I made those."

"You did not." I carefully lifted one from its delicate paper wrapper and took a bite, closing my eyes to savor it. The cake would have been a light sponge, but it had been soaked in—what? Cranberry syrup? Maybe some orange as well? "This is *delicious.*"

"Thanks." He looked pleased.

"How long did it take you to make these?"

"Two hours? It wasn't so bad, though I'm always messy at cutting out the shapes."

"How do you even have *time* for this?"

He raised his brows. "It's not like I'm putting on an epic play or entertaining relatives or trying to seduce anyone. It's just me and my moms."

Right. "Well, it's great."

He looked past me. "Is that him?"

I followed his gaze and nodded.

Tyler eyed him critically. "Cute, if you like the type."

"The type?" I echoed, amused. "You mean tall, dark, and handsome? Yes. I do."

"He's not *that* tall."

I didn't deign to reply. Isaac, at well over six feet, had several inches on Tyler.

He gave me a sharp smile. "And how's it going? He's everything you ever wanted?"

"Pretty much."

"Hmm." Tyler cleared his throat. "I looked up the sailors."

My head jerked up. "Really?"

"Yeah. There's a database of crew lists and a newspaper article naming the ones who died. Two were in their forties and fifties, but the first mate . . . he was twenty-six. This was his second trip to South America."

Twenty-six. He would have been twenty-four when he left, when the girls were seventeen, fifteen, and fourteen. Which made the argument for Shoshana more compelling, if he'd been the sailor. Well, hopefully, eesh. "What was his name?"

"Charles Turner."

"Did you look up the crew who lived? It still could have been one of them."

"I did, yeah. There were four guys in their teens and twenties, so they can't be ruled out. But if the sailor survived, why would she have the quarterboard? Why wouldn't they have gotten married?"

"She could have kept the board because she was sentimental? And he might have left. The whaling era had basically ended—a lot of guys were joining the Union army or going out west to look for gold. Or it could have been because of their religions."

He frowned. "You think religion was important?"

"In the 1840s?" I shot him an amused look. "Yeah."

"There *is* separation of church and state."

"There's . . . a bit of separation," I relented. "I think Nantucket was pretty chill as far as religion went, because Quakers ran it. But I don't think people in the nineteenth century were giving three cheers for inter-anything marriages."

"Fair. It'd suck, though, if they could have been together and weren't."

"Yeah. Though that's pretty normal, right? So many factors go into the choices you make. If it was Shoshana . . . maybe her family pressured her to choose someone in the family business. Someone who understood where she came from. Or maybe she chose Nathaniel, her father's apprentice, because he felt safer. More secure."

"What would you do?" Tyler asked. "Pick the safe choice or the exciting one?"

"In terms of romance or other things?"

"In terms of anything."

I looked out over the crowd, people milling in their holiday best, couples standing shoulder to shoulder, catching each other's eyes. I wondered what all their stories were, who chose the safe path versus the exciting one. If either path was better than the other, really. "I don't know. I don't even know which I think would be right. Exciting is exciting, but is it real?"

"It's worth experiencing."

"It depends on what you want in the end. If Shoshana wanted

a stable marriage and for her family business to succeed—maybe she made the right choice." I looked up at him. "What would you want? If you ever *did* want something long-term."

He glanced across the room to his moms. They stood with their backs to each other, talking to separate sets of people, but we could still see their hands held behind their backs. "If I wanted something long-term . . . I'd want to get it right, you know?"

I did know. "How would you know if it was right?"

"I think it would feel easy. Like"—he looked at me—"like I could be me."

And I felt a zing. Because I felt like I was being me with Tyler, and I thought he might feel like he was being himself with me. I felt like we clicked. And I felt like—

I felt like I'd felt three and a half years ago, but I refused to go down the same dead-end path again. We had struck a deal, nothing more. "Want to meet my great-uncle now? I still owe you three meetings."

Tyler's lids lowered, reminding me of nothing so much as a cat about to pounce. He nodded over to where Isaac stood in a clump with Noah and Abby and a few others. "Let's talk to Isaac first."

"What?" Alarm fizzed through me at the idea of Tyler and Isaac being in the same space. "Why?"

"He works for your uncle. He'll have the scoop."

"I'm not sure that's a good idea."

Tyler raised his brows. "What are you afraid of?"

"Nothing. As long as you don't embarrass me."

"Please." He scoffed. "This'll make him notice you more."

My mouth fell open. "Excuse me?"

Tyler shrugged, nonchalantly confident. "If he sees you with me, he'll think other guys are interested in you, and pay more attention. Supply and demand."

"You're ridiculous." I glanced over at Isaac. "Besides, I don't want to give him the wrong idea. I don't want him to think I'm— you know, interested in someone else."

"It might make him competitive."

I considered. In TV shows and movies, I liked when two boys had a heated confrontation over a girl, but it turned out in real life, the idea made me squirm. "I don't think I'd like someone who got more into me because he saw me with another guy. It wouldn't feel genuine."

"Fair."

Still, a flicker of curiosity taunted me. "What about you? If you saw a girl with another boy, would you want her more?"

His expression made me think I'd surprised him. "No," he finally said. "I'm not interested in people who aren't completely interested in me."

"Hmm," I said. "You do like to be the center of attention."

"It's because I'm naturally the center of attention." He bopped the center of my forehead like I was a puppy. "It's good for the world to be in its natural order."

I rolled my eyes at him. "Okay. Let's go."

I marched over to Isaac, though I tried to alter my gait into a less militaristic movement as we reached his circle. "Hey, guys," I said brightly, then turned to Isaac. "This is Tyler. Our neighbor. Um, this is his place. Well, his moms', obviously."

Beside me, Tyler brimmed with silent laughter. "Hey."

Isaac nodded. "Hey."

"Tyler, my man." Ethan slung his arm over Tyler's shoulder. "Great party, loving the floating tea candles."

"Thanks, I worked really hard on those."

"They're no joke. Also, I appreciate how all the adults are going crazy over the photo booth."

We all paused to consider half a dozen women posing in front of the DIY photo booth, wearing cocktail attire and silly hats, their drinks in a small cluster on the floor.

"Anyway," Ethan said. "You know what would really take this party to the next level? If we could get drunk in a different section of the house from the adults."

"Noted," Tyler said. "This way."

He led a dozen of the older teens at the party up to his room, which I took in surreptitiously. It was neat in name only, as though his parents had told him to straighten up before the party. Several pairs of shoes poked out from under the bed, and scarves had been flung over an armchair. The walls were sage green, the bedspread white, and three framed ink prints hung above the bed—a map of Nantucket, a ship, and a whale. Both books and small, pretty things stuffed the shelves: gleaming stone paperweights and shells and decorative stones.

The group of us settled on the floor, leaning against the bed and the walls, lying on the dark-green rug. We'd brought wine, Cisco beer, and a handle of vodka. Ethan idly spun a dreidel he'd brought from home.

Tyler nodded at it. "Shira and I meant to play a dreidel drinking game the other night. Could be fun."

Ethan stuck a finger in Tyler's direction. "Excellent plan, Nelson."

"We don't actually know any dreidel drinking games," I said.

"Google does," David said, pulling out his phone. "Aha!"

Abby and Noah exchanged their own set of glances. He raised his brows; she shrugged and nodded.

"There are literally a million results," Ethan said. He read for a minute, then started snickering. "Fatal Dreidel!"

Uh-oh.

The rules were simple: Nun, no drink. Shin, you drink. Hey, you chose someone else to drink. Gimel, everyone drank.

"Who starts?" I asked.

"Me, obviously," Ethan said, spinning the top. It toppled on shin. "Aw, man." He took a shot.

It was easy to play, easier to get drunk. By the time I landed on my first hey, twenty minutes in, I could already feel the effects of my earlier champagne and the vodka. I raised my cup to Isaac. "Hey, Isaac."

Next to me, Tyler scoffed. I ignored him and focused on Isaac. Amazing how when you were tipsy, it became immediately easier to hold eye contact.

Isaac lifted his cup to me, and we drank.

"So, Isaac," Tyler said as the dreidel continued around the circle. "What's your deal?"

I stiffened but didn't see how to stop Tyler without Isaac seeing me run interference.

"I'm interning for their great-uncle," Isaac said, as though the question was completely banal.

Tyler tilted his head. "Isn't it weird for someone to bring their intern on a family vacation?"

Isaac shrugged. "Arnold and my grandparents are family friends."

"So you got the internship because of nepotism."

"Tyler," I said sharply.

Isaac didn't look overly bothered. "The introduction didn't hurt."

"Yeah, I'm sure vacay with his family doesn't, either."

Pretending to be placing my hand behind my back, I gave Tyler a quick pinch and was rewarded by his intake of breath.

The game continued. I was aware of Tyler's knee against mine, blazing hot, even through his pants and my tights. His turn came and he spun, the dreidel toppling to hey. I looked up at him, expecting his gaze to find mine.

Instead, it slid past, and latched on a girl on the other side of the circle. "Hey, Amy."

The flirtation in his voice was undeniable. She blushed and raised her cup. I felt a hot, unpleasant tightness in my chest and took a quick sip of my drink even though it wasn't my turn.

"Hey," I hissed a few minutes later, when everyone else was wrapped up in a story Ethan was telling. "You were being a little aggressive there, don't you think?"

He pursed his lips. "What do you mean?"

"You were poking at Isaac."

"I was making conversation."

"You accused him of getting his job through nepotism."

"Well, he did, didn't he? And I didn't *accuse*. I'm scoping it out. If it worked for him, it could work for me."

"Whatever. Just play nice, okay? I want him to have a good time."

He stared at me. "Fine," he finally said, his gaze flicking to Amy. "It's a party. We should all have a good time."

My chest tightened, but I tried to ignore it. Instead, I looked over to Isaac, concentrating on his familiar features. He caught me looking and smiled.

The tightness in my chest released. Good. This was going exactly how I wanted it to. I sipped my drink.

At some point, we devolved into an intense conversation about the right order in which to watch Marvel movies. "Is it like Narnia?" Abby asked. "Strong feelings of publication date versus author's preference?"

"What's author's preference?" one of the other girls asked.

"Like, chronological for the world."

"Sure," David said. "You could do chronological and start with *Captain America*, which is set during World War II."

"Isn't *Wonder Woman* World War I, though?" Ethan said.

David stared at his older brother. "I can't talk to you ever again."

"What?" Ethan looked blankly around at the group. "What did I do?"

I turned to Tyler. "Do you have a strong opinion? As the resident comic expert?"

Tyler stiffened, his body momentarily as tense as I usually felt at parties. Then he returned to his normal, charming self. "Whichever," he said. "I'd probably go by release date."

("I thought you'd be *proud* of me," Ethan was saying mournfully to his brother. "I'm so impressed I knew *Wonder Woman* was about World War I."

"*Wonder Woman* is *DC*, you idiot," David said.)

Tyler had told me he'd stopped telling people he read comics. But superhero movies were so mainstream, and my family made me so comfortable, I hadn't thought twice about what I'd said—I'd almost wanted to show off Tyler's knowledge. But Tyler had spent so much time tailoring how he appeared to other people. Maybe he didn't like showing any aspect of himself he hadn't preapproved for display. I'd made him uncomfortable.

"Sorry," I whispered. "I know you don't like . . . sharing stuff about yourself."

He shot me an unreadable look. "I don't mind."

Obviously he minded. He minded other people's opinions so much, he'd learned to hide away his hobbies and blend in with the popular crowd. But maybe, like me, he was trying to let down his walls more.

Isaac landed on hey. "Hey, Shira," he said with a small, almost shy smile in my direction, and a bubble of delight welled up in my chest. He had picked *me*. That had to mean something, didn't it?

I leaned over to clink my plastic cup against his. "I like your sweater," I said, the compliment, like eye contact, made easier by the alcohol.

He smiled in return. "I like your dress."

I sat back down, beaming to myself. Tyler frowned at me as the game and conversation moved around the circle. "You shouldn't just reuse compliments," he said under his breath, so only I could hear.

"What?" I whispered back, confused.

"You said you liked his sweater; you told me you liked mine.

You should find something real to compliment people on, not say the same thing to everyone."

"I like both your sweaters," I said, slightly taken aback. "Also, sweaters are kind of an easy thing to compliment people on. But I meant it both times."

"Whose do you like more?"

My lips parted, and I tried not to crow. "Tyler Nelson. Are you jealous?"

He frowned. "It's just, mine's objectively better made than his."

"Okay, then," I teased. "You win the rich fashion snob contest."

His frown deepened, and he polished off his drink.

We continued playing until we finished the alcohol we'd brought up, leaving everyone pleasantly tipsy but not too buzzed. Well, except maybe Ethan, who was either a surprising light-weight or had managed to get ahold of those shots earlier. "I'm so hungry," he said, sending plaintive eyes in my direction.

I shook my head. "It's not my job to take care of you."

"Feed me, Seymour," he sang. "Feed me salt-and-vinegar chips."

"You're a baby."

"I'll grab more snacks." Tyler stood. "We could all use them."

"I'll help." It would be my cousins devouring most of the food and drink, after all. I followed Tyler down the hall, down the stairs, and into the kitchen, where a cornucopia of party foods had been laid out.

"You seem like you're having a good time with Isaac," Tyler

said stiffly, grabbing a twelve pack of seltzers from the top of the fridge and putting it on the table.

"I am. He's great." I beamed at Tyler. "You think he likes me?"

Tyler looked up. "Well, he should."

I sighed happily, boosting myself up to sit on the kitchen counter, my legs swinging. I pulled a blue corn chip out of the open bag next to me and munched on it. "Honestly, I didn't think this would work. I thought I'd still be too awkward or weird and he wouldn't want to spend any time with me at all. And maybe he only is because I'm the only option, but I feel pretty good about the idea that if I convince him to give me a shot *now*, it'll carry through to when we get home."

"It's not all about *him* giving *you* a shot." Tyler sounded irritated. He opened and shut the fridge and cupboards, pulling out salt-and-vinegar chips and a jar of salsa and a chunk of Manchego. "You're more of a catch than he is."

I kicked my legs and smiled, delighted. "Why, Tyler. I didn't know you cared."

He frowned at me. "I'm serious. He's lucky you're giving him the time of day."

I laughed. "I never would have guessed *you'd* be the one hyping me up."

"I just don't think you should see Isaac as some far-off star, your Hanukkah miracle or whatever. He's fine, I guess. But you could do better."

"Oh-ho! Could I!" I ate another chip. "I haven't though, so I'm thinking I couldn't."

"You haven't been open before." Tyler ripped open a bag of cheese puffs, dumping them forcefully into a bowl. "You probably shut down every possible moment before it happened."

"Shut down a moment?" I undid my hair clip, shaking my hair out and running my fingers through it. "How so?"

"You know. You move away, you talk through it."

"I don't know what you mean." I shook my head. "I don't think I've ever had a moment."

He looked up at me. "Yes, you have."

"Nope." I licked the salt off my fingers. "Or maybe I don't recognize them. What do they look like?"

He crumpled up the cheese-puff bag and shoved it in the trash, hard. Then he walked over to where I sat on the counter, standing alarmingly close to me. With me sitting up high and him standing, we were almost exactly the same height. He stared directly into my eyes. "They look a lot like this."

I swallowed hard. "What do you mean?"

"Or," he amended, "they'd look like this if we stopped talking. And kissed."

I stared at him, at his blue eyes, his rose-brushed cheeks, his golden hair. My heart pounded frantically against my chest. I couldn't breathe.

Then he walked away, leaving me feeling like I'd narrowly

avoided being hit by a freight train. "Course, you have to be into the person."

Right. He wasn't into me. And I was into Isaac. "Of course."

"But honestly, Shir, it feels like you're going after Isaac because you want more friends. Maybe you should be putting all this energy there."

"You're wrong. I want Isaac." I paused. "Okay, *and* more friends. He's like a two-for-one deal."

"Right. The best-friend-you-can-kiss scenario. So, what, you feel like you have some really strong connection with him? Like he could be your best friend?"

"What?" My legs stopped swinging, and I stared at Tyler, taken aback by the realization. "Well—not yet. No. But that's because I don't really know him yet. I *like* him. I'm just still figuring him out." I let out a frustrated sigh. "Things aren't as easy for me as they are for you. Dating Isaac would make things easier."

"Why do you think things are easy for me?"

I threw my hands up. "Because you're comfortable hooking up with anyone! I'm not. I need all this—this exploration, hooking up, whatever, to be in a situation where I feel really safe and comfortable."

"And Isaac makes you comfortable," he said flatly.

The room spun slightly, not quite pinned down by gravity. "He *could*, maybe."

He looked at the bag of chips. "Do I make you comfortable?"

"You make everyone comfortable," I retorted. "That's what you do." I jutted out my chin. "And what about you, Tyler? How often does someone make you comfortable?"

He stared at me, silent, then pressed his lips together and shook his head. "I don't know."

I hopped off the counter, grabbing the bag of chips I'd been munching on, the salsa, and the seltzers Tyler had pulled out. "Anyway, we should go back up."

I headed upstairs, trying not to care if he followed.

CHAPTER
SIXTEEN

The night ended with us tramping back across the lawns between Tyler's house and Golden Doors, too impatient and intoxicated to wait for cars. I woke to rain against the eaves, and through my window I could see slate-gray sky and a slow, steady drizzle. Cold and sleepy and reluctant to leave my cozy cocoon, I scrolled through my phone. I opened my messages with Olivia. **Merry Christmas!** I wrote, followed by every festive emoji.

Then a half-remembered comment from my conversation with Tyler last night resurfaced. Maybe I really should try harder to strengthen the friendships I had. I pulled up Meg from school on my phone. Maybe we weren't going to be best friends. But I'd never know if I didn't try.

> **Me:**
>
> **Merry Christmas! Hope you're having fun in Florida**

After I sent the text, I closed my eyes and clutched my phone and took several breaths until my heartbeat returned (almost) to normal.

And not two minutes later, she replied. **Thanks!! Very humid, my hair is giant ha. Happy Hanukkah! How's Nantucket?**

I blinked at the text, happiness uncurling in my stomach.

> **Me:**
>
> **Good! So much family time. And food, yum.**

I sent a photo of the latkes from earlier in the week.

> **Meg:**
>
> **Delicious! See you soon xo**

I clutched my phone to my chest, an overwhelming sense of happiness crashing over me. Maybe I could have closer friends. Maybe it wasn't too late. Maybe I imagined walls where they didn't exist.

I listened to Miriam's breathing beside me and Abby's soft snuffles from the air mattress, drawing strength from these comforting noises, from the gentle patter of rain. In one fluid movement I brought my phone back up and found Tyler's messages. We hadn't exactly fought last night, but we had been odd and tense, and I hadn't been precisely sober. I never fought with anyone, except for Noah, and then only along the lines of what show to watch or what food to order. With him in college, we didn't even have those anymore.

Should I apologize to Tyler? Was there anything to apologize for? For telling him he made me comfortable?

After an embarrassing amount of consideration, I came up with the deeply brilliant **Merry Christmas**.

I immediately received a reply: **Thanks. Merry six candles to you**.

I closed my eyes, taking several deep breaths while two slow tears of relief leaked from the corners of my eyes, my mouth pulling up in a giant smile. Then I pushed myself upright and headed to the bathroom to get ready for the day.

When I went down to breakfast, I was still smiling.

The great room smelled like coffee and eggs and bread. I spotted Isaac sitting next to Great-Uncle Arnold. But then I saw Noah, alone for once, sitting on the sofa eating scrambled eggs. I hesitated, glancing at Isaac, then filled my plate and dropped down on the couch next to Noah. "Morning."

"Morning."

It used to be so easy to talk to Noah, when we lived on the same block and saw each other all the time. We didn't have to make conversation; conversation just happened, floating in the air between us, bred by boredom or frustration or inanity.

With him gone, it felt like everything had changed. Now there had to be some sort of reason for us to talk, other than griping or killing time. "How's college?"

"It's good."

"Good?" I wheedled. "What about, like, exciting? Wild, debaucherous parties?"

He smiled slightly. "Some of those, too."

"Do you like your classes? Are you taking another one at the arboretum next semester?" Noah might not kill it in the communication department, but he had occasionally sent me pictures of plants he'd taken care of at the giant nature park in Jamaica Plain.

"Yeah, I'm going to keep working with the same professor. And I'm taking another biodiversity class, with the prerequisite out of the way."

"Good." Noah had always been happiest outside, surrounded by plants, and I was glad he didn't plan to give them up. I glanced at the hallway. "How are things with Abby?"

"They're good."

I pried, because otherwise what was the point of basically being siblings? "Good enough you brought her here for Hanukkah. Aren't her parents sad?"

"She says they understood. Since we don't get to see each other a ton."

"Do you feel like you're missing out on any typical college experiences? Like you worried about Erika?" When he'd broken up with his last girlfriend, he'd talked a big game about thinking she shouldn't have a high school boyfriend dragging her back from college life.

"Oh." He ruffled his curls, so like mine, and looked sheepish. "Uh, maybe with Erika it was more of an . . . excuse."

"Harsh."

"I didn't like her as much as I like Abby. And I don't feel like I'm missing out on anything. I'm still doing stuff and making friends."

If he wasn't bent out of shape about it, I wouldn't be, either. I ate a forkful of eggs, considering how to phrase my next thought and if it was even worth bringing up. It wasn't like I could do anything about it. But . . . maybe worth mentioning? "It's kind of weird, you not being home."

"Yeah?"

"Yeah. I feel like there's no one on my side anymore, at Shabbat, or whenever we go out. It's just me and all the parentals. It's a little lonely." To my shame, I could hear my voice get scratchy, and I forced a smile.

Now Noah looked a little worried. "But—you have all your friends, right?"

"Oh yeah," I said quickly. "But you know, they're not—well. They're more people to go *out* with, you know? Not, like, stay home and watch a movie."

"True," he said slowly. "They are a little . . . But I thought you liked that? Or you didn't mind being home alone?"

"Yeah. It's fine. They're fun. Sometimes I do want someone to just hang out with, though." And Noah had been my person to be low-key with, hanging out in one of our living rooms or at Grandma and Grandpa's before they'd moved full-time to Nantucket.

He nodded several times, wearing his thinking face. "The good thing about college is if you like to stay in and watch TV constantly, so do a million other kids you can be friends with. I know it sounds dumb when the parents say 'It's a fresh start,' but it really can be. You can be whoever you want."

I swallowed. "That sounds nice."

And it did. I didn't *have* to be silent all the time, because I was nervous about how people would interpret what I would say. I could try being friendlier, more outgoing. If people didn't know how out of character it was for me, maybe it wouldn't feel so embarrassing to text people and ask them to hang out.

"Look," Noah said, leaning forward. "What's going on with you and Tyler?"

"Uh." I fumbled my piece of toast. "Hmm?"

"It's not my business. But. You guys are spending a lot of time together, and last time . . ."

"Last time I was a kid."

Noah scowled. "You were really upset."

"It was a long time ago. I overreacted."

"He's not—if you want—he's not the kind of guy who wants a girlfriend."

"No, I *know*," I said emphatically. "That's not what we're doing."

Noah set down his fork. "I don't want to know."

"No! Noah—he's teaching me to flirt," I blurted out.

Noah blinked. "What?"

Oh my god. I couldn't believe I had admitted that to *Noah*. How embarrassing. "Never mind."

"He's teaching you to . . ." Noah's expression turned thunderous. "That doesn't make any sense."

"Forget I said anything."

"Shira, you don't"—he made a frustrated noise and raked a hand through his hair—"you don't make good choices about Tyler."

"Thanks a lot!"

"I'm not trying to be mean. You have a blind spot around him. You like him too much."

"I don't like him," I hissed. "We're not doing anything. And even if we were, you're right, it's not your business. It wouldn't affect you at all."

His voice softened. "I don't want you to get hurt. I'm . . . I hate when you're sad, Shira."

"Oh." That . . . was actually kind of sweet. "Well, you don't have to worry. I'll be okay."

"Okay," he said. "Okay."

"Besides," I said, "I like Isaac."

Noah's mouth fell open. *"What?"*

His reaction was so over-the-top that I started giggling, and then he started laughing, and then everything was all right between us.

Twenty minutes later, Ethan plunked his plate down next to us. "Guys. Real talk. I think I might be a brilliant thespian."

I tilted my head. "Are you sure, though."

Ethan stretched his exceedingly long arms over his head. He'd wound up with several inches more than the rest of the Barbanel cousins, courtesy of his father, though neither of his brothers were quite as tall. "I nailed my last reading. Ask the purple flower. She said, 'That's *exactly* the energy we're going for.'"

"So she basically called you a maniacal despot."

"'Maniacal' is a strong word." He tried to steal my toast. "How about charming despot?"

When breakfast had been reduced to scraps of crust, we migrated into the downstairs TV room with most of the family. *The Sound of Music* was on, as it always seemed to be this time of year. I sat on the couch seat closest to the armchair Isaac had chosen, and we smiled at each other, but with the triplets at my feet and Miriam at my other side, there wasn't privacy for a conversation. Besides, my family treated *The Sound of Music* like *The Rocky Horror Picture Show,* with well-worn commentary: how *young* Julie Andrews looked; how many children there were (seven, one more than the Barbanel siblings in my father's generation); the hotness of Christopher Plummer. Everyone sang along aggressively to each musical number, even Dad and Uncle Harry, whose voices could charitably be called "bad."

Outside, the rain melted away the snow. The sky was an endless, uniform gray, the depth indecipherable. It made everything all the cozier, being cocooned inside with my family. This was my ideal kind of day, all the Barbanels laughing over inside jokes and bantering and simply being together.

As the credits rolled, Iris slid over to my side. "We need another rehearsal."

"I'll have to bow out of this one." Even if I wanted to spend the day hanging out with my family, I needed to make progress with Isaac. I felt like we'd started to get somewhere last night, and I needed to keep our momentum going. "But I'm sure it'll go great."

Three identical expressions of dismay faced me. "Why?" Iris asked.

"It's because of Isaac, isn't it," Rose said. "You want to hang out with him."

Lily gave her sister a scandalized look. "She doesn't like *Isaac!*"

"Yes, she does," the other two said.

"We'll give Isaac a role," Iris said. She looked at Lily. "I'm sorry."

Lily let out a long-suffering sigh. "I understand."

"Wait, what?" Sometimes the three of them moved too fast for me.

"Isaac!" Iris hollered, jerking Isaac's attention away from his phone. "We need you. You'll be Holofernes."

He looked at me, bemused, then at the triplets. "I'm sorry?"

Lily turned to me, her limpid eyes wide. "Shira, you're Judith. I'll be the handmaiden."

"But you're Judith!" I said, alarmed she was giving up her large, juicy part.

"No," Iris said, dead set already, a familiar voice and expression, Grandma in miniature form. "This makes more sense from a casting direction. Obviously, it pains Lily to give up the role, but you'll be able to play the parts more realistically." She gestured to Isaac. "The audience will take your pairing more seriously, while they would have seen Lily and me as a farce. You'll have chemistry."

Chemistry. I would have died from embarrassment if I wasn't so busy being amused at the triplets' careful consideration of audience opinion. I faced Lily. "I see. Are you sure?"

She nodded, self-sacrificing, the captain going down with her ship. "It's the right thing to do."

"Okay, then." I gave Isaac a dry smile, then remembered I wasn't supposed to be dry and tried to let it warm up. *Don't be snarky. Don't be cold. Beam.* "You in?"

He smiled right back at me. "Why not."

Iris nodded, problem solved, then looked around at each cousin as though eye contact was a contract. "Time for rehearsal!"

"I can't," Ethan said, draped over an armchair. "Don't make me. I'm so hungover."

"You shouldn't have had so many shots, then," I said unsympathetically, and shepherded everyone upstairs.

Rehearsal lasted for several hours, though we never quite made it to Isaac's and my scenes. He was learning how to take over the known world, and I was telling my town leaders to suck it up and get better at standing up to imperial forces. The triplets were focused on the Maccabee story line, making sure the blocking for the battle scenes fit their vision exactly.

We traipsed downstairs around five for Chinese food: scallion pancakes and braised eggplant with garlic, spinach-and-mushroom dumplings, three treasures, sautéed spinach, lo mein. We lit the candles languorously and ate in the glowing light.

Six candles tonight. Somehow I always was surprised by the sixth night—a little shocked, a little saddened, unable to understand how so much time had already passed. Hadn't it just been the first night, me and Tyler, the shammash and a single candle? Or the second night, the menorah mostly empty, the days ahead showing such promise? Now seven candles glowed before me, four to the right of the shammash, two to the left, and so much time had already slipped away.

After dinner, most of us ended up back in the cousins' room. I was determined to catch Isaac's attention before we went to bed, to do *something* just the two of us, but it was hard with a mob of others listening to our every word. Isaac joined a group playing video games, and I reluctantly settled on a couch next to Rose, skimming my phone while she marked up a script. She was the quietest of the triplets, but when she let out a loud sigh I could tell she wanted to talk. I nodded at the script in her lap. "The play's going well."

She looked up quickly. "It's not bad, is it?"

"It's great. And very inventive, how you twine both the story lines around each other."

"Thanks." She riffled through the pages. I could see her notes, stage directions, and dialogue tweaks. "If it works, I want to do it at school next year. This is—like, we're workshopping it. But I think it could be really good. If I fix some of the laggy bits and figure out how to make the stories parallel each other a little more."

"Did you write the whole play?" I had a vague feeling that Rose did most of the writing, while the others contributed ideas and direction.

"Most of it. Iris likes to plan the big announcements and denouements and fights, and Lily likes the romantic stuff, but mostly I write everything." She flushed. "I mean, they do a lot. Iris is the most organized, and Lily can really act."

"I'm impressed by all of you," I said. "How long did it take you to write it?"

"I started working on it this summer I guess?" She tucked a strand of hair behind her ear. "I want to be a real writer, you know."

Damn. Even my twelve-year-old cousin knew what she wanted to do with her life.

As she focused back on her edits, I stared out the window at the waning moon and the scattered stars. How were people so sure of what they wanted to do with their lives? I pictured Shoshana Barbanel walking through Golden Doors dressed in a giant crinoline skirt, trying to decide between one of two paths: marrying her father's apprentice or choosing her lover.

Not that we knew it was Shoshana—yet.

Who had the marital choices for Barbanel girls in the 1840s even been? A quick search told me the number of Jews in the US had increased from three thousand to three hundred thousand between 1820 and 1880, so hopefully Shoshana, Louisa, and Josephine had had a decent pool of bachelors to choose from.

A new thought struck me like a bell. I'd looked up Nantucket families earlier when trying to find sources referring my family, but my family's strongest circle probably lay outside Nantucket, in the Jewish families of New Bedford and Providence and New York. *Those* were the families whose correspondences I should be reading, who might know the personal lives of a Barbanel girl in love with a sailor.

I started with the in-laws of the three girls. Shoshana's husband, of course, had been her father's apprentice, the son of a family friend from New Bedford who had moved to Nantucket when they were teenagers. Josephine had married a New York merchant, and to my delight, his family's letters had been preserved and digitized. I hit pay dirt reading a letter from a Josephine's future mother-in-law, written in 1843—six years before she got married and two years before the *Rosemary* was destroyed:

The Halperns brought their guests, Mr. and Mrs. Barbanel of Nantucket and their three charming daughters. Shoshana is seventeen years old and the eldest, though it was made clear she has an understanding with her father's apprentice. Josephine, the middle, seemed rather headstrong, though of course my Samuel has his own stubborn nature, and I do not think a woman with a similar countenance a bad match. (Though perhaps he needs someone softer? It is so hard to tell, and, of course, he refuses to tell me and his father what he wants. Perhaps he would run right over a meeker personality.) The youngest, Louisa, is only fourteen, and bookish.

They shall stay three days . . .

Excited, I pulled up Tyler's messages and attached the screenshot, then froze. Was it a faux pas to text someone anything on Christmas besides *Merry Christmas*? Wasn't this day supposed to be devoted to family?

But I really wanted to tell Tyler. I pressed send.

> **Me:**
> **A description of the three**
> **daughters! Not the "X daughter**
> **is madly in love with an ineligible man"**
> **I was hoping for, but kinda cool**

Tyler:
I'm betting on Josephine.
It's always the headstrong one.

> **Me:**
> **Thought it was always the quiet ones?**

Tyler:
You know I'm still really banking
on it being Shoshana

> **Me:**
> **My least favorite theory.**
> **Let her be happy!**

I was so entrenched following different internet pathways, I almost didn't notice when the gamers disbanded. It was past nine, and my last chance to get any alone time with Isaac today. "Oh, hey," I said as he walked by me, as though a thought had just occurred to me. "Do you think we should practice our lines?"

"Sure," he said. "Where?"

Somewhere private, where no one would barge in on us. If it was warmer, we could go to the gazebo (how very *The Sound of Music*), but in this dark, drizzly weather, no one was venturing outdoors. "We could try the library."

The library was a small room where Grandpa often lounged when he wasn't in his study. It was in the older section of the house, with low ceilings and old, warped glass looking out over the lawns. I liked it because there was only one entrance, instead of serving as a pathway between other rooms like the music room or the downstairs parlors.

I settled in Grandpa's ancient leather chair while Isaac sat in its matching twin across from me. Old books lined the walls: an encyclopedia set, travel books, thrillers by Michael Crichton and Palmer and Connelly. I pulled the small chain of the tasseled lamp, and a warm, orange-yellow glow pushed back the gloom. Outside, rain still pattered down.

We flipped open our scripts, scanning for our scenes. Isaac grimaced. "I hope the triplets don't expect me to memorize any lines."

Erm. They most definitely would. "Maybe a few? You're helping them out, though, so I'm sure they'll appreciate whatever you're willing to do."

"Cool," he said. "I think we start on page forty-nine."

"Okay." Judith had just taken matters into her own hands: after her local menfolk failed to stave off the invading Assyrian army, she put on her best dress (relatable), ate sacred foods (less relatable), prayed real hard (occasionally relatable), and set off to infiltrate the invaders. Stunned by her beauty, soldiers escorted her to General Holofernes's tent when she arrived, because probably a dude had written the original text.

Our scene began with stage directions:

> JUDITH *enters the tent preceded by two soldiers holding*
> *silver lanterns.* HOLOFERNES *reclines beneath a gold-*
> *and-purple canopy.*
> SERVANT: We present Judith of the Hebrews, who has
> come seeking sanctuary.
> JUDITH *prostrates herself; the servants raise her up, bow,*
> *and exit.*

Isaac started reading. "'Be steadfast, woman, and have no fear. I have never harmed any willing to serve Nebuchadnezzar. But your people have brought war upon themselves by insulting the king. Tell me—why have you fled them and come to me?'"

"'Listen to me, my lord,'" I read, flushing a bit to call Isaac *my lord*. "'You alone are known to be good and powerful in Nebuchadnezzar's kingdom, and your brilliance is known throughout the land.'" I gave Isaac a quick smile. "Bit of a suck-up, isn't she?"

He returned the smile. "I'm guessing it's going to work."

We traded lines back and forth in the dim lamplight. Judith expounded on the reasons she'd come, fooling Holofernes into a false sense of security. He rewarded her with her own tent, where she stayed for four days.

On the fourth day, Holofernes told his eunuch to invite Judith to a private banquet. Isaac leaned forward, his soft voice backed by the distant patter of rain. "'Go and persuade the Hebrew woman to come and eat and drink with me. For it will bring shame upon me if I let such a woman go not having enjoyed her company. She will laugh and scorn me.'" Isaac glanced at me, amused. "As we all know, it's a horrible thing for a man to be laughed at."

I smiled, trying to look dazzling. "Then you better enjoy my company."

We stared at each other for a charged moment.

Then I skimmed down, past the eunuch asking Judith to join Holofernes, to her answer. "'Who am I to gainsay my lord? Whatever is pleasing to him I will do. This will be a joy for me until the day of my death.'"

In silence, we both read the stage directions:

> JUDITH *dresses in her finery, while* HANDMAIDEN *spreads a blanket on the ground before* HOLOFERNES *for* JUDITH *to come recline on—which she does.*
> HOLOFERNES *burns with desire for* JUDITH.

I looked up again and caught Isaac looking at me. My heart rate increased; my tongue darted out to lick my lips. "Um," I said. "I think it's your line."

"Right." He swallowed, hard. "'Drink now and be merry, for you have found favor before me.'"

"'I will drink now, my lord, because my life is magnified in me this day more than all the days since I was born.'"

Once more, our gazes locked. My breath came fast, and Isaac shifted in his seat before offering me a smile. "They definitely sleep together, right?"

The tension broke, and I smiled back. "I think he's too drunk. Look—stage directions say they drink and drink, or at least the general does, until he collapses in exhaustion."

"Pretty ballsy of Judith."

"Very. Listen to this." I read out the stage directions following Judith's last line as she stood beside Holofernes's prone body. "'Judith strikes Holofernes's neck twice, cutting off his head. She wraps it up in her blanket, then leaves the tent, hands the head to her handmaiden, who puts it in her food bag.'"

His nose scrunched up. "I hope they don't plan to reuse the bag."

"I'm sure they can wash it first."

He laughed, and I felt a surge of satisfaction. I'd made him laugh. This was the first time I'd felt like we could actually have something, like it wasn't all in my head, like maybe Isaac could like me. I decided to push my luck. "There's blocking, too, you know."

"Hmm?"

"You know. Follow the stage directions."

"Right. You mean . . ." He flushed.

I nodded, heady with nerves. "I'm supposed to recline." Feeling dangerously bold and terrified, I moved from Grandpa's armchair to the couch, lying on my side, trying to look both casual and irresistible. "Then you come over to drink with me . . ." I pretended to offer a glass.

"She should have poisoned the wine." Isaac stepped forward to take my insubstantial glass.

I smiled. "Good point. I guess you sit or something . . ."

He sat, almost cautiously, on the floor before me. He never took his eyes off mine.

"And then I—we're supposed to be . . ."

Suddenly we were so close, I couldn't breathe.

"Well!" I said brightly, bolting upright. "Then I kill you."

He laughed.

"I guess we should go to bed?" I said, still so, so bright, far too bright for any mood lighting.

"Sure."

We walked in silence upstairs, awkwardly close, me half a step in front of him, and the tension returned. We had been so close. We'd said such lines to each other—ridiculous ones, but seductive all the same. We'd held eye contact.

We reached my room. The hall was dark, mere bits of light sliding out from behind closed doors. I felt like throwing up. I wanted something to happen, or I wanted nothing to happen. I had told Tyler I didn't recognize moments, but maybe I did, and I shut them down because they terrified me.

Maybe I should stop running from them.

"This was fun." I forced myself to wait, despite wanting to melt into the floor. I lifted my head and met Isaac's eyes.

"Yeah," he said, and hesitated. "It was."

There was a long, drawn-out silence, where neither of us moved, where I kept my face lifted to his, where it became harder and harder to breathe. Then his face tilted and came slightly forward, slowly, giving me time to back away, to rebuff the moment, to disappear.

But I didn't.

And he kissed me.

He drew back. "Good night."

"Good night," I said automatically.

He walked away, turning the corner toward his room and disappearing. I stayed in the hall, fingers pressed to my lips.

And I thought, *I have no idea how to kiss.*

CHAPTER SEVENTEEN

In the morning I showed up, panicked, at Tyler's door.

He opened it after my three frantic texts, took one look at me, and frowned. "What's wrong?"

Standing there on the doorstep, facing a boy in his pajamas, I blurted out the most embarrassing statement of my life. "I don't know how to kiss."

"What?" Tyler's eyes, formerly hazy with sleep, widened.

I was fairly certain kisses were supposed to be passionate. Robust. I'd spent *so much time* fantasizing about kissing, I expected I could whip up a fifteen-page essay on it. And, having read enough romance novels and talked to Olivia in great detail, one of my main tenets on kissing was that it would come naturally.

But it hadn't.

Which meant—

Maybe—

I sucked at kissing.

"I've never kissed anyone before. Well, now I've kissed Isaac, but I don't know *how*. What if I can't do it? What if I'm bad at it?"

Something flitted across his face, and he gave me a close-lipped smile. "You can't be bad at kissing."

"I bet you can," I said darkly. "You can be bad at anything if you set your mind to it."

His mouth twitched, like he was reluctantly amused, despite also potentially being sleep deprived and having barely finished celebrating the birth of his savior/ye olde pagan tree ritual. Which reminded me. "Also," I added. "Merry Christmas! How was your Christmas?"

"Fine, thanks for asking."

"Great." I paused the minimally acceptable length of time before continuing with my panic. "I'm freaking out over here."

"You'll be fine."

"Will I, though?" I asked. "I have no idea what I'm doing. People act like you'll know what to do when you mash your mouth against someone else's, but where do your noses *go*?"

"To be honest, I've never really thought about it."

"*I'm* thinking about it, and I can't figure it out. Do they kinda slide against each other? Are your noses basically kissing, too? *I don't like thinking about noses this much!*"

"Don't get offended," Tyler said cautiously. "But I'm going to suggest you take a couple deep breaths."

"I'm offended!" I yelled, then took a couple deep breaths. Right. Yes. I was essentially having a meltdown, which I preferred to do in private. I breathed in through my nose and out through my mouth, holding at the top and the bottom of the breath, making myself take in the world around me. The rain from yesterday had stopped, though it'd melted most of the snow, and the sky was a pale blue, spotted with low clouds. The temperature felt almost warm in comparison with the weather earlier in the week, as though spring might rear its head during these last few days of the year.

"So," Tyler said, apparently no longer deeming me a human teakettle at risk of blowing. "Why are you telling me this?"

He knew. Of course he knew. I lifted my chin, hot and embarrassed. "I need help."

"Oh?" he drawled, refusing to fill in the blanks. "Help with what?"

I swallowed my embarrassment and my pride and mumbled down at my feet. "I need you to teach me how to kiss."

"I'm sorry." Tyler cupped a hand around his ear. "I couldn't hear you. What did you say?"

I glared at him. "Will you teach me," I gritted out, "how. To. Kiss."

He let the moment stretch out, long and tight and taut.

"Honestly, Shir," he said, light as a feather, "if you wanted to hook up with me, you could just say so."

"I don't." My hands curled into fists, tendrils of heat coiling inside me. "It's an extension of flirting lessons."

"You don't need *lessons* on kissing. It's natural."

"How do you know? Babies can't even talk at first because they need two years to understand language."

"Kissing isn't like learning a language."

"Isn't it?"

His mouth twitched. "Okay, yeah, I guess it is, but not in the way you mean." He pinched his nose, and his flippant air fell away. "Shira, you shouldn't kiss someone for practice. You should kiss someone because you like them."

"I told you." I tried to ignore my burning cheeks. "I like practicing things."

His expression shuttered. "Well, I'm not comfortable being used as 'practice.'"

His words hit me like a blast of freezing air, and I drew back. "I'm not trying to use you. I thought—I don't know. I thought this was what we did."

"Excuse me?" He sounded cold.

"You know. Helped each other out." I took in his extremely icy expression and cringed. "Sorry. I didn't think you'd be . . . insulted."

"You didn't think I'd be *insulted* you only want to kiss me in order to be good at kissing someone else?"

Honestly? No. "Um, no. You like casually hooking up."

"I like hooking up with people who specifically want to be with *me*. Which isn't what you're saying, is it?" He gave me a razor-sharp smile. "Unless it is."

My heart started beating wildly. "Uh," I stumbled. "Uh, right, no."

"Right." He looked at the sodden snow. "If you want to learn how to kiss so you can kiss Isaac, learn with Isaac."

I sucked in a breath. "Right. Sorry I suggested it."

"No worries," he said, voice smooth. He leaned against the doorframe, expression dismissive, like I should probably take myself out with the trash.

I hesitated. I hadn't felt bad about a conversation with Tyler this entire trip; I'd been comfortable saying whatever I wanted to him. But now, it turned out I *liked* Tyler. "I didn't mean to insult you or hurt your feelings. I thought—I don't know, I thought you might even think making out with me might be fun?" I winced, saying that out loud. I really thought a lot of myself, didn't I?

His anger, which I hadn't been expecting before coming here, seemed to grow. "You think I'd really want to hook up with you, knowing you were thinking about Isaac?"

"I wouldn't be thinking about Isaac," I said in a small voice, then stopped, not sure if I was making things better or worse.

"I wouldn't have expected *you*, of all people . . ." He shook his head, clearly disgusted.

It made a small pit open up in my stomach. "You wouldn't have expected me to what?"

"Everyone always thinks I'm so casual about everything, but I thought you, at least, didn't buy my act," he said, blinking furiously. "I thought we got each other."

"We do," I said, because we *did*, and it was suddenly really important to me that he knew that. I felt like I did understand him, how he had created this whole facade, built his own walls with polished exteriors, controlled exactly how close he let people get to him. He was like me in so many ways, except strangers read my walls as standoffishness, while they didn't even know his existed. "I really do. But I didn't think your comfort hooking up with people was an act."

"It's not. But it's different with you, Shira." He looked away, toward the ocean and the horizon. The sun crept up, pushing back the gray of night and the endless darkness of the sea.

"Because I used to be so obsessed with you?" I asked in a small voice.

"No, of course not. Because—I don't know, because I feel like we've been honest with each other, and this wouldn't be honest."

"Oh." I bit my lip. "I'm sorry."

He focused his laser-bright eyes on me. "Also, I don't get it. You've made it clear you're not comfortable hooking up outside of a relationship, so why is this different?"

I swallowed. "I guess I'm comfortable with you."

His face was unreadable. He looked . . . not mad, exactly. Shut off. Not the way he normally did with me, and not the friendly facade he usually plastered on, either. "But you don't want to date me."

"No, of course not," I hurried to assure him. "I didn't—I wasn't trying to imply we should date or anything. I'm interested in Isaac. I just meant—I like you. As a person." His eyes flicked up to me, and I offered a tentative smile. "I think we're friends."

His eyes widened with surprise. "You do?"

I raised my hands. "Maybe we're not! Obviously I suck at friends. But I feel like usually I'm on surface levels with people, and I feel like we're beyond that, so yeah. I think we're friends."

He studied me.

"We don't have to be," I said hurriedly. "I can take it back."

He shoved his hands in the pockets of his pajama pants, squinting at the glaring gray sky. "I guess we can be friends."

"Cool." A rush of relief poured through me. I hadn't realized how much it would matter that Tyler and I were okay, that we could keep being honest and open with each other. "Good. I'm glad."

He gave me a small smile. "I mean, you clearly need more friends."

"So do you," I shot back, and he laughed, and I felt another surge of relief. We were okay. "You're coming to the party?"

"You still need to introduce me to your great-uncle."

"It'll be a great introduction. The best introduction."

"I'm counting on it," he said. "See you tonight."

✳ ✳ ✳

Golden Doors was more chaotic than usual when I returned. Two aunts sat on the foyer's staircase, having mimosas and a gossip, while upstairs I could see Uncle Gerald patiently untangling a knot in his sobbing four-year-old daughter's hair. Deeper in the house, someone played piano—probably Dad, given the loud and angry Beethoven, Dad's normal response to the stress of so many family members.

"There you are." Uncle Jason caught me standing by the entrance of the great room. "Come help with party prep."

In the summer, my grandparents hired caterers for parties. But tonight would be a more intimate affair, and so we cooked everything ourselves. For the rest of the morning and afternoon, all the cousins wound up in the kitchen—or at least the lucky ones did. Some of the middles were put on cleaning duty, which was a hundred times worse.

I wound up next to Noah, chopping ingredients for a tagine: onions, sweet potatoes, carrots, tomatoes, apricots. Noah and I had made a hundred meals together and easily fell into the rhythm of swapping knives and trading cutting boards. Next to him, Abby measured broth and healthy doses of coriander, turmeric, and cinnamon into the Crock-Pot. Isaac joined, on salad duty, and I sent him a tremulous smile. We had kissed last night. Was it normal to feel so weird around him? Should I be trying to find private time? Should we *talk* about it?

He smiled back and kept chopping tomatoes. Even though I should probably want to steal him away, I was relieved to have a buffer of cousins around us. I'd rather kiss him again than have to talk about it. Also, without any practice, I was back to being terrified that I sucked at kissing. Isaac's lips might touch mine once more and be like, *Nah, bro, none of this.*

Olivia arrived an hour before the Hanukkah party started, and we escaped upstairs, where we found Miriam already hiding. She looked up from her book as we came in. "Did you only now get free?"

"How did you escape?" I took in the silver slip dress she wore. "Are you wearing my dress?"

"Can I borrow it?"

"You're supposed to ask *before* you put it on." I swatted the back of her head lightly, then picked up a pair of black-and-silver earrings from the vanity. "Pair it with these."

I pulled on a blue-velvet dress with a high neck and a short skirt, adding my Star of David necklace and threading in long, dangly silver earrings. As Olivia and Miriam talked about the books they'd read, I did my makeup at the vanity, finishing my ensemble with cherry-red matte lipstick. I swiveled around. "How do I look?"

"Stunning," Olivia said.

Miriam eyed my lipstick. "Can I try that one, too?"

We headed downstairs as the grandfather clock in the great room struck six. Only family milled about, no guests yet present. Gone were the signs of how we'd spent the entire day cooking. Tablecloths had been draped and flowers arranged. All the candles had been lit—not just in menorahs but in hurricane glasses and in the center of flower arrangements. Food lined buffets: sufganiyots topped with powdered sugar and bursting at the seams with strawberry and raspberry fillings; wide bowls filled with applesauce and sour cream near a potato farm's worth of latkes; endless amounts of fruits—berries and baked pears and pineapple chunks.

"Point out Isaac," Olivia whispered at my side.

I searched him out, my whole body primed with nerves. But it didn't feel like I had felt for the past year when I searched for him in a crowd; instead of wanting to home in on him, I almost wanted to know where he was so I could . . . avoid him? Was this what happened when you kissed and you were bad at it? You were so wretchedly nervous you never wanted to see the other person again? "He's next to Ethan."

"He's cute."

"I know." Cute, and he'd kissed me. "Really cute."

Olivia slid me a look. "So why are you standing here with me instead of talking to him?"

"I don't want to abandon you."

"So we go over there together, and I gradually distract your cousins so you can talk to him privately." She bent her head toward Miriam. "Miriam will help. We'll be great wingwomen."

"Okay. Right." I took a deep breath and squared my shoulders. "Let's go."

We integrated ourselves in the circle with the boys. True to her word, Olivia expertly cut our circle of seven in two, with me and Isaac on the outskirts. I forced a smile, trying to squish the unpleasant nerves twisting around in my stomach. This was *good*, talking to Isaac. This was what I wanted. "Having a good time?"

He smiled back. He was so good-looking, not in Tyler's pretty-boy gilded way, but solid, handsome. He felt steady. "Yeah. It's really . . . something."

I tried to see the party through his eyes, all these adults who'd known each other for decades, all us cousins with our lifelong bonds. Probably a little boring to him. "What are the parties you usually go to like?"

"Most of them are dorm parties, so . . ." He shrugged.

"Dorm parties sound *amazing*." Ugh, too overeager. "I mean, everything about college sounds amazing to me."

"Seriously?" He sounded skeptical. "They're pretty different than this vibe."

"Oh, well, this isn't my vibe. This is my family's."

He tilted his head. "And what's yours?"

"Oh, um. I guess I'm not so much of a partier. I don't *mind* them," I said hurriedly, in case he adored them. "But I'd rather hang out at home. What are college parties like?"

He laughed. "Sloppier."

We lapsed into silence. I'd thought, after last night, I'd be better at talking to Isaac—but the conversation still came in spurts and jerks, instead of a smooth banter, an ebb and flow.

The room was filling with people now, guests arriving, their voices rising as they came in and falling as they joined groups. My attention skipped to the door every time a new person entered the room. Stupid. I wanted to be focused on Isaac, wanted to be totally into our conversation.

Tyler entered the room.

Our gazes connected. My throat went dry and I licked my lips. A bundle of nerves swarmed like bees in my belly.

Okay. Obviously I wanted to keep hanging out with Isaac, but I'd promised Tyler an introduction to my great-uncle, hadn't I? Actually, I'd promised him three, and none had happened.

How did I extricate myself from Isaac while making it clear I wanted to keep talking to him?

"Hey, Isaac. Shira." Tyler appeared at our sides, summoned by my indecision. He wore the nice white sweater I'd seen him in two days ago and a pair of dark-blue pants. Hanukkah colors. I would have smiled, if I wasn't frozen. "You look gorgeous."

I felt like I'd been sucker punched. He thought I looked

gorgeous? Wait, no, he was back to flirting, as natural to him as breathing. "Um. Thank you."

He reached out and ran his hand along my sleeve. "Is this velvet?"

I yanked my arm away, glancing at Isaac, who watched both of us noncommittally. How could Tyler just *touch* me like that in front of Isaac? I'd told him I didn't want Isaac to think I might be interested in another guy.

Of course, I had touched Tyler's cashmere sweater the other day, but no one had been watching.

I swallowed. "Yup."

Friends. We were friends. Friends talked at parties.

"You're in New York, too, right?" Isaac asked Tyler.

"Yeah, NYU. You?"

"Columbia."

"Mm." Tyler turned to me. "Shir, what are you drinking?"

"Um. Hot chocolate. With Baileys."

"Let me try." He plucked my mug from my hand and sipped it. "That's good."

Okay. I clearly could not handle the two of these boys in the same space; I was about to spontaneously combust. "Let's get you your own! Isaac, I'll be right back."

I practically dragged Tyler away, speed walking to the drinks station. "You can't just drink from my cup."

"Why not?" He grinned at me.

"I don't know, germs? False impressions of intimacy?"

"Don't you ever share drinks with Olivia?"

"That's not the same and you know it."

"No?" His eyes danced.

I rolled my eyes at him. "Here's your drink," I said, handing him a spiked hot chocolate. "Now let's get you an intro to my uncle."

"Oh yeah. That."

I led us over to where Uncle Arnold and Aunt Shelbie talked to my father. "Hi, Dad," I said as we approached. "Have you seen Mom? I wanted to check if we have more sour cream."

He pushed his lips together thoughtfully. "I saw her talking to Melissa Garcia earlier, in the foyer."

"Okay, thanks." I waited for his eyes to flick behind me. "You remember Tyler, right? From next door? Tyler, this is my dad, my great-uncle Arnold, and my great-aunt Shelbie."

"Nice to meet you." Tyler nodded at the adults.

"Hello, Tyler," Dad said. "How's your break going?"

"It's good, thanks. Hanging out at home, mostly."

And with me.

"You're at NYU, right? What are you studying?"

I shot my dad a surprised look. I expected *Mom* to remember details of neighbors' lives, but not Dad so much.

Oh *no*. Did Dad know about Tyler because my family gossiped too much, and Mom had told Dad we were hanging out, and now Dad was paying attention?

Tyler looked equally surprised. "Um, yes, sir. Psychology." His gaze flicked toward Uncle Arnold. "But I'm also considering a BS in business. I took a Business and Society class last semester, with Professor Rivera."

"Not Steve Rivera?" Uncle Arnold looked interested. "He's an old colleague of mine."

"He's very complimentary about your work, sir."

Uncle Arnold snorted. "He thinks I sold out."

Tyler smiled. "He says he's only bitter because he's jealous."

Uncle Arnold laughed. "What business track are you interested in?"

"Digital and entrepreneurship," Tyler said promptly. "I'm also taking a media studies class next semester, and I'd like them to intersect."

"Are you, now," Uncle Arnold said with a slight smile, clearly familiar with people trying to cozy up to him.

Tyler valiantly plowed ahead. "In fact, I'm trying to find an internship to help me explore it more."

Uncle Arnold's eyes gleamed. "Well, we have plenty of internships at Danzigers. You'll have to send over your résumé."

Tyler blinked and looked like he might pass out. "I'd love to. Thank you."

I tugged on his arm. "We should really find Mom," I said, and politely excused us.

"Did that actually just happen?" Tyler asked. "He said I could send him my résumé?"

I patted his cheek. "Nepotism. It really works."

"That's horrible."

"I know."

"Am I a bad person for taking advantage of that?"

"That's between you and your therapist. More importantly, do you really *want* to do this? You like psychology. It's not your job to impress your grandparents."

He pulled at his hair, then smoothed it over and found a mirror, clearly aware of the staticky nature of the fine strands. "If I can try, though, shouldn't I?"

I was debating how, exactly, to change his mind when Ethan bounded over to us, ceaseless in his energy. "Tyler! Here you are! With Shira! Again!"

"Hey," Tyler said. "Here you are. Sharing your observations. Again!"

Ethan laughed. "How was your Christmas?"

"Merry." Tyler grinned. "It was good."

"Any great presents? I hear Christmas has lots of presents." Ethan looked mournful. "We only get socks."

"We also got candles," I reminded him. "And you love socks."

He perked up. "True." He extended his feet like a ballet dancer, each clad in green-and-gray argyle. "They make my ankles look great, don't you think?"

"You have beautiful ankles," Tyler assured him.

"What did you get?" I asked Tyler, curious what his parents, the people who knew him best in the world, would have given him.

"A lot of books," he said. "We mostly give each other books and food. Keeps things easy."

"You should try socks," Ethan said. "They'll love them."

During the short conversation with Ethan, the triplets had started circling, like cats eyeing a goldfish, reflected in triplicate. They finally coalesced before us, looking at Tyler with undisguised curiosity. "You're here again," Iris said.

"People keep saying so," Tyler said with equanimity. He took in the three of them, Iris in a black jumpsuit, Lily in a floaty, romantic blue dress, and Rose in a skirt and T-shirt. "I would have thought you'd be in purple, white, and rose."

The triplets gave him the kind of terrifying blank expression only masterable by preteens. He flinched. I smothered a smile.

"You're very original," Iris said flatly.

Tyler rallied. "How's the play going?"

They regarded him silently for a moment, as though measuring if he was worthy of a response. "Good," Iris finally said. "Though not everyone has memorized all their lines." She cut her eyes to me.

"I've mastered my lines," Ethan said cheerfully. "I'm an imperialistic king. It's great. I think I'd be great at conquering places."

"In Shira's defense," Lily said kindly, "she switched roles. She has a new set of lines to learn."

"Really?" Tyler asked. "How come you switched?"

"We wanted to give her a chance to play opposite Isaac,"

Lily said. "Now they have a lot of scenes together. She seduces him."

Tyler coughed, whacking his chest as he cleared his throat. "Really."

"Yep," Iris said. "Then she chops off his head."

Tyler let out a loud, startled laugh. "Got it."

"You guys should go talk to Lisa Walsh," I told the triplets, deciding no more talk about Isaac was necessary. "She owns the boutique on Chestnut. Go tell her how much you like it."

The triplets bobbed their heads and began wending their way toward Ms. Walsh.

"They do your bidding." Tyler sounded amused.

"For now," I said. "I live in fear of the day they rebel."

"If it makes you feel better," Ethan said, "Uncle Arnold called them a beautiful bouquet earlier and I thought they were gonna murder him." He clapped Tyler on the back. "I'm gonna get another drink. You kids have fun."

Tyler waited until Ethan was gone, then lounged against the wall behind him. "So you seduce Isaac. How very topical."

"Art mimics life," I said. "Or something along those lines."

He smiled briefly, opened his mouth, closed it, then opened it again. "Don't get mad."

I braced myself. "Okay, so I'm getting ready to get mad."

"Why are you here with me instead of hanging out with Isaac?"

I hesitated. "I had to introduce you to my uncle."

"Shira." He made my name sound like *Come on.*

"What?" I said defensively, a slow discomfort starting to build inside me.

"Look, it's just . . . You seem like you're actively avoiding him. You don't seem very comfortable with him. How can you say you want to date him?"

I felt like he'd driven over me in a bulldozer. "Why do you even have an opinion on this? You've never even been in a relationship. How would you know what makes a person want to be in one?"

"I know a good relationship should be based on being able to talk. On *liking* each other. Not getting drunk or hooking up."

"Wow, thank you, I really needed your advice on my life. And we didn't 'get drunk' and 'hook up.'"

"You've literally spent a week asking for my advice."

My face was hot enough to boil eggs. "Yeah, because I *want* to get better at talking and opening up. Because I'm not content to keep everyone at a distance and give people fake smiles and a fake persona."

He reared back as though slapped, his skin paling. A tight, long silence stretched between us. "Got it," he said, but his voice came out whispery and soft, a trail of smoke about to dissolve.

I felt suddenly very small. "Tyler—I'm sorry, I didn't mean that—"

"You know what, Shira?" he said. "I'm not the fake one. You're the one fooling yourself, telling yourself you want Isaac just because he looks good on paper, because he'd be easy to be with. Just like Shoshana went for her father's apprentice instead of her sailor, just like your grandfather married your grandmother—"

"Leave my grandparents out of this," I whispered harshly. "And leave Shoshana out, too."

"You wouldn't have asked me to teach you to kiss if you were really into Isaac. You're just too scared to go after what you really want."

My jaw dropped open. "And what do I really want, then?"

"You tell me. If you're brave enough to say it."

But I couldn't say anything at all.

"Fine. You want fake; here it is." He smiled at me with almost vicious politeness. "I hope you're very, very happy with Isaac," he said. He drained his mug and lifted it to me. "Cheers."

And he walked away, leaving me feeling both furious and like I was going to cry.

So that had gone very badly, very quickly.

I moved through the party in a whirl of confusion and rage. I hadn't meant to tell Tyler he was fake. But he shouldn't have told me I didn't know what I was doing with Isaac. Which, in fact, I didn't, but it wasn't any of Tyler's business. And if Tyler wanted something, if he was—god forbid—jealous, he could damn well say something instead of putting it on me.

And actually, even if he was jealous, who cared? He didn't want to date me, so what could he possibly want? Simply for me not to be with someone else? For me to spend all my life obsessed with him, like he'd wanted the Barbanel girl to wait for her sailor lover forever?

I decided to get drunk and hook up with Isaac.

Isaac had been cornered by the Avillezes. They were enthusiastically grilling him about Columbia, and I waited until they'd been beckoned away by a couple across the room before swooping in. "Want to go for a walk? Unless you'd like another set of adults to ask about your major."

"A walk would be great," he said with much relief, and followed me into the foyer so we could grab our coats. We passed Tyler, talking to Ethan and David, and I smiled at him sharply. He straightened, face blank, and looked away.

Don't think about Tyler, I told myself. Tyler was incidental. Isaac was the point. Isaac had always been the point.

Tension coiled through my body as we wrapped ourselves in outerwear and circled back into the gardens. I was painfully aware of our arms, close to brushing. Okay. Focus. I wanted this to happen. I wanted to be open with Isaac. I wanted to create a romantic moment and a genuine connection.

We walked through the garden, the stars and moon sliding silvery light over the pines and juniper trees and dormant flower bushes. The air tasted cold and crisp. When the path approached the edge of the cliff, I took us over to a stone bench some distant ancestor had installed, which had a view of the sand and the sea and the sky.

We sat. In the past, I would have been painfully awkward, utterly silent. Anything to keep the boy beside me from knowing I liked him. Now I crossed my knees, leaning them to the left so I angled toward Isaac. "Chilly."

"Yeah. But very pretty," he offered.

We could, potentially, have sat there forever in silence, drowning in the wind and cold, the moon bright, the sea black. But I had to make my own moments. I looked at him, focusing on the curve of his jaw, the line of his lips; holding the moment out; urging him to fall into it. This was *Isaac*. I wanted Isaac.

He looked at me quickly, then away, then back again, and offered a slightly nervous smile. "What?"

I tried to smile. The nerves within me coiled and banked, like frantic animals trying to escape confinement. Why wouldn't he kiss me? Should I kiss him? What if he didn't *want* to kiss? Maybe he regretted last night. "Nothing."

I was too much in my own head. I needed to think like Tyler— more confidently. Or think *less*. Try to live, instead of letting the possibility of failure and embarrassment freeze me.

Isaac smiled awkwardly. Maybe the same nervous energy darted through his body. Though now, oddly, my energy had begun to rebound, my pulse slowing enough I thought I might go into hibernation. Maybe I'd used up all the energy I had and only had seconds left before collapsing.

If so, I needed to use them.

I lifted my head, scooched an inch closer, and kissed Isaac.

He kissed me back, pressing his soft, closed lips to mine. Then he pulled away and smiled, the same hesitant smile. I smiled back, mortification starting to uncurl in my belly. "Is this—I wanted—is this okay?"

"Yeah," he said, and touched his lips back to mine.

Okay. Yes. Good. Exhilaration shot through me. We were kissing! We were kissing.

It was . . . fine?

His mouth was warm, the pressure from his lips pleasant. His hands stayed by his side, and I wasn't sure what to do with mine, so I placed one on his shoulder and kept my lips on his. Okay. Now what? How long did we do this for? Why hadn't I made *someone* tell me about noses?

Actually, our noses seemed to be fine.

Weren't tongues supposed to be involved? My tongue remained quite firmly in my mouth, and to be honest, I couldn't argue with its placement. The books I'd read always went for "mimicking another dance" imagery, but our tongues mimicked no dance, and I for one did not plan to induce it.

So I was a touch surprised when Isaac slid his hand up the front of my dress coat. I shied back slightly, and now it was my turn to smile awkwardly, then look away at the moon and the sea. My heart raced and I wasn't sure what to do, wasn't sure why I wasn't more into this, wasn't sure where Isaac's head was at.

"Oh, wow, sorry!"

I looked up and saw Abby staring at us, before she made an apologetic moue and vanished in a blur of flying brown hair. Mortification rushed through me. Isaac jerked back so violently he almost fell off the bench even though we were alone again. I stared at him, then after Abby as though to make sure she'd really vanished, then back at Isaac. "Oops."

He'd turned sallow. I'd never appreciated the descriptor until now, the way his skin gained a greenish tint in the moonlight. "Do you think she'll tell anyone?"

Did I think she'd *tell* anyone? What kind of a question was that? "Noah, I assume."

"Oh." He scratched the back of his neck. "Yeah."

I frowned at him, then directed the frown toward the sea. It shouldn't bother me, how appalled he looked at the idea of other people knowing about us. Maybe he was deeply private. Or hated PDA. And, sure, maybe it made sense to keep us a secret, especially since we hadn't even discussed what "us" meant. We should keep everything under wraps until we figured out what we were doing.

But for whatever reason, it bothered me, the instant scooch away.

Worse, it bothered me how it only bothered my pride, not my heart.

Because this was *Isaac*. Isaac, who I had a crush on, who I wanted to date. But when he'd pulled away from me, my reaction was only slight irritation.

I should be wounded. I should want Isaac to shout about us from the rooftops. *I* wanted to shout about us from the rooftops.

Except.

Except I didn't, did I?

"We should head back to the party," I said, trying to keep my voice level, trying to keep my roiling emotions under control.

"Cool."

We retraced our steps through the garden and approached the house across the lawn. The French doors framed the glowing warmth of the party, the laughing people, the menorahs, the cocktails, the fancy dresses. I didn't want to be in there right now, didn't want to have to smile and play along. Tyler would. Tyler could plaster on his politician's face and make people feel good, but I wanted to process, to think. "Actually, I think I'm going to stay out here a bit longer."

"Oh. Okay, cool. Good night."

I waited for the door to open and close behind him, letting out a burst of warmth and laughter. Then I groaned, leaning my head back toward the spinning stars above me. I breathed in the black night, the cold salty air, the hushed rustle of the trees.

I should have been more upset about Isaac, and I wasn't. I should have been less upset over fighting with Tyler.

It was obvious, wasn't it, or it should have been obvious, if I hadn't been so damn determined not to see it: I wasn't upset over Isaac because he wasn't the person I wanted. Isaac had been nice, a dream—someone with potential, and it hurt to see potential vanish.

Tyler . . .

Of course I hadn't wanted to admit it. How could I? I'd made a stupid mistake, fancying myself in love with Tyler Nelson three years ago. I liked to think I wasn't the kind of person who made the same mistake twice; I was the kind of person who learned from them. Fool me once, after all . . .

I texted Olivia: **Sorry I disappeared. Are you still here?**

GOOD you disappeared!! She texted back. **At least I hope so** **I headed home but coffee tomorrow?**

Me: Yes please.

I reentered Golden Doors through a side door, climbing a narrow, little-used staircase and winding my way to my room, ignoring the sounds of the party below. I threw myself on my bed, feeling a particular kind of morose, all dressed up and nowhere to go, sad and lonely and mad. I felt outside myself, looking inward like I was a character in a movie, and maybe not a very sympathetic one. Poor little rich girl.

I rolled over and stared at the ceiling.

God, I liked him. Two sides of the same coin, they said about love and hate, and sure enough, I'd plastered up the first emotion with the second. Now it'd been scraped away, like a paper label dissolving off a glass bottle. Tyler wasn't exactly the person I'd fallen for the first time, but he certainly wasn't the heartless playboy I'd imagined after. He was kind to my cousins and interested in how people ticked, smarter than I'd given him credit for, funnier than I'd realized, and he'd opened up to me in a way I thought he rarely did for anyone else.

I liked him so much, and I wanted him to like me, too.

He *did* like me, too. That was almost the worst of it. I hadn't imagined the way we teased each other, the flare of attraction, the electricity between us. *Too bad we want such different things,* he had said when we fell off the sled at the bottom of Dead Horse Hill, and he was right. We didn't want the same things, so the best thing to do was to say, *Too bad, how unfortunate,* and move on.

I rolled over on my side. This was fine. I had gotten over Tyler Nelson before; I could do it again.

A tear slid out of my eye, hot and stupid, streaking down my cheek to the pillow, followed by another and another. At first, I wiped them away, then gave up, feeling my lashes turn spiky. My chest heaved uncontrollably.

The door opened and Abby entered. Horror immediately marked her face.

"My *god*!" I barely corralled the urge to throw my tear-drenched pillow at her. "You're everywhere."

"I'll go," she said quickly, and closed the door.

More tears leaked out of me, this time from guilt. What was wrong with me? Why did I always react so badly, so sharply to things? Why couldn't I get a grasp on my emotions and think through how I wanted to respond to people, instead of exploding like a boiling kettle or staying utterly silent?

The door cracked back open, and Abby peeked in, her concerned brown eyes looking even bigger than usual since she'd pulled her hair back in a messy bun. "Look," she said hesitantly. "I know we don't know each other really well, but if you want to talk . . . Talking usually helps."

"How can it help?" I asked starkly, but I managed to pull myself upright, curling my knees into my chest. "I like someone who doesn't want to date me. There's literally nothing to be done about it."

"Ah." She slipped inside and quietly closed the door. "Tyler?"

She'd just caught me making out with Isaac. "Why are you asking about Tyler?"

She spread her hands. "Because it seems like . . . Tyler."

I dropped my head to my chest. "I'm an idiot."

"What happened?"

The story poured out of me. "I can't believe I was so stupid. I knew better than to fall for him again."

"You shouldn't beat yourself up for liking someone."

"I wish I liked Isaac," I said. "I *did* like Isaac."

"I'm sorry."

"Me too." I took a deep breath. "And—sorry if I haven't been totally welcoming."

She waved a hand. "You have been. Don't worry about it."

"I don't have a ton of good friends," I said stiffly, not even sure why I was telling her this. "Casual friends, yeah. But I don't connect with lots of people." I gave what I hoped looked like an easy shrug. "But I guess you're going to be around awhile."

"I hope so." She looked down and smiled, a small, private one, then looked up and smiled wider at me. "Noah always says really nice things about you."

"He does not," I scoffed. "I'm sure he barely mentions me."

"No, he does. He pays a lot of attention to what you like and how you're doing. And he always sounds really proud of you. He obviously thinks of you as a sister."

I picked at my nails, feeling like something soft and tremulous had inflated my chest. "Mm."

"He showed me some of your skating videos. He said you could be great at whatever you wanted."

My gaze flew to hers. I never would have expected Noah to show anyone my old videos. "I wasn't good enough to go pro."

"He said—he said he hoped it was a good thing, not continuing to compete. He hoped you'd be able to like it again if it didn't carry so much other weight."

"He's never said any of that to me."

A tiny smirk. "Well, Noah's still working on communicating his emotions."

I let out a genuine bark of laughter. "Yeah." Sliding her a sidelong look, I added, "Communication's not always a Barbanel strong suit."

She rubbed my back. "I don't think it's most people's."

Feeling better, I headed to the bathroom to scrub my face and pour a cold glass of water and get ready for bed. "Okay," I told my reflection. "You're okay."

And I thought I probably would be.

CHAPTER EIGHTEEN

n the morning, I strode into the great room on a mission, approaching a clump of middles. Few of the adults had made it down yet, probably nursing off the side effects of last night's party. "Has anyone seen Isaac?"

Oliver looked up from his sketchbook. "I think he might be outside?"

I popped into the backyard. Lumpy gray clouds blanketed the sky, and the trees stood out against them, barren save the eternal evergreens. Isaac sat on a decorative bench that I wasn't sure I'd ever sat on in my life. I shoved my hands deep in my coat as I approached. "Mind if I join you?"

He gave me a quick smile. "What's up?"

I sat next to him, kicking my feet out in front of me in the snow. "Can we chat about yesterday real quick?"

He looked alarmed. "Uh—sure?"

I braced myself. Having this conversation made me want to curl up and die, but it was important, and it was honest, and it was real. "I had a good time last night," I said, which, okay, was *not* honest and real, but felt like an acceptable white lie.

He smiled. "Me too."

Oh no. I was the absolute worst. "But I wasn't being entirely honest with myself about what I want right now and—I've had *such* a crush on you, Isaac, but I sort of figured out—I don't actually think I'm in the right place to date you. I'm sorry."

"I don't want to date you." He sounded so appalled I forgot what I was saying for a moment.

I blinked. "What?"

"Don't get me wrong, I like you! I'm down for—you know. But us dating wouldn't be a good idea. I mean—you're hot and confident, but I work for your family."

Hot! Confident! I couldn't believe I'd fooled him into thinking I was confident. Apparently fake it till you make it really worked. "Oh. Uh. What did you think we were doing?"

He shook his head. "I dunno. Having fun? I don't normally do this."

"Do what?"

He waved a vague hand. "Hook up on vacation."

Oh. For whatever reason, I'd assumed everyone save me was an expert at hooking up. "Right." I gave a slow nod.

My previous words seemed to be catching up with him because he peered at me uncertainly. "You have a crush on me? I'm really flattered. But—"

I held up my hands. "It's okay! That's what I'm saying! I also don't want to date."

"Oh." He relaxed. "So we're good hanging out."

"Right," I said, then started laughing, a little hysterically. "Only, literally I mean hanging out. I don't mean hooking up."

Now he looked disappointed. "Oh. Okay."

This was awkward, but weirdly having this conversation felt less excruciating than anticipating it. "I'm sorry. I'm probably messing this up. I'm not used to talking about stuff."

"Nah, it's good you brought this up. Always better to lay stuff out. I'm cool just being friends." He looked at me speculatively. "I sort of thought you were into the boy next door."

The boy next door. I tried to sound casual. "A bit, maybe. But it wouldn't work out."

"Why not?"

I cast him a wry look. Did people who had hooked up talk about their other wannabe relationships? Well, I could use a guy's perspective and advice. "He's not looking for anything serious."

"Ah. Got it."

Okay, no advice, then.

I pushed to my feet. "I'm gonna head back in—but I'll see you later?"

He smiled at me, a nice, easy smile, but it didn't make my heart swoop or my pulse pick up. "See you."

I felt lighter, freer as I walked back through Golden Doors. Who knew having clarifying conversations could make you feel so good? I felt like I'd disposed of some of the tense anxiety I'd been carrying around all week. A bit of nervous energy remained, but it felt more positive, friendlier, instead of dragging me down.

I wound up in the piano room by the mini grand, my fingers drifting over the keys. They were so familiar, even after so many years of ignoring them. I pressed my fingers down and a minor seventh sang out, melancholy and somber.

Maybe you didn't have to be brilliant at something to enjoy it. Not such a novel idea, and yet . . . it was hard for me to internalize. What was the point if you weren't brilliant? Wouldn't it hurt too much, knowing you'd never reach the top? Or could you simply love something anyway, a love without envy and self-criticism, based solely on joy?

I sat down on the bench, the ghost of my younger self taking control of my muscles. I hesitated, unsure what I was doing, unsure if I'd remember how to do this. How long had it been since I had played? I'd gone cold turkey; when I didn't place in the Harrington Concerto Competition at age twelve, I'd stopped lessons all at once and focused on ice-skating.

I flipped through the songbook on top of the piano, a compila-
tion from classical composers. I paused at Debussy's "Nuages." I'd
loved this song so much. Growing up, I'd played it in this room,
from this book, so often. Looking at the music felt like revisiting
an old friend. I hesitated, then set my hands over the keys.

The music filled the room. It hooked inside me, slow and
haunting. My hands were more confident than I'd expected, my
eyes focused on the notes. I'd forgotten what playing music could
do to me, how it could tug something out of my chest and unspool
it, how it could be physical and emotional at once.

The good thing about music was you didn't have to think, you
could simply pour all your emotions into playing. I wasn't sure how
much time had passed—two, three songs?—before I realized Noah
was in the room. I paused. "Hey."

My father had taught me the basics of piano when I was very
small, before my parents put me in lessons. I felt like half my childhood had been stuck in recitals with other cousins. But not Noah.
Noah had quit after the first year, because Noah could be a stubborn brat (a family trait, it had to be said). For a while, though,
we'd played together.

"You don't need to stop," he said.

I'd rather talk than play, but I was almost done with the song,
and there was something satisfying about someone else listening
to me be good.

Because I *was* good. Not great, and not peak me, since I'd gone years without practice. My hands were stiff and my notes occasionally jarring. But I could be good again, if I wanted. This could come back to me.

Noah reached out to turn the page half a measure before I did. I shot him a startled glance, then finished the last half page of music, throwing in a bit of overdramatic shoulder movement, like when I was really little and pretending to be Beethoven. Noah grinned as I ended, which had been the point.

I swiveled to look at him. "I didn't know you could read music still."

He smiled. "I'm not completely illiterate."

"No. But you haven't played for years."

"I can follow along."

I nodded. I'd been sad when Noah refused to play anymore, since I'd loved playing with him. But if he could still follow music, maybe he still had muscle memory. "Do you think you could play 'Heart and Soul'?"

He looked surprised, then contemplative. He nodded as he placed his hands to the left of mine. A surge of emotion washed through me, and I had to close my eyes against it. I'd missed Noah. Then we plunged into the familiar music, the '50s progression coming easily on my part despite years without playing this melody.

When we came to the end, I looked up and saw we'd gained another visitor. Grandpa stood in the doorway, listening silently.

His face, so weathered, seemed more relaxed than usual, like the lines had been softened. "Very nice," he said before slipping away.

I looked over at Noah, who'd gone very still watching Grandpa's disappearing back. "Do you think Grandpa would be sad if Grandma left him?" I asked.

Noah plucked at keys: a melodic fourth, a discordant third. "I don't think she'll leave him. I think this whole thing with her brothers, with her stock, is about making Grandpa suffer a bit, since she suffered when she learned she wasn't his first choice. Making him afraid she'll give control of the company over to her siblings. But this is her family, her home, so I don't think she'll leave."

Interesting, but not an answer to my question. "But do you think he would be sad if she *did*?"

He frowned. "Sure. He's been used to her being at his side for decades."

"Yeah. But what I mean is, do you think he loves her? Obviously he loved Abby's grandmother when they were young, but you can love multiple people, right? Do you think they've been happy?"

He looked at me, serious, and I realized he'd thought about this, too, and it also bothered him, the idea our grandparents' marriage might not have been as strong as we'd thought. "I hope so."

"Me too." I thought about what could make you happy; I thought about the music moving through my body, about Noah playing a duet with me, about my skates cutting across the ice, about Olivia laughing over shared croissants, about the beauty of a Nantucket winter. About my family being happy, and how much that mattered. "I like Abby."

He smiled, and it transformed his face, lifting away the clouds and making him look like a kid again. "Yeah. Me too."

I curled up on a couch in the great room, and the adults slowly trickled in, going straight to the coffee carafe. As had become my habit when I had a bit of downtime, I searched through old letters for mentions of the Barbanel girls instead of scanning my socials. After all, looking at other people's posts bummed me out. Far less depressing to look for, say, mentions of ship-wrecked sailors.

I paused. I'd been looking for mentions of the girls, but had anyone mentioned the *wreck*? Even if shipwrecks were common here, I had the date—if I narrowed in on Nantucket letters and newspapers and diary entries from the week or two following the disaster, perhaps I'd find something.

My burst of being impressed at my own brilliance carried me through for about half an hour before my interest started to wane. I found a handful of references to the *Rosemary*, but none that conveniently said "And Shoshana/Josephine/Louisa sobbed and clutched a sailor's body."

I'd almost decided to give up flipping virtual pages and scanning cramped, faint handwriting when I saw the familiar double *B* and long *L* of my last name in the diary of a Nantucket merchant's wife.

> *Came across Mrs. Sarah Barbanel, which was unexpected—nice family, but they don't tend to gawk. She looked melancholy, so I asked her if she'd known anyone on board, and she said not for a very long time.*

Wait.

Mrs. Sarah Barbanel? The girls' mom? Marcus's wife? I supposed the island was small enough she might have known a sailor her daughters' age, but still . . .

What did I even know about Marcus's wife? I pulled up the images of the family tree on my phone, but she wasn't marked with a maiden name. She had married Marcus in 1826. Where had she come from?

Before I'd thought it through, I'd pulled up my messages with Tyler, ready to text him this latest development. Then I paused. No. Tyler and I were done, weren't we?

Or were we friends?

I couldn't make this decision about Tyler right now, but I could learn more about Sarah Barbanel. I popped into Grandpa's study, practically jittering with excitement. "Hi, Grandpa. Can I ask a few more questions about early Nantucket?"

He looked up and broke into a smile. "Always."

I perched on one of the old wooden chairs. "Do you know anything else about Marcus's wife? Like her last name or birthday."

"Let's see." Grandpa pulled out one of the now-familiar binders and flipped pages. "Marcus's wife . . . Ah yes. She was a Fersztenfeld." He nodded decisively, like the name meant something. "Born 1804."

"Who were they?"

"One of the old New York families. You should ask your grandmother about them."

"You could ask her," I suggested.

He patted my hand. "Best if you do, sweetheart."

I headed to the sunroom, stepping through the door to find Grandma sitting across a wicker table from Great-Uncle Arnold. Neither of them appeared to be speaking.

"Oh." I paused, a smile pasted on my mouth, even as my eyes narrowed. "Sorry to interrupt."

"You're not, dear," she said smoothly. "My brother was leaving."

He didn't speak for a moment, then nodded and slowly raised himself from the chair. I half expected him to creak and fall, but he walked with his slow, awkward gait, nodding at me as he passed. "Shira."

"Hi, Uncle Arnold."

At the door, he turned and paused, another laborious process. "Think about what I said, Helen."

She smiled thinly. "I always do."

I watched Uncle Arnold go, then turned back to Grandma. "What were you talking about?"

"When did you become such a nosy child?"

"I got it from my grandmother."

Her mouth twitched. "I was never nosy."

"Yet you somehow always know everything going on. Which I aspire to be like."

"You just have to make everyone tell you everything."

I dropped down in the chair closest to her. "Tell me everything, then."

That won me a laugh. She brushed her fingertips lightly against my cheek. "When I was your age, I thought I had the whole world figured out."

"Did you?"

"No." She scoffed. "But I was too blind to see otherwise." She raised her brows. "What did you burst in here for?"

"Oh. I wanted to know more about Marcus Barbanel's wife, Sarah. Grandpa said you might know about her family, the Fersztenfelds."

"Did he," she said. She took a seat at her desk, before a monitor where she kept all her windows greatly enlarged. "They're still around, yes. I might have some correspondences from Laurie

Fersztenfeld from years ago when I was looking into some family genealogy on my side."

Everyone had really been sticking close to each other for a dozen decades, hadn't they?

"Her niece wrote a book about all their old stories." Grandma lifted her reading glasses so she could peer at the screen. "She says she sent me a copy? Hmm. Let's go ask your grandfather."

Back through the house we went to Grandpa's study. He was notably surprised to see us both. Grandma marched up to him. "You have a book about the Fersztenfelds."

"I do? Here?"

"Where else would it be?" she asked. "You have all the family history here."

"I don't remember a book about the Fersztenfelds."

"You probably never read it. Laurie Fersztenfeld sent it to me years ago. It's a small volume."

The three of us divided up the shelves, searching title by title, until Grandpa finally pulled out a slim, unmarked volume with a triumphant "Aha!"

"Good." Grandma plucked the book from his hand and placed it in mine, then swept us out. I glanced over my shoulder at Grandpa, and caught him watching her with a forlorn expression.

I caught up with her in the hall. "You met Grandpa around my age, didn't you?"

She shrugged. "A few years older, but yes."

"How did you meet?"

"Through family friends."

"No, I know, but—the first meeting. What was it like?"

"I'm not sure I remember the first time we met, but the first time I noticed him . . ." She smiled distantly as we reentered the sunroom. "Someone was having a party outside the city. It was spring—Passover. The younger kids were hunting for the afikomen, and we'd both been sent along, but we felt too old to be peering between books or under couch cushions. Not that anyone had put the afikomen under a couch in years, not since Arnie stood on it to reach a mantel, and crushed the matzo into a hundred pieces." She laughed. "Grandpa and I sat on the porch steps as the kids looked, and he offered me a light."

"You *smoked*?"

Her eyes danced and she took a seat on the couch. "You think you're the only one who's ever been young? Besides, it was different then."

Pretty sure nicotine hadn't been different, but sure. I dropped into a chair across from her. "When did you start dating?"

Now she looked out the window, at the shadowed snow, the white-capped trees and twiggy branches. Sunlight filtered through puffy clouds, turning their edges blindingly bright. "He asked me out for ice cream when I was twenty. Ice cream, then roller skating."

"Sounds very 1950s," I teased. "Were poodle skirts involved?"

She laughed. "I'd be careful mocking old fashions. You kids keep recycling decades; you'll be back in poodle skirts soon enough."

"Do you have pictures?" I was pretty sure I'd seen some old photos of Grandma, but not in a while.

"Lots. We were always going to parties and . . ." Her expression dimmed. "But it turns out he loved Ruth the whole time," she murmured. "He was seeing her, too. None of it was real."

"But he married *you*," I said. "He wouldn't have if he didn't love you."

She smiled gently. "You're right, I'm sure."

I was silent a long moment. "I don't care about you giving your brothers your shares because of what it means for the company or whatever," I said. "But—I get scared about what it means if you *want* to give them your shares."

"What do you mean, dear?" she said, gaze piercing.

I swallowed. "It would mean you and Grandpa aren't okay. And if you're not okay—that would mean you were unhappy. *Are* you unhappy?" I asked, a little desperately.

She opened her arms, my not-very-physically-affectionate grandmother, and I moved to the couch and curled up next to her. "Oh, my dear. It's not always easy to be happy."

"I want you to be."

She stroked my hair. "Sometimes I'm happy. It comes and

goes. It's not something you lock in once, forever."

"That sucks."

"Yes." She laughed, then sighed. "Inside, we're all sixteen-year-old fools about love. We want it to be eternal. Unbending."

"Maybe it is."

"Maybe." She looked out the window. "For the people who fell in love in the first place."

I left, worried. If Grandma thought Grandpa had been in love with another woman but married Grandma anyway, she'd think her whole life was a lie, any happiness she had felt founded on falsehoods. But how could Grandpa have not loved her? The other woman had been a dream, part of his youth, not part of his life.

I retreated to my room to read the book on the Fersztenfeld family instead of ruminating on my own. Could it have been Sarah Barbanel—Sarah Fersztenfeld—who loved a sailor once? A woman who, like Grandma, hadn't been born a Barbanel but had married into the family. A woman who might have been happier as someone else.

I'd been so focused on the lovers being young. I'd wanted it to be Josephine or Louisa—and I'd even rather it had been Shoshana setting aside a lover to marry someone new. Not another story of a full lifetime confused and unhappy. I wanted to know that the woman who'd lost a lover had found happiness at the end.

I skimmed the intro pages, the tiny font set closely together. The Fersztenfelds had moved from Germany to New York at the turn of the nineteenth century. They set up a clothing shop and had five children, the first of whom was Sarah. She was described as the wittiest and most headstrong of the daughters. At seventeen, she was sent to finishing school in Boston. No more mention was made of her until she resurfaced as the bride of Marcus Barbanel of Nantucket.

Headstrong. Like her second daughter, Josephine.

I unearthed the scrap of napkin I'd scribbled notes on.

1819: ships make it to Hawaii (seashells)
1850s/60s: photography shows up (no need for painting!)
1813–1845: Rosemary whaling
1845: Rosemary sinks

In 1845, Sarah would have been forty-one. She'd arrived on Nantucket at age twenty-two, in 1826. The dates worked.

Had Sarah known her sailor before she arrived on Nantucket and married Marcus, or had she met him after? She could have been a new, scared bride. Or a young mother, or a harried woman with three children pulling at her skirt. Did she maintain the affair for twenty years, until the ship sank? Did it last only a season, or half a decade? *Not for a very long time*, she'd said about knowing anyone on the *Rosemary*, but by then she'd already been married for two decades.

It was so much easier for me to think the girl who had hidden away the chockpin and the shells and the painting had been a girl my age, still trying to figure her life out, still unsure what made her happy. It hurt more to think it might have been Sarah Barbanel, an adult, a wife, and a mother. I wanted to think by the time you grew up, you knew what made you happy. But maybe no one did.

Had Sarah resented her marriage to Marcus? Had she wanted to escape it, had she seen Golden Doors as a prison? Why had she married Marcus in the first place? Had resentment grown or dissipated?

Did Grandma resent her marriage? Did Grandpa?

God, I wanted to talk to Tyler. I wanted to tell him about Sarah and Marcus and the sailor. I wanted to talk to him about Grandma and Grandpa. I wanted . . . him.

But it was easier to think about other people's wants and desires than my own, so I called a convocation of older cousins, summoning them to my room for privacy's sake. Noah and Abby, Ethan and David and Oliver, and Miriam.

"I think Grandpa needs to do something," I said. "To fix things."

"Like what?" Noah asked.

"I don't know. Apologize? The adults are acting like this is about stocks and power, but I think it's really about

Grandma being hurt. She's unhappy. She thinks Grandpa has been in love with Abby's grandmother their entire lives, and her whole life was a lie. She needs to know he's sorry and he loves her."

"You think an apology from Grandpa would fix their whole relationship," David said skeptically.

"Not like an 'I'm sorry you feel hurt' apology. A real apology. If he gets that he messed up and owns up to it."

"A grand gesture," Abby said.

I nodded. "Exactly."

"But what if he doesn't love her?" Everyone's eyes swung to Miriam. She flushed. "What if she's right, and Grandpa never loved her? Then she'd be right to be mad."

"He can't have stayed in love with Abby's grandma forever," Noah said softly. "He and Grandma built a life together."

I nodded at Miri. "If he doesn't love her, and they're unhappy, maybe they shouldn't be together," I said. "But they shouldn't not be together because of a lack of communication, because one of them was too proud or foolish or blind to mention how they felt. I think we need to give Grandpa a little guidance. We have to . . . create a moment for him, a moment where he can step up. And hopefully he'll take it from there."

"How do you create a moment?" Abby asked.

I looked out the window. The sun had set and turned the world blue. Tyler could recognize moments, and maybe I could, too. Maybe anyone could learn how to create possibility and hope if they wanted to.

My grandparents were as stubborn as I was, as likely to reject a moment as to lean into it, unwilling to get hurt. So we needed to create a moment they couldn't reject. We had to get Grandpa to actually talk to Grandma, to not be stiff and locked down, but open and willing and talking.

Outside, I could see the moon—crisp and white and oblong— and a million stars beginning to shine in the early evening sky. Free light in the darkness, not oil controlled by people but the one thing we could always count on.

"It's the last night of Hanukkah," I said. "Aren't we due a miracle?"

CHAPTER NINETEEN

"We're pushing the play back," Iris announced to the family over dinner. "We're very sorry, but we need a few more days for it to be perfect." She nodded solemnly to Uncle Arnold and the other Danzigers. "We're sorry you're going to miss it."

He nodded back, equally as solemn. "I'm sure you'll be wonderful."

With Isaac leaving, Iris had reclaimed her role as General Holofernes, and I'd been demoted back to handmaiden so Lily could be Judith. Which, honestly, sounded perfect. Instead of the performance, we celebrated the last night of Hanukkah the way I had for most of my life, watching the candles flicker and burn, surrounded by family and food. A minor holiday but a beautiful one, with all my family in one place.

In the morning, we gathered to see the Danzigers off. No one seemed too distressed by their departure. The five-night visit had clearly been long enough for everyone. "You'll keep in touch?" Great-Uncle Arnold asked.

Grandma gave him a wintry smile, which she then extended to the rest of us. "Yes. I certainly will."

Then, not waiting for the Danzigers to depart, she turned on her heel and walked away.

I went over to Olivia's house afterward. In her bedroom, a bubble of teal and pink, we watched a nonsensical Christmas princess movie, a plate of illicit cookies between us. (Food was not allowed in Olivia's bedroom for fear of crumbs summoning mice.)

Honestly, watching an American girl bumble around a tiny fake country in the Alps because the media had mistaken her for the prince's betrothed and he needed her to keep up the pretense was very soothing. A menorah even showed up at one point when the prince and the American girl attended a holiday fair. There were probably two Jews in the tiny fake country of Ellinnia, but I'm sure they appreciated it.

The movie required very little attention to keep up, so we chatted through most of the B story line.

"To be honest, I thought kissing would be more exciting," I said. I'd texted her the main details yesterday—the rise and fall of Isaac Lehrer, in my heart at least—but now wanted to get to the good stuff.

"Exciting how?" She popped the rest of her snickerdoodle in her mouth and offered me another.

"I don't know. I wasn't expecting fireworks, but it felt very . . . manual."

She giggled.

"Stop!" I said, but a few half giggles escaped me as well. "I'm serious. It felt . . . fine? But boring. Not very adventurous?"

"Harsh."

"I don't mean to be harsh. It just wasn't super exciting."

"Okay, like, what are we working with here? Too much tongue? Not enough tongue?"

I dropped my head into my hands, my cheeks hot. "No tongue. Zero tongue. Just—we kissed."

"Oh. Hmm. Well, sometimes you need to train someone in kissing, you know? To be perfectly honest, Jackson wasn't a great kisser when we started dating."

My jaw fell open. "You can train someone? What, like you graded him on a rubric and gave him feedback?"

She laughed. "No, he was just, like, kind of slobbery? I did a lot of positive reinforcement. You know—appreciative noises when something worked for me." Her cheeks darkened, and she cleared her throat. "Anyway! You shouldn't be worried, you'll figure it out."

"Wait, no, tell me more about these 'appreciative noises.'"

She rolled her eyes, grinning. "I made it very clear what I liked, you know?"

"Olivia. What hidden depths."

"I try," she said. "So how do you feel? You've been obsessed with him for a year."

I reached over her to snag an oatmeal raisin cookie. "I'm kind of . . . relieved? It was so much work to talk to him. He's hot and smart and I *wanted* to like him, but I didn't really know him, and now . . . I don't know, there's nothing there between us. I'm more bummed out about losing the idea of a boyfriend, instead of being sad about actual Isaac." Tyler's volley came back to haunt me, that I wanted an easy boyfriend instead of a connection with someone I really liked.

I pushed both boys out of my head. "What about you? Jackson gets in later today, right?"

"Wait, no, first. What about Tyler?"

I slumped, looking out the window at the gray sky. "I don't know. We had this weird fight that made me think he might be jealous—but we want different things. I want steady and reliable, and he wants fun and uncommitted, so even if we *are* circling each other, it doesn't matter, because no future would make us both happy."

"Hmm," Olivia said, her tone more measured than usual. "It's good you realize you don't want the same thing. So you don't jump into something and wind up miserable."

"Right. No." I pushed my hair behind my ears. "I'm definitely not going to do that."

After the movie ended, we went downstairs so I could gather my things and head out before Olivia picked Jackson up at the ferry. While Olivia ducked into the bathroom, I wandered over to the piano, which stood in its own personal alcove. A songbook lay open at the march from *The Nutcracker.* Tentatively at first, I began to play, then more and more sure, ending with a cheerful, confident few notes.

When I looked up, Olivia stood there. "I thought you didn't play anymore," she said.

"I don't."

"You sounded very good for someone who doesn't play."

"Thanks. Is this what you're dancing to at the New Year's party?"

"Indeed." She did a pirouette. "How do I look?"

"Like a perfect Clara."

She regarded me. "You could play, if you wanted to. Mom's planning on it, but she really doesn't want to—she'd rather be captaining the ship."

"Oh no," I said quickly. "I haven't played in public in years. I'd mess up."

She shrugged. "Just putting it out there."

I set off along Cliff Road toward Golden Doors. I could have called someone to pick me up instead of embarking on an hour-long walk, but today was on the warmer side, and the road's incline churned enough heat in my body that I unzipped my coat and stuffed my hat in my pocket. At home, I routinely walked more than an hour through the heavily trafficked grid of Manhattan; it was soothing to instead walk by myself on an empty road.

The light was soft and malleable today, fading in and out of thick, undefined clouds. There were no shadows, but an ever-present glare as I took in the island's barren beauty. The trees were stunted and wizened from salty air, patches of snow still lying thick in the wood. The ocean, when I could see it, was a shimmery blue-gray, fading into the washed-out sky.

When I reached the turnoff to the long, private drive leading toward Golden Doors, I looked instead to the left, where Tyler's home lay.

It wasn't Hanukkah anymore. The season for miracles had passed. And I wasn't sure I believed in miracles, anyway, not ones handed down by an all-seeing power. But maybe I believed in the miracles you made, in the leaps you took. I believed in small miracles, in realizations and understanding and belief.

I believed it was a miracle to like a person who liked you back, in the same place, at the same time.

Last night, I'd watch eight nights' worth of candles flicker and burn, a celebration of god or oil or light. We all wanted to push away the dark, metaphorical or real, and if you could, shouldn't you? Sarah Barbanel might not have been happy. Grandma might not always be happy. But if I could find happiness, shouldn't I grab it with both hands and hold on?

Being around Tyler made me happy. I didn't know what would happen if I went to him, if I told him I wanted him. But I was tired of not speaking up because I was afraid of being laughed at; I was sad I'd stopped doing things I loved just because I wasn't perfect at them. If Tyler rejected me, I'd be upset, but I'd move on. I would have tried. I'd regret it if I didn't tell him how I felt.

I kept walking past Golden Doors until I reached the next turn. I walked down the drive to Tyler's house. The treetops rustled in the breeze, which snaked its fingers down my nape and billowed up through the bottom of my jacket. The sun had dropped during my walk, and now that my pace had lessened, the temperature felt stark and bitter.

Walking around the side of the house, I paused below the window I thought belonged to Tyler and pulled out my phone.

Me:

Clack clack

Clack

This is the sound of a rock being thrown against your window

I am not ACTUALLY going to throw a rock because 1) weird and 2) what if I break the glass

Tyler's window flew open, and his head popped into sight. "Shira?" he called down. "What are you doing here?"

"Surprise!" I shouted back.

"Wait right there," he said, and vanished, as though I'd come here just to go away. I shivered as I waited, but he was quick, not even putting on a coat or shoes before coming outside.

"What's going on?" he asked. "What's wrong?"

"Nothing's wrong," I said. "I just . . . wanted to talk to you."

"Okay," he said warily.

"First off. Isaac and I didn't pan out."

His eyes widened, and he took a step forward. "What? Are you okay?"

"Totally! It's a good thing."

His mouth parted slightly, and he looked confused, then pressed on. "What happened?"

"We weren't a good fit. I mean, he didn't want to date me, but it turned out . . . I don't want to date him, either."

"Oh." He shoved his hands in his pocket. "I'm sorry."

"Don't be," I said forcefully. "I'm glad."

His eyes were disconcertingly bright. "Why are you telling me?"

Energy fizzed in my belly, a deep fear of putting my feelings into words. I looked everywhere but at him—his house, the snow, the sky, Orion shining bright. "I thought maybe we could talk about what this means for us."

His gaze, on the other hand, remained centered on me. "Why would it mean anything? You got your flirting tips. Your uncle said I could send him my résumé. Nothing's left."

My stomach felt hollow. *Nothing's left.* Right, of course. We'd only ever been a bargain.

Except.

We *liked* each other. Being around him made me happy. "Maybe we could have . . . a new bargain."

"No," he said abruptly, so hard I took a sharp breath. "If you want something, Shira, you have to ask for it. I'm not striking any more deals."

"Right." I felt like I might float right out of my body and into the sky, buoyed by the air I couldn't seem to let out. "I don't want to be with Isaac."

"So you said."

"I do . . . want . . ."

He waited, still and frozen as a statue, the most beautiful boy I had ever met, the first one I had ever wanted and the one I still wanted, and I couldn't say it—I couldn't dash my words against the cold stone of him and be shattered once more. "Never mind," I said, and turned.

He was at my side in an instant, cutting in front of me,

grabbing my hands in his. His face was inches away, his skin flushed and eyes bright, feverish and gorgeous in the cold. "What, Shira? What do you want? You have to say it."

"You," I whispered.

He closed his eyes, and for a moment he looked like an angel in prayer, like his prayer had been heard and answered. "Okay," he whispered back, the word a sigh, ringing with relief. But then his eyes flew open. "Is this because you want more . . . lessons? Training?"

I almost said yes. It would have been the easy answer, to say I didn't want him but an education, to pretend I saw him as a convenient teacher. But we had been so honest with each other. "No. I want you."

Our eyes connected. He stared at me, frozen and beautiful and terrifying.

And then, before either of us could say anything else, Tyler's mom poked her head out the door. "Shira? Is that you? Why don't you kids come inside, it's freezing out here!"

Tyler leaned his head back, exhaling a white cloud into the sky.

I gave a tentative wave. "Hi, Mrs. Nelson."

"We might as well," Tyler said, speaking sotto voce. "It'll be more comfortable inside."

I trailed them both in.

"Would you like a peppermint whoopie pie?" Elena asked. "We made them yesterday and have far too many for ourselves."

Would I like a peppermint whoopie pie? In general, yes. Would I be able to stomach a peppermint whoopie pie at this particular moment in my life? Unclear.

"They're very good," Robin said from the kitchen counter when I entered. "Ten out of ten. The cookie recipe was much better than the one we used last time. More cocoa, less sugar."

Elena smiled at her wife. "Look at you, you could take over my job as a food critic."

I accepted the chocolate cookie sandwich on a plate, the pink filling dotted with crushed candy canes. "Thank you."

"Robin didn't want to put pink food coloring in the buttercream," Elena said. "But I think it's more fun this way."

"Definitely," I said. My stomach kept turning over and over.

We sat at the table and chatted about my relatives and the upcoming New Year's party at Olivia's and other banal things, and my heart climbed higher in my throat with each second, and I tried to pretend every bite of cookie didn't scrape against my throat like broken glass. Finally, enough time had passed to politely escape. Tyler stood. "Okay. We'll see you later."

"Thanks for the whoopie pie," I said, following Tyler out of the kitchen.

"Leave your door open!" Robin yelled after us.

I flinched, and darted a look at Tyler. "Are we going to your room?"

"Do you want to?"

I gave a small, nervous shrug. I had suggested—well, *something*—and where else would said something occur? Or be discussed? "Okay."

"We're not actually going to leave it open," he said, mounting the stairs. "They won't check immediately." He glanced back at me mischievously. "Unless you want to go back outside?"

"No. Um. No."

He threw open his door. Unlike the other night, when his room had been forcibly cleaned, things were strewn everywhere—clothes on all surfaces, bed unmade, jackets and scarves slung over a chair and piled on the desk. The closet door had been flung wide open and revealed a rack of expensive shoes and endless sweaters organized by color.

I shouldn't have eaten the whoopie pie, which now rolled in my stomach like a ship batted about in a heavy sea. Nervous energy spiked through me.

"So." He leaned against his desk. "What did you come here for, Shira?"

I cleared my throat. "You said I wasn't going after what I really wanted. That I was picking what was easy and looked good on paper."

"Yes." He watched me carefully.

"Maybe you're right. It's not how I thought of it, because I liked Isaac, but maybe I really liked the daydream I had of him."

"Which you gave up on."

"Yes. Because he's not who I wanted."

"Oh?" He stared at me, unmoving. "And who do you want?"

I pushed the words out, stark and clear. "I want you. I want this." I swallowed hard. "I'm utterly terrified, but I think about you all the time."

"*All* the time?" He pushed himself straight and came toward me—sauntered, really. "What do you think?"

God, he was beautiful. I thought about how determined I'd been not to fall for him again, how I'd sworn no feelings could ever develop for him a second time. And here we were, and the way I felt for him was too big for words to describe, like a balloon in my chest stretching larger and larger, big enough to encompass the both of us. "Tell me if it's just in my head like it was last time," I said quietly. "If I'm the only one who feels this."

"It's not," he said, just as softly. "Or this time, it's in mine, too."

I closed my eyes in relief. "So what do we do? What do you want?"

"I want the same thing I've wanted since we were snowed in together."

"Oh?" I said a little breathlessly. "And what is that?"

He took a last step forward, closing the gap between us. And *this* was a moment, and we were in it. "To kiss you."

I was terrified and excited and frozen. "You don't have to butter me up."

"I'm not buttering you up." He brushed his fingers underneath my chin, tilting it upward slightly. "I'm being honest."

"I"—I couldn't get the words out, couldn't say the same thing even though *god* I had thought about him constantly, even when trying not to, only to have the thoughts infiltrate in the twilight before sleep—"Tyler, I—"

"Yes?" he murmured. I could feel the heat of his body. He looked down at me from so very, very close, his eyes twin sapphires, his hair palest gold. "What do you want?"

"I want—I want to kiss you," I whispered.

The way this boy smiled, starting small, then blossoming full and wide . . . His smile was a spider's web, beautiful and complex and impossible to escape, and I didn't want to escape it. "Even if you don't know what to do with your nose?" he teased, and I broke into a startled, unexpected laugh, and he bent his head the last few inches and pressed his lips to mine.

His mouth was hot and firm, and this was *Tyler*. I was overwhelmed by sheer sensation, by the bolts of heat sparking through me, by the pressure of his lips on mine, by the heat of his hands on my waist, pulling me closer, until our bodies pressed against each other. His tongue nipped at the seam of my lips, slipping through them, sliding against my own. And I couldn't help but respond, leaning into him—

I pulled back. "Oh my god," I gasped. "What was that?"

He smirked at me, infuriatingly smug. "*That* was kissing."

"That was—that—" I licked my lips, watched his eyes fall to them. I swallowed. I needed to get ahold of myself. "You're, uh, not bad at that."

Apparently, my coolness didn't work, because his smirk broadened. "You're not so bad yourself."

"I'm not?" I paused to think. I *hadn't* been thinking, I'd been following. But it had worked right. "I was—I did okay?"

"Jesus Christ, Shira," he said. "Yes."

I held up my hands. "Just checking."

"Let's check again," he said, and put his hands on my waist and pulled me forward.

Oh god. Sensation. It poured through me, swirled and pooled. It was heat and craving and delight. I wanted to be even closer to him; I wanted every inch of us to be touching. I pulled myself higher and tighter against him, my arms wrapped around his neck, and he made a small noise. I pulled back and stared at him, at those eyes so close they made me dizzy, and I remembered to breathe and dropped my arms and broke away.

My breath came in pants. "Wow."

"Agreed," he said, almost laughing.

I was still having trouble breathing. Kissing! Who knew! "This is great," I told him emphatically. "I am in full favor of doing this forever."

He laughed. "Good."

"Wow, *who knew*?"

He kept grinning at me, his face all crinkled up, his nose looking a little scrunched. "I think a lot of people. I think that's the whole point, of, say, biological imperative."

"Wow. Well. I'm really for it."

"Better than with Isaac?"

I shoved at him. "You're terrible."

"Sorry," he said, his mouth twitching. "That was inappropriate."

"You're saying the right words but smirking too much."

"Better wipe the smirk off my face, then," he said, and we were kissing again. I hadn't known you could *feel* like this. I hadn't known time could disappear, thoughts could slip away, sensation could totally, utterly take over—

We only stopped after hearing a noise terrifyingly like one of his moms walking down the hall. "Should I go?" I asked, sitting on the edge of the bed. "I don't want you to think I only came over to make out with you—"

He grinned. "Didn't you?"

"No! I mean, yes. But I also don't hate hanging out with you."

He shrugged, almost managing to look perfectly nonchalant, but he couldn't quite hide the smile at the corners of his lips. "We can hang out."

So we hung out. I told him about Sarah Barbanel. "I just want her to have been happy," I said mournfully. "Even if she lost her lover to the sea, or if they broke up for other reasons. I hope she got to be happy in the rest of her life."

"Maybe she left behind some writings."

"Maybe," I said doubtfully. "I feel like my grandpa would have mentioned if she had, though."

He bit off a leg of a gingerbread man from the plate Elena had brought us in a not-so-subtle check-in we were luckily prepared for. "An affair with a sailor is dumb though, right?"

"What d'you mean?"

He ate the man's other leg. "He's on land for, what, a couple months, before shipping out for years? Not very satisfying."

I thought about how I'd fallen for Isaac without really knowing him, how spending time with him lessened his appeal. "Maybe it made the affair easier. She could picture him as the poetic ideal of a lover, without spending enough time with him to get irritated."

"Not real love, then."

"No. But I think imagination can be almost as powerful."

My phone pinged. Mom checking if I'd be home for dinner. "I should probably head home."

"You want a ride?"

"You don't have to."

His brows rose. "Suddenly you're going all polite on me?"

"Fine." I felt a shivery type of pleasure. "You can drive me the two minutes home."

We said goodbye to his parents, and in barely any time we were in front of Golden Doors. I could feel my nerves building back up on the short drive over. Now what? I'd run over and told him I wanted to kiss him, but what did that mean for the next few days? What did that mean for us? Should we talk about this? We should talk about this.

But instead what came out of my mouth was "Good night."

"Good night," he said, blue gaze sharp and bright.

What the hell. I leaned forward and he met me halfway, lips firm and warm under mine. The heat surged back up within me. Was it depletable, this heat, or did it last forever?

"What are you doing tomorrow?" Tyler asked when I pulled back, his voice a murmur.

"Tomorrow?" I echoed, hazy. "I don't know. I'm not doing anything."

"Want to hang out?"

Yes.

CHAPTER TWENTY

"Shira!" Mom called through my bedroom door the next morning. "Can I come in?"

I raised my head from the pillow, sleepy and confused. "Um . . ."

Then I saw Abby's bed, unruffled. "Quick," I hissed at Miriam. "Mess up her sheets."

Miriam leaped from our bed and threw back Abby's covers, then punched the pillow down with impressive foresight. She threw herself onto the vanity's bench just as my mom pushed in the door.

Mom didn't even glance at Abby's bed, her face flushed with righteous determination. "We're making chocolate babka."

"Are we?" I asked warily. My family did pretty well on the cooking front, but baking had never been our strong suit.

"Yes. And it's a fourteen-step two-day process, so we need to get started."

"We . . . ?"

"Get dressed," she said. "I'll see you downstairs in five minutes."

"It takes me an hour to shower and get ready!" I shouted after her, but she was already on her way out.

Miriam and I exchanged alarmed looks. "Two *days*?" my cousin echoed. "Have you done this before?"

I shook my head. "Never. But you know Mom. When she gets an idea in her head . . ."

I got dressed, memories of the night before blazing through my mind. I'd gone to bed high on shimmery excitement, but now uncertainty rippled beneath my skin, making me as jumpy as a deer. Yesterday had been amazing, but what had it meant? Tyler said he wanted to hang out today, which I assumed meant make out. But did it mean anything else?

I was getting ahead of myself. Best to enjoy the day and not go digging up any problems before they happened.

Downstairs, I tried to keep my head down, afraid anyone would be able to read what had happened by glancing at my face. Unfortunately, Mom called me over. "There you are. How hot do you think one hundred and ten degrees is?"

I studied her cautiously. "Hot . . . ?"

"Put your finger in here," she said, sliding a Pyrex measuring cup filled with milk toward me.

"This can't be sanitary." I stuck my finger in. "That feels warm, not hot."

"We killed the last round of yeast," Aunt Rachel, Noah's mom, said. She sounded woeful. "Google says if your milk is too hot, the yeast will die."

Okay, apparently they couldn't tell anything had happened. "You guys remember that you're *very bad* at yeast, right? That's why we leave the sourdough to Uncle Gerald."

"'Bad' is such a strong word," Mom said. "We're . . . not great at it."

"I'm going in." Aunt Rachel poured a full packet of yeast into the milk, then added a pinch of sugar. She looked up, alarmed. "Should I have added the sugar *first*?"

Mom and Aunt Rachel stared at each other in horror, then turned to their phones for internet advice. "I'm getting coffee," I said.

I took my mug over to Grandma in her armchair and sat on the loveseat kitty-corner from her. "Morning, Grandma."

Grandma watched her daughters-in-law. "They're baking."

"They're trying," I agreed. "It'll be a valiant effort, in any case."

"I could never bake," Grandma said. Her gaze focused across the room, and I turned to see Abby and Noah entering, both of them freshly showered. "Her grandmother baked."

"Did you want to bake?"

Grandma's tone turned thoughtful. "Not really."

"Well, then."

Grandma laughed. "I suppose you think I'm silly, being jealous of a dead woman."

"No," I said. "Because it's not really about her, is it?"

"No," Grandma said after a moment. "It's not."

"Shira," Uncle Gerald called. "You have a visitor."

I barely kept myself from vaulting to my feet, certain my face had turned bright red. My heart stuttered to a stop then continued on, double pace. Tyler stood in the doorway of the great room. Oh my god. I had made out with him for hours last night. His hand had gone under my shirt, his body had pressed down on mine . . .

His arrival had to be a good sign, right? Unless he planned to say yesterday was a mistake.

"Hi," Tyler said.

"Hi," I said.

He was *gorgeous*. He'd always been gorgeous—I'd first noticed him because his laughter sounded like music and because he looked like a young Greek god—but it had been an unattainable beauty and then an irritating beauty. Now, for the first time in ages, I felt like I could soak him in without awe or bitterness. I felt, almost, like he was *mine*.

Only he wasn't mine. We were friends who had kissed, and no more.

To convey all this, I said, "We're making babka."

"What's babka?" He came to my side. "Hi, Mrs. Barbanel. Ms. Levin."

"It's a chocolate pastry." To my mom and aunt, I said, "Tyler made the mini chocolate-and-cranberry cakes at the Christmas party." I felt a surge of pride in Tyler, which made no sense, given I had nothing to do with Tyler's skills.

Mom started to respond but was interrupted as Rose came barreling into the room. "Shira! We need you!" She pulled to a stop and stared at Tyler. "You. Again."

"Guilty as charged."

"You can't have Shira; we have precedence," she said quickly.

"The babka has precedence," I told her. "I'm supervising these two."

Mom rolled her eyes. "We're not children."

Rose and I didn't laugh, but we didn't not laugh, either.

"Okay, Rose," I said. "Lead on. Tyler can come with us."

Up in the cousins' room, final touches were being put on scenes and costumes. With the play delayed several days, the triplets had decided they had time to tweak several scenes and make a whole warehouse full of props. Rose led me over to one corner, where Gabe and Iris were essentially frothing at the mouth. Iris noticed me first. "Shira! Tell Gabe he *has* to be an elephant. We need more elephants in the scene where the Maccabees are harrying Antiochus and his army, and he *refuses*."

"It wouldn't make sense." Gabe jutted out his chin, a

twelve-year-old lawyer in training. "I'm the *king* of the Seleucids. I can't pop up as an *elephant*. It'll confuse the audience!"

"You're the king in the *other story line*. It won't confuse anyone," Iris said hotly. "And you'll be wearing a trunk and ears. They won't recognize you."

"It undermines my authority as an imperial emperor."

Iris whirled on me. "*Shira*! Tell him! It's my play."

"*I'm* the talent," Gabe said. "It screws with my performance if I have to transition back and forth from emperor to elephant."

I rubbed my forehead. "How many elephants do we have right now?" Was *I* an elephant? Surely I would know if I played an elephant.

"One. Oliver. No one's going to be impressed by an army with only one elephant."

"I think one elephant is still really impressive." I chewed on my lip. "What if Gabe isn't an elephant but a general? So you get another impressive soldier but Gabe gets to retain his, ah, imperial, militaristic attitude."

"I suppose," she said grudgingly, then looked behind me. "I hope you don't expect a role."

Tyler spread his hands. "I could be an elephant, if it helped."

Iris turned bright red and looked away. "You can build sets and make props."

"Yes, ma'am."

"We don't have to make props," I told Tyler, because what if he had only come here to make out, not hang out with my giant, demanding family? Though he hadn't indicated he wanted to so much as brush my shoulder with his again.

He grinned at me, his real smile. "It sounds fun."

We made swords, cutting blades and pommels out from cardboard with X-Acto knives, wrapping the blades with tinfoil. "Arbiter of elephants and emperors." Tyler's eyes twinkled. "I'm impressed."

"Elephants, emperors, video games, toys, blankies, dreidels—I've done it all."

"I'm surprised you're not the captain of team sports."

"Are you kidding? I like a chance to relax," I said automatically, then paused. I'd actually never even considered team sports, I'd been so focused on piano and skating, and teams suggested a camaraderie I wasn't used to. But I supposed keeping my family on task was practically a sport.

"Since Isaac's gone, who are you seducing?" Tyler snagged a leftover sufganiyah from a nearby plate, taking a bite and getting powdered sugar all over his fingers and mouth, not to mention raspberry jelly.

Relief bloomed in my chest. So we were still flirting, at least. "Why? Are you angling for the role?"

He valiantly tried to lick himself clean, catlike. "If you have to seduce *someone*, I'd rather it was me."

"You should be so lucky." I grabbed a tissue from the box

nearby and handed it to him. "Anyway, I've been demoted to handmaid."

"Maybe the handmaid needs to seduce someone." He raised his brows. "An off-the-clock soldier. I bet the two of them would have a great time when Judith is beheading generals."

"Maybe." I said, heat curling through me. I wanted to scoot closer to him, to climb onto his lap and twist my arms around his neck, only we were surrounded by my family, and I didn't know if I'd be brave enough even if we weren't. Tyler flirted with the same ease as breathing, so while I wanted this to mean he liked me as much as I liked him, it could simply mean we'd established a solid friendship. "Probably only in order to murder him, too, so they could get away without witnesses."

"At least he'd die happy."

I rolled my eyes. "You're too much. And you have jam on your cheek."

He wiped at one cheek. "Gone?"

"No."

He wiped at the other cheek and failed, then looked at me imploringly. I leaned closer and smoothed the jam away, then, without thinking, licked my finger. Our eyes caught, and something sparked in Tyler's. A matching heat lit deep in my stomach, the embers of a blazing desire.

I looked away. Part of me wanted to think it was impossible for me to feel so strongly for someone and not have it be matched in return. But I'd made the mistake of thinking that before. Tyler liked me, yes, but you could like someone without wanting to date them. And Tyler had explicitly said he didn't see the point in relationships. You had to believe what people told you. I couldn't let myself get swept away by delusions of romance.

I swallowed a groan and concentrated on the sword before me.

We spent the afternoon making props for the triplets, an easy camaraderie between us edged by fire every time our arms brushed or eyes caught. As we fit cardboard helmets to the littles' heads while they squirmed and giggled, I found myself laughing so hard my stomach cramped. Looking around, I found everyone in similarly good moods—Noah and Abby fake dying in a corner, Ethan and Gabe monologuing in tandem, Miriam and Oliver leading a revolution, David helping the triplets. It made my chest so full, it hurt.

Smiling, I looked up at Tyler, only to see a look of naked longing on his face. "Are you okay?"

He started, and an expression of easy comfort fell back into place. "Yeah, why?"

I pulled a face. "Tyler."

He made a face right back at me. "Fine." His gaze wandered through the crowded room. "I guess my moms' wanting a big family rubbed off on me."

"Ah." I started coloring a curved piece of white cardboard red—the plume we'd put on Gabe's helmet to mark him as a general. "So if you bring your moms back into the family fold by, say, landing an internship at my uncle's company and impressing everyone, you might get your big family, too."

He gave me a startled glance. "Maybe. Yes. I've considered it."

"But you have no idea if a job would change your mom's relationship with her parents. And it seems to me like if your parents and grandparents are fighting about how you were raised when you turned out pretty well, they have deeper issues."

"Ugh." He pulled on his hair. "You're not wrong."

I smiled. "I'm never wrong."

"I wish I had a magic wand to make everything better."

"Don't we all. But I think anything with your moms and grandparents has to come from them."

"Isn't it like what you're trying to do with your grandparents, though, with the play? Making them better?"

Our plans for the play would, fingers crossed, make my grandparents remember they'd once liked each other. "I guess I'm trying to create an opening for them to talk to each other; I'm not trying to do something for them to react to. It needs to come from them."

He blew out a breath. "So you think I shouldn't email your uncle."

"You should if you want to. My dad says it's important to explore all paths you're interested in, to make sure you're settling on the right one. But I think if you do, it should be for *you*, not for your parents or grandparents."

"Hmm," he said. "Maybe. It'd be ironic if I landed an intro to the CEO of Danziger Media and decided I didn't want it."

"If you ever want more family, you can borrow some of mine."

"You joke," he said, taking in the room full of cousins, "but I like them." His phone buzzed, and he glanced at it. "Shoot, I told my moms I'd be home to help with dinner."

"Oh." Disappointment weighed down my stomach. Would he leave now? I'd had a great time hanging out, but I'd sort of thought . . . Well, I shouldn't have bothered thinking anything. "Okay."

I walked him to the door and watched him lace up his boots. Here he'd given me all the flirting advice in the world, and I couldn't think how to use it to any avail; all I wanted was to kiss him, to tell him I liked him, and I still found those things hard. "Thanks for coming over."

"Of course. I had fun."

We both hesitated, neither of us moving. I smiled up at Tyler, all nervousness and anticipation, like an effervescent bubble, my emotions shifting, swirling colors, and inevitably going to pop. Tyler looked almost nervous. The moment stretched.

Then he was leaning down and his lips brushed against mine. I rose up to meet him, hands sliding up his chest before weaving through his hair. We were in the foyer of Golden Doors, and anyone could walk in or by at any second, and yet I didn't have any control over myself; I didn't even care. I pressed up, intensifying the kiss, awash with heat.

Then footsteps in the hall brought me to my senses. We broke apart, breathing hard. "Wow," Tyler said, his eyes wide. "We should have found a time to do this earlier."

Delight rushed through me. "It's a very crowded house."

He looked around, as though a private space would suddenly spring into being. "Do you want to—I don't suppose there's anywhere—"

"Miri and Abby are always running in and out of our room," I said regretfully. "And all the other rooms sort of bleed into each other."

"Well." He looked rueful. "I guess that's the one benefit of having a small family."

I laughed, giddy. He liked me. Or at least he liked kissing me. Maybe we'd spend the rest of break kissing.

"What are you doing tomorrow?" he asked.

"Depends." A smile played around my lips. "Got any good ideas?"

"Turns out I'm really good at making tinfoil swords."

The smile pushed so hard at the corners of my cheeks, it hurt. "I happen to know somewhere your skill will be appreciated."

"See you tomorrow, then," he said, and with a quick brush of his thumb against my lips, he was gone.

✳ ✳ ✳

Back upstairs, I faced a tribunal of cousins. "So," Ethan said. "What's the deal?"

A very good question. What was the deal? I wanted Tyler, and Tyler wanted me—but what did wanting *mean*? Tyler was probably used to this state of limbo, but I wasn't, and this not knowing what we were doing made me feel wobbly and on edge as soon as Tyler disappeared from sight and the serotonin from his presence vanished.

"There's no deal," I told the expectant David, Noah, and Ethan. "We're just friends."

"Okay," David drawled. *"Friends."*

"I like him. As a person," I said firmly. "But nothing's happening between us."

"It looks like something's happening," Noah said.

"It's not." Then, with a burst of bravery, I lifted my chin. "Actually, you know what? Even if something was, it'd be fine. I can do what I want."

"So something *is* happening," David said. "I can't believe you didn't tell me."

I glanced at the middles playing video games on the other side of the room. "Shh." Then I looked at Noah. "You don't have to protect me."

"Right," he said, like he understood my words intellectually if not emotionally. "Yeah."

"Look, I *like* Tyler. He's smarter and funnier and more interesting than I think any of us had given him credit for." I thought about how Tyler had looked when he was watching my family before he'd realized I was watching him. The length he was willing to go to to impress his grandparents, so his moms could have the big family atmosphere they missed. How he'd wanted to know why I liked him, and the way he always asked questions instead of answering them, and how his polished facade circled him like a force field whenever he was around other people. I thought about how much Tyler, like me, needed friends. "We should give him a chance."

The boys looked at each other skeptically. "You're the boss," Ethan finally said. "If you say he's in, he's in."

"That's what I thought." I looked at David, who nodded, then at Noah. "Noah?"

Noah frowned, then finally released it with a sigh. "Fine. We'll give him a chance."

A burst of satisfaction ran through me, and I beamed at my cousins. Maybe that had been the point of this holiday all along: not romance or lessons in flirting or even kissing Tyler Nelson, but figuring out friendships. Not just for me, but for Tyler, too. Because maybe we needed those more than we'd realized.

And maybe, miraculously, we'd get them.

CHAPTER
TWENTY-ONE

ut, okay, in addition to friendship, I really wanted to
know what Tyler and I were doing.

I couldn't fall asleep, tossing and turning and staring
at the ceiling for hours, listening to Abby and Miriam
breathe. When I was with Tyler, I felt on top of the world, but
when I had a minute to think about what this was—or wasn't—I
felt unsettled, unmoored. Unease rippled beneath my skin. I
wanted, very clearly, to date him, but what if Tyler just wanted an
easy hookup through the end of the holidays?

I ached whenever I thought of him, and I thought of him all
the time.

I knew I should talk to him, but what if bringing up dating
made Tyler think I was clingy and obsessive and he called it all
off? In which case, sure, his loss. But also very definitely my

loss. Maybe, instead, I should maintain the status quo, and Tyler would realize he was having such a great time and that he wanted to date. Maybe I could be cool and chill and casual.

I rolled over and squeezed my eyes shut. I was driving myself insane.

Finally, finally, I fell asleep, and when I came down the next morning after sleeping in, an unexpected sight greeted me: Tyler, standing next to my mom and across from my aunt, carefully measuring cocoa, sugar, and flour into a mixing bowl. Mom held a measuring cup full of melted butter and watched Tyler with the kind of furrowed brows I reserved for difficult chem homework.

"Hi." I stared at this bewildering trio, my focus landing on the odd man out. "What's going on?"

He looked up, and I noticed a dusting of cocoa powder on his cheek. My entire chest felt warm and full to see him here. "I came over to see if you wanted to go for a walk. But . . ."

"You can't have him," Aunt Rachel said. "We're desperate."

"There's so many more steps," Mom said. "I thought day two would be the easy day?"

Tyler studied the recipe. "Day two can be the easy day. If you make the streusel and filling and syrup the day before," Tyler said, then flinched under their combined glares. "Sorry."

I smothered a smile. "I can help."

"Grab the dough," Tyler said. "I'll make the simple syrup." He poured sugar into a measuring cup of water and popped it into the microwave.

"Why don't we let you kids finish this off!" Mom said brightly.

I glared at her. "No. You break it, you buy it."

Mom gave a beleaguered sigh, but I noticed she was very excited to stir the butter into the flour mix to create a streusel topping for the cake.

I wanted to believe baking with my family meant Tyler was into me more seriously—who baked babka with their friend with benefits's mom?—but honestly, Tyler really liked baking, so I couldn't use that as evidence.

By the time we finished, we were all covered in dough and chocolate. Tyler and I retreated to the kitchen sink to scrub ourselves clean. He glanced over at me, shamefaced. "Sorry I came over with no warning. I thought I'd get a chance to check if you wanted to hang out before . . . hanging out for an hour."

"Are you kidding? Now I get to have cake for breakfast. If you hadn't appeared, they might have given up." I dried my hands, then handed him the dishcloth. "You're good with parents."

"I'm good with everyone."

I rolled my eyes at his cockiness. "Yeah, but you seem like *you* with them. You're relaxed."

"Guess fifty-something women are my people."

"I shouldn't be surprised."

The babka came out delicious. We didn't even have to send

around a middle to collect anyone; the family came tripping out of the woodwork like children lured by the Pied Piper. "This is very good," Noah said, which might have been the first nice thing I'd ever heard my cousin say to Tyler.

Tyler looked down at his plate, his cheeks pink. "Thanks."

I could have sat in the great room forever with my family and Tyler, but then my phone pinged. I looked at Tyler. "I told Olivia I'd meet up with her and her boyfriend—"

"Cool." He started rising from his seat beside me on the couch. "I'll head out—"

"No, I meant—Tyler." I grabbed his arm. It felt good and secure, and I tugged on it because I could, and it made him look down at me, gaze serious. "Do you want to hang out with us?"

He blinked. And stared at me. "Okay."

Something good fizzed in my belly.

In town the four of us wandered from shop to shop. Jackson was a quiet, serious guy who liked birds and snowboarding. It was easier to bring Tyler to hang out with him than with my cousins: he didn't know the ins and outs of Tyler's and my history, or at least didn't care. The four of us were easy together, laid-back and playful, and I didn't see Tyler put on a fake smile once.

At two, we squeezed into a table at Born & Bread for sandwiches. Jackson told us about his family's Christmas drama, and Olivia gave us the update on her family's New Year's party. "There's all these rules about *The Nutcracker*," she said. "You're not supposed to have Clara and the Nutcracker dance a pas de deux, and you're not supposed to have any dancing when the tree grows or the overture is played—you're supposed to be concentrating on the music."

"Not sure Tchaikovsky reckoned for twenty-first-century attention spans," Jackson said.

She stuck her tongue out at him. "I'm pretty sure we can handle five minutes of music before squirming."

"Speak for yourself."

Olivia looked over at me. "Change your mind about playing for us?"

"I'd probably suck even if I wanted to," I said. "I haven't played for anyone in years."

"Eh, it's a pretty easy arrangement."

I opened my mouth to say no, then paused. "I wouldn't want to screw you guys up if you've already practiced with your mom playing . . ."

Olivia leaned forward. "Oh my god, no, pretty sure she'll be so busy hosting she's going to play it from the stereo if her dignity allows."

"Well . . . if you want to send the sheet music over . . ."

"Yes!" she squealed. "Maybe you can also wear a tutu."

"Pass."

Olivia and Jackson headed back to her place, and Tyler and I drove out to Madaket to walk along the beach. Papery grass grew between the cliffs and the water's edge, and brown seaweed lay on the sand. The world was carved in four: the land, the sea, the shore, the sky. White crests lapped against the sand. The wind whipped across the Atlantic, harsher than on the other side of the island, uninterrupted for thousands of miles. We bent our heads as we walked, hats pulled low, everything all dull yellows and gray greens, clouds streaking the washed-out sky.

Then the setting sun emerged from behind a cloud, fierce and blinding. It made the ocean unbearable to look at. The white-hot reflection of the sun stretched to the shore, seeming to come right to our feet. I looked at Tyler. I wanted to ask him what we were doing, what he *wanted* to be doing. Though maybe he didn't plan so far out; maybe he was simply enjoying the time we had before we returned home. Was the secret to happiness doing what you wanted in the moment and not worrying about the future? Not dwelling on the past if it didn't work out?

"Are you happy?" I asked.

"Very existential." Our feet left prints in the hard, wet sand. "Do you mean right now or in a larger sense?"

God, I didn't know. "A larger sense."

"I'm generally happy," he said. "I wasn't as a kid because first I was bullied, and then I thought everyone was stupid, but now . . . NYU's pretty great. I feel free to act however I want since no one expects anything from me."

The blank slate of college. It sounded amazing. If I wasn't aloof Shira Barbanel, who could I be? "Do you act differently than in high school? Less . . . polished?"

He shot me a wry glance. "I guess I still . . . prefer to ask people about their interests instead of tell them about mine, but it feels better than it used to. I think because I'm more interested in what they have to say than I used to be."

"How so?"

He shrugged. "When I started high school, I asked people questions to draw them out, to get them comfortable and liking me, not because I cared. I thought people were boring, basic. Now I like talking to people about their passions. Makes them come alive. And you learn something."

"But you should also be talking about *your* passions."

"In my defense, they don't usually ask."

"*I'll* ask," I said, feeling oddly protective of him. "Hey, Tyler. Bake anything exciting lately? Read anything good?"

He burst into laughter.

"What?" I fought back a grin. "I'm serious! I want to know what you're reading."

"I know you are." He reached out and tucked a curl behind my ear, and I froze, startled by the intimacy of the gesture. "I'm rereading Squirrel Girl, a series from when I was a kid—I have some of the collections here. And my moms gave me the *Bread Baker's Bible* for Christmas, so I've been reading the intro." He tilted his head. "Why are you asking about being happy?"

I didn't move, unwilling to when we stood so close. "My grandmother and I were talking. She said it's not easy to be happy. And . . ." I hesitated, looking out at the sea, squinting at the sun. "I was thinking about how I'm happy on Nantucket but not so much when I'm not here. But also about what I need to be happy. I used to think I needed something *epic*."

"Like how you felt about skating?" he asked.

"Yeah. Something . . . capable of filling every hour of every day. Something burned into my muscles and my mind. But—those things burned me out, too. They burned away my joy in them."

Maybe something less obliterating would actually make me happier.

"So what do you want now?"

I looked at the water, now the color of sea glass—translucent green, a sheen of gold sun glossing over a streak at the horizon—then back at him. "Maybe the same things as before but with less pressure? Maybe the people who I like being around." I swallowed. "You make me happy."

He smiled, soft and real. "You make me happy, too."

So maybe we could keep being happy. We could carry whatever this was from the contained snow globe of Nantucket back to New York. I wanted to ask him if he wanted that, too, but I was scared I'd hear something I didn't like. And that would ruin everything.

So I stood on my tiptoes and kissed him. Kissed him until we'd generated enough heat that our jackets were redundant, kissed until our lips were chapped and we were as close together as we could possibly be on a beach at sunset in a dozen layers.

When the sun had drowned itself, and it was too dark and too cold to stay out any longer, we went back to his house and sat in the living room and talked. I hadn't known talking could be so easy with a boy, hadn't known thoughts and words could expand forever, hadn't known how fun it was to say nothing with someone you liked.

We had dinner at his house, and when I left, I invited him to Golden Doors the next day like it was the easiest thing in the world, and he said yes.

"Oh, you're here," David said when Tyler entered the cousins' room the next day—the last day of the year. "You can be on Shira's team."

"What?" Tyler asked. He shoved his hands in the front pocket of his sweatshirt, looking confused. And adorable.

"It's you, me, Abby, Ethan, Gabe, and Rose. Against that lot." I gestured at Noah, Miriam, Oliver, Iris, Lily, and David, then went back to cutting up small slips of paper. "I hope you're good at this."

"At . . . what?"

"Shira's a shark," David said. "But not a very good one."

"Oh, come on," I said. "The fact you couldn't recognize my fin as a fin was pitiful."

"She clomped." Ethan straightened his arms and clapping his hands together before his face to illustrate. "Like an alligator."

"Sharks clomp, too!"

Abby took pity on Tyler. "We're playing charades, apparently."

"Salad bowl," my family corrected her in unison.

"Charades," she said again. "With multiple rounds and rules."

"They're never going to let me forget the shark thing," I muttered to Tyler as he sat next to me. "But they're the fools. Ha! I had a *fin*." I waved my hand by my side to demonstrate. "Do alligators have fins?"

"How long ago was the shark thing?" Tyler asked.

"Three years," David said. "We have long memories."

"I noticed."

"Did you know elephants really do have long memories?" Oliver, our one elephant for the play, slotted in. "Their matriarchs lead herds and remember their friends and locations."

"Like sperm whales," Tyler said, sliding a glance at me. "And Nantucket girls."

"Clearly whales and elephants and Nantucket girls know what's up," I said, distributing pieces of paper. "Everyone write down seven nouns. First round is describing without saying the word, second is one word, third is charades, fourth is charades under a blanket."

"Under . . . a blanket?"

I suppressed a smile. "I said what I said."

Then I started laughing, and after a bemused moment, so did he.

Salad bowl dissolved around 3:00, and the cousins split into smaller groups—the triplets made last-minute preparations for the play, a group went to eat, Miriam and Abby pulled out books. I tugged Tyler away. "Come with me," I said, feeling bold and adventurous and *fun*, and I liked the feeling, liked feeling pretty and desired and a little bit wild. "I have an idea."

"A good idea or a bad idea?"

"All my ideas are good." I led him to the third floor, to the very center, and flourished my hands at the attic door.

"You're kidding."

"You're right. It's a *great* idea."

We pulled down the ladder, and Tyler gestured to me to go up first. I did, remembering the last time we had done this. "I thought you wanted to look at my ass last time this happened."

"Shira! I am a gentleman," he said with mock-affront. "I would *never* admit that."

I laughed and climbed into the attic, then pulled the ladder and door up behind me once Tyler had followed. "Nice place," he said. "You wanna look for some New Year's decorations? Trip over some floorboards?"

"I don't hate it." I took a seat on one of the old wooden chairs and tried to look up at him flirtatiously. "In fact—ah!"

The chair had not, apparently, been resigned to the attic because it no longer matched its downstairs brethren but because it no longer had structural integrity. A leg had given out, and I crashed forward in a rumpled heap.

"Are you okay?" Tyler rushed over, kneeling by my side.

"Ugh." I rolled over. "I think I bruised my hip. But otherwise, I'm fine."

"Are you sure?" He peered down at me with concern.

I lifted my hand and tugged at his shirt collar. "Would you like to kiss it better?"

His concern melted away, replaced by a smile. "If you insist."

God, I liked him.

And I liked this so much. It was passionate and exciting and new and addictive, and I wanted to kiss him forever and ever; I wanted to lie next to him and feel his skin against mine, the inhale and exhale of his breath, feel the cold of his toes—I wanted all of it. All of him.

Maybe this *didn't* have to come to its inevitable end. Maybe we could continue in New York. We weren't so far apart, not if you hopped the 1, 2, 3 lines. Tyler might not want a high schooler showing up at the dorms—I could not imagine anything less cool for a college boy—but I was a city girl, and I knew all the places tourists liked to go. And Tyler was still sort of a tourist, wasn't he? He'd only been in New York one semester. We could go to the High Line and Chelsea Market, and I'd show him the best parts of Central Park and ice cream in the East Village, and we'd go to the Brooklyn Botanic Garden and—

No. Tyler wasn't looking for a girlfriend or a tour guide, and I wasn't looking to torture myself. I would live in the moment. I would accrue enough experience over the next few days that I would have the confidence to embark on actual relationships.

I took a deep breath, trying to focus on something beyond Tyler and me. "Do you think there's any other secrets hidden up here?"

"You could knock on every floorboard to find out."

"Maybe I will." If there were other secrets, I wanted to find them. I wanted to know more about Sarah. Had she been unhappy with her husband or her marriage? How long did her affair last, and who was it with? "I get a teen hiding away her ex's stuff, but an adult doing that somehow seems . . . sadder." I wandered over to the secret compartment. "Maybe we missed something."

Tyler watched me as I pulled up the floorboard. "Careful. Maybe there'll be mice."

"Ha ha." I swept my phone's flashlight around the hollow, and once more only found dust and cobwebs. But out of curiosity, I reached my hand in, trailing my fingers around the bottom and the sides. Just in case.

The fourth side wobbled.

"What was that?" I said, wide-eyed.

"What?"

"Look—the fourth side—it didn't feel stable."

Tyler came over, and we both lay down on our stomachs to peer at the long wall of the cubbyhole. I poked at it once, twice, and then it swung inward.

"Jesus," Tyler whispered. "I can't believe we missed that."

"We're the worst Sherlock and Watson ever."

"Who's who?"

"Obviously I'm Sherlock. *Duh*." I reached inside and pulled out a wrapped bundle. Very carefully this time, I checked for any other objects or fake walls. Nothing.

We placed the bundle on the floor between us. It was a coarse sackcloth bag. From it, I drew a pair of trousers, a belt, and a long strip of cloth.

"I don't get it," Tyler said. "She kept her lover's clothes?"

But I wasn't looking at the trousers or the belt. I was looking at the long band of cloth: thick, sturdy cotton; ten inches wide; a dozen or more feet long. My breath came faster as I slid the fabric through my fingers. "These weren't her lover's clothes."

"Who else's would they have been?"

I thought of the painting we'd found, of the young, handsome man dressed for sea. I thought of what Sarah Barbanel had said, about whether she'd known anyone on the whaleship. *Not for a very long time.* I thought about how Sarah had gone off to

350

finishing school and disappeared from the record until she married Marcus Barbanel. "Hers."

He stared at me.

Sarah hadn't been in *love* with a sailor. She'd *been* one. "She could have used this cloth to bind her breasts. She could have been the young man in the painting. The chockpin wasn't a gift—it was hers. She wore it, used it. The seashells belonged to her. It was all hers."

"Women weren't whalers in the 1800s," Tyler said.

"Some were. Women disguised themselves as men to join the Civil War. And the American Revolution. Whaling captains' wives sailed with them. Maybe Sarah never went to finishing school. Maybe she went to sea."

"And what, continued even after getting married?" Tyler asked, still skeptical. "The quarterboard came from way after their marriage."

"She didn't have to have been on the ship when it wrecked. She could have sailed on it, decades before."

"Maybe," Tyler said slowly.

"You looked up the sailors from the time of the wreck, right? We could look up the crew from earlier, from when Sarah left for finishing school." I pulled up the photo with the dates on my phone. "She left home in 1821 and married Marcus in 1826."

Tyler pulled up the New Bedford whaling database, which contained crew lists for almost a hundred years. He pulled the voyages out of New Bedford for the *Rosemary* in the early nine-teenth century, including a departure in 1821. "We can compare the names here to the voyages before and after," I said. "She wouldn't have been on those—she would have been with her parents or married—but if there's a name on this list only . . ."

We compared the lists, scanning for a name unique to 1821, a name a girl called Sarah Fersztenfeld might have found easy to answer to.

Sam Ferston. Sam first appeared on the *Rosemary* in 1821, and never again.

Sam Ferston. Sarah Fersztenfeld.

A rush of satisfied adrenaline washed through me. It all made sense. It all clicked. I leaned back and grinned. "Sam Ferston. That's her."

"Still conjecture," Tyler said.

"Sure," I agreed, searching *sam ferston* on my phone and coming up with no results. And yes, even if Sam Ferston had been around for more than one ship voyage, he might not have a huge internet footprint. But he might have a tombstone or a marriage turned up by Google. "It could be a coincidence. But it'd be a good coincidence." I stared at the name again. *Sam Ferston.*

"You have to admit, it sounds pretty wild."

"It does," I agreed. *Wild.* How apt. She had been wild. I lay down flat on the floor, staring in stunned contemplation at the peaked wooden ceiling. "I think I'm right, though. It feels right."

Tyler lay down as well, in the opposite direction so only our heads were next to each other. "Yeah. You could be."

"Can you even imagine? What a terrifying, brave thing to do. Disguising your identity, choosing a new one. Choosing a new life."

"Why would she even do it?"

"Why wouldn't she?" I gestured at the peaked ceiling, at the world beyond, at history. "Freedom. Choice. Options. She grew up in a time when girls worried about marriages and husbands if they wanted a secure future. Maybe she wanted something else. Something more out of life. Maybe she wanted adventure. Passion."

"Seems like a pretty dangerous adventure."

"Well, she only lasted one trip." Was that why she stopped? Because the grueling nature of life on a whaleship, of hunting and traveling, took more out of her than she'd expected? Or had she been discovered? Had she tried something she thought would make her happy, only to realize it wasn't at all what she wanted?

But at least she had tried.

I rolled onto my stomach, propping myself up on my elbows so I could look into Tyler's face. The light slid across the unfinished attic, long and languid and golden. "We've spent all this time thinking this was about a woman who built her life around a man. Who was sad about a lost lover or a forced marriage.

But we missed the whole point, the whole story. Sarah's life was about *her*."

Tyler nodded. "Though in our defense, it was way more likely to think a nineteenth-century woman's secrets were tied to marriage."

Was it? Or had we thought that merely because it was the story we were used to hearing, the one we'd heard so many times we forgot others existed? It would have been even harder, I imagined, to choose to live a story you'd never heard before, but Sarah had. She'd known what she wanted to do, and she had done it. She'd done something hard and stressful and dangerous. She'd done it for years.

What if we all did that? Burst through the confines of other people's expectations and grabbed what we wanted. Maybe it hadn't made her happy forever—maybe she'd been forced to give up sailing too early, or she'd given it up because she hated whaling—but I found it both invigorating and bittersweet that she'd created a treasure trove not about a man but about her own life. What would I put in such a box? Skates and sheets of music? But what if I didn't have to lock them away forever? We didn't have such hard lines around my passions as Sarah had around what she wanted to do.

I didn't know if Sarah Barbanel had been happy. But I knew she'd been brave.

I wanted to be brave.

CHAPTER
TWENTY-TWO

I arrived at the Phans' an hour and a half before the party started to run through the song with Olivia and her sister before the guests arrived. My family and Tyler's would both be arriving later in the main crush.

Olivia and Kaitlyn both wore white Romantic tutus, the long, gauzy white skirts giving them a dreamy appearance. "You look gorgeous," I told them.

"So do you," Olivia said. She nodded at my dress, red with black detailing. "I love this."

The Phans had a particularly impressive foyer, sporting a two-story ceiling, perfect for displaying their elegant Christmas tree. The piano had its own private alcove to the side, and I warmed up as Olivia and Kaitlyn put on their pointe shoes. As expected, they nailed the dance; both girls had been in ballet for over a decade. Afterward, the three of us—along with Jackson—helped their parents with last-minute preparations.

The Phans had taken *The Nutcracker* theme seriously: their house, usually cool colors and simple elegance, had been transformed into a Victorian mansion. Golden cords held back red-velvet drapes framing the windows, plush red carpets lined the floor. Multiple small conifers had been added to their collection of houseplants, and their impeccably decorated Christmas tree stood at the bottom of the stairs, where the sisters would dance.

"The tree grows," Olivia told me.

"I'm sorry, what?"

"It's a key part of *The Nutcracker*. Clara shrinks down to toy-sized, and the tree grows."

"Trees don't actually grow, though."

Olivia grinned. "Hate to break it to you . . ."

"You know what I mean! Christmas trees don't grow. They're dead."

She pushed out her lower lip. "Now I'm sad."

"How does it grow?"

"You'll just have to wait and find out."

The Phans had made a feast for the evening: spring rolls and banh mi and sticky rice, salads and tiny cannoli and French 75s. We straightened things up right until the clock ticked eight, and guests started arriving.

I'd always loved New Year's—I always spent it with my family,

after all—but I'd never been the kind of person who made res-
olutions, or, god forbid, stuck to them. Sometimes, as midnight
struck and people counted down, I flung some half-baked hope
into the universe with the same amount of thought and foresight
I put into making a wish as I blew out my birthday candles (none).

But tonight, as Olivia, Kaitlyn, and I got ready for the performance, I realized I did have a resolution. I wanted to be more
confident. I wanted to define myself, be who *I* wanted to be as
opposed to letting how other people perceived me be a factor. I
wanted to let people in more. I wanted to take risks. Perhaps not
ones as drastic as disguising myself as a man and going on a
multiyear voyage, but whatever my version of that might be.

By nine, everyone had arrived: my family, in one massive
influx of dark-eyed, curly-haired brunettes; friends of the Phans
who had been convinced to come to the island for the holiday;
and islanders I had known my whole life—year-rounders who had
slowly warmed up to some of the summer people.

I saw Tyler and his moms arrive. He'd changed outfits since
the attic, trading his sweatshirt and jeans for a gray sweater and
darker gray slacks. Every time I saw him, my heart rate picked up.
He scanned the crowd, and when he found me, a smile bloomed
on his face, and I could feel a matching one on mine.

The crowd shifted, and I lost sight of him; too many people in
fancy outfits blocking my view. And I didn't have time to think
about Tyler, anyway: with almost all the guests here, I could see

Olivia's mom looking round, getting ready to officially welcome everyone to the party and for the ballet sequence to start.

I stood by Olivia at the piano, both of us trying to wrangle our nerves. I swallowed, hard. Here was another thing I could do—something else I'd always felt too embarrassed to say out loud. "Can I tell you something kind of silly? Or—sentimental?"

"Please." Olivia ran her hand over her hair, which had been pulled back in a tight, high bun. "Especially if it's going to distract me from performing in front of fifty people. God, how can your cousins do a play for *fun*?"

"Because it's only for family." My throat felt tight and I felt ridiculous and stupid, and I pushed through it anyway. "You're my best friend."

She stared at me, her face unchanging. My stomach sank. *Oh.*

God, why was I such an idiot? Of course this was a stupid thing to do. Who just told someone they were your best friend out of nowhere?

Wait. No. That was a bad thought. It wasn't *embarrassing* or stupid to like Olivia so much. Even if she didn't feel the same way.

Then she blinked. "Wait—you're not adding anything else?"

"What?" Now *I* was confused.

"You're not saying, 'You're my best friend, *but . . . but* you really don't know how to dance, *but* you should tell your mom to stop making you dance, *but* you're spending too much time thinking about where Jackson's going to school and you should go wherever you want'?"

"No, I—I just wanted to tell you you're my best friend."

"Shira!" She hugged me. "You're so sweet! You're my best friend, too."

"No, I mean—" This conversation had not gone how I expected. I didn't want her to return an empty platitude; I wanted her to know how sincerely I meant it. "Not just here on Nantucket, but everywhere. You're really my best, best friend."

"Are you okay?" She looked worried. "Is something wrong?"

"No." I shook my head quickly. "Um. I hadn't said it before. So I wanted to say it, because I want to be better about—I don't know—having friends at all. I feel like I keep most people at arm's length. But not you."

"Hey. Shira." She cupped my face in her hands. "You're my best friend, too."

My chest felt like it was full of so much air, like the whole world was air. "Really?"

"Really! Of course! You've always been my best friend. I love you."

"Oh." My voice came out higher than usual and I blinked rapidly, emotions I'd kept inside bubbling to the surface and bursting and dissipating—fear of rejection and anxiety and tension—leaving relief behind. "I love you, too."

"Oh my god, are you going to cry? Don't cry." She hugged me

again, longer this time. "I mean, you can cry, but your makeup is so good right now, and your mascara isn't waterproof."

I started laughing and pressed the heels of my hands beneath my watery eyes. "True."

She rubbed her hands up and down my arms. "Also, you'll make me cry, and I'm about to dance, and everyone's going to stare at me."

I grinned at her. At my best friend. "Okay. You're going to be great."

"Hello, everyone!" Olivia's mom clinked a spoon against her glass from the foyer stairs. "Thank you for coming!"

The crowd quieted. I looked around and saw my family, saw Tyler looking right at me again, and joy filled me, so bright and real it hurt.

"It's so wonderful to have so many of our friends and family here on New Year's Eve, especially since we know this is a bit farther than a commute to the South End." There was a gentle ripple of laughter. "But we're thrilled to get to spend time with all of you, and to get to share Nantucket, one of our favorite places on earth, with so many people who haven't been here before." She thanked several people in particular, adding a few light jokes before finishing: "And so to wrap up our year, we'd like to treat you to a performance of 'The March of the Nutcracker' from *The Nutcracker*, performed by my daughters, Olivia and Kaitlyn, and accompanied by their friend Shira on the piano."

She gestured, and the lights dimmed for most of the room. Only a few stayed on at the base of the stairs where Olivia and Kaitlyn would dance, along with my little light to read and play music by.

And the tree grew.

Okay, it didn't really grow. But it must have been on a small platform, like a standing desk, which rose several feet. From somewhere, a projector cast larger green branches against the existing tree and walls. Everyone laughed and applauded. Mrs. Phan nodded to me, and I took a deep breath and started to play.

✳ ✳ ✳

Olivia was wonderful.

I didn't see much of the performance as it happened because I was looking at the piano, but I could feel the energy in the room, hear the applause—and immediately afterward, I saw the video Olivia's mom had taken, which confirmed said greatness.

I couldn't get over how much *fun* I'd had, playing "The March" from *The Nutcracker*. I'd never thought about a live performance as being a good thing for either piano or skating; I'd thought of them more as a ring of judgment—or literal judges—there to tell me I hadn't done as well as I'd hoped. But this audience hadn't been here for me, so they felt easier to confront. It was *nice* to be part of this. It felt less like pushing myself hard and more like . . . floating. Relaxing. And happening to be part of something beautiful.

After the performance and the immediate review of the performance, when Olivia and her sister had been enveloped in well-wishers, I looked up, and Tyler stood before me.

"You were great," he said.

"I was decent," I corrected, but a small smile escaped me. "Thanks."

"How'd it feel?"

"Pretty good, actually. *Really* good."

"Good."

We smiled at each other. Just smiled, foolishly, happily. I didn't have to have something to say to Tyler—though I almost always had something to say—and I could still stare at him, and it didn't feel awkward or weird; it felt normal and good and easy and right.

"Also," he said, his gaze running down my red dress, which slipped and slid along my body, "you look stunning."

"Thank you," I said, smoothing my hands over the fabric and looking up at him shyly. "So do you."

"You're consistently stunning, in fact."

I laughed. "Too much," I told him. "Any more flattery and I'll explode."

He looped one of my curls around his finger. "We'll work on that."

That made it sound like we had a future, didn't it? If we'd be working on something together? Or was I reading too much into everything he said?

"Hey," I said, recalling something from the back corner of my mind, where it had been lurking for almost two weeks. "I have a question."

"Okay."

"Did you know I was on the plane? When we both flew here from JFK? Because I was *stunned* to realize you were."

"Are you serious?" He looked taken aback; his mouth actually parted in surprise. "We sat in the boarding area together for an hour."

"We did?"

"I kept trying to catch your eye. I thought you were purposefully ignoring me."

"Really?" I gaped at him. "Wow."

"I boarded after you. I sat a dozen rows in front, but—you seriously didn't notice me?" He shook his head when I shook mine. "Guess you really were over me."

"I'm still over you," I told him, in my constant quest to keep his ego in check.

"Don't worry," he said wryly. "I know."

I grinned at him. God, I *liked* him. "But you know," I said. "You're not so bad."

He took my hand, stroking my palm. "You're not so bad yourself."

An indefinable joy washed through me. I wouldn't forget this, the holiday lights and music, the way Tyler looked at me, the glow in my chest. Not if I lived to be a hundred years old. I'd never forget the way Tyler made me feel.

The rest of the party passed in a blur of conversation and Tchaikovsky and the swish of velvet. I sat on the floor of the Phans' open living room, wedged between Olivia and David, Tyler nearby. I ate too much and laughed until my stomach hurt. At some point, all the teenagers ended up outside, playing an impromptu game of freeze tag, surrounded by the stars and wind and sea.

"I love the stars here," I told Tyler, looping my arms around his neck. I tilted my head back, drinking in the night. Spots of light lay scattered across the black-velvet heavens. When I glanced at Tyler, I found him with the oddest expression on his face. "What are you thinking?"

"There's this old Russian fairy tale," he said slowly. "About two old people who desperately want a daughter, so they build her out of snow and she comes to life. But when spring comes, she melts away."

"But she returns the next winter," I said. "Doesn't she?"

"I guess so," he agreed.

I tilted my head. "Why were you thinking about it?"

He shrugged. "I guess you remind me of her."

"That's weird." I patted my cheeks with my giant mittens. "Don't think I'm made of snow."

He laughed, a long, unexpected laugh, and pulled me into a

hug, wrapping his arms around me and smothering me with his body. It felt amazing, being folded up in his embrace, warm and safe and like I never, ever wanted to leave. He tucked his face into my hair. "Shira," he murmured, and it was my name and a laugh and an endearment all at once.

I leaned my head back slightly, not enough to pull away, but enough so our faces could be aligned, so I could stand on my tiptoes and press my lips to his.

Just shy of midnight, we crowded back inside in time for the countdown, taking coupes of champagne or sparkling apple cider and joining the crowd of adults. Tyler stood next to me, or I stood next to him, and emotion as fizzy as the bubbles in our drinks coursed through me. This was what you spent your life chasing after: not work or success or genius, but whatever brought you this level of happiness and joy and comfort. This was what made life good.

"Twelve! Eleven! Ten!"

For me, it was these people who made me so happy: this collection of family and neighbors and friends, people I had known my whole life. My parents and my grandparents, my aunts and uncles—all people I loved more than words could describe.

"Nine! Eight! Seven!"

My cousins, who made me roll my eyes and laugh, who made me *me*.

"Six! Five! Four!"

Olivia, who had always been at my side, who had always let me in.

"Three! Two! One!"

Tyler. Who kissed me as the clock struck midnight, tasting sweetly of sparkling apple cider. Who was not what I had thought but so much more, so much better.

And as everyone cheered and raised their glasses, the implacable realization rose inside me. An obvious one. One I should have seen coming a hundred years ago, or at least two weeks ago. One I'd been trying to ignore.

I had fallen—deeply, irrevocably, stupidly—right back in love with Tyler Nelson.

And that meant I had to end things with him.

CHAPTER
TWENTY-THREE

The next day was January 1. New Year's Day.

Though I'd been up past midnight, I woke early to a light snowfall. I stared wide-eyed out the window, then threw my blankets off, climbed out of my cozy cocoon, and started getting ready.

Showered, I checked my phone, only to see a message from Tyler: **Good morning—happy new year's day!**

I stared at it, hands shaking.

A few weeks ago, I wouldn't have been able to fathom initiating a conversation about relationships with anyone, let alone two in a few days, but now . . . Tyler and I didn't want the same things. We worked in this bubble of Nantucket, where we lived next door and could wander over and make out and be casual. But in the real world?

I wanted more than Tyler wanted to give. I wanted everything. I didn't think it was bad or a flaw that Tyler didn't want a relationship the way I did, but settling for something I didn't want would make me miserable. And I didn't want to be miserable.

I texted him back: **Any chance I could come over this morning? Tyler: Sure.**

I shook the entire time I got ready, not that it took me long. I didn't bother with makeup or jewelry or hair, just pulled on leggings and my favorite sweatshirt, then dashed across the lawns. The morning light was still new and fresh, the gentle snowfall almost magical.

I texted once I arrived, and he immediately opened the doors, holding a finger to his lips. "They're still asleep," he whispered. He took my hand and we silently raced up to his room, stifling our footsteps and giggles.

Once there, though, I remembered I hadn't come over for fun. I sobered as I sat on the edge of his bed. He glowed at me. "Hi."

"Hi," I said back, and swallowed.

And then he kissed me, and all my thoughts fled from my head.

I kissed him back. He pulled me closer, so close I could feel every hard line of his body. It was addictive, not just kissing but this firm warmth, this contact up and down every part of me. We fell backward into his bed. I could do this forever, the press of our bodies, the play of our tongues. I pressed a hand to his shoulder, spreading my palm across the corded muscles. His hand slid under my shirt; his other skimmed up my leg, coming to a rest on my outer thigh.

God, I wanted this boy.

Too much.

Recalling myself, I put a hand on his chest to ward him off. "I don't think we should do this."

He sat up immediately, putting space between us. "Sorry—I didn't mean to pressure you—"

I rushed to correct him. "No, you didn't pressure me, you were fine—"

"Are you sure? We don't have to go any faster than you want to—"

"No, I mean—I meant"—I took a deep breath—"I meant, we shouldn't do any of this. I don't think this is a good idea." I waved a hand between our chests. "Us."

His expression froze. "You're breaking up with me."

"What? No," I said automatically, because we weren't dating. "I mean—*can* I break up with you?"

"You can do whatever you want." He gave me an icy, polite smile. "I get it."

"You—you do?" How could he get me breaking up with him when I wasn't? I was telling him I couldn't casually hook up because I couldn't bear for him to not want this as badly as I did.

Because I couldn't be casual with Tyler. With Tyler, I wanted everything, and having an undetermined amount would destroy me. If I agreed to that—if I let this go on, this foggy, uncertain state—I'd be responsible for making myself miserable. And I wasn't going to do that. I knew what I wanted, what would make me happy, and it wasn't fragments of his time, it wasn't uncertainty, it wasn't being casual. I couldn't hope eventually he would come around to wanting to be with me. I'd constantly be on edge, spending my time overthinking every comment of his, always wondering if it would end.

Maybe it was too late to keep my heart from breaking again over Tyler Nelson, but at least I could make it a clean break. I wouldn't help him slice off tiny slivers. I knew what I wanted, what I needed. *It's too bad we want such different things*, he'd said, and damn, it was. It really, really was. But I knew what I needed to be happy.

"Of course, I get it." Tyler stood and started pacing across the room. "You've made it perfectly clear I'm not the kind of guy you'd ever seriously date."

"I'm sorry—what?" My brain did a poor job of sifting the meaning from his words. "What are you talking about?"

"I'm no Isaac. I'm not ambitious and smart and focused and all those things you like."

"Right," I said slowly. I put that aside for the moment—"Okay, but I'm not breaking up with you, because we're not together. I'm saying—I can't do what you do, casual flings. I don't *want* to do that. I want to date someone, one person, exclusively."

He frowned. "Wait, so—would you date me?"

I frowned back at him. "You don't want to date me."

"Yes." He pressed his lips together and looked away, the color in his cheeks heightened. "I do."

I stared at him a long time. "I'm confused," I finally said. "Because for the last two weeks, you've made it very clear you don't do relationships. For the past several *years*, honestly. Why would you suddenly be interested in one?"

He pulled at his hair. "I thought being in a relationship would make me feel tied down and uncomfortable. Maybe because I didn't really like the idea of letting someone in. I didn't really want to be myself around anyone. Didn't trust anyone." He shrugged. "But I trust you. You make me feel comfortable. Being around you feels . . . easy."

I stared at him.

My silence might have cracked him, because his voice sounded uncertain. "Unless you're not interested?"

That stabbed me. I jumped off the bed and took a couple quick steps up to him. *You remind me of the Russian snow girl story*, he'd said. Did he think I would melt away? That he wouldn't see me until the next time we were on Nantucket? "God, Tyler, *yes*. Of course I wanted to date you. The only thing I want in the *world* is for you to want to be with me. But . . . wow." Letting in people was one thing; letting in Tyler Nelson, who could be wrapped around my heart in an instant, quite another. "I'm surprised you're interested."

"I think we both shut people out," he said quietly. "In different ways. With different kinds of walls."

"I agree," I said, equally soft.

He looked up, eyes vulnerable. "I don't want any walls with you. Usually I feel like I'm performing, making other people feel comfortable. And *I* never feel so comfortable." He took a deep breath. "You described a partner as a best friend you get to kiss. I haven't had a best friend in a long time. But I like the idea of both of those with you. I don't want to go home and all of this to vanish."

"I don't, either," I said. "But I already fell for you, Tyler. I don't want to make the same mistake again."

"You fell for an idea in your head when you were a kid. This is different."

True. But because I had let him in once, if I let him in again, he would instantly be back in all the old spots he'd filled. "What if you break my heart?"

"What if you break mine?"

I stared at him.

"I *like* you," Tyler said again. "I like how smart you are and how curious, and I never know what you're going to say, and you keep me on my toes, and I like when you let me in and I get to *see* you. And, Shir. What if it's really, really good?"

"I don't even know how to think about this," I said.

"Start with—do you like me? As a person? As a friend?"

"Yes."

His shoulders dropped with relief. "And you like making out with me."

I narrowed my eyes at him. "It's all right."

"And—if you didn't have, uh, historical data about me—you would say yes if I asked you out."

I looked at him.

I thought of Grandpa this time, not Grandma. Grandpa, who had loved a girl when he was young but hadn't gone after her. Who might always have wondered, *What if?* I thought about Sarah Barbanel, who had been brave enough to do a wild thing. I thought about miracles, about light, about how important it was to push back the dark when we had a chance.

Screw it. Screw being sensible, and protective of myself, and closed off. If he broke my heart, he broke my heart, and I would pick myself up and move on. "Fine."

He looked at me questioningly. "Fine . . . ?"

I folded my arms. "We can give this a shot. You can, like, give me your chockpin if you want. Not that Sarah's sailor did that, actually, since he didn't exist."

A slow, radiant smile started to grow on Tyler's face. "You sound very enthusiastic."

"It's still important to keep your ego in check."

He bounded across the bed and enveloped me in a tight hug, resting his chin on top of my head. "I thought you were going to say no," he whispered, and I could hear ragged emotion in his voice. "I thought you wouldn't want me."

I tilted my face up so I could see his, resting a hand on his cheek. "Of course I want you. I want you so much." I kissed him, and I could feel us both trembling.

Slowly, slowly, every single of inch of me started to relax and expand, like I'd been carrying around a tension my entire life I hadn't known existed. I could hardly believe it. I wasn't sure when I would believe in the idea of Tyler and me actually lasting. Not today, certainly. Probably not tomorrow. But I was willing to try.

"Oh," he said. "I looked something up last night when I got home, when I couldn't fall asleep right away."

"Yeah?"

"The captain's logs." He grabbed his laptop, bringing it over to the bed so we could both see it. "From the *Rosemary*. I thought the captain might have mentioned Sarah, or Sam Ferston at least," Tyler said. "But I found something else." He turned the screen toward me.

Picked up a passenger, Marcus Barbanel of Nantucket, in Philadelphia, the log read. *Will be returning him home as we head there next.*

"Marcus boarded the *Rosemary* in 1825, on the last leg of Sarah's trip," Tyler said. "They reached Nantucket in May and married three months later."

I touched my finger to the words. There was no way to know the reason Sarah left the *Rosemary*, if it had anything to do with the passenger she'd met, if he even knew about her disguise at the time. But.

Maybe she didn't have to stop sailing because her identity had been revealed. Maybe she met a man on a ship, and they sailed together, and she liked him. Maybe she decided to make a home with him. Maybe she decided there was a different way to be happy than the one she'd originally imagined.

You couldn't ever know anything for sure. But you could hope. You could trust. You could try.

"So are you my boyfriend, then?" I asked. "Or is this more casual dating?"

"Shira Barbanel," he said gravely. "I would very much like the honor of getting to call you my girlfriend."

I laughed. "You're a nerd," I said, and bit my lip, and felt once more like I held too much happiness to possibly contain. This might be the most foolish idea in the world. *Fool me twice*, people might say to me a month from now, but I didn't care. I believed we were going to work, that we were going to be together. And if I was wrong, if we were wrong, so be it. Right now, we worked. Right now, we were together. Right now, I believed we would prove true.

We would have to wait and see, and what a vision to look forward to.

✳ ✳ ✳

That night, we put on the Hanukkah play.

We dressed in the most elaborate outfits we could create. I wore a white blouse with long puffed sleeves cinched at the wrists, tucked into a red maxi skirt I stole from Aunt Liz's closet, with a gold silk scarf wrapped around my waist. Abby and I drew dark eyeliner and dramatic lipstick on everyone who wanted it.

"I never knew a handmaiden could look so good," Tyler said, giving me a small, conspiratorial grin. He'd spent the afternoon helping various cousins run lines or find last-minute details for their outfits. He'd moved furniture around the great room, setting up a temporary "stage" by the fireplaces, bringing out wobbly cardboard columns for the temple and moving potted plants. He even helped the littles hand out programs to the somewhat bemused adults. The audience barely outnumbered the cast: twelve parents, two grandparents (and baby Steffie)—along with Tyler's parents, who Iris had magnanimously allowed him to invite.

The cast piled on couches with less direct views of the cleared-off area functioning as a stage, dressed in flowing skirts and cardboard armor and whatever non-denim pants the triplets had deemed historically accurate enough. Tyler sat beside me as the triplets strode out to enthusiastic applause. Lily wore a long skirt and a scarf holding back her hair. Rose, as a rebellious

Maccabee, wore . . . leggings and a white blouse? Sure. Iris, who should have been wearing General Holofernes's armor, wore a black turtleneck.

"Here we go," I whispered, squeezing Tyler's hand.

"Welcome, everyone!" Iris shouted. "Welcome to *The Maccabees and Judith, a Hanukkah Story*." She looked at me, and I gave a slight nod. She took a deep breath. "We have a casting change to announce. The part of Judith will be played by Mrs. Helen Barbanel, and the part of General Holofernes will be played by Mr. Edward Barbanel."

The adults gaped. My grip tightened on Tyler's hand, and I tried not to break into nervous giggles. This had been my idea, after all, and maybe a terrible one, but what the hell.

Grandma looked like she very, very badly wanted a drink. "Oh no, dears," she said, her voice diamond-hard. "We wouldn't want to interfere."

"But you have to," I said, so wide-eyed and earnest I heard one of the boys snort. "It'll make the play better."

"We don't know the lines," she said flatly.

"Don't worry," David said. "None of us know our lines. We're reading from the script."

"Actually, I know my lines," Ethan said.

"Do you know the kind of noises elephants make?" Oliver demonstrated with a long trumpeting noise. "I have other lines, but those are my favorite."

Honestly, sometimes I thought I needed a whistle to keep my cousins' attention.

Miri, at least, stayed on task, leaning forward from her seat to look at our grandmother. "Please, Grandma. We really want you to."

"Please," the middles and littles echoed. I deployed four-year-old Eva, giving her a gentle nudge so she would go forward and hug Grandma's leg, staring upward.

Then, to everyone's surprise, support came from an unexpected corner. "Why not," Grandpa said. "Let's have a go at it, Helen."

Grandma narrowed her eyes, intensifying the human-melting beams directed at Grandpa. A silent standoff resulted, indecipherable on the outside, but perhaps they were using sixty years of history to read each other's minds.

But then: "Fine." She tossed the word out almost dismissively. "If you all insist."

"This way," Iris said. "We'll get you into costume right away."

"Costume?"

I got to my feet. "I'll help."

Grandma waved me off. "I don't need your help." She got to her own feet, but she didn't brush me away as I followed her to her room. "I assume this is all your doing."

"A collective effort," I said. "We thought it would be fun for you to have a more active part in the play."

"I don't need an active part."

"But you'll get to murder Grandpa. Won't that be fun?" I flipped through Grandma's closet, which consisted of a lot of soft pants and structured jackets and sweaters. Cardigans and button-downs, everything exquisitely tailored. Not many dresses befitting a widow from two thousand years ago.

"Is this some sort of clever ploy? You think we'll be on better terms just because I get the chance to enact a vengeful fantasy?"

"I would never go so far as to call us clever."

If she'd been less elegant, I would have called the noise she made a snort. "Honestly, you children."

I pulled out a dark red floor-length gown from her closet, the kind of thing Helen Mirren might wear to an awards ceremony. "Here."

She took one look at it and scoffed. "That's hardly appropriate."

"Why not?" I gestured to my outfit. "I'm wearing a hodge-podge of clothes, and I'm not even playing a part." Lily had once more given up her role as Judith, and would play the handmaiden.

"How long have you been planning this?"

"There's no plan," I said, then smiled. "However, you might wonder why we pushed the play back in the first place."

"And here I thought you simply didn't want to include my brothers in an enjoyable evening."

"Grandma! We're not actually the worst." I paused. "Are we?"

She patted my cheek. "Everyone has room for improvement, my dear."

Ouch.

She changed, and I helped her zip up the dress. She already wore makeup—she always did—but I convinced her to change out the diamond studs in her ears for long, dangling rubies to match the dress. "I'm sorry if we should have been nicer to Uncle Arnold and everyone."

"Don't worry about it, darling. He understood."

Well, I might worry, but maybe not right now. I handed over Lily's old script. "Your lines are highlighted."

She looked down at the script, then gave me a coy smile. "I suppose it won't be *such* a hassle to have to kill him."

We returned to the great room, and I took my place next to Tyler. "Did you survive alone with my cousins?"

"They haven't beheaded me. Theatrically or otherwise." He studied me. "Do you think it'll work?"

"I have no idea. It's up to them now." I turned my hands palms up. "They've been so stiff with each other lately. I wanted to give them a chance to be goofy. I thought if they remembered they could be loose and relaxed, they might remember they liked each other. If they do like each other. I wanted to give them a moment."

"Even if it meant sacrificing your own role."

"Well." I leaned over so I could whisper in his ear. "Pretty sure the handmaid seducing the soldier is not a PG scene."

At the front of the room, Iris cleared her throat. "After twelve years of rule," she projected, "Alexander the Great died . . ."

The play went exactly as expected, which was to say all the littles cried from confusion or exhaustion at some point, Oliver took his elephant role exceedingly seriously, and the triplets committed to a hilarious degree. Gabe managed to hurt himself on his fake sword, Abby and Noah made eyes at each other through their whole scene, and Ethan spoke in a very bad British accent. Everyone laughed the entire time, which pleased everyone but the triplets, who expected their masterwork to be treated with more gravitas. But it was hard to be serious when baby Steffie started crawling around during battles, wanting to be part of the excitement, and when David went off script with commentary whenever he felt like it.

Finally, we reached Grandma and Grandpa's scene, the same one Isaac and I had rehearsed. Grandma wore her gown, more befitting a gala than an afternoon at home, and Grandpa had been rustled into a suit jacket and tie. "'Take courage, woman,'" Grandpa read, "'and have no fear in your heart.'"

At first, as they read their lines, they sounded stiff and cold, but they slowly unwound. By the time Grandpa offered Grandma a goblet full of cranberry juice and said, "'Drink and be happy with us,'" Grandma smirked at him broadly.

"'I will gladly drink, my lord,'" she said. "'For today is the greatest day of my whole life.'"

Stage instructions encouraged Grandpa to keep drinking until he passed out. He set down his drink and very, very carefully lowered himself to the ground, groaning slightly as he made his way. This worried enough of the adults that Uncle Harry and Aunt Rachel hurried over to help him down, then hovered nearby in case he needed help climbing to his feet.

Grandma stepped forward. "Pick up a sword!" I whisper-shouted before she could get started. She looked startled, then accepted one from Iris, who'd dashed forward with the very best of our tinfoil attempts. Sword in one hand, script in the other, Grandma said, "'O Lord, in this hour, look graciously on the work of my hands. Now is the time to shatter the enemies who have risen against us.'"

She bent down (maybe we should have thought more about old people enacting these scenes) and struck her tinfoil sword lightly against Grandpa's neck, once, then twice.

"I am dead," Grandpa announced, off script. "You have killed me."

And Grandma, to my surprise—to everyone's surprise, given the looks I saw the aunts and uncles exchange—threw back her head and started laughing, a sound filled with pure, utter delight.

So did Grandpa.

"You're ridiculous," she said, her voice almost coquettish. "Get up, old man. You're going to hurt yourself lying there."

And she offered a hand to help him up.

EXCERPTS FROM THE TEXT LOG OF SHIRA BARBANEL AND TYLER NELSON

JANUARY 20

Tyler:

I'm back tomorrow do you want to pick me up at the airport with a bouquet of flowers and balloons

Me:

Lol sure what's your favorite kind of flower

Tyler:

Roses duh

Jk but how about dinner? I need to drop off my bags at the dorm but I could meet around 6.

Me:

That sounds great!

JANUARY 29

Tyler:

You left your Thai at my place

Me:

NO

Tyler:

Do you want to come back and get it

Me:

Yes I am turning around right now

FEBRUARY 3

Tyler:

Wow my legs are . . . sore?

Who knew ice skating made you sore

Me:

I, for one, am stunned by this news

FEBRUARY 9

Tyler:

Hey what are you doing Friday

Me:

Friday

You mean

The 14th?

Tyler:

Yeah that day

It's a day

This month

Me:

I dunno

Thought I'd wake up

Go to school

Maybe eat some food

Tyler:

Wanna eat food together

Me:

Let me check my calendar

Ok yes

MARCH 3

Me:

DAMMIT I just realized I left my
pho yesterday

Why am I so bad at this

Also why didn't you tell me

Tyler:

Don't hate me

I may have eaten it

MARCH 20

Tyler:

SPRING BREAK I'M FREEEEEE

Me:

Wow I've literally never heard you
be so excited about anything in your life

Tyler:

It's only because

I'm excited I get to spend so
much more time with you

Me:

Tyler that is too much

emotion I can't handle it

Tyler:

Is your poor little robot heart

going into overload

Beep boop bop beep

APRIL 1

Tyler:

Happy birthday!

Me:

Thanks but uh my bday is

actually tomorrow

We made dinner reservations??

You know its Monday today right

Tyler:

APRIL FOOLS

Me:

I can't tell if you set me up or if you

genuinely messed up

APRIL 9

Tyler:

I'm downstairs

You'll know me because I'll be the
one in the reed basket

And the loincloth

Me:

You're not as funny as you think you are

You ate, right?

Tyler:

I thought this whole thing was
a meal? A four hour meal?

Me:

Haha

Hahahaha

You're gonna get one dry cracker
and one bitter herb dipped in salt over
the next two hours

Tyler:

Dipped in SALT?

Me:

It's the tears of our ancestors

Don't worry, I'll sneak you a clif bar

APRIL 20

Me:

There are 15 other women
here and they're all wearing pastels

Why did you not tell me to wear a pastel

Tyler:

In my defense, you look very hot in red

Me:

I WANT TO BE WEARING A PASTEL

Tyler:

Calm down you'll upset the bunny

Me:

There is no bunny

What is up with all these LIES

Tyler:

You have lies too!

What do you call the leave-the-door-open dude

Me:

Who, Elijah? Trust me, no children are sad
when they realize they'll never meet Elijah

Tyler:

I mean do you really want to meet
a six foot tall easter bunny

Me:

WHO DECIDED THE BUNNY
IS SIX FEET TALL

MAY 2

Tyler:

Do you wanna come to a
Derby party Saturday

Me:

Heck yes I do

If I get to wear pastels

MAY 16

Tyler:

You forgot your pizza

I ate it

JUNE 6

> **Me:**
>
> This is fun!!

Tyler:

Why do you look so surprised??

> **Me:**
>
> Because it's a pre-prom party!
>
> With other people!
>
> I thought I would hate everything about it!

Tyler:

Except for my dapper presence, tho, right

> **Me:**
>
> Yes except for that

JUNE 22

> **Me:**
>
> I'm here
>
> Where are you

Tyler:

I'm very easy to spot

Me:

Are you tho

There's like 500 people getting off the ferry

Tyler:

Yeah but

There's only one guy

Holding 10 balloons

Me:

I assume this would be a

dude selling balloons?

Tyler:

You would be incorrect

Me:

TYLER

You have BALLOONS

In the shape of WHALES

Tyler:

Four people have actually tried to
buy some from me already

Me:

Pocketing my phone so I can hold

my bags and make my way to you

Tyler:

Bon voyage

Love you

Me:

Love you too

ACKNOWLEDGMENTS

I thought a lot about friendship while writing this book. Shira hungers for closeness because I did, too, while writing *Eight Nights* during the winter of 2020 and 2021. My friendships turned largely virtual: we communicated via Slack and text chains, and held movie nights and happy hours over Zoom. When I saw my friends in person, we layered up and huddled by the heat lamps suddenly ubiquitous throughout Boston.

But we still managed to stay connected, celebrating and laughing and venting through our computer screens. My friends are some of the purest and best parts of my life, and I love you all. Thank you for your ceaseless and unwavering love and support. Thanks to my writer friends, who understand the highs and lows of this strange corner of the world we're in.

Special thanks to my amazing agent, Tamar Rydzinski, who always has my back, who listens to my smallest questions, and who is excellent at bouncing ideas off of. Thanks to my film agent, Mary Pender. And many thanks to my editor, Gretchen Durning, whose long and loving edits chiseled the final tale out of my drafts, and who made Shira and Tyler shine.

So many people are involved in bringing books to life. I'd like to thank everyone at Razorbill and Penguin Teen: thanks to Delia Davis and Heidi Ward for copyediting; Marinda Valenti for proofreading; Lori Thorn for the beautiful interior design;

Danielle Ceccolini for this stunning warm, wintry cover; Miranda Shulman for production; managing editor Jayne Ziemba; Vanessa DeJesús for publicity heroics; and Susie Albert and Casey McIntyre.

I occasionally borrow from reality from my stories, like in the case of the painting owned by Tyler's moms. It belongs to my former roommate, Nisa, and hung in our apartment for several years, and remains one of my favorite pieces of art. I also know absolutely nothing about skating or piano: thanks to Diana C. for reading my word salad.

Shout-out/eternal gratitude to my parents, who will never be convinced my books aren't about them, and who will always be mostly wrong and a tiny bit right.

I've been so lucky to get to explore more of Nantucket as I write these books, and I'm deeply grateful to all the people who've taken the time to talk to me, from tour guides at historic homes to museum guides to shop owners. I've taken some artistic liberties with the exhibits and plaque text at the Nantucket Whaling Museum for the story; any mistakes are my own, and I hope I accurately conveyed the sense of the place. While "The Nantucket Girl's Song" isn't on display, you can get a print from the gift shop (I did!).

The very best part of being a writer is connecting with readers. Thank you so much for reading and reviewing and reaching out. Your words make all of this worth it.